THE SEA MONKEY TOMBS

THE SEA MONKEY TOMBS

A Novel

Christopher Noël

ISBN #: Softcover 0-7388-3419-X

This book was printed in the United States of America.

To order additional copies of this book, contact:

Xlibris Corporation

1-888-7-XLIBRIS

www.Xlibris.com

Orders@Xlibris.com

1-NOEL

The human flair for self-invention and -dissemination animates *The Sea Monkey Tombs.* It explores—and pokes fun at—how we'll stylize reality in our own image, often obsessively. Archimedes said, "Give me a place to stand and I will move the world." Each of three main characters seeks a redeeming leverage.

Christopher Noël is the author of a novel, *Hazard and the Five Delights,* and a memoir, *In the Unlikely Event of a Water Landing.* He lives in Vermont and teaches in the Master of Fine Arts in Writing Program at Vermont College.

LATE OCTOBER, 2006

When a man labors and halts himself into orgasm, which is the better comparison—a mighty cascade, or a cricket trapped in a closed hand?

We find that men of science will gang up, like Crick and Watson, working in teams to reach their fond horizons. I can hear them congratulating themselves and calling for more light, like a high buzzing in my ears. I can't hear myself think, except to wonder—Has someone told them that the world is listening, always listening for its own long definition, drawn out through all their words and thoughts?

Hypothetically, say that some guy chokes a woman nearly to death because she's too persistent and because he's had enough of all her meagre equipment. What does she do? Similar case: a scientist becomes abruptly disgusted by the narrow scope and sameness of his inquiry. So now, how does the woman retaliate? Old knee to the groin? Hip check to the ribs? Or does she go subtle instead, fight back less as a woman than as an inquiry? Isolate what bothered the man and slip it under a microscope, fine-tune the focus and make him feast his eyes until he begrudges, gurgling, "This, *precisely. I could never have dreamed it."*

Remember, science is often forced to demonstrate the plainest truths through myopic repetition. But this takes patience, and how am I supposed to breathe when, these heady days, the young Cricks and Watsons are starved for sensation, for the sexier results, and when every time one of them reaches toward an evasive likelihood and grabs hold, shouting "Eureka!", he's closing his hands around my throat?

"Actually, sir," said the boy, faintly scowling, standing from the metal chair, backing toward the office door. "I should be going; um . . ." He gestured to the wall, to the recently mounted pen-and-ink of the famous fish, *Scombridae vagrantitus*. ". . . Real pretty picture, sir."

"'Sir'? Since when, Eugene? We're partners. Yes, my wife just had that drawn for me." Professor Henry Trapuka stood, too, behind his desk. "We're extremely lucky to have gotten the funding from the department. It was nip and tuck this time around. We'll leave Tuesday at dawn . . ." He stepped to the map that covered the back wall of his office. "And this is our destination, Grand Manan Island, New Brunswick, where, as you know, *Titus* spends these early weeks of autumn."

"Yeah, I know."

"I can count on you, then? For the expedition?"

The boy slipped out into the hallway, all except for his hand—"I know, I'll try, I'm not sure, I'll get back to you"—which waved crisply and disappeared.

"Boy"? Yes, Trapuka knew better; Eugene was beginning his second year here in marine biology, a devoted protege (the eighth in an underwhelming series), winning the mentor's esteem by sitting hunched in transcription of notebooks full of elaborate behavioral specifics. At the same time, Eugene had played the gangling adolescent—ducking and bobbing beside Trapuka's considerable expeditioner's build—with oblong head and pasty face, and a perpetual frown that Trapuka came to accept, last year, as a sort of endearment. But now, Eugene having returned from some obscure summer fun in Northern California, this frown had turned into wary distance and surmising glances, the boy shifty-eyed and seeming pressed beneath the weight of some private joke; and there, sounding from down the hall—a quick waterspout of laughter.

Trapuka shook his head, clearing it of this fruitless enigma and focusing instead upon his one chosen enigma. Index finger touching wall map in reliable, pre-trip ritual, he traced *Titus's* autumn itinerary. She hugs the East Coast, riding the Gulf Stream up past Maine, last craggy jowl of the continental United States, before striking northeast to abandon the Stream's temperate flow, and by mid-October hitting Grand Manan Island, Bay of Fundy, where the water is always murderously cold; here, she gorges on herring and other small fry for thirty-two to thirty-six days, before setting out again to open sea and the far north, making Baffin Island by early November.

Unless, that is, she decides otherwise.

He swept his hand over the vast territories outside this route, from the Gulf of St. Lawrence to the North Labrador Sea, *Titus's* winter playground, where her irrepressible whimsy drove her, certain years, to side-swim this limited program altogether, to pass undetected by any of the research vessels and posts in the Maritimes with which Trapuka was in steady contact, nor yet to arrive where he himself may have travelled and lain patiently in wait for her. After all, one could only attempt to intercept her on her likeliest path, where the paper of the map had worn down through the years and, blue sea rubbed gray, had finally grooved and pilled.

Trapuka leaned in and blew some of the tiny pills away. The route remained valuable, terminating all the way up here, at Frobisher Bay, Baffin Island, this inhospitable arrowhead of water where, he'd determined, it pleases *Titus* more than eighty percent of the time to overwinter, though it freezes tight, and though other fish are busy streaking south, south, south. This behavior had always been evinced by his colleagues, and even the occasional brazen student, as proof of *Scombridae vagrantitus's* singular retardation. That, and the fact that she seems, seems, mind you—though Trapuka had come up empty in every attempt to link her definitively to these local legends—to hurl herself in her numbers, during the darkest days before and after the solstice, against the underside of ice sheets across the Bay, producing an eerie tattoo that can be heard at first as far inland as the village of Gudock, and that then becomes fainter, until by early January one must cock one's head in a favorable wind even to make her out from shore. Baffin lore spoke of drowned seamen growing nostalgic and famished, each year at Christmastime, for the lights and soups of the human world.

Though he would have to concede if pressed that chances were slim of a robber's breaking in and prying open the five file crates that bore his eighteen years of research findings, Trapuka double-locked his office door. He hurried through the dim basement corridor that ran the length of the Oceanography Building. There was so much to accomplish before departure, but he took a second to reach out and pat the bony shoulder of ancient Professor Gelancy as he shuffled by, muttering, stooped and in-bound for yet another long night over the microscope. Gelancy had made his name in the late sixties by proving incontrovertibly that mussels propel themselves along seabeds during immaturity in a manner almost identical to that of oysters, whereas it had always been lazily assumed that their method of propulsion was much more akin to that of the clam. All the man needed now in the way of mollusks was shipped to him directly; nor did he even seem aware of those who—like Cousteau and Trapuka and Melville—were cursed with ambitions that only the high seas themselves could match.

Thirty-nine hectic hours later, Trapuka sat savoring a bowl of cooling oatmeal aboard the "Grand Manan III," a modern, smooth-going ferry that made the hour-and-a-half crossing between Blacks

Harbour, New Brunswick, and the Island. Through the window was the surrounding platter of sea, dulled by low cloud cover. But what he watched instead, and bitterly, were the tourists out on deck, leaning against the rails, shivering in the wind, beaming. And Eugene stood among them, showing square shoulders and looking smart in black pea coat, maroon scarf, Greek fisherman's cap, planted at the prow, leading the way through scraps of fog. Trapuka couldn't believe this was the same cringing boy except when, every few minutes, the boat's horn would blast suddenly and he would buckle to the left, raise his hands to his ears.

But the tourists. They struck their dramatic poses. How they courted this bracing wind, liked to feel it lashing their faces, numbing them with the absolutely safe yet absolutely unmistakable beginnings of death—it charmed them to themselves, though it could never teach them a single thing. They reminded him sadly of his wife, Jonna, how she'd test her nerve also in such meager, self-governed ways—such as taking "the flume ride!" at fairs—whenever they'd go someplace with their daughter, Ellie. Jonna would silently pronounce herself daring and sound. On his early expeditions, though, she'd been sullen and bored, so he'd stopped including her. Ellie was a different story—a great soul awaiting its moment.

Trapuka pushed the last bite of oatmeal around inside his mouth, letting one raisin sing on his tongue. He lifted from his briefcase the latest issue of "Ichthus" and leafed quickly through, yawning yet vigilant. Although he knew that he alone was seriously in pursuit of *Titus,* certain pesky amateurs (like Nolan, that drifter!) occasionally dipped into these waters, so far frivolously, but one day—it could happen to the best—he might find himself swamped and cast under by some act of research piracy.

He swallowed the raisin, rescued as ever by the stunning conservatism of the oceanography community. Long before he ever witnessed her in the flesh, it was in the pages of this very publication that Trapuka had first met his fish. She'd been discovered strangely pitched up along the Nicaraguan shoreline in groups of three and five. The accompanying article—a fortunate bolt for Trapuka just when his thesis advisor, Doctor Rulon Fells, world authority on krill, was threatening to drum him out of school for his lack of a topic—went on to hazard a link, based on local descriptions, between this Central American phenomenon and the maverick ice-tappings reported by the Baffin Islanders.

Yes, one morning three years later, while on a ship helping to monitor reef decay in the western Caribbean near the Grenadines, Trapuka and the others aboard "The Sebastian Quick" began to notice anchovies leaping out of the water, as they do whenever a school of predators has arrived beneath them. All hands crowded belowdecks to peer through subsurface portholes, expecting to see barracuda or marlin; Trapuka knew immediately what he was seeing, and that he'd replay this moment forever. But he held his tongue, bit it, in fact.

His watch read twenty minutes before ten.

There was no mistaking that profile—long snout, upper and lower jaws ridged with fine teeth, body arched equally on ventral and dorsal halves, hind end tapering quickly until as slender as a girl's wrist before the translucent spread of crescent tail.

She was preparing to feed, working together to corral her prey in a pincer maneuver, fins on her back and belly positioning her with breathtaking precision. The untrained eye—liable to gloss over that slight bevelling of the skull above the fixed eyes, eyes which give nothing away—could so easily mistake her for her larger and much more common cousin, the tuna.

Granted, the tuna is a proud and worthy species, containing under its taxonomic umbrella albacore, billfish, shipjack, sailfish (the only swimmer to better the speed attained, on land, by the cheetah), the marlin, bonito, and wahoo—all of which are considered to be, hydrodynamically speaking, very close to the ideal. But next to *Titus?*

Cheers out on deck, shouts of "Look! Here's one . . . oooo, and back there, two more!" Trapuka didn't have to look; as always, porpoises were performing their bright little tricks in the water.

A delicate webwork of muscles around his right eye began to twitch. Eugene had mixed with the tourists and was now permitting a woman—attractive, but much older—to explain her camera to him. He took her picture with it. Then together they played at focusing and shooting into the waves below.

Certainly, porpoises were more intelligent than, say, halibut, yet people constantly mistook for genius their propensity to show off. He'd never been swayed by Doctor Lily's coddled prodigies; in fact, it was his private contention that, inasmuch as porpoises and whales, no less than tortoises, seals, walruses, and sea lions, originally took to sea from land, the entire category "mammals at sea" is highly suspect. Small matter that the aquatic invasion occurred fifty million years ago, because it was evident to Trapuka that the imperialists continued to lord it over the natives as if they had stormed in just yesterday.

Trapuka covered his face with his hands, trying to draw off the electricity responsible for the twitching, but those prima donnas leaping down below in the limelit surf, those people applauding, hopping, snapping pictures that would show smudged dots, if anything, and on top of it all his feckless protege, seduced—they acted as generators to sustain the twitch.

He went to the men's room, sat in quiet. After a while, as he expected, his mind brought him new distractions. Ten-year-old Ellie giggling recently with a friend ("My daddy is a fish-trainer, but they won't do a thing he tells them to!"); Doctor Cardoval, old graduate school colleague, after several drinks at the conference last fall ("But, Henry, what I mean is . . . I mean, exactly how long are you planning . . . I'm thinking about your standing, your talents . . . maybe branching out a bit"); his wife Jonna's facial expression, as though puzzled with herself, while he unwrapped the pen-and-ink drawing of *Titus* she'd gotten for his forty-sixth birthday last spring, just days before she took Ellie and left home.

He'd first seen that look in Jonna's eyes twelve years before, the time he'd placed a call to Jacques Cousteau himself. By some stroke of luck, he'd been able to link up directly with "The Calypso," which was at that moment anchored off Portugal, where down through sixty feet of bottle-green water, the remnants of Atlantis seemed to be bubbling up out of hot-spring craters.

"Doctor Cousteau, hello-bonjour to you, sir. . . . Oh, yes, and I'm terribly sorry to disturb you this way, but I've been sending you letters for some time and, and I thought—Oh, allow . . . I'm Trapuka, Henry Trapuka, Doctor Trapuka, that's right, from the United States, I've been on the trail of *Scombridae vagrantitus* and I can report some very peculiar behav—What? She is related to the tuna, but this hardly—Yes, oh yes, sir-monsieur, I'm very well aware of that, I myself have many demands on my time, but I'm a great admirer of your work, which is the only reason I'd presume . . . No, yes, uh, yes, absolutely not, would never wish to cause you—thank you, yes, thank you, but maybe some other—"

Nightfall. Henry Trapuka stood on the northernmost headland of Grand Manan Island, leaning into a stiff wind and watching the last of the day's sheen over the Bay of Fundy fade toward the horizon. The temperature had dropped at least fifteen degrees with sunset, so that now his oilcloth poncho, thick fur-lined boots, and wool cap were strict necessities. All around, scrub grass, chalky rocks, and salt-stunted pines chafed audibly against the gusts. His ageless van stood nearby like a hulk of shadow between two great boulders. Stuffed with supplies, this travelling research station had made the crossing, once again, in the lower hold of the ferry. Far out to sea, at the dim back of the world, a green light blipped periodically.

He lifted a palm-sized tape recorder to his lips.

"October 25, 2006, Grand Manan Island. Have completed set-up. Ready to turn in. At dawn will begin survey of eastern shore with aid of assistant . . ."

He sighed. Speechless but not without a certain bounce, Eugene had pitched in for a while late this afternoon, carrying boxes and equipment from the van, assembling the tent and helping to inflate the twelve-foot rubber launch, before twilight reminded him of food and he hiked off toward town. Trapuka had called after the boy, "Don't forget, we've got an early morning," and then put baked beans on the cook stove.

"According to my usual source, a Mr. Dana Russell, proprietor, Island Boat Tours, Inc., *Titus* has been on site for a month already—unprecedented—and has massed in the tape grass at Seal Cove. Apparently idle, apparently not feeding. Also, locals have reported isolated beachings on the east coast. This means trouble, or some expanded trickery. We may learn more tomorrow, but I wish you were here, Ellie, it's a little lonely on this outlook. There will be a time for that yet. For now, your father needs beans and good sleep."

Meanwhile, more than eight hundred miles to the southwest, a roomful of widowers politely hushed. Ross Zingman, veteran group member, watched tonight's new man—red-faced Matthew Glennon, essentially bald in his early thirties—turning an ear of corn carefully in his hands, trying to find voice, then resigning to a whisper. "While I was still in the air, she 'succumbed to her injury,' is how they put it. I was a little too late, which is just one more thing I guess I didn't—" He rubbed his eyes with the heels of his hands; even the top of his head was flushed. Zingman had often seen it go this way, an awkward start; he himself had been mute at first. "She wasn't even where she was supposed to be, that night. She was lost, and she was on foot." Matthew Glennon's wife was found dead just three weeks ago under circumstances he wasn't ready to disclose any further, but which the papers had termed "suspicious"—Sheila Glennon had been away on a business trip in Virginia, this much was clear.

Seven members were attending tonight's Cobhouse session. Two of them, Gilbeau and Mezzanotte, had lately abstained from active participation, staging some obscure protest, sitting in one corner of the room, dressed too formally. That left four to coax the story from this neophyte widower, without putting him under too intense a microscope. Having corn to shuck eased the tension, but he seemed consumed by guilt, surely not an uncommon reaction to early grief—Zingman had nearly choked on it himself, two years ago, when his wife Andrea died—but bearing tonight a distinct element of emergency, as though Sheila Glennon were still out wandering.

"This is a place," Patrick Tenzer said, opening his arms up to the comfortable living room, "where nothing is off-limits. Say it all. But please," he added, indicating the many untouched ears of corn remaining on the round table at the center of the room, and the oaken barrel to one side, "do shuck with us." Tenzer was the group's founder, a retired doctor of fifty-six who looked closer to seventy, with gray hair and jowls that seemed to pester him; he'd smooth them with his thumbs. "Do. I know that it's odd, but you'll find it helps more than you'd expect."

For a minute, nothing sounded but the diligent squeak of corn work, everybody on task (including Matthew Glennon, gamely) except for Gilbeau and Mezzanotte, the disgruntled forty-year-olds in their dark suits, sitting stiffly in straight-backed chairs, arms crossed. On the wall behind these protesters hung Estelle Tenzer's beige kimono, printed with lime-green willow trees and brown swallows in flight through a creamy sky. According to Tenzer, she'd worn it only a few times, for nostalgic ceremonies with relatives from Japan, who knew her by her girlhood name, Peilo. It was six years ago September that Estelle tripped over a sprung tie on the Bismark Railroad Bridge and fell off, landing fifty feet below on the riverbank among dry brambles.

"Well, I can tell you all that my Jessie stayed alive for eight hours after the horse threw her," said blonde-bearded Stanley Keillor, kindly breaking the silence. Of course, the regulars had heard every detail many times, but during the first year one needs to say what happened again and again; also, it was crucial, just now, for the new man to have a model. Zingman had considered jumping in, but Andy's death from cancer honestly didn't make such a good story.

"For a while," Keillor continued, tapping his fingers on the oily front of his red-and-white-checked shirt, "they were pricking her all over with these pins, trying to see if she'd, y'know, flinch at pain, even though she was not conscious." Matthew Glennon put his face in his hands. "To figure the extent of the paralysis. This was before the MRI showed it was severed, her spine, snapped. But lots of people live.

"Anyway, what I'm trying to say is that I sat by that bed the whole time staring at her, her face but also her skin where they were pricking her, which she never did flinch at at all, and I kept noticing details I'd never seen before. This freckle or so, the exact shape, or a little chink of fat on her calf. There was this inoculation mark on her shoulder, from when she was a girl, I guess. I knew about it, but I never thought it was so shiny. Other things, bigger. Her whole jawline seemed like a stranger's, even though she hadn't hurt it in the spill."

Matthew Glennon, face still buried, wept into corn silk. "Especially when I touched it," said Keillor. "There was a birthmark on her temple, like a light coffee stain under fine hairs. Brand new, as far as I was concerned. I remember thinking stupid things like, y'know, hey maybe if we can prove any of this, we can get the whole situation . . . reviewed."

Keillor laughed gently at himself, so the others joined him, even Gilbeau and Mezzanotte, in their corner.

During a loud, lasting pause, the amateur wiped his eyes. "When the plane landed in Richmond and they . . . took me to see her, I just sat there for a while." No longer whispering, his voice was weak and astonished. "Then, I stood up. I went to the men's room but I came right back." His body shook a little. He tossed his first finished cob onto the table, took two more, but his fingers only stroked their matte casings. "I washed her off, even her neck and behind her ears, with one of those brown paper towels from the dispenser. You know, it's not true, what they say about bodies getting stiff in two hours. Sheila's hands didn't, anyway. I just kept on squeezing both of them, smelling them, breathing on them like in winter until the coroner arrived. I know that must sound pathetic."

"Actually, not," Zingman put in, yanking at a leathery husk, peeling it back like the old pro, and understanding that because he was, for the moment, still a well-known figure in town, his words carried value for newcomers. "It always seemed to me," he said, leaning toward the trembling man, "like two separate ideas, my wife dying and her hands dying."

The first time Zingman spots Andrea Parker, nine years ago, she is digging up sod on a cloudy day in front of the courthouse. He thinks that she seems like an emblem and he halts on the sidewalk, watches her from a distance, feeling a little embarrassed not to know her already, and know her well. In her hand is a small silver trowel, with which she hacks surgically at the grass, producing squares that she lifts out, pinning them against her chest, walking them (in her knees) to the edge, where the squares are piling up. They are large enough so they flex and flop, yet maintaining impressive structural integrity. Her hair isn't visible yet (it'll be brown), held bulging beneath a green baseball cap. Her face looks smaller than it ever will again, as it tilts to check the sky for rain. Digging each square out of the ground requires that she fight its thousand roots, but gingerly, or else the roots will snap off too high and cause trouble later. Zingman can start filling in the nuances of her craft, even from fifty feet away. A minute earlier, he was walking with a cup of coffee in his hand, feeling sleek and cagey with ideas for a new short story called, "Slippery Morning, Slippery Knife," and now he feels inept and bloated by being caught, catching himself, on the outside of this woman's life.

He almost doesn't want to know her name; she's meaningful enough. He steps ten feet closer, sips coffee, asks himself what she's an emblem of, and decides he'll take on that question like a quest. She's teasing another square of green grass from its bed. With her trowel, she saws precisely around the perimeter a second and a third time. She sets the tool aside and then fits both hands down in underneath. By her sweaty face, eyes edged leftward, he can read exactly how her fingers are going through the roots, loosening them, low, like painful tangles in hair. This is how she does it.

"And then we started trying to get down from the campsite, me carrying her, her walking a little whenever she could." Simon Reese was mid-story. His wife Theresa had passed away last summer from acute viral pneumonia while they camped at Lake Sunapee, in New Hampshire. "See, her lungs were filling up with fluid, fast. Just overnight, it got such a hold of her. This was four years ago this Saturday, four years. Seems like much longer or much shorter, but not anything like four *years.* So she was on my back, Theresa, completely out of it, raging fever, coughing, babbling about some character named Swim Prell, from a movie, until we finally got to the ranger's station and he put in the call. He gave her ibuprofen and helped her onto this mildewed old cot to wait for the rescue truck. I know I've said all this before, but here's something else. The other day it popped into my head for the first time, something that happened while she was laying there. She wasn't focusing on me, or answering any questions, but what she did do, then, made me so happy. She just cried. For half a minute, that's all. And it wasn't any big thing, either. She was too weak to even put her hands to her face. It was more of a casual type of thing, like you do . . . well, like maybe a kid would, if they lost something that belonged to them but it didn't matter much. I'll tell you, I was relieved, I was filled with relief, for some reason. I thought it meant she would get better, like crying means you have a future?"

Later, on the same day Robert Jenwaugh strangled me, I went swimming at the local YMCA. I'd never been there before, but it reminded me very much of the pool I took lessons in as a girl.

"You brought this on yourself, Harriet," he'd explained to me. When I came to and he left, closing my apartment door so carefully behind him, when I'd tried getting up and walking to the bathroom, my legs were weak. This is what reminded me of the pool in the first place, the way that after swimming your legs will wobble, marvelously. I gathered my things and rushed downtown. I didn't spend energy on fury or thinking big; I didn't retaliate, I escaped. Because I didn't have time. At the center of my brain was the black cube, which has always meant unconsciousness unless I can keep it small. It says, "Your future vanishes as fast as I can grow."

Robert Jenwaugh had put all of his weight on me, nearly collapsing me.

I drove, hardly blinking, to the Y. The most I could get myself to feel was a kind of pale disappointment, garden-variety, just as if I'd lost some contest, though lost it by a million miles. Focusing can arrest the black cube. I looked at parking meters, ladies' shopping bags, swinging, rusty trikes in alleys, cats on steps, the grills of oncoming trucks.

"You do see how you brought this on yourself." Robert Jenwaugh had stood above me, hands on hips. His thumbprints were still vivid on my windpipe, I mean vivid on the interior of my windpipe—for days,

I didn't look into a mirror. "Don't you? What was all that?" He'd pointed to the bed, where I still struggled merely to breathe evenly. "I mean, you lost complete control, I think you'll agree, Harriet."

Using my inborn knack, I slipped into the water and performed a simple crawl, lap after model lap, without wasted motion, easier for me than walking, than sitting still. My breathing resumed, slim but steady. I'm a shadow when swimming; the afternoon pulled long and late, and through blue water I lost enough dimension, I outshadowed the cube in my brain, shunned it, collapsed it.

Early morning. A red-and-white-striped buoy with a bell on top. Ten thousand swells charging him from out to sea, then letting him off with a minor jostle before heading hard again for the rocks. And above, the sleepy alarms of gulls as unimaginative as the blue sky they drifted through.

Sitting in the launch, motor off, Trapuka drifted as well, two hundred meters from the southern tip of the Island—happy, happy. The sun had been up for less than ninety minutes, and he'd already managed to cover the entire thirteen miles from tip to tip in a first, general inspection, skimming in his yellow launch by the three small coastal towns, like old friends—Seal Cove, Castalia, Point Orange. Despite clear sky overhead, down here hillsides of fog hid homes, dockyards, whole seaward communities from view. Just after sunup, he'd nodded in passing toward the narrow, misty mouth of Seal Cove; he was familiar with the extensive bed of tape grass in there, the flat brown blades rising forty feet to brush the surface. This afternoon, he'd revisit the Cove.

Directly below, sonar showed a sloping pebbly floor and scattered small fry at six fathoms. No sign of *Titus* so far, which only made more plausible her grouping inside the Cove. He yanked the outboard motor alive and headed toward shore, to begin a closer pass from south to north.

Eugene had not returned at all last night. Trapuka had left the

Coleman lantern burning low, but when he awoke it still hissed white hot on the aluminum table outside the tent. He'd written a note; the last few years of his marriage to Jonna had schooled him well in terse communiques. "Eugene, Have begun survey. You proceed with interviewing locals, as discussed. Keys in ignition if needed. MOST appreciative."

And then he'd single-handedly dragged the rubber launch down over the craggy, twisting pathway to the water.

He veered north, just twenty meters from land, raised his field glasses, and began a meticulous scan of the shallows, the many small pools left behind by ebb tide.

Yes, it was true that Trapuka himself had never found her pitched up on shore, as had so many indifferent Nicaraguans. In fact, he'd never once held her, alive or dead, in his hands, an astonishing fact which he'd always taken as a reflection, somehow, of their mutual respect. He'd only encountered her in open water, where her behavior was on full display. He counted himself fortunate to have dived among her on so many occasions, experienced her casual attentions, her tasteful disregard of him, to have photographed the majestic show as she surrounded him, swirling, caused him to feel—what?—sewn up, tucked away, discovered.

But others would see in the still pictures only the standard roil of a school disrupted. For so long, he'd pointed out the hidden patterns, without prevailing. And yet—he fondly recalled from zoological history—hadn't it taken Pavel Sucek himself nearly thirty years to properly record and share the structure behind the fabled dance of the alabaster hornspinner, keeping the faith amid all that laughter? And nearly as long again for Armando LaPolombara, in arthritic pain, to lure those shyly promiscuous apes from their damp caverns, present them to a doubtful world?

Indeed, *Titus's* particular virtue had proven inordinately difficult to read, much less to explicate. Trapuka had written of it as "a self-concealing wherewithal, a secret urge to slip that tight categorical noose, 'fish,' in favor of a new, more capacious one." He'd spent his best energies since the age of twenty-eight documenting this elusive virtue, trying to cast the cold light of science upon it, had caught nuances of behavior much too subtle and numerous to inflict piecemeal upon the lay public; no, in order to reveal her boldly, Trapuka must write the entire coherent book of her.

He'd been building the case diligently from the bottom up, toward the day when he might crown it by surprising his subject in an attitude more conclusive than any so far witnessed, unveiling the truth behind her ten thousand surreptitious winks and indications, let these rise into place, finally fill in the whole startling picture, give the world eyes to see.

When Trapuka had proceeded nearly a mile up the coastline, he began to hear sharp inland laughter. There, above him and behind a dense partition of fog . . . two laughters, really. One young and female, flirtatious? The other older, more the master of itself, male. His field glasses failed to penetrate to the source.

He returned his attention to the tidal pools, adjusting the glasses' heavy little focus wheel with his thumb. The laughters, though, seemed to follow him along for minutes, until the moment he saw what he saw—a small flap, like a leaf, lifting off the quiet surface of a pool in the sand.

He angled that way, then leapt overboard and felt the cold knives of the Fundy pierce his bare legs. He towed the launch by its rope through the last, foamy waves, stranded it on the rocks, his eyes always pinned to the flap, flagging him in.

The pool was lined with red-furred stones smelling of old ham; knuckle-sized hermit crabs vanished inside their hijacked shells; minnows darted everywhere; and here, noble at the center of it all, none other than *Titus*—one of the young, not quite a foot long. She listed badly, discolored in six inches of water. Bands of belly-white ran through the ordinary blue-gray of her back. A delicate veined tail picked itself up off the water, wind-drying, then wilting down again. Three immature fin-pairs paddled silently at her side as though nothing were wrong. And her one visible gill, gashlike, spread immodestly every few seconds.

Trapuka lay his hand gently against the skin. Of course, this broke all protocol—the last thing a weakened creature needs at such a time is to be racked by a great shock. But the fish made no reaction, merely sank to the shells and pebbles.

Again, the laughter from above! And now, too, an hysterical effort to hush. Trapuka stood. The fog had thinned just enough to show a grassy bluff, twenty meters high, overlooking this beach. And much too near its edge—his van, white and muddy, with a crumpled spot toward the rear, where Jonna had backed into it. Eugene, capless, leaned against the driver's-side door, speaking to a girl with a green scarf over her hair, a dark pocketbook in her hand.

He yelled, "Move it away from there!"

The two checked with each other, as though play-acting, then the girl looked down at him and raised a hand to her mouth, ready to shout. But Eugene covered this tiny bullhorn with his own hand, and they struggled together, giggling like naughty children. Finally, she shook free and called, "C'mon up!" Trapuka sighed, deciding to leave the fish in peace for the moment.

The climb had him huffing. He stood bent, hand against the back corner of his van. Eugene hung his head, but not in shame (grinning like a prankster). The girl left his side and stepped up to Trapuka, arm extended. "I'm Pauline Ard, Professor Trapuka." They shook. "Welcome back to the Island. You know, I used to see you in town when you first started coming, ten years ago, wasn't it? Or more. Oh, yer assistant here"—she glanced back at Eugene who, without lifting his head, put his index finger to his lips, shhhh—"yer Eugene, he's been safe with me, don'tcha worry, found him wandering the streets last night, me and my mother, took him in for a bite. One glass of homemade beer and he sang for us!"

Trapuka nodded, as if to say, 'Well, of course that's Eugene for you.'

"Flopped on our sofa for the night. Didn't you?"

Pauline shoved the boy in the shoulder, and then, smiling forcefully, turned back to Trapuka, who'd caught his breath and now stood straight, but somehow bewildered. What was it? No, this girl didn't have particularly arresting eyes. Then why was he staring? Was it that she thought she spotted an interest in his face so that hers reflected a distant sort of flowering awareness of this interest, even though it did not exist? He'd only just begun to delve into these and related questions when a fetid odor caused him to look down. He heard himself gasp, like a sound effect; it wasn't a pocketbook she carried in her left hand but *Titus,* an even smaller specimen than the one on the beach, perhaps eight inches.

"Oh, this," said Pauline. "Pity, yeah." She handed it over, stiff and curled. "But it's not the only one, they're everywhere. Folks've been collecting 'em for weeks. Make a great stew, I hear—not often we get a brand new treat. Oh, I'm sorry, Professor!"

Trapuka passed the dead fish back and forth gingerly between his hands. Eugene slung an arm over Pauline's shoulders, staring at his mentor with a challenging directness; Trapuka turned his suddenly heavy eyes inland, resting them on a level, cloud-bearing field.

"That's right," breathed the boy. "That's been my . . . my first finding so far."

"Ah."

Nobody moved for a long while. They all listened to the surf below and to the flapping of the girl's scarf in the breeze. Trapuka tucked *Titus* into the pocket of his windbreaker, nose-first. He pictured steaming black pots.

"I know what," said Pauline. She invited them back to her house for breakfast, and then helped Trapuka to haul the launch up the hill and slide it into the back of the van.

They drove through Point Orange and Castalia, brief towns with simple wood-frame homes, post offices, grocery stores. Every now and then, he'd spot on a front lawn or porch a messy heap or neat stack of the specimens, ready for cleaning and cooking. All very young . . . a whole generation lost? Trapuka had to force himself each time not to stop and gather her up.

Pauline lived in what seemed the only brick house in the community of Seal Cove. Her mother greeted them at the door. Mrs.

Ard was shorter and rounder than her daughter, but her eyes led with that same scarce flowering claim of minor irresistibility. She was overjoyed to see Eugene again—a mainland husband for the girl?—and honored to meet a well-known American scientist.

"Yer right-hand man here was modest," said Mrs. Ard, "but we got the word out of him, sir, yer being the next Jacques Cousteau and all that."

With a stifled snort, Eugene led his prize by the hand indoors and up a nearby staircase. Before she disappeared, Pauline could only crane her neck to look back, smile, and shrug.

Mrs. Ard showed Trapuka into an airy, high-ceilinged kitchen, with dried herbs hanging from beams, sat him at a wooden table, and thirty seconds later, while she hummed an unfamiliar tune and started preparing muffins somewhere behind him, he sipped from a tall, warm, sweet brown beer—a breakfast blend?—while gazing out the window at a pair of little rusty birds who played about a clothesline. He studied how extremely well they played, attacking, parrying, dodging one another far too subtly to be followed and interpreted by the awkward melon of the human mind. For this reason, even as they delighted him, the birds' movements also began to insult him. He hid his face in his hands and brought up *Titus* instead.

During experiments conducted to chart her responses to stimuli—to various foods, to scents of shark and other foe, to different-colored pulses of light, etc.—there were times of course when she'd behave like any other fish; yes, he would concede that these made up the majority of instances, even the vast majority. But this only served to sweeten the minority, straining it down into a sort of observational concentrate.

On one historic day three years ago, for instance, off this very island, he had precisely measured her degree of hesitation before a cloud of sardine parts. Always before, she had leapt upon such a cloud with dispatch. Her hesitation that day bordered, so it seemed, upon the coy. But indeed it was "bordering upon" that spoke volumes, because *Titus* never allowed herself any out-and-out display of subtlety. Hers was a subtlety cut on the bias, which amounted, perhaps, to the very same thing as a straightforward normalcy, yet shaved, just once over, by the keenest of razors.

The pale pink sardine cloud expanded slowly near the surface in the sunny water while Trapuka crouched at the bottom, fifteen meters down, behind a large boulder, a frond of seaweed waving before his mask and camera.

Titus split and approached the cloud from two sides, military-fashion, as was her wont, ready to surround the prey should it attempt to flee, and then, seeing it had no such intentions, she converged and fed, as was also her wont.

What set this episode apart, however, was the pace and nature of the convergence; whereas previously she had always perceived the cloud's inanimacy from a distance of between seven and ten meters, and had then pounced immediately, entering that frenzied state, now she proceeded with caution, or, more accurately, mock-caution, well past the point at which she must have known better. Nor did she fail to pounce once she had reached the edge, or, more accurately again, the edge of a narrow margin surrounding the cloud.

Yes, he had snapped many pictures.

A failure to pounce would have passed the whole event off as a simple lack of appetite; but her use of this margin was a master stroke, neatly dividing *Titus* from herself even as it wed her with who she'd always been, because by refusing to pounce until it was nearly too late, she made a dodge toward abstinence, but again, in pouncing with fervor when still distinctly removed from the first bloody chunks, she asserted her hunger, alluded to having abstained, and shattered the illusion of abstinence, all at once.

Frond still waving casually before his eyes, Trapuka witnessed this insanely clandestine satire, *Titus* blending style with desire in proportions suggesting nothing but the driest humor in the entire sea, and he said out loud (the word spilling from his regulator in a rising column of bubbles), "Exquisite!"

And this was just one example.

He swigged his breakfast beer, draining the glass. If he were alone, he might lay the specimen out on this wooden table and cut into it with Mrs. Ard's sharpest paring knife. Start checking for a disease process—in the intestines, along the spine, and if time permitted, in the brain.

"So you've worked with that Cousteau, then, have ya, Professor?"

"Well, I," he said, sitting upright and trying to clear his head by raising his eyelids unnaturally high. "I would report my findings, um, periodically." He patted the outside of his jacket pocket, where the body was still firm against the fabric. "Though you know, the poor man died some time ago now."

"Oooo, can I take that stinking fish for ya?"

"No, no, that's all right, Mrs. Ard. Thank you."

"I see." She sat opposite him, setting before herself a short green bowl or wide mug of hot tea or coffee or broth or cider; he couldn't smell because the yeasty fumes of beer filled his head. She took a long sip and then smiled so that the tip of her nose veered minutely to the left. "I see," she said again. Trapuka sensed a difficult question building, something to do with life itself, but just then Pauline stomped into the room and dropped with great self-conscious heft into the chair beside him. Scarf gone now, her silly-grinning face announced her suddenly as no older than fifteen, maybe sixteen. Eugene followed and sat too, beside Mrs. Ard, but guilty, slumping, perhaps because of this announcement.

He looked to Trapuka, but Trapuka offered him no secret nod between men.

"You know," said Pauline. "I used to see you floating out in our Cove. In your diving suit, there." She laughed. "I thought you were a spaceman!"

Back then, she'd been much younger than Ellie was today. He'd recently written his daughter a birthday card: "Seems like it's always your birthday, this time of year. And here I go again, out to sea. You remember that island from the pictures. Well, it never changes, so that's where you can think of me. How about joining me next year, to celebrate double-digits? My God, little girls should be more like islands, don't you agree? Take centuries to change, sometimes even shrinking."

Lightly, he touched Pauline's tabled wrist. "I only wish I could say I remember you."

"Oh, maybe you saw me anyway. I watched you from the pier."

They nodded wistfully. Mrs. Ard got up and went to the oven behind him; its door squeaked and the aroma of muffins—what sort of berry?—breathed into the kitchen like a consolation that swells until it takes the precise shape of what's missing.

The woman put a plateful of the tall brown creations down on the table. Pauline took one for herself, then handed one across to Eugene, who might have wept if she had not. "Thank you," he said, but he didn't eat. Trapuka threw one to the cook, who caught it, laughing, and then he broke one apart beneath his own face, where it exhaled steam.

"You'd've seen Toad, then," said Pauline, buttering two perfect halves. "He was old by the time you came around, Professor. What a dog. I'll show you pictures, maybe you'll recognize him." She bit and chewed, bit and chewed, with a hitch, as though to march-tempo, pausing for an instant whenever her teeth met. She swallowed, rested three fingers on Trapuka's forearm. "Toady."

He watched Eugene's head wobble on its pale stem. Then Pauline pointed down to the crispy tail sticking from Trapuka's pocket. "I used to wonder what it was like, spending so much time with an animal that way. I used to think, you know, that man must be right at home with those fish. He must know what they're thinking, almost. I mean, sometimes I used to stare into Toady's eyes, when we were left alone, flopped out on the bed together, and . . . and I felt like we understood each other more than, you know, more than just a dog and a girl. Because he wouldn't look away, that's the reason. Other dogs, always, but not him. Like we knew each other, really, like we were breaking through a wall, like he wanted to tell me, 'All that barking I do, and fetching things, you know that's all for show, Paulie.'"

She took her three fingers off his forearm and sighed, then rolled her watery eyes. "Crazy, right?"

Strangled still, I seemed to fit better through the water—I'll concede it—and swam on into the evening, until the pool was empty except for me. They issued last call, issued it again. I finally stopped and clung to the side, letting my legs dangle like weeds, sending breath against the smooth tiles. When I was seven, eight, I was always the last one out like this. I used to feel anxious, delicious, the taut pain of trouble enhanced somehow and brought high by the many little tiles, their flawless lines and their blue.

Since some staff member was certain, any second, to shut off the main ceiling lights, I prepared myself, grievously, to climb out of the pool, but I understood that by reintroducing myself into gravity I'd be diminished, I'd be giving the black cube a whole fresh chance at my life. I stayed, going only so far as to place my bent elbows up on the grainy deck.

Hovering there at the edge, on that recent afternoon, I smiled, because how had I forgotten for twenty-five years that swimming can accomplish this, can restore possibility like an accurate wind righting a tipped cart? Imitating myself as a child, I breathed against the tiles, and heard my breathing reflected, timid and grateful, because of the delicacy of breath's channel, so easily crimped off, the tiles so slick they mocked sex, although as I remember, when I was eight they'd openly suggested it. Shivering, I let my bottom lip drag into the top of the water, so that each breath contained a trace of drowning. This used to suggest sex, too, and I found it still did, well enough.

When the lights banged out, echoing on the far ceiling, no more than a second went by before I could hear Robert Jenwaugh's orgasm—his petty murmur, some cricket chirps—from today, as he lay there beside me in bed, beating off, including the woman only laterally. I got him to mount me soon after, but this he used to gain leverage, to do me in.

The girl who hid in the pool past lights-out could find, in being so dangerously late, a taste of the opposite. She was early in life; that was the secret inside the excitement. Late-season water weed, I hung in pitch black and tried to recollect a specific ball of electricity that toured the girl's gut one day when she was shattering the YMCA rules, the visitation that meant sex was planning for her already—and that it would be thorough, and that it would be best.

Trapuka cut the motor and the launch slid smoothly over tape grass, then slowed and did a half turn inside Seal Cove.

A mid-afternoon sun made him and the girl surprisingly hot in their wetsuits, her equipment leased from a Mr. Felcher in Point Orange, a small man who repaired pilings.

Trapuka harnessed his reserve tank onto Pauline's back and briefly reviewed things for her, showed her how to breathe through the regulator, how to make air-tight the face mask. Then he tended to his own equipment while she worked her feet into a pair of black flippers.

Soon, they sat face to face, perched in the bright afternoon on the two cushiony side tubes of the launch and squinting at each other out of their masks' oval windows. With a finger, he conducted her in a steady-breathing exercise. She did fine, though her window fogged up.

"That'll clear," he told her, and took his regulator back into his mouth. They nodded "ready," then tipped backward together into soft pewter, quickly found each other again, afloat, and caught hold of hands (all four), inhaled and exhaled carefully, touched base with eyes, nodded "ready" again, and left the friendship of the glittery surface. He'd told her that one has to swallow repeatedly during the first ten meters of slow descent, in order to clear the pressure building behind the eardrums, and they did so now, sinking feet-first past swaying blades of grass. Below, spears of sunlight led Trapuka's vision along curving stalks and into a thick collapsing night.

He didn't expect to see *Titus* yet; sonar had placed her at five fathoms, thirty feet. He checked the girl's face once more; her mask had cleared, but her eyes themselves seemed foggy now, unsure. She was listening, he understood, to the lonesome metallic sound of her breathing, and to her air bubbles (her little life) leaving her behind and hurrying to the surface, already far above. Why had he put this child in such danger?

All of a sudden, though, she let go his hands, upended herself with startling grace, and dove head-first into a well that seemed to open for her in the grass. He found a well of his own and plunged into it, but Pauline was half lost behind the shifting weave; so he crossed into her well and dove after her bubbles.

"Look, Jonna," he said in bubbles. "This is the spirit, do you see?" Only a few weeks ago, his wife had finally agreed to meet him for the first time since she'd left, but only at a neutral site—a little league baseball game in which their daughter, until it rained, was pitching beautifully. And somehow, in the safety of the terrific thunderstorm spent under bleachers, between bites of her hot dog, tiny rectangles of relish caught in the fuzz of her upper lip, she'd blithely tossed off the suggestion that maybe his fish behaves the way she does only in response to him, that this might say more about his relationship to *Titus* than about *Titus's* to her fellow creatures.

He'd stared at her. She cringed when the next thunderclap struck like a gavel, and then, when a mighty flash lit her up, she appeared for an instant in her true form—an old woman with silver hair and the charcoal planes of a face dead set against glory.

Pauline bounced. Or so it seemed. She sprang suddenly into his arms. Sunlight being low now, he took his flashlight from his diving belt and trained its beam into her eyes; they were calm, even merry. Then they notched up and focused behind Trapuka's head and, behind hers, he saw why—the school rising massively around them.

He expected her to scatter or circulate. She did nothing but continue to rise, finally closing over their heads, quicksilver cooled to lead. Trapuka and Pauline grabbed hold of each other.

She then pretended (old trickster) to go back to sleep, no easy matter for one lacking eyelids. She seemed like many sad statues of herself; never had she behaved this way, but then, neither had he. He reached out toward her, at her nearest; his gentle poking test did not alarm but merely tilted her, which told him what he instantly understood he'd already known—she was not pretending, she was desperately ill. His mind began scrabbling, scraping together a plan.

And his body became aware of the muscles in Pauline's arms and shoulders vibrating, to get a tighter hold on him, and he switched off his flashlight, put it away, then clasped his hands together behind the rocklike metal of her tank, returning her pressure. Soon, he'd swim her back up and release her into gravity again and into its custom of pulling us down rather than toward one another. And then, so the plan formed itself, he'd break camp and escape in the van with the healthiest specimens available, and whomever else, race back southwest, where he envisioned one place to go, not far from his home university—a wild chance for her future.

But for another moment, he and Pauline would remain here, breathing and secured inside the exhausted multitude. The girl didn't represent Ellie or Jonna, because nothing was required of her, in the dark. There was light enough only for all the failing eyes, free now from sport, from tactics, to study the two at the center—though what she'd learn *Titus* would never tell. She'd keep her findings secret, secret.

Next evening, the Cobhouse met again, called into a rare Friday session. Zingman wasn't free tonight, but he dropped by for a few minutes, because Matthew Glennon needed to talk. "That's all I could do, was sit there, after I landed and they took me to her. I forget if I told you, I got up and walked to the bathroom, got some of that brown paper out of the thing. So I could wash her off. She had a little mud there on her neck. I don't know why she had that mud, though." This time through, the man's voice hit a firmer pitch. He stretched and yawned, but not because he was sleepy; he craved oxygen. Beneath his blue t-shirt, he had a puffy belly, which until now he'd hidden by slumping. In his own seat, Tenzer smoothed his jowls with his thumbs, eyes closed, paying strict attention.

Zingman glanced at his watch—7:17. He had a class to teach at 8:00. He stood at the edge of the living room, having no other choice; otherwise, he feared he'd never get himself out the door. 7:18, and tonight he was on foot, to enjoy the Indian summer evening. The YMCA building was half a mile from here, so he approached the table and set down two denuded ears of sweet, pale yellow corn—which Tenzer would take to the soup kitchen, as ever—and tossed his husks and silk accurately into the oaken barrel. "Well, guys, it looks like I better say goodnight."

Matthew Glennon had been watching him, looking anxious.

"I'm sorry," Zingman told him, extending his hand. "I mean it, I'd really stay if I could. Let's you and I have lunch this weekend."

"We'd been fighting." He accepted Zingman's handshake, but put new information into the air. "She was on me hard about something, which I thought was unfair. But as it turned out, she didn't know the half of it. Before she left on her trip, she made tons of her specialty, eggplant ratatouille, partly out of hostility, I think, making a point." He rubbed vigorously above his temples, kicking up wispy clouds of hair. "That's how it seemed at the time. She loaded it into the freezer for me, enough packages wrapped in foil for the nights she was going to be gone. I haven't touched a single piece."

The speaker gazed into space. Zingman didn't know how he'd get away, suddenly didn't wish to. "I think it's strange," said Matthew Glennon, "how they put it that way, 'succumbed to her injury.' I almost thought, how could she have an injury if she was so far from home? Don't most injuries happen within the home, or nearby?"

He stood up and shook Zingman's hand again, this time apologetically. "It's okay, Ross. Actually, that's about it for me tonight, anyway. There's a million things going through my mind, and I guess I'm not ready to say them." He turned and ventured unsteadily down the hall to the bathroom. Zingman waved to the members, exchanged his customary hug with Tenzer, who seemed all bones beneath a faded cardigan. His last image was of Gilbeau and Mezzanotte, eyes damp but still sitting with arms crossed, frozen in place like the swallows on Estelle Tenzer's kimono, behind them.

Breathing the warm breeze, trying to get it all, passing beneath streetlights, one of which flickered pink, Zingman enjoyed this reliable post-Cobhouse solidity, the respite from strict hopelessness; even the very faint green stains on his palms always worked for him like a badge of struggle.

Patrick Tenzer had come upon the corn method quite by accident. After Estelle's death, he'd joined the State Organization for the Recently Widowed, an up-beat club that believed less in quiet talk than in distraction through staged social events. One afternoon, at a barbecue/dance party, he found he could best avoid people's overtures if he tended conscientiously to shucking the corn, sitting at a picnic table, producing a mound of husks, blinking tears loose and recalling for the first time since her death—he later told Zingman—Estelle's peculiar way of waving hello or goodbye with the heel of her hand pushed forward. He learned that this nearly violent act of peeling back and yanking off rough green layers to reach the silky threads and smooth thin-skinned kernels made it easier for him to focus and to cry.

From then on, Tenzer stayed at home with his six-year-old daughter Mathilda, whose longing for her mother was "just like a fountain."

When Katherine Selden, a casual acquaintance, died of complications from diabetes, and her husband Paul started dropping by, Tenzer offered him some of the corn he'd taken to stashing in his refrigerator; they sat together at the kitchen table, Paul filibustering upon the topic of Katherine, while a green pile grew great before them. And the Cobhouse was well born.

Zingman stepped briskly along Bigelow Street, believing he could cope with the home decorations. On both sides of him, Halloween characters mocked, icons of his chosen craft. From a nearby window, a black-paper witch in lethal silhouette shrieked, "Eeeeeh! Look at the Hangdog, Wife Dies and He Hasn't Written a Word in Twenty-Six Months . . ." Three grinning skulls on three porch pillars cried out in unison, "Hoooo, We Concur, Poor Thing Can't Scare Himself Anymore, World's Been Drained of Strangeness . . ." A squat mummy with green-glowing eyes whispered from a lawn, "Ahhhh, But Don't Let's Worry, He's Found A New Calling Now—Distinguished Professor at the YMCA!"

The skulls made a valid point. He'd only taken the teaching job on the off-chance that it might persuade him again that the world crackles with strangeness, with imaginative possibility. "Creative Writing 300: Advanced Horror!" The "advanced" and the exclamation point were pure frill, for group morale, and his own.

The witch was wrong, however. Last week he began a new story, entitled "Tag." It wasn't, perhaps, very good, but at least it was, and he hoped to read it aloud to Mr. Ruthbar, his friend and best listener. He'd invited the man to his apartment tonight for one of their patented readings, and then afterward, at midnight, maybe they would watch the television broadcast of "Wombdwellers: A Pre-Natal Nightmare," starring Lucas Haas and Claire Danes, the movie made from Zingman's 2002 novel. He and Andy had poked great fun at it in the theater three years ago, not long before her first symptoms. Of course, she'd groaned at the cheeseball acting, but she had to admit that at least Claire Danes was convincing as the hugely pregnant crossing guard, months overdue.

Zingman's watch showed that he now had less than twenty minutes till class. He decided to trot, but his eye was soon drawn to a tall window with yellow light. He stopped before it, remembering that their own windows had seemed, at night, no less peaceable and pardoning. Sometimes, on walks by alone, he used to let the house sneak up on him, then do a double-take. When Andy had died he'd lost not only the woman, but just exactly this as well, this lit window.

The curtains parted to reveal a red-headed teenage boy, peering out apprehensively. Zingman raised his palms—stained their faint, innocent green—and was on the verge of mouthing some mealy explanation for his presence on the lawn when the boy let the curtains drop shut. Zingman quickly resumed his way.

The mystery woman is, he figures out, a landscaper for the City, but it takes him three finished projects—courthouse lawn resodding; shrubbery upgrade at the elementary school; rock garden installation behind the Department of Natural Resources—before he can stop observing and approach a sapling and start clearing his throat. He knows she'll return to the sapling after her break because it lies on its side, roots packed in burlap.

During two long brunches, he hardly eats, drinks coffee while listening to Andrea Parker talk and watching her spread piece after piece of toast with blackberry jam, bite out semi-circles, leave the crusts. Her hair, free of the baseball cap, has turned out to be a dull color, which is a relief—at last, something about her that's not spectacular. He asks questions about her work, which she is glad to describe in exquisite detail, using her hands so deftly compared to his own two lugs fumbling with the mug that he finds it possible to forget he's ever felt inspired, to wonder whether, secretly, he may not already have passed his prime somehow, ripened and begun a subtle rotting. At twenty-eight, he's never been in love; he's suspected this, and now he knows.

Applying blackberry jam to a scone, she tells him, "I'm planning to teach a minicourse in topiary up at the state college next month," and to Zingman this sounds virtuous, sounds, in fact the more he thinks about it, like only the single most unassumingly bountiful statement ever uttered. He pretends to consult his menu, watches her blinking, watches her laugh briefly at herself for trying to spread jam evenly over the rocky crags and ledges of the scone. This task, he tells himself, must be especially troublesome for one practiced in the smooth forms of topiary.

"And what will you cover in your first meeting?" he asks. She locates a napkin and a pen, right away makes a sketch.

Tire rubber chirped on asphalt. Whirling, Zingman saw a dirty white van of the bread truck variety, speeding this way beneath a series of streetlights. It swerved several times, at one spot even mounting the curb on Zingman's side before careening off and streaking past him, engine roaring. Was the driver actually wrestling for control of the wheel? Rectangular brake lights stammered then stayed red, the van undergoing a severe left turn and then squealing to a halt somewhere out of sight.

Catching his breath, Zingman watched a crepe-paper skeleton, dangling from a clothesline, dancing in the last swirls of displaced air, laughing derisively. "Awwww, Nothing Ever Happens To Him Anymore, Nothing Ever . . ."

Zingman followed, trotting once again, and found himself entering onto a broad asphalt plateau. A sign read "ARCHIMEDEAN PRODUCTS, INC." The parking lot was half full; here and there, streetlights glowed in cone-shape. And beyond, a colossal steel and glass structure jutted many stories into the sky, with hundreds of dark windows, and hundreds of others, shining bright. He scanned the lot until he picked out the culprit, parked thirty feet away at a random slant in an otherwise empty section, just outside one of the spreading cones.

Like some stealthy cartoon cat, stepping high and silent, enjoying himself for a change, Zingman approached, careful to remain at a forty-five-degree angle to the rear bumper, in the presumed blind spot of the driver's-side mirror. Soon, he could make out in this mirror a dim wedge of shoulder, shifting uncomfortably.

Unlike a cartoon cat, Zingman checked his watch. He really ought to quit this game; after all, he had a job, like all those people up there, in the windows of the Colossus—miniature workers absorbed in tasks, crisp shadows lifting things, putting things down, consulting with one another. Then again, not all of them were industrious. In a window midway up was the silhouette of a woman, just sitting, and who, unless his eyes were imposing strangeness where none existed, removed a pair of glasses and began striking herself on the side of her head repeatedly with her hand.

Inspired by this behavior, Zingman crept onward. When he'd come to within fifteen feet of the blocky van, he froze at the sounds, inside, of a ferocious muffled argument between a man and a woman. He couldn't make out the words, listening with his head tilted at various settings until, at last, the man's voice sliced out— ". . . that it rests solely with us . . ." After laughing rather cruelly, Zingman believed, the woman's voice calmed itself, forging, if tone could be believed, a diligent chain of logic.

He remembered Matthew Glennon's allusion to conflict with Sheila, and his stomach braced, his knees weakened, and so he thought he'd simply take a seat on the blacktop, which, when he did, turned out to be warm from today's unseasonable sun.

He studied the green on his hands, a steadying meditation.

Andrea's hands are clean, alarmingly so, the soil of her livelihood banished now from even the merest pockets beneath her nails, though at their brunches Zingman has found that trace endearing, an enticement to his imagination. He can't understand, here at dinner, sipping wine, how he deserves even that focused labor, much less the woman as a whole, in her creamy sundress, sitting with him on a terrace under a vast umbrella in mild evening air. There will be no sketching on napkins for her tonight; she's adopted a differing spirit. Finishing a salty olive, her eyes slant past his left ear. "You're very skilled, you know, with all those questions. I'm not saying they're not sincere, because obviously"—she places the pit in a small bowl—"you're interested in my answers. But you've always got the next good question loaded up, don't you?" When her eyes shift to his right ear, Zingman assumes they're pointing out his strict limits, and he can only agree. "After I got home last Sunday, I suddenly realized what a little racket you're running!" She laughs into her merlot. "Trying to build me like a statue out of my answers. It's flattering, but it's also kind of . . . it is, it's a bit of a racket."

She insists that tonight, he talk. When he admits he's a writer, she says, "Well, well," grinning like a crack sleuth.

"There's one for Andy." She picks up another Spanish olive, but he can't quite bring himself to go ahead and say he writes dark fantasy or horror fiction, much less to offer examples of any particular plots, for fear she'll see him as an iffy bet, a kind of perpetual adolescent drifter; she's thirty-one, and probably doesn't wish to squander time. This is years before he starts work on Wombdwellers, his breakthrough novel, the idea for which will

-NOEL

hatch from their marriage. His first two books, although published, have sold poorly and received starkly mixed reviews.

He tells her a few childhood stories, typical only-child woes and spoilage. Andrea listens but, deflected, tears her napkin into lengthy shreds and vows, he can tell, a solemn ban on such exotic, modern details as topiary.

Therefore, at last ditch, when the paella arrives, Zingman invites her to the city zoo, where at least he knows he's highly accomplished at gazing into the Seaquarium. "It's a place that's been very important to me. I meditate there about my novels. The fish are so . . . they're peaceful," he says, then hears himself sounding horrendously simplistic, so he adds, "and inside there, I've always thought it was beautifully . . . landscaped." Now he feels worse than ever, because what he's referring to with that word so carelessly flung—the boulders and the swaying sea plants—is, as she'll soon find out, a) just a jumble, and b) under water.

Canned yet voluminous, the voices inside the dirty van swelled once more, although still unintelligible; and now it seemed that the conductive materials out of which the vehicle was built threw the contours of this clash into a kind of gorgeous relief, making whatever was at issue seem like the overblown plot of a tragic opera, balming through abstraction the pain of Ocracoke. Man and woman, stripped to their essences, locked in a duel in which the entire questionable future of love on earth hangs in the balance.

Nine minutes till "Advanced Horror!" Fearlessly, Zingman got up and shuffled into better position. Soft breezes played in his ears like cloth, making him laugh a little. Now, through the window, he could see that the driver must be leaning back in his seat, because visible, only, was the profile of the passenger who was pleading her case by means of urgent chopping gestures with both arms. Zingman cupped his ear, clearing away the folds of wind, and received splinters of sense—". . . every wasted minute you say . . . just the one school . . . stop to think . . . never, NEVER . . . way I used to watch you from the pier . . . you promised my mother." Then, she splintered even further, into tears.

Prompting Zingman to begin a respectful retreat. Except the driver's door flew open and a large man emerged, wearing a wool hat and heavy boots. Zingman was going to call out, "Hi-hey-don't-worry-sir-I-was-just-passing-through," but the man didn't notice him, fiddling instead with a set of keys, isolating one, and proceeding to stomp directly to the back of the van. While he unlocked and heaved open the doors, the woman climbed much less briskly from the passenger side of the cab and proceeded, out of sight, toward the rear.

He stepped right up to the van and leaned his shoulder blades against it, as though waiting for a bus. He sniffed a foul-smelling wash, like a breeze off a weedy beach at low tide. He felt the chassis buck; the man had hopped inside. He heard splashing liquid and the man's voice again, now low, cooing to someone in there.

Oh, the woman was just a girl. She entered Zingman's view and stood hugging herself, dressed in a muddy knee-length sweater, a drab scarf over her hair, tied primly beneath her chin. Her cheeks were blotched red. She coughed twice. Then she saw him.

"Oh!" She backed away.

"Hi-hey-don't-worry." He went to her and held out his hand. "I'm Ross Zingman." They were directly behind the open double doors; the fishy odor was strong. She considered the hand—could she tell it was green?—but the man appeared abruptly on the threshold, unshaven, fiftyish, face splattered with water drops, a framed extremist of some sort. Zingman offered the hand to him now, while using it also to point up to the Colossus, where the tiny silhouettes in the windows kept up their good work; on the instant he couldn't relocate the woman who'd struck herself, earlier, so impressively on her own head. He formulated a plan to say, "I've lived in this city for years but I don't know what this company produces, and I was hoping you could tell me," but he'd only cleared "I've" when the man gave an embarrassingly intimate moan, sprang onto the pavement, and shut the doors with two terrific bangs, then pressed his back against them, looking down on Zingman from his superior height, eyes quickly reading him like a list of bad ingredients. Zingman dropped his hand.

"I'm Pauline," said the girl. It was more than the cheek blotches; her pretty face seemed wholly smudged by some large regret. "But I'd advise you to move right along, then, sir. My . . . friend and I have some urgent business here."

"Well, yes, I'll be on my way . . . but first, and I hate to ask," said Zingman, buoyed by this person's evident concern for his welfare. He addressed the man again. "I can't help wondering what you've got inside here, and why you were in such a hurry back out there on Bigelow Street. Nearly took me along with you!" It occurred to him to step up and chuck the man playfully on the shoulder. But instead he said, "Not a bomb, I hope!" and laughed naturally. He'd always wanted to be the type of guy who would chuck a total stranger on the shoulder, oh, not habitually, by any means, but under the right circumstances and if the spirit moved. The man took one step forward, made a wide swing with his arm, and landed a powerful blow with his open hand to Zingman's head.

A sunny Sunday morning. Movers are cleaning out the house, new owners due on sight. Zingman stands in the front yard, seeing things through the movers' eyes. He's let the lawn go since Andy; weeds choke the flower beds. Two men grapple with the bedroom mattress, squeeze it out through the front door that suddenly looks as small as a keyhole. They lay it on the grass, as if inviting him to sleep. He wants to sleep. He's been doing little else for months. After that, another man carries the round mirror from the upstairs bathroom out this same front door, carefully down the porch steps and across the lawn. Zingman can't help looking—the mirror shows blue sky, shows a red-orange smear of autumn leaves, shows a terrible moment of the sun itself, before resting on the ground, leaned against the trunk of a young tree, where it reflects nothing, nothing but the fixed yawn of infinity.

His knees are failing. He's not alone. Someone stands beside him, holding him up, the same man (though he doesn't know it yet) who has been writing him gentle letters for months, inviting him to join his widowers' group. "I know, there is something very wrong," says this man, "about a mirror out of doors." He helps Zingman to sit down on the grass, then he goes and picks up one of the movers' thick pea-green protective cloths, marches straight to the mirror, and wraps it up carefully.

"Who are you?"

"I'm Patrick Tenzer."

He was not alone. "Told you, I told you!" said Pauline, helping him to his feet and leading him rapidly back toward Bigelow Street. "I'm awfully sorry, sir. You're going to have a bit of a bump on the head, there. But like I told you before, you better not stick around—he gets crazy when it comes to his . . . to his babies."

Zingman hustled numbly down the middle of the street, turning once to see his guardian angel trudging back to her post, her long sweater brushing the backs of her knees. She rounded the corner and disappeared. And still looming, the Colossus—had it actually enlarged with distance?

As to the woman in silhouette, Harriet Corrigan sat at the edge of the company cafeteria, nursing a bad earache and a terrible crush; both were more painful now because of what had occurred nine floors below a few minutes back, while, in a long windowless room, she inspected cultures of mold.

Down there, no silhouette was possible for her—*though in shadow I'm at my peak.* Prior to riding the elevator, Harriet had been on the job, perched atop her metal stool, feeling roundly on display. Hoping for her crush to arrive, and not to arrive, she'd kept glancing left down the length of the lab, like a sight through the wrong end of a telescope.

In front of her was ample distraction—thousands of plastic petri dishes, each two inches in diameter, lidded and labeled. Her job was to take them from their shelves one by one, lift their lids, and run her eyes caringly over the circular khaki tundras, noting what pinpoint villages of gray-green mold may have arisen since last inspection, then recording the results on her keypad. The task never required so much as a basic microscope, and this condition itself often sickened her—being forced to attend to gross trivialities.

Speaking of which, she'd been rid of men for two years, ever since Robert Jenwaugh—*don't have to strangle me twice.* Her latest quandary was what to do now that she was infatuated with a woman, for the first time. *Well, first since early in high school, though then I wanted to be Elaine Hemmings, not to touch the girl.*

Harriet rapped the side of her head three times briskly with the heel of her hand, as though jostling an ache meant improving it, and opened the next dish, an apparent dud—but then, they could fool you. Those few cultures that burgeoned would win through to the next stage of enforced evolution here inside Sector F3 of Archimedean Products, Inc.—Agricultural Bacteriology Division, Porcine Microintervention Subdivision. Pig diarrhea, that's essentially what it all came down to. Mega-agri-business. At first, she had managed to find it amusing that—after completing her graduate work in the formation of spermatozoa within the germinal epithelium of the seminiferous tubules—she was now a member of a crack team busy engineering a spore whose sole reason for being was to be introduced into hogs' small intestines, there to infiltrate and disable invader bacteria that decimated farmers' stock by causing extreme dehydration. Such diseases were constantly mutating, so the work was never finished.

Harriet had languished down here in "The Pig Trough" for thirty-seven months. It was exactly the sort of lucrative but mindless position—trafficking in commercial biotech—that had become traditional for young post-grad researchers in the nineties and early aughts, while they lobbied for rare slots in the top university labs.

She capped the last dish of the day—yes, a complete failure, #4412, a wasteland, although its culture was 9999.9978% genetically identical to the most rousing success stories. She replaced #4412 on its shelf, tapped it lightly farewell, then entered a score of zero in its column.

Harriet clicked out of the database, took off and folded her thick glasses—what she called her frog glasses—and slid them into her lab coat's breast pocket. She rubbed her eyes, then gazed in welcome soft-focus at the pale-blue monitor screen set into the wall beneath the shelves, where the screen saver was a message in fancy yellow script; it floated up from the bottom, paused midway, then exploded, shrapnel of characters shooting off hypnotically beyond the four corners. It was something her mother dreamed up and used to recite, soberly, when Harriet was feeling lowest—THE WORLD IS ALWAYS LISTENING, LISTENING FOR ITS OWN LONG DEFINITION, DRAWN OUT THROUGH ALL YOUR WORDS AND THOUGHTS.

She tried to enjoy this calm before the storm. Most of the day crew had already gone home, but soon the night-shift would fill this narrow room with their annoying habits of banter and fellow-feeling. It was the price to pay to be able to whiff, coming from one neck in particular, a lilac perfume. For the past twenty-five weekdays running, Pepper Sarles, fresh blonde recruit out of Berkeley, would report for duty in her crisply starched white lab coat—face alive, not a single cell of self-doubt in her entire body—and dance about on her stool announcing late-breaking genetic news from her hot sources on the West Coast, spell-binding her devoted band of male subjects—Franklin, Nomura, Kirby, Butterfield, O'Callahan, and Pollard, these men who, even Nomura, were privileged sons of the British microbiology machine, descended from Crick and Watson, who had worked out the form of the DNA molecule back in 1953. This Franklin was no relation—he'd answered her caustically—to that Franklin, Rosalind, who'd labored right alongside Crick and Watson in that immortal lab in Cambridge, England, until of course the men were on the brink of their discovery, whereupon they'd kicked her out, dooming her to obscurity.

Harriet yelped quietly and cupped her right ear, rubbing it, knowing this was useless; the ache throve far inside her head, a culture more momentous than any found in these petri dishes. Freshly dizzy, she lay her hands flat on the counter.

For days, the ache had measured itself bearably, a tightly held pocket of pain right above her jaw-joint, its only sound an occasional throaty sizzle that she could even imagine to be the gentle applause she'd someday earn from the recombinant DNA research community. But ever since yesterday evening, she'd been granted certain brief eavesdropping privileges. For a moment, the ache's most private workings would leap into focus. Some clamoring business was underway in the fleshy rooms nearest her brain, sounding like construction, with gears, pulleys, winches. Or, at other times—such as right now—when she'd cock her head and rap her temple, the sound would shift into a quieter, more diligent operation. *Someone is chiseling in there, trying to finish me off by rendering accurate and honorary busts of James D. Watson and Francis Crick.*

She rushed to the bathroom, twenty feet away, leaned over a deep stainless steel sink, waiting while her nausea passed. She peered down into the throat of the drain, to a metal cross, which was, she'd always noted, an odd universal in drain design. She managed to breathe herself back from the brink, then sighed, long and with feeling, which sounded bulky, pleasing, in this chamber.

Harriet splashed water in her face and stood up straight, though keeping her eyes shut. A mirror was never a friend to her. She'd long ago marked the pathos in the fact that her passion lay in isolating and manipulating genes while she herself had been dealt such a dismal hand.

Turning, she opened her eyes upon a small cloud of bathroom gnats—*mmmmwell, we meet again.* Month after month, this company-wide infestation had survived the finest poison pellets and fumigations, been driven back into the plumbing system, but had always rallied and re-emerged. She drew her fingers through their busy midst, smiling. Actually, she kind of liked them and cheered their returns; they seemed a favorable tribe, somehow sent, making her musey and self-approving, forever shimmering on the outskirts of things, like herself.

Back at her station—too sick to face her, not on my game, when does my game begin?—Harriet made ready to escape and go home. She picked up wallet, car keys, and—"No, no, you dopes!" Pepper's voice belled the length of The Pig Trough, causing a clutch in Harriet's gut; but she didn't look. Usually, the lilac scent would tip her off, but today Harriet wasn't sniffing so well. "That's just because you've only known cell division to occur in that limited way," Pepper continued, "in nature's creaky old method." Her subjects laughed very hard. "A teacher of mine in California is developing an enzyme that can stimulate receptor sites in T-RNA within the nucleus. You're right, Tom, there's nothing so surprising there, but get this—my guy Barnes has shifted the emphasis from protencartic to intratencartic, which has opened some doors, let me tell you. It's fission made into a spectator sport. It's turbo-fission, you've never seen anything like it, I swear, just wait till this hits."

Yes, the girl would certainly go places in this organization; chances were she'd lift herself out of here and up to Hormone Synthesis within the year.

Harriet sighed and set car keys and wallet back down on the counter. For solace, she reached up for petri dish #2939. Occasionally, one would please her. She took out her frog glasses and, after removing the lid, used one lens as a magnifying glass. Though probably not cut out to be the savior of the hogs, this variation had abruptly bloomed into a lush jungle valley—orange fungal stalks packed together, each stalk topped by a striking black sphere; and then the spheres themselves wore a delicate lavender fuzz. No bare patches, none. Unbridled, joyous growth . . .

"Corrigan! Yoo hoo, Corrigan!"

On her way, Pepper carried in her hands a bright silver bowl heaped with dark leafy salad. Dish #2939 fell onto the counter, bounced, clattered on the floor, settling upside-down by a foot of Harriet's stool. Fool.

"You okay? Looking a little pale there, I'd say," Pepper called; if she'd noticed the error, still she grinned abundantly.

Never before had the woman visited Harriet's own station. They'd spoken briefly just a few times up in the cafeteria. Harriet quickly pocketed her frog glasses, wondering whether to stand or remain seated, then told herself that after all Pepper had still covered only half the distance. As she walked she fit a great forkful of spinach leaves, plus one prettily speared coin of carrot, into her mouth. There was still time, maybe she would choke and collapse. I take it back, I take it back. Behind Pepper, mouths agape—

Franklin, Nomura, Kirby, Butterfield, O'Callahan, and Pollard glared at Harriet, frozen in their incredulous poses and their rumpled labwear, coffee mugs suspended. *Hey, I agree with you, don't ask* me.

"You're not feeding yourself," said Pepper, arriving, "is all." She gathered and forked another mighty knot of foliage.

"'Harriet' is fine," she answered, startling herself, then stood up and startled herself again by accepting the offered bite, by letting her teeth clamp the tines and hold a moment, against the pull.

"Well, young lady," Pepper laughed, setting the bowl atop the now empty stool, kneeling to scrape the dashed jungle up off the floor, placing it on the counter, preparing another bite of salad. And all with a fluidity that made Harriet want to hire this person to show her around the world. "I knew I had a clear sense about you. Here, have another, 't'sa way."

Pepper stared at her face, no doubt registering the low pedigree. "Mmmm, you do seem awfully pale."

"Gawtuneewek."

"What? Chew."

"Sorry. I said I've got an earache, no appetite, kind of dizzy, all clogged up, you know?"

Pepper produced as if from thin air a little square blue packet of Kleenex, opened it, pulled out and fluffed a single sheet with the elaborate respect hands reserve for virgin tissues. Harriet took the gift but did not insult it by contact with her nose.

"No wonder you're sick, this end should be called The Sty, not The Trough." She waved through a cluster of gnats Harriet hadn't noticed, dispersing them. "What are these? Taking a refresher course in basic mutation, are we, going all the way back to fruit flies?" She hissed. "Oh, it's those again, from the bathroom . . . thought we got 'em with the exterminators my first week . . . men in uniform, hoooo boy! So now they're in our workspace. Corrigan, we've gotta get out of this stinking hole."

"It's 'Harriet'." But she couldn't meet the blue eyes, fumbled instead with her wallet and keys, and with the precious fragile tissue gift. *Good Lady, why do you torment me?*

"Okay, listen . . . Harriet. I've been watching you, admiring your covert style." *Torment me.* "Mine's different. I've been thinking." Pepper placed one of her hands on Harriet's unappealingly down-sloping shoulder. "We need to organize, you, me, and eventually the other women in this company. All twenty-three strong of us. Get some priorities addressed." She took in another bite of salad, munched it thoughtfully. "For instance, did you realize that precisely zero company funds go into gene therapy research for ovarian and breast cancer, even though it's a huge market and there've been really promising results—hell, the Brits have been on this for years."

Harriet hated having one more thing to admire about her, a moral compass, but she said only, "You know," shrugging off, though gently, Pepper's hand, still looking anywhere but at her eyes, "it's always been sort of hard for me to . . . take these men seriously . . ." She picked up her keys and wallet.

"Ha! Join the club!" Pepper brushed dismissively with the back of her hand up toward Butterfield and the others.

"I mean specifically British men. I've had a grudge ever since I was a girl, since Crick and Watson. You've read *The Double Helix,* what those two did to Rosalind Franklin?"

"Well, that, as they say, is ancient history, sweetheart. Grudges never changed a thing. And men are much weaker than you think. We've got work to do, but let's talk over some food upstairs? It's more secure in the cafeteria, with that hubbub. Okay?" She replaced her hand in the very same spot, finger for finger.

Harriet dropped keys and wallet on the counter. "All right. Um, now?" She picked them up.

"Couldja give me twenty minutes?"

Harriet put them down.

"Have to placate the boys for a while. You know how that goes."

"Mmmmm."

Pepper removed her hand and stretched hugely, yawning. "All part of the master plan, like my little thing with Garvey."

"Him? Oh, my God."

She laughed. "I know, he's cute—I shouldn't be so cold. But would I be seeing him if he didn't have his hands on the levers of power, or one lever, at least? Plus, there's more going on in that boy's head than you might guess. I—" She glanced over her shoulder; apparently one of those boys had made an impatient sound. "I'll fill you in."

She took up her silver bowl and started to turn, but caught sight of the blue wall monitor. "What's this about?" She read the sentence softly aloud, finishing, ". . . DRAWN OUT THROUGH ALL YOUR WORDS AND THOUGHTS."

Harriet looked her dead in the eyes. "Just something my mother used to tell me, when I needed to hear it."

(What she didn't say was that whenever she would go to her mother, while growing up, asking why science had made her an outcast from the human fold, her mother would reply, "Nonsense," massaging her daughter's temples as though she could actually keep her brain company, physically, in the way a brain sometimes yearns for. "You, you're just biding your time. Do you want to know why it seems so quiet around you?" Harriet would nod every time. ". . . listening for its own long definition, drawn out through all your words and thoughts.")

"Ah, very nice. My mom wanted me to stay with her in the woods and blow Goddamn glass. See you in twenty." And Pepper was away.

Harriet blew her nose, violently, depositing a goodly stock of phlegm into this holder cruelly petite for the task. Which pointed up another of the thousand ways she'd found to divide the human species, and yes, she fell into the category of those who will gaze, almost adoringly, into their own full tissue.

Nor did this attention escape the attention of Franklin, Nomura, Kirby, Butterfield, O'Callahan, and Pollard, who, although more than ready now to welcome back their own and hear further news about the latest alternatives to mitosis, continued to stare past her for the moment at Harriet with tilted, queasy faces, Butterfield's even out-and-out mortified. She arced the immoral wad perfectly into a nearby wastebasket, where it made a tired "bonk."

After riding the elevator seven floors up, Harriet had slumped her heavy self into her usual red-plastic chair in the corner of the busy dinnertime cafeteria, at a small round table by a window. Now, she tried not to overhear snatches from neighboring tables—". . . looks like Hell . . . no, over there . . . oh yeah, still in The Trough . . . she's a lifer down there . . . ha ha ha . . . typical Corrigan, right . . . verge of passing out whenever you look at her . . . does not work and play well with others, ha!"

Her left nasal passage was clogged. Through her right, she tried to guess by aroma alone the newest concoctions of Archimedean's master chefs, offerings housed in those glass cases across the room. Yes, one could of course side-step the most venturesome treats if she wished for no more than, say, a cheeseburger, fries, and a shake, but since the unorthodox fare represented the only evidence Harriet had encountered of company playfulness, she tended to investigate, though by nose alone, never tasting anymore.

Tonight, only a muffin would do, blueberry, or perhaps corn. She put on her frog glasses, but still felt dizzy, not quite ready to cross the floor—the roomful of eyes, the wait in line, the small talk. So she took her ordinary dodge, turning to gaze out the window to bathe her eyes into the dependable salve of night. But this time, something caught her eye—a boxy truck of the kind used for heists in low-budget movies of the '70s and '80s, speeding into the parking lot far below, skidding to a halt by a streetlight. After its hasty parking job, she watched it for a minute. Nobody got out; nothing happened. It wasn't very clean, and it had a large dent in its side, toward the rear.

When nothing further happened, she raised her eyes, sought

and found again the wideness and depth of sky, and in order to distract herself from the upcoming conversation with Pepper, she inhaled diligently, undertaking once again to tease apart the aromas, separating the rich smoky over-smells of frying meats and strong coffee from the thin, enfeebling under-smells of the unholy marriages.

During her first three weeks on the job, chipper, Harriet had helped herself to several of the novelties, most of which could be had free of charge, because here was the ideal volunteer testing pool. Employees favored the mood-elevating cheeses that came from genetically altered cows and goats whose lacteal glands now rained out milk laced with serotonin boosters; and they also raved over the navy blue stick candy formed from the spew of "super-bees" re-engineered to secrete royal jelly instead of honey, which sticks Harriet saw, until the project was abruptly cancelled, protruding from mouths throughout the building. Archimedean hearts beat bravely, fist fights and romances flaring in the halls. A dismal failure, though, was the line of fruity, diagnostic soups, which, if you were ill, would stain your urine various colors, depending on the type of disease that afflicted you.

But before she knew better, Harriet had found herself actually enjoying a salty gray pate made from enhanced human pituitary glands, then mashed and applied to wheat crackers, that is until the morning rheumy-eyed Eve Culbertson from the front desk, showing every day of her seventy years, snitched to Harriet that there were hormones in this pate that stop the aging process . . ."in its tracks," she said, explaining that she'd been eating the stuff here for fourteen years. The old woman set her face at its best viewing angle and batted her eyes a few times, which made a remote spongy sound. "These men are certified geniuses, don't you agree?" "Well," Harriet had answered. "It certainly is spreadable."

She blinked, realized she was looking not into the sky anymore but down at the company grounds, at the lit statue of Archimedes—discoverer of leverage, shouter of "Eureka!" . . . father of Crick, Watson, and every other man who'd been in position to use his mind as fulcrum, his privilege as lever, to advance the cause of science. Archimedes, who reportedly said, "Give me a place to stand and I'll move the world."

When Harriet took off her glasses and administered one more series of raps to the side of her head—*that ought to hold me*—she pronounced herself minimally fit to stand. But below, another character had, at some point, entered the stage of the parking lot—*the playlet goes on, does it?* As if to hold her at the window, a tiny man was overplaying his part, sneaking, so it seemed—although he was in full view—across the lot toward the dented boxy truck. But just before he'd reached his goal, what did he do? She laughed, then stifled herself. *Men. Can't seem to go a single minute without referring to themselves in some way.* He actually sat down and began—how rich—staring at his own hands. *Eureka!*

Archimedes and now this sneaking man. They reminded her, indirectly yet vividly, of poor Henrietta Lacks, long-dead cancer patient, victim of science. One night, right here in this very room, Harriet had sampled one of the dark chewy humps that were forever showing up behind the sneeze-guards, preparations conspicuously unnamed in their innocent green ceramic bowls. While the hump was certainly dreadful, it wouldn't have made her so sick if it weren't for its shocking resemblance—recognized only afterward—to a famous tumor. Eight weeks before her death, back in 1951, a surgeon at Johns Hopkins had removed much of Henrietta Lack's twenty-six-pound cervical tumor, then kept it going in his lab. And although this doctor was now dust, himself, those aberrant cells were still "alive" today, having grown not into a science fiction monster but into a sprawling mass, sustaining themselves and multiplying, used ever since, worldwide, for cancer research.

Harriet had once even invited herself to Baltimore, to visit a prospective boyfriend (who had other ideas). She'd gone to Johns Hopkins and gained access to the storage facility, was saddened to find that Henrietta's cells were housed in a fleet of mere gray tubs in a chilled basement vault. Under bluish light, they looked like malignant oatmeal, faintly rummaging; she could have bent down and touched them (since one cannot "catch" cancer), caressed them, more than half a century after they'd first flinched into being on the surface of a young woman's cervix.

Well, she must have missed something, down in the parking lot, because the sneaking man had vanished. Now Harriet saw two figures behind the boxy truck, where the back doors had been thrown wide open. It was a woman and a different man; they appeared to be playfully dancing. Momentarily, she found this an enormously comforting picture—how they neared one another and then receded, arms flailing, feet stamping . . . how they inhabited a world of biological business-as-usual, where flirtation still reigned, still succeeded—until the woman suddenly closed the gap and poked the gentleman, hard, making him stumble backward! *Oh, my miniature companion, you have seen the light already. Do not give him a blessed inch!*

". . . 'and so it was that Death came to Jake Raftery, less like a shadow than like a springer spaniel, beseeching, darting in and out of reach, yipping, yipping, yipping, always the yipping—or is that, he wondered, only the sound of the last of my wind whistling, whistling, whistling through this stiletto hole in my chest-cavity?'"

"Masterful use of repetition, there, Penny," Zingman said, nodding at her and then around the table at his nine "Advanced Horror!" students, who nodded back respectfully in the acidic fluorescence that fell from above. "Definite improvement since last draft."

The whole left side of his face, where the man had slapped it, seemed to have become a hive of stinging ants, not bees, and not especially large stinging ants either, but tiny, insidious, quietly invading ants. The corner of his mouth had become involved in the swelling too, and this gave his words a slightly iffy taint, as though completely insincere, which would be an exaggeration.

"So, Penny, you've got to promise us another installment next week. Am I right in believing Mr. Jake Raftery has a few tricks up his sleeve, yet? Mmmmm, thought so! Okay, so, ah, Vivian, how would you like to go n—"

Vivian had been coiled; she leaned toward the base of her chair, reached into her blue denim book bag, so that Zingman could see the top of her stiff brown hair—frosted at its peaks like baked Alaska in reverse—and the overlarge aqua beads of her necklace floating out before her and swinging, swinging, as though through the vast empty space of possibility, making him slightly nauseated.

"'Fear is a cheap generic item, available to all in this liquidation sale we call living,'" she read, laying a two-inch-thick manuscript out before her and fastening her hands onto its upper corners, like a water skier ready for the first violent tug.

"'Ah but Terror, my friends, Terror is top-of-the-line, name brand, accept no substitutes. Yes sir, Terror will cost you. Terror will take you to the cleaners. What's that? Not sure you can afford it? Ha ha ha ha ha ha ha ha ha! In the market for Mere Apprehension? Right this way, then, we'll proceed down this corridor here, following these signs. I only hope . . . I only hope nobody has switched them on us; there are some tricksters about, you know. . . . Ah, here we are at the door marked Anxiety Annex, and what have we over there? Why, it's the ever-popular Department of Palpitations, just across from this narrow door—The Writhing Room. My, my. Shall we try the knob? Very well . . .'"

Zingman became aware—thank God, before anyone else—that he was drooling from the corner of his mouth, where his lips were puffed up to the point of slackness. He gingerly slurped, and followed this by a casual wipe with his sleeve.

His slapped ear had tuned out; his other ear joined it now in sympathy. He watched Vivian turn the first page over, place it print-side-down next to the stack, and then continue mouthing words. This soundlessness allowed him to observe the woman more affectionately. Something about her reminded him of his mother. Was it a personal philosophy that barred blinking? Was it the way her lips seemed to revere her words so much they hated to let go of them? Or was it maybe that both women were named Vivian.

". . . 'At last, the longed-for day had arrived,'" he heard, checking in. The rectangular table seemed to have lengthened until it was a plank along which her words made for him. "'The one Gladys had chosen as her personal Independence Day, the day on which she would make Mr. Baird and the rest of them regret until Hell gained dominion over the Earth that they had ever forced her to clean out those gerbil cages . . .'"

Even with his mouth impaired, Zingman successfully executed (without nostril-twitch or chin-rumble) that most diabolical and indispensable of the teacher's tricks—the closed-lipped yawn.

That earlier Vivian, his mother, had disliked his first forays into making horror stories, calling them "inappropriate and mean-spirited." But this caused a remarkable thing to occur, he noticed. One day, while he was reading to her one about mothers killing and grinding up their children, putting them into bottles in the spice rack or smoking them in a pipe, "Ahhhhh, ahhhhhhhh, now that's refreshing!", a little blue vein rose at the side of her neck. From then on, instead of looking to her eyes for approval, he'd watch the vein, in cahoots with it, smiling to see its silent applause for him. Eventually, at age seventeen, it provided the inspiration for his first published story, which appeared in none other than "Rod Serling's Twilight Zone Magazine."

"Vein Glory" featured an ugly duckling girl who turned into a great seductress, gorgeous in every particular, except that whenever she became sexually aroused, this strange vein, running down her neck, became thick as rope—pulsing, with smaller veins criss-crossing it all over—and extended all the way to her shoulder, where it vanished into the "holy sanctum of her innards, where it belonged."

Because she always wore plenty of scarves, shed them only in total darkness, a man could sometimes miss the fact long enough to became intimate with her, until the moment a hand of his would land there, and that's when "his prick would be quite undone, believing itself no match for this mighty display of blood's true potential."

Naturally, she tried tourniquets of silk and lace, but these stanched more than she bargained for—apparently her brain was heavily dependent upon this source.

"However," Zingman had written in a crucial, final-twist paragraph that he now knew to be worthy only of "Advanced Horror!", but which had seemed back then on par with Mr. Serling himself, "love's extemporaneous, if anything is, and Sweet Sophie found someone, quite by chance, to call her own. He loved her not despite her vein but because of it, and, he insisted, the mind that it fed so generously. Sophie came to love herself as well. Truc was shy and never smiled because he had lost most of his teeth during childhood due to poor dental habits and the crushing poverty of life in the Old Country. In fact, she noticed more gum than tooth in there, wide stretches of plain pink shelf, which felt very nice indeed rubbing against her neck, pinching the vein (something that he was extremely fond of doing), just as if he were attempting to bite through, which made her feel deliciously light-headed. Perhaps it was only the condition of Truc's mouth that gave him his profound lisp, which was why she found it so difficult at first to make out his accent, that subtle, subtle Transylvanian drawl . . ."

When Vivian paused to draw breath, Zingman pounced. "This reader is hooked, see." He placed his fist out on the false-woodgrain tabletop as though offering a provisional trophy. "The very idea of someone plotting revenge but forgetting that she is blind. What'll she do? What'll slip her mind next, I can't help wondering. Well, it appears that unfortunately we need to move along."

Vivian seemed about to cry, bugging eyes asparkle. It was very warm in this small room.

"No, no, oh," Zingman said, "rest assured . . . soon, soon, soon . . ." He couldn't think of any other words. "Soon, soon now, we'll be back to this, this 'Gladys' you've created for us." He found he liked the word "now" inordinately well all of a sudden; it was a friend to him. Why had he never given it its full due?

"Um, now then, who's next? Who hasn't yet shared any writing with the group?"

"That would be me . . ."

"Oliver, my good man . . ."

Oliver nodded his great bald head, and it seemed like the

beneficent act of a bishop. A Bishop of Horror? This man's waxen face appeared incapable of supporting blood-flow, and he was Zingman's favorite. Zingman swallowed, realizing that he was actually bright with hope.

Oliver cleared his throat for fully half a minute, and during this time Zingman recalled the strange event of learning to whisper, a big day in his life. No one had had to teach him, but it was difficult, and it prefigured everything. He was only six. One night, after his mother had tucked him into bed and tiptoed from the room, he tried. It came out as a croak, even louder than his normal voice; his mother came lunging back in, afraid he was choking. He'd calmed her down—patting her hands, telling her, "I was just pretending to be a troll." When she left again, he lay there trembling, thrilled, and practiced until he'd worked his whisper down to a wisp no one could possibly hear but himself.

He found he could say all kinds of things this way that he'd never thought of before, scary things that made the air turn ripply, made the room tilt just a little. "Is the monster here yet?" "Eggs are breaking in my head." "Give me that knife, give it to me." "Daddy's a standing-up mouse." "I will wash your mouth out with soap, Mommy!" He dove under his huge downy pillows, screaming.

Oliver's throat was not yet clear, apparently, but he let the project drop. "A MODEST REBATE FROM THE GRAVE, by Oliver F. Griffith, First North American Serial Rights, 2006, Chapter One."

A sort of speechless physiological simmer around the room said that he had command of his audience.

An abrupt swell of laughter from behind Harriet. Without looking, she could picture the regular tableful of hale, handsome top execs. They were sharing tall tales from the history of bioengineering. That penetrating voice belonged to Mr. Jack Garvey—and he'd be the tan one, wearing a tie that depicted scarlet hemoglobin molecules against an electric yellow background. "As you know, raptors are to say the least kind of my deal, so you'll believe this. Here I'd stumbled on a way to produce a bald eagle the size of a pigeon, a genuine bald eagle, small enough to fit in your standard toaster oven. If I'd gotten the backers, I'd've outfitted a factory to mass produce the damn things. Nothing easier. And the public would jump all over it, a chance to chow on our national symbol . . . little lemon sauce, some basil . . . I was going to call it, 'Eat Up America!'"

Vice President in charge of Enzymes, Garvey had accosted Harriet, her third day on the job, caught her snooping on the fourteenth floor. "Corrigan, is that you?" He recalled her from orientation. "What're you doing way up here, so far from Home Sweet Pig Trough? Actually, though"—he crooked his index finger, up next to his eye, beckoning—"this gives me the opportunity to tell you how impressed I was, just going over your file, in my office right down there, down the hall. So I gather . . ."—cornering her, breath smelling of brandy, having apparently taken time to review her dissertation, where she'd distilled her five years of research on the processes by which the male gamete is first formed in the seminiferous tubules of the human testis, the coiled thread-like passages thickly lined with germinal epithelium from which arise the spermatozoa (germ form to the eventual gamete), this lining itself having become her prime focus, Harriet having advanced our understanding of the intricate choreography by which a small number of proteins and enzymes conspire to manufacture the twenty-three chromosomes of the mature sperm cell—". . . I gather you could stand there and tell me all there is to know about my balls, Corrigan?" He let his clipboard fall between them like a drawbridge, spanning belly to belly.

"Well, if you mean—"

Up drawbridge, and he was against her, moaning to the effect that *his,* thanks, held riddles, stubble rasping her chin and lips, until the soft brandied flesh of his tongue projected between her teeth and she stamped a row of tiny holes—*simply tear at perforation and keep for your records.*

Over her shoulder, now, this same man was broadcasting further exploits, and predicting others, such as a falcon he planned to create that would revolutionize the camping industry; it could be trained to lift hikers' gear and fly it to the top of the trail. "Set it down gently on the summit, hunt and eat all night and be perched and ready for work again at sunrise!" She noticed that the parking lot scene had shifted; both figures were now at the swung-open back doors of the truck, loading something into a bag, the woman not helping.

Well, look at that, would you? They must be making some sort of special delivery. Imagine having a normal job for a while, where I could deliver things that people have been waiting for, where everyone would be glad to see me.

Harriet put her frog glasses back on and rose to her feet, turned and headed for food. The circle of men at the nearby table rose too, but just partway, flashing mock lady-present grins. She waved vaguely in their direction, which caused them to glance at one another as though her gesture had settled a bet amongst them.

Harriet headed for the golden-railed back-and-forth course, mercifully unpeopled, but she was too slow; a bustle of women and men from marketing filled in the line ahead of her. It seemed to her that all her life, whenever she'd stood at the back of a line like this, she'd remain the last even as she progressed, so she was initially glad to sense bodies arriving behind her, until she turned to Franklin, Nomura, Kirby, Butterfield, O'Callahan, and Pollard. "Corrigan," they said, as one man, under his breath.

She wondered how they'd managed to make it all the way here to the seventh floor without their young muse.

"You don't mind? I'm famished!"

Pepper had slipped in front of her and faced her now with a nearly clownish wince of contrition, shoulders hoisted.

"Between you and me, who was I kidding with that salad? I've got my eye on a strawberry shortcake, that one there, third row, see it?"

"Those aren't strawberries."

"Hhhyes. Listen, I really just wanted us to get the chance to talk a bit, like I said, without all the . . ."—she jabbed an eyebrow toward her subjects—". . . distractions of Ye Olde Trough."

This woman's radiant face, swaying so near, understood all too well that it was a rich fund, and though it seemed to spend itself on Harriet with impulsive gusto, they both knew this to be an illusion, that Harriet could possess none of it, not really. The fierce and playful blue eyes, full of schemes, made Harriet picture her own, muddy brown, the eyes of a mole, constantly disappointing. Not generally understood by the lay public was that genetic kinship among Earth's species, at the molecular level, had emerged in the twentieth century as far more striking than any differences. It could only be easy, then, for this insightful charmer to tell that Harriet did indeed share her eyes with those of the lesser rodents; her flaking skin with the common clover moth; and surely, swaying within range, she'd pick up the musty odor of the cherrystone clam, at which point Harriet's cheekbones would loom, finally too close, courtesy of the mandrill baboon—severe, upswept, designed to ward off fondness like shields. The lilac perfume entered the vacant nasal passage, seeping into Harriet's sinuses, traveling along her eustachian tube, and quickly finding the deep nest of her earache, where it rallied the tiny industry of pain.

"Most *distracted* distractions I've ever seen!" Harriet said.

Pepper's laugh consisted of "sh-sh-sh-sh," leaving open the possibility that she meant for Harriet to shut up.

"All right. Now, listen. You see Jack over there?" She waved to him, but he pretended not to notice. "Oh look, he's doing the wily bit!"

"Mmmmm."

"Or 'The Hawk,' as he's known only to intimates."

Harriet lost her appetite, even for a muffin.

Although Butterfield et al were speaking amongst themselves, Pepper's voice frizzed into a whisper. "I'm telling you, he's not so bad, once you get past his ego, or learn to *ride* it, more like. And plus, like I said, he's not just bluster. Fact, he's extremely smart in certain ways, and really well connected around here. I'd actually known—ahhey!" She whirled. "You stink!"

But Garvey, having pinched her, and grinning wolfishly, or hawkishly, was already sidling off toward the salad bar, where he picked out a single black olive. On his return trip, he gave them a wide berth, feigning fear of retaliation. "Talking about me again? My ears are ringing off the hook."

"Topic Numero Uno. Dominates the mind of woman." Pepper rubbed her backside meaningfully.

"So tell your new girl friend there I'm not rabid, will you?" He winked at Harriet and popped the olive into his mouth. She searched for something else to look at, and found, unfortunately, only Butterfield's distorted face, their mutual cases of nausea gnashing together.

"Okay, what was I saying? Oh, I'd known the guy almost a year before I finally gave in. And presto, he hired me here! Used to send me blocks of Pepperjack cheese, get it? Horrible stuff. So now to get back at him I give him marigolds, because they stink, like he does.

"Anyway," she continued, "I've been making, oh, inroads lately. I mean, I haven't figured everything out yet, haven't gotten downstairs . . . for that I'll need your help. I'll explain later. But I've been in his house several times and seen some pretty wild stuff . . ." She checked to make sure nobody was eavesdropping, but somebody was, leaning small and self-conscious against the avocado tiles of the wall, holding a black telephone receiver.

It was the red runt, as Harriet had privately dubbed him, though his name tag said "Mr. Ruthbar"—a short retarded man, always flushed, with one small hand and one big hand. He presided over the salad bar, and over the removal of empty steam trays from the serving line.

Startled, he began punching in a phone number with his little hand, pudgy, always more active than his large hand when he'd do his work.

Harriet whispered, "Downstairs? Downstairs here?"

"Oh, honey, yes it's here. Way down, though. He's got some kind of major project going on, and you can't get to it by the regular elevator. He almost cracked the other night, after a bottle of red wine and my best lasagna. He had in his Goddamn fridge a giant pair of lips, you heard me, made apparently from living tissue. Would I lie to you, Corrigan? So I said to him—"

"Mr. Z!" the red runt shouted into the phone. "Hey, Mr. Z. Mr. Z. You home? It's me. Pick up the phone, it's me."

The runt's round face was wide open, dead-pan, but his voice twanged with a cryptic urgency. His greater hand enwrapped the receiver, nearly concealing it.

"I gotta mop the floor in back, but they got a bell in there so I can hear the phone. You got that number, I gave it to you. Remember you said I could come over tonight. I can take the bus to your house after—"

His flat face jolted to life, folding inward and twisting furiously at something just before it. He made several swipes through the air with the baby hand. Harriet couldn't see what the problem was, until . . . *Oh, you bathroom gnats, even here.* "Jesus, this place oughta be shut down!" Pepper laughed.

"Gotta hang up, be talkin' to you later!" said the red runt.

He stepped crisply off down the linoleum gangway that ran beside the kitchen, hard-soled shoes clicking above the clank of pots, the splash of water. Attached to his belt, he wore an oversized ring of keys, which jingled emphatically.

"So, Corrigan, how about if we get together 'on the outside,' as they say. Some time tomorrow? Say, before your shift, breakfast? I'll bring my notes. You bring yours, wink-wink."

Perhaps Harriet would have relaxed enough to let Pepper take her on as confidante; more likely, she'd have snapped, seized the woman around the waist and tossed her into the air for Butterfield and the boys to catch, as do tuxedoed dancers their sequined star in Broadway musicals—if from the echoey corridor just outside the cafeteria archway a woman had not yelled "Ahhh no!" and stolen the attention of the entire room.

"Keep your voice down, Pauline, I'm asking you."

"I am not a child, Professor. Let's go back to the truck, please? Go get something to eat?"

Into the silent cafeteria stepped a big man holding a brown canvas duffel bag that bulged at the bottom.

It's you, of parking lot fame.

Bulky boots, dark wet clothes, a haggard, unshaven face. Surveying his audience angrily, he yanked off a knit hat to free long, unruly hair.

The young woman, still unseen around the corner, sounded as if she'd swallowed dust. "So you are forgetting what you promised my mother, that's it? You said you'd look out for me, like I was your own."

Hands on her hips, she entered, stunned at the reception. They stood side by side, throwing off a strange, brackish odor. She was not a young woman, was maybe fourteen, shivering, bedraggled, sweet face bleached of all color except for red around the eyes. She wore a drab green scarf over her hair, like someone from the 1960s, and a dirty example of one of those thick, knee-length, British Isles sweaters, wooden buttons up the front.

The bulge at the bottom of the man's duffel bag dripped onto the gray carpet. A small puddle was forming.

"Well," he said, his voice even within this one word casting about for an appropriate pitch. "I must tell you that I have a bomb inside this bag. I will expect your cooperation. First of all, my . . . assistant and I will require your largest bowl filled with lukewarm water."

The bomb twitched once, individual drops joining to form a strand of water—splashing in the puddle—before turning back into individual drops. The splashes could be seen but not heard, because of the gentle laughter in the room.

"'Marsha wasn't about to laminate the truth, not here, not now, not while she lugged Claude's artificial heart's nuclear power unit, on its nine-foot extension cord leading to his chest, up the rocky incline behind her wildly scuttling husband. "Claude," she whined, heaving for breath, "I must tell you something, slow down, for the love of Pete." But his ruddy stone-cutter's laugh thanked her not for her luggings . . .'"

Oliver's initial gravity had deserted him, his voice lifting in pitch, becoming attenuated; he dipped and swayed and bobbed in his seat like an enormous broad-beamed puppet. His listeners snuck peeks at one another.

"'The man halted only long enough to toss back a sweep of sandy hair with a hand briefly free of gripping-duty, then he was off again, Marsha in tow, panting, like a Mongrel of Ambivalence. For she loved him too, damn it all, she did! The sun, a nuclear power station in its own right, to be sure, glared down upon the newlyweds ironically, and Marsha glanced up at it, then glanced at the shoe-box-sized unit in her hands, then let out a laugh which glanced off the sheer humorless walls of Ketchkemethy Gorge. "Let's put it this way," she said to herself behind the goodly screen of her laughter, which had succeeded in arresting her demented heartless groom. "That unit up there does not come equipped with one of these!" She held the unit up for Claude to see, index finger poised over the off button . . .'"

The puppet stopped reading and froze stiff.

Everybody got older.

"Please, go on," said Zingman.

"No."

"Why?"

"I am not being taken seriously."

Several students had indeed tittered, and so they and the others now took turns reassuring Oliver, reporting sensations of painful suspense, two women—Heather and Arlene—even reaching over to stroke his black-sweatered forearm. And thus, speaking through clenched teeth, Oliver deigned to emit the chapter's concluding paragraph, having haughtily vaulted over the intervening material: "'. . . Claude's hand crushed Marsha's shoulder. "Don't you ever," he bellowed, "ever," he barked, "ever, ever lose control with my heart in your hands, is that clear?" And he was off again, scaling desperately toward the sky, almost as if he resented Marsha's father's breakthrough research, which had returned him to life, removed him from the Golden Scrolls of Eternity, kept him down here tethered to plutonium, confounded to no end. Tenderly, while crawling up untender rock, Marsha wept for poor earth-bound Claude, gruff man of peaks, man of valleys too.'"

With that, the author gathered up his manuscript pages, rose from his chair, and marched out of the room, slamming the door behind him.

Following a surprisingly brief pause, "What are those?" said doughy, insecure Mrs. Flynn. This was the first she'd spoken in class.

From somewhere underneath Zingman's shirt, several of the tiny frenetic flies had emerged and now zipped around before his chest. Ever since Mr. Ruthbar's last visit, three weeks ago, the insects had beset Zingman; he would see them flying in his apartment, feel them tickling inside his clothing or see them emerging into the air. He'd shower, scrub, change clothes, and then sure enough, especially when it was warm, out they'd come again. Mr. Ruthbar worked in some cafeteria, of all places.

"Well, all right," Zingman ventured. "Let's take this opportunity to practice, to meet mystery with mastery, like we did last week with those ink blots I brought in, yes? Mr. Schupack, care to take a shot?"

"Mmmmm, oh, jeeez, okay, okay, so I'm looking at them and I'm thinking . . . I'm thinking mites, like the mites that got all over my daughter's baby rabbit last winter, we had to spray—"

"Form of a story, remember." Zingman leaned back, away from the flies.

"Right. Sorry, so mites." He tugged at his beard. "'The whole class looked on, watching the small hovering swarm of harmless insects, not suspecting that . . . um . . .'"

"'Little suspecting,'" entered Vivian, bursting back to life, "'that each one of those insects carried a miniature payload of Zorobrenalon, deadliest toxin known to man, developed by the world-dominating scientists of the People's Republic of China, sent to this country-'"

"Or no," parried Schupack. "How about, 'Developed by Marsha's father to kill Claude, early in Chapter Two, and then sent to destroy a certain innocent horror class who had dared to giggle, dared to disrespect . . . Mr. Oliver F. Griffith!'"

Zingman joined the laughter and applause. Vivian pouted. "And the first symptom of the poison," Schupack chirped, "is—it turns your hands light green!"

Zingman made as if to be aghast at the sight of the stains on his palms.

"Must . . . warn . . . others!" said Vivian, reviving.

"Good show, people," said Zingman. His watch read 8:51 pm. Almost there. His eyes darted around the table, and as they did so, he was conscious of the fact that they were "darting," that he was thinking of them as such, and that cliches were fast becoming the currency of his mind. He noticed Heather had only a short paragraph in front of her. Depending on its contents, he might have a crush on this woman.

"Well, now, we just have time for one little selection more. Heather, how about you?" She twinkled at him from beneath auburn, flipped-up bangs.

"No title yet, sorry."

"Hey, listen, that's okay. We're all in the same boat here, Heather, a life boat, struggling against the current that's trying to pull us out to sea, and that sea is . . ."

Everyone was nodding, first at Zingman and then at one another, even though their teacher hadn't actually said anything at all. The worst part, though, was that he was nodding as well, and vigorously, which made the assaulted portion of his cheek, standing out on its fattened own, discernibly wobble. Oh, he thought, I'm terribly confused.

He realized that all he wanted right this moment was to go off somewhere, sequester himself and meet with mastery his own unfolding "Mystery of the Filthy White Van."

Jacob hauled seaweed, nutritional kelp, and . . .

No.

Carl was a maker . . . of chowders, fine seafood chowders, and tonight he was to deliver ninety gallons of his best to a company called "Archimedean Products, Inc." What he hadn't counted on, however, was feisty young Pauline, secret agent for Progresso Soup . . .

Or should it be entitled, "I, Colossus Worker"?

Heather continued to await her cue, checking the bridge of her nose with her fingers as if to make sure it had not gone soft over time. Oh well, perhaps, by some providence of inspiration-by-proxy, out of her mouth would flow the very tale he needed. He tipped his head back a bit, raised his eyebrows, and this proved cue enough for Heather.

"'Words failed her when Butch, rigid with confidence, swung open her labia like Old West saloon doors. All chatter ceased inside the place, folks cowering, clearing chairs and tables out of the way, but eager for a good old brawl. Except, in the far corner, the piano player's sad tune played on. Before he could even order a drink and strut his rude stuff, the tune made this strong man weep, grow limp, sink to the floor, and then crawl backward out through the same doors. She had this effect on men.'"

"Sweetheart," Pepper called out, marching across the cafeteria toward the damp couple and laying a palm on the man's chest. "Hey, our bowls are your bowls, believe me; why don't we cut the routine and let's take a look in this very interesting bag of yours?"

"Oh, Miss," blurted the girl, but Pepper snatched the duffel and set it on the floor, knelt to unzip it, and peeked inside. "Well, well!" But before she could reach in, the man produced from behind his back some sort of spindly gun, raised and lowered its metal butt with sharp force on top of Pepper's head, sent her into a tight fetal curl.

Several in the room let out absurd whoops of protest. The girl with him wheeled and sought the nearest wall, hid her face against it, crying, arms flung up on the tiles.

Harriet couldn't breathe; she stared at Pepper's hunched back, now so narrow and without spirit. At the center of Harriet's brain, a black cube started to grow; she was going to faint. Regretting the need, she hooked both hands over one of Butterfield's muscular shoulders, which he permitted. When she exhaled onto his neck, he raised the collar of his lab coat. She glanced once more at Pepper's body and at the man hulking above it, who seemed, at least, bewildered, staring down at the gun in his hands. Then, she closed her eyes.

Robert Jenwaugh had looked bewildered, also, when last she'd seen him, the night he strangled her. That was two years ago, the last visit of the black cube. *Maybe tonight, it'll be the YMCA pool for me again.* Oh, the man had claimed he hadn't choked her, not really. He seemed to be waiting for her eyes to open, like a cue, because his mouth beginning was her first new sight. "I was only trying to push you off me. You were out maybe twenty seconds. Thirty, tops." His voice didn't even tremble. She was lying in her bed, and he was standing above her. Outside the window, rain lashed the window. "You kept coming at me, practically gave me no choice. You see how you brought this on yourself, don't you?" She couldn't talk, because she was relearning how to breathe; the black cube, too, paused as if recalling itself. Harriet envisioned her own windpipe, dented by his thumbs. She'd never suspected a windpipe of being so tender. Robert Jenwaugh got himself dressed, and only now, now that he'd made his points, did he betray any anxiety, having difficulty with his slacks, losing balance. Gathering up his cigarettes and his keys, scooping his change from off her bureau, he added, "I mean, you lost complete control, I think you'll agree, Harriet . . . darling." He closed her front door with infinite delicacy, so that the final click rang out. The rain let up just so she could hear this ringing.

The truth was, she *had* lost control, giving him the mandate he needed to slam her back onto the mattress, pin her wrists beneath his knees, and to oppose her fit with digging thumbs. Even as she stared up into his purpling face and heard the taut piping song of her breaths and felt the black cube expanding to blot away her future, Harriet's mind understood this episode as only the most recent in a lifetime series of botched retaliations. Perforating Garvey's tongue, for instance, had guaranteed her a career in The Trough.

Yes, she'd attacked Robert Jenwaugh brutally on the bed, not striking him, but trying, like some scrawny succubus, to kiss him and to hug him, and here's why. All he liked to do in bed, anymore, was to lie next to her and happily masturbate while touching parts of her with his free hand, his right, lazily, as though to placate her or to remind himself, generally, what the topic was. He'd wend his hand between her legs and feel her there, fingers leafing through her folds as through the pages of a small, boring book.

At the sound of a chair hitting the floor, Harriet released Butterfield's shoulder and opened her eyes. It was Jack Garvey's chair, fallen over backward as, at the middle of the room, he jumped to his feet, hemoglobin tie flying up and landing over his shoulder. He stretched his arms out toward the scene at the front, pointing with both index fingers, and shouted, "Excuse me! Excuse me! Excuse me!"

"As you can see," said the man up front, "this is a high-powered spear gun. It is loaded. Here is the aluminum shaft with a barbed manganese-steel tip, designed to penetrate the skin of sharks. Please be assured that as a man of science I have no desire to harm any living creature, and without provocation I will not do so again."

"We," said Garvey, indicating his tablemates, "we, too, are men of science."

"Don't insult me! You and your colleagues in this company are the precise opposite of science. I've been following your activities from my headquarters," the man said, "not far from here, and I understand exactly what you are capable of, how well you care for the dignity of the natural order. Unfortunately, there isn't enough time to review your crimes against nature. We find ourselves at this moment . . ."—he glanced over at his partner, still pasted to the wall, regarding him balefully—". . . in a position of dire need. I have come to you for help, to save a dying species from extinction. You might say I'm giving you a chance at redemption . . . Gentlemen, ladies, please have a look at your newest project, *Scombridae vagrantitus.*"

He set aside the spear gun and peeled back the duffel bag like gift wrap, letting out more of the held water and revealing a slate-gray fish that lay on its side, glistening, gills sucking at the useless cafeteria odors, its whole sleek body vibrating with advanced oxygen deprivation.

"First, as I said, I'll need a very large bowl, filled with water at room temperature. And yes," he said, removing a vial from his pocket, holding it up. "I do have saline solution." Some people laughed at him, which he seemed to take as a sign of progress. "And then, if you can spare me a few hours, I would like to acquaint you with the creature you'll be rescuing from oblivion."

Nobody moved, except the twitching fish.

"NOW!"

One of the hair-netted women in the kitchen began filling a crystal punch bowl with water, glancing at the black telephone on the wall.

Zingman held his breath to turn the key in the lock, listening for any hint of strangeness within the mechanism's familiar gristly rearrangement. The door to his small apartment swung open without creaking, then only clicked shut behind him like any door in a humdrum universe.

He noticed, blinking in the darkness, two messages on the answering machine. One, he trusted, was from Mr. Ruthbar, his friend and finest audience, who used to sit in the old house and listen to Zingman read aloud from what he'd just written. Recently, the man had visited several times, swinging by the apartment after work, chatting and watching tv. Tonight, tv meant "Wombdwellers: A Pre-Natal Nightmare," but first—fresh new fiction to share. Zingman switched on the living room light and tossed Vivian's manuscript, *The Cost of Terror,* toward the desktop, where it landed, exactly suffocating his own slim tale, "Tag."

In the refrigerator, he counted no fewer than eight jars of spaghetti sauce, each from one-third to two-thirds full. He usually judged it safest to buy new, since you never could tell when mold would spring up, those colorful formations on any given tomatoey surface. Now, he selected three suspects, carried them to the sink, unscrewed their gummed lids, and sure enough—bright yellow and blue dots decorated the musty little worlds inside. He ran hot water, poured the sauce down the drain.

In Andy's kitchen, there is never mold, unless, in summer, she forgets about an onion, rolled to the back of the crisper, or Zingman has left a loaf of grainy bread on a humid countertop. They moved into their house in August, 1998, one week before the wedding, and now they have spent three seasons here.

Today is a Saturday in early June. She reads a magazine in the backyard while he is upstairs in his office, supposed to be revising a piece of fiction but glancing out the window at his wife in her reclining lawn chair. On such an ordinary afternoon, his mind naturally slides to the opposite extreme, taking stock, finding that indeed there is strangeness to consider even today, hypothetical alarm. No wind blows outside, which reminds him that although he and Andy have been breathlessly happy—like two kids playing house, yet permitted limitless sex—they've also been, at another level, holding their breath.

Below his office window, she turns the pages of her magazine. A bird flits across the yard, thirty feet up, but she doesn't notice. She's wearing only her red shorts and a gray sports bra, its gray lighter now than it was half an hour ago, when she'd just finished jogging. Her legs are thin and muscled. She tans well. He does not.

Looking at her, Zingman remembers having once, as a child, read a little horror story about a boy who is hit and killed by a car. His mother always loved his two brothers better, because they were rugged, outdoorsy types, whereas this one was pale, effete, hardly left the house. Instead of reporting the accident, she stretches the dead boy out in the grass, under a beating sun, and watches him bronze up nicely. Zingman forgets the author, but if it were not for the car accident, he'd assume this was from the Grimms, because their bleak, unapologetic plots shone throughout his youth. His favorite also happened to be the shortest of their tales, "The Stubborn Child."

> Once upon a time there was a stubborn child who never did what his mother told him to do. The dear Lord, therefore, did not look kindly upon him and let him become sick. No doctor could cure him, and in a short time he lay on his deathbed. After he was lowered into his grave and covered over with earth, one of his little arms suddenly emerged and reached up into the air. They pushed it back down and covered the earth with fresh earth, but that did not help. The little arm kept popping out. So the child's mother had to go to the grave herself and smack the little arm with a switch. After she had done that, the arm withdrew, and then, for the first time, the child found peace beneath the earth.

Zingman has never been sure just exactly why he loves such stories, but they make his ankle bones sting, his eyes water, with plain clasping joy. Even meditating on the note of unease in his new marriage brings him a little shudder of suspense.

Now her magazine is splayed on the grass. Andy has fallen asleep. She breathes easily, and he doesn't doubt that he adores her; he has to hold himself back from abandoning his fruitless desk, slinking downstairs, across the lawn, and massaging her legs. Her affection and her physical presence is much more reliable than the effort of composing solid fiction, but touching her while she rests also connects him surreptitiously with his trade. One thing he likes about the human body is that even when apparently at peace, it is a fragile vile of ready nightmare, always an instant away from bursting its tentative seams and spilling its contents. One can relax only because one feels enlightened—the substances and rules of physiology have been named and understood, no? But in themselves, they have no names, none, and they occur, what's more, in utter darkness, a darkness which rises constantly from within us, pushing outward and outward against sheer, naive skin.

Andy tends to disagree, by main force, whenever Zingman has the nerve to advance such notions, disagree at least that they have merit within daily life. Either they go between book covers or else they fall into the category of what she has continued to refer to as his "racket"—a system of melodrama and projection that, she believes, often blocks him from true experience. Once a week or so, they have some version of this exchange:

"It's what I do. It's my imagination scouting around, looking for paths."

"For pathos, don't you mean? It's as if you feel you need more emotion, Ross, and you have to sneak it in from elsewhere. Looks like a smuggling racket."

"Hey, sometimes it comes looking for me, if I'm open to it. I may have to prime the operation at times, or do a kind of mental dance to call the brainstorm, a dramatic little dance, sure, but when it works, what finally comes doesn't seem like melodrama at all."

"I'm oversimplifying, I know. The racket's kept you going fine long before I appeared."

"No, not 'fine,' and you're right, too, Andy. I can feel just so . . . dried out sometimes, when my writing's going absolutely nowhere. Like I'm in Death Valley, waiting to be rescued."

"I thought that's where I came in."

"Oh, yes, yes, yes, you are my salvation, and—"

"Okay, all right. But you're talking about the part I can't expect to reach. It's like you get into suspended animation. What's my role, just add water?"

"Well, in my case, it's more like, just add *wind.* My best ideas feel like strong wind, arriving. I love wind."

"Me, too."

"And can we also agree that what we've got on our hands is a simple difference of opinion on the nature of thought?"

"We could . . . if saying that didn't mean I'd have to become an official racketeer myself."

Down below, Andy turns onto her side, liberally, as though she believes she's on their king-sized mattress, and so she's lucky to stay aboard the recliner. It's 2:54 pm. The air outside stays motionless. He glances at his computer monitor. The short story he's reworking makes no room, he knows, for good ole radiant love, for a family life and the counting of blessings. But that's not its business. It thrives on twisting fate, the worst case, and everything that eludes the grasp.

Zingman quits his desk, marches himself downstairs, and out the back door. He sits in the grass at the foot of the recliner, lays his hands on her lower left leg. Andy wakes up smiling but—in the way of the massage recipient—doesn't wish to break the spell, remains mum. He sets to work, avoiding the deceptive blade of shin and concentrating on the slick bolus of the calf muscle, encountering it with all ten fingertips, pressing it back and forth and to its very limits, looking at it, wondering that it may be isolated and shifted such a great deal within its housing, trying to prove he's able to take Andy's presence literally, to know it and to care without importing emotion from a further story. Edging his fingers partway underneath as though to lift the muscle free, he causes her to hiss and squirm, eases off but barely, sustaining the pressure, all of which ought to mark the success of his trial. However, not for the first time, or for the hundredth, he suspects that he doesn't quite deserve this woman, a common complaint, he's sure, among men who've somehow landed striking beauty. For him it's worse, though, because of the racket, and because he can't put this enterprise aside more often and simply be with her in the moment, he experiences a vague and musty remorse in his chest, an acrid tinge of decay, like an unclaimed bowl of peaches or grapes. Someone once told Zingman that he lets his friendships die on the vine. Friendships are one thing.

Andy hisses again, and—he's been sternly kneading—he spares her calf muscle, lets go. As she emerges from her haze of mild trauma, she's laughing. "I had a short dream about you just then."

"Oh, yeah?" He tries to bob his eyebrows sexily, but knows it comes off only silly.

"No, you're going to hate it." Sitting up, she blinks down at him, lovely face shining. "It was more like a snapshot of you, your eyes. What are those kind of extra eyelids some animals have, like cats or lizards?"

"'Nictating' eyelids, I think."

"You would know that, they're right up your alley."

"Now wait a minute, I've never had a liz—"

"Semi-transparent. A film you draw across your eyes."

Andy's own brown eyes are almost frightfully unveiled, beaming and fresh and suddenly filled with the pronouncement, "See, here's how to be eyes. Open. Nothing to it."

Zingman hit PLAY, and the answering machine readied itself with a series of clicks and maneuvers that seemed both superfluous and strictly necessary. While the tape rewound its two messages, he returned to the kitchen and snapped a fist of spaghetti in half, fed it into the pot of boiling water, stirred till the sticks yielded, then lowered the heat of the neighboring burner, beneath the pan containing an Italian sausage and fennel sauce, marginally mold-free. "Leeeeeeeeep! Ross, it's me." Patrick Tenzer. Zingman rubbed his eyes, eyes which, with Andy's death, had lost their ability even to nictate, which is only what they deserved. "I know you're teaching right now, but I wanted to warn you that we've got a little . . . situation on our hands. Gilbeau and Mezzanotte have spoken to me, outlining several . . . oh, call them grievances, I suppose. [Sigh.] Which I won't go into here on the phone. They need to speak with you, Ross. They trust you."

Zingman smiled, kept stirring the spaghetti, recalling how at the beginning, in this city, he had been something of a star in the realm of grief, heavily recruited both by the Cobhouse and by the State Organization for the Recently Widowed, although the latter was by far the more powerful outfit, its many local chapters staffed from the ranks of social work graduate programs, women and men well-intentioned and empathic but for the most part sadly unschooled in any personal course of mourning. Zingman learned that SORW, as a "caring public resource," was too much interested in ushering the bereaved through the "stages of acceptance" and then jollying them with party games and field trips.

"Anyway . . ." Tenzer's tinny voice picked up after its pause. ". . . I hope you can make it, tomorrow afternoon at 2:00, my place. We'll sort this whole thing out. I'm sorry. Ross, they want changes, and as you can imagine, that hurts me. But I'll just . . . I'll see you tomorrow."

Zingman braced himself for the possibility that the second message would be from Gilbeau or Mezzanotte himself.

SORW enjoyed free reign over the widows, while the Cobhouse competed in the arena of widowers only, scanning the feet of articles and obituaries for those four golden words, "Survived by her husband." And then began the recruitment tactics, the battle for the hearts and minds of the region's aggrieved. SORW barraged candidates with flashy brochures containing color photos of convivial gatherings, of sad yet single women and men, of tall goblets of red wine, of couples waltzing. The Cobhouse took a subtler, more aesthetic approach, sending a short, comradely letter with stirring passages from the literature of loss, such as Shakespeare's "Give sorrow words; the grief that does not speak/Whispers the o'erfraught heart/And bids it break"; Matthew Arnold's, "We are wandering between two worlds, one dead, the other powerless to be born"; Edmund Wilson's 1932 journal entry: "Margaret—her death which deprived her of the things we have in life made them seem worthless to me—I couldn't enjoy them. . . . A loyalty to her made me less loyal to life itself."

Soon, a slight breeze comes through, making Andy shiver. Today, Zingman can't even enjoy seeing a person shiver, a symptom he normally holds as dear as some do the sight of prayer. Still sitting at her feet in the grass, he can't look up at her eyes anymore. His own feel ashamed and diminished.

"What's wrong? Is it the nick . . ."

"Nictating eyelids, yup. So let me get this straight—do mine come across from the sides, Andy?"

"No, from above, just like your regular lids, you dope! You're not that monstrous to me yet." She does a little wag of the head, as if ridding herself of old, faded confetti. He grabs her right foot and starts massaging the sole with his thumbs.

"You liked that second book."

"Oh, God. That's not the point. Of course I did."

She did, although the central premise of *A Toast for Grief Among the Infants* is that a suicidal sorrow can afflict the extremely young, and for no other reason than that they have grown weary and dispirited, already, with the pressing weight and cruel limits of incarnation.

"Don't forget, I went and found it in the library when you were still too scared to admit to me you wrote horror."

"I remember, Andy. Thank you." And he expands his attention to the flesh of her foot, reaffirming its contours with his fingers as though he's molding it into being.

But he's sad, because she's on target with what she pictured in her dream—this is how he's felt, occasionally, when his approach to reality has seemed too mediated even to himself. Sort of ironic, though, how a dream invented an image that's not anatomically accurate and yet is more accurate than anatomy. He thinks that this irony alone might go to demonstrate his general thesis; yes, he thinks so; but then, to think so is only to nictate again. She's got this monster in a trap.

"Let me guess, you prefer it when I compare you to that buried kid." He nods. "Because it rewards your self-image, stuck down in the grave, such a restless soul." She pats his hand. "That's why you wanted to read that fairy tale to me in the first place."

From the ground, he reaches up to his wife, wildly beseeching. "Put me out of my misery, strike me, oh grant me peace beneath the earth."

"'Fraid I just don't have the right kind of switch, you Stubborn Child."

"Leeeeeeeeep. Mr. Z! Hey, Mr. Z. Mr. Z. You home? It's me.

Pick up the phone, it's me." Mr. Ruthbar! "I gotta mop the floor in back, but they got a bell in there so I can hear the phone. You got that number, I gave it to you. Remember you said I could come over tonight. I can take the bus to your house after—"

Zingman punched the seven digits, used his unslapped ear to listen for the connection, while on the tape his friend concluded, "Gotta hang up, be talkin' to you later!"

". . . and believe it or not, ladies and gentlemen," said Trapuka, pacing before his audience, "that one small episode, which may not at first glance appear so noteworthy, can be regarded as yet another reason why I have liked to say that she is at heart a rambunctious reactionary! As if we needed another reason. Questions?"

None. He'd been lecturing, tonight, for perhaps two or three hours (where was a clock?), but had only begun filling his captives in on all they should know about Titus in order to compassionately replicate her cells; already many of them had fallen into what could only be described as a magic sleep, sitting rigid, eyes fixed on invisible points before them, or draped over tabletops, blinking with mechanical regularity.

Beneath Trapuka, as he paced, lay the presumptuous blonde woman, still unconscious and curled up next to the fluted glass punch bowl that contained the specimen. The spot on her head where he'd been forced to strike her had not bled for long. An hour ago, he had paused between topics and leaned down to rearrange her hair, covering the wound.

Pauline Ard slept on the floor in the corner of the cafeteria, exhausted after four cheeseburgers and two milk shakes. He himself had refused food, anticipating exactly that outcome after three full days without sleep.

Yes, events had certainly overtaken the patient decorum of

science, and Trapuka had been required to sacrifice experimental elegance for expediency, so that finally, after these eighteen conscientious years, the cause would now lurch forward with ungovernable speed. Each expedition, he'd found, calls forth its own unsparing improvisations.

Three times already, the absurd man with the flamboyant yellow tie had interrupted important aspects of the case, had risen and attempted to take control of the situation, until Trapuka simply stopped pacing and placed the speartip against the downed woman's temple, which caused the man to snap his mouth shut and sit back down. Now he, too, appeared glazed in trance, hands folded neatly before him.

The lone reasonable soul among the captives had proved to be a sullen-faced, loose-limbed woman whom he had allowed to act as sentry for him. Some catch of sincerity or despair in her voice had persuaded him to listen as she respectfully approached him soon after the unfortunate incident. She'd leaned close to explain, in a whisper her co-workers couldn't overhear, that "at this time of night, we don't expect many more people to come in here. But there will be a few. I can stand just outside the door, if that's all right, sir, and head them off, tell them there has been a 'Degree Six Biohazard Spill,' that they should return home immediately, that the authorities have been called and are on their way."

He liked her and, oddly, trusted her; she spoke in an anemic monotone, unperturbed, not trying to curry his favor but merely interested in helping to avoid further violence, ticking off her good thoughts by extending the long fingers of her right hand one by one, striking them softly on their ends with the index finger of her left.

Twice so far during her watch, Trapuka had heard footsteps nearing behind him, and then an expert performance, followed by the sound of the feet rushing off down the corridor. Insubordinate cries for help from here among the captives had only served to confirm for the interloper the danger of which she had warned.

Whereas in truth the danger lay in the depths of the sea. *Titus* was gravely ill, as a species, not merely as a school. This conclusion had forced itself upon Trapuka when he and Pauline had returned from their dive and he'd examined several individuals in the sunny bed of the rubber launch.

They were dead, essentially, from a condition affecting respiration—their gills were badly inflamed. Industrial toxins off the U.S. Atlantic Seaboard were the scourge of the ocean. Dozens of chemicals could be detected now even two hundred miles offshore; and it only took one, sometimes, to exploit a particular species' weakness, to compromise her fragile immune system, while leaving every other species unaffected.

Trapuka's knees had been threatening to buckle for some time now, and so, before the room could become aware of his fatigue, he sat down behind the bowl. He'd planned to say, "Nobody move. Let's take a short break before our next topic: 'Her Natural Foes and Patterns of Evasion.'" But nobody moved anyway, so he yawned and reached into the bowl, ran his fingers along Titus's extended jawbone; she jerked away, and he smiled. The specimen seemed to have recovered somewhat, at least to regain the sickly condition in which she'd been taken from the waters of Seal Cove; she bumped about, bruising herself, skin already nicked and scored by her many traumas—desiccated dorsal ridge in the air above the tap water—inside the fancy punch bowl normally reserved, no doubt, for well-funded company galas.

Back below, Pauline had helped him to cull through dozens of prospects before selecting and bringing to the surface the two youngest fish, in slightly better shape. These had survived inside the deflated launch, slung hammock-fashion in the back of the van and filled with bay water. Until he was dropped off at the university, Eugene had lain moaning and cursing beneath this sling, dripped and sloshed upon for eight hundred and twenty-two miles, suffering the complicated after-effects of Mrs. Ard's sweet brown beer.

Trapuka leaned back against the cool wall tiles and regarded the dormant roomful, workers capable of transforming this one specimen into a plenitude, if they could be convinced or coerced to apply their dark art; and then he spied for the first time a clock far off on the wall, visible at an extreme angle—nearly midnight! He'd been talking much longer than he'd supposed.

He sighed, then noted with surprise that he felt more peaceful at this moment than he had in all the days since Jonna had taken Ellie away. Again, he stroked *Titus,* and again she jerked, kicked up water. The woman on the floor beside him spasmed mildly, but no more than one might do during ordinary sleep. "You will both be well," he whispered.

Trapuka rested his head back against the tiles. Yes, he was peaceful, because at least he had acted, and something in his decisiveness had created a situation with its own rules, its own strange normalcy, an implicit schedule. He allowed himself to rest his eyes, and remembered the first sea creature he'd ever studied, and lost, long before he had learned the skills of radical advocacy. It was a gift brought back from a business trip to the Jersey Shore when Trapuka was nine, younger than Ellie. His father presented it to him in its small Styrofoam box. His father was sixty-two, died seven months later of a ruptured aorta, on a business trip to Orlando.

Henry opened the lid of the box and was disappointed to find only a round bluish shell no larger than a medium marble. His father explained—and he realized then that the man had never explained anything to him so carefully before—that a living animal, called a hermit crab, was hidden inside this shell, and that it would come out if Henry was patient enough. The shell rolled back and forth on the pocked white floor of the box. His father handed him another, larger shell, said that the pet store owner had included this as part of the deal, because the crab would need it, because when it outgrew its current home, it would switch.

In the backyard, Henry took his pet out of the Styrofoam box and sat cross-legged in the grass, letting it rest after its long trip and get used to life on his palm, letting himself get used to believing without seeing. When he peered into the shell's flared opening, his eyes followed that first twist of spiral in there while turning the shell minutely, and then suddenly he did catch sight of several pink quills that might be legs squeezing away, trying to make it around the bend from the boy's eyes, stopping with just the points of the feet stacked over that horizon. (This was the first time Henry had ever thought of the idea of naturally intelligent behavior.)

Sometimes, if he held the crab in his fingers absolutely without trembling, those points would start to slide forward, tickling his vision, retreating only when an eye back in there must have recognized the huge and dangerous shade of Henry's head. He placed the shell in the dry bathtub, alongside the larger shell, and sat on the closed toilet to wait.

Eventually, the crab did poke feet, legs, and suddenly a fearless little head out from under the shell's flared hood. Henry snuck his own face over the tub's porcelain rim and saw the two chocolate-jimmy eyestalks, two pinching-claws—one big as a sunflower seed, the other almost invisible but pinching anyway—and then the mouthparts, just bristly flaps that Henry stared at and stared at, trying to understand their hinges.

He was about to run and get his father and mother and sister Nicole, but then decided, no.

The animal clicked around, its shell light as a mushroom, but didn't seem ready to leave it behind and set out yet for the new home. Henry thought he would name the crab, but not until after it made the switch; once, he held his breath when it crawled right up to the other shell and kind of leaned its own against that one for a moment before scuttling onward.

The ringing telephone caused everybody to leap in their chairs, and then Trapuka heard the trot of sturdy shoes coming from behind the kitchen, a person making for the phone on the wall.

Mr. Ruthbar didn't pick up until the seventh ring. "Hey, guess who!" said Zingman. "What? Yes, of course you can come over, in fact I'd hoped . . . Hey, Mr. Ruthbar, I was wondering, do you remember that story I read you a long time ago, when I was still living in the house, that one called 'Lip Service'? Mr. Ruthbar?"

A woman's voice, wanting to use the phone, took away his friend's attention, and then a far-off male voice, probably the boss, reprimanding. When he came back Mr. Ruthbar told Zingman not to worry.

"Well, no, I wasn't worried, exactly. He's your boss, not mine. I'm trying to remember, though, what you said about that story. The story made you feel like what? A fish in a bowl? Really?" The man always reported how a story made him feel using vivid images, but Zingman didn't recall this image. But maybe it was good news, a fish in a bowl being at least somewhat akin to a reader hopelessly caught within the writer's spell. He'd lately been meaning to resurrect and rework that old piece from before Andy's illness, when Mr. Ruthbar used to drop by the house at night and they'd steal down to the basement for Zingman's private readings. In "Lip Service," people occasionally find themselves transported to an evil version of our earth, but it's nearly impossible to tell the difference because this other earth is exactly like ours in every respect except one—after a meal in a fine restaurant, your waiter will bring you, in addition to the check, a small silver plate on which sits a perfect pair of red wax lips. You're doomed.

Through the phone came a terrific crash. The clumsy goof had probably been holding some tray full of food while talking on the phone—Zingman pictured blood-red julienne beet slices—and become so excited reliving "Lip Service" in his mind that he'd dropped it, splattering and staining everyone.

Next, Zingman heard more chaotic noises, and shouts, and cries of agony, all of which made Zingman want to laugh, seeing zany kitchen hijinks, pratfalls, workers pretending to be mortally wounded, lurching. Was this little man constantly the butt of their jokes?

When he tried to raise the conversation again—"Mr. Ruthbar, hello! Mr. Ruthbar?"—he only got a hollow repeating percussion, the phone striking against a surface. He hung up, shaking his head, reflecting upon how different was the tenor of lives other than his own.

"Hello, cafeteria. Oh, Mr. Z., it's you. I fell asleep in the back! Yeah, I can come over to your place. Right now?"

It was a mentally defective man, small, flushed, holding the receiver with an outsized, bony hand. He hadn't yet seen anything abnormal in the room; Trapuka noted that the man needed all his concentration just to conduct his conversation. "Yeah, yeah! Sure I remember you reading that story to me, Mr. Z. It made me feel like—"

The ringing had woken Pauline, who now left her corner and approached the little man with a meaningful wave; he saw her, but still only her, and wouldn't acknowledge her appeal. He shook his head, holding out a ridiculous paltry hand to halt her advance.

"Sir," said Pauline. "I have to use that phone. Look what's happen—"

"Listen!" Trapuka stood and took several steps toward her. "This is not your affair anymore."

The man on the phone looked from Trapuka to the blonde woman curled on the floor, and then to the fish in the punch bowl; and the vague round face twisted itself into a knot of dismay that seemed extraordinary even for one so clearly accustomed to misunderstanding issues of any subtlety.

"Don't worry, my friend, I'll explain," said Trapuka.

"Yeah, yeah, I'm here," said the little man into the phone.

"Don't worry." He scratched his head. "Okay, let me think. That story made me feel like . . . like a fish, a big fish inside a bowl."

Trapuka said, "This poor woman, lying here, she's my wife, and she's very sick. We've come here to—"

The would-be hero in the flamboyant yellow tie stood up, as he had several times already. "No!"

The man on the phone smiled at him. "Mr. G? Hi! What's everybody doing?"

"Just go back . . . you know where, do it NOW, run and finish your chores, you've got a lot of work to do, remember? And keep an eye on everything for me. I'll be down soon!"

At "soon!" the hero chose to charge, covering the distance in seconds, reaching for Trapuka's throat, giving him barely time to raise the spear gun and pull its trigger. A terrific crash from back in the kitchen said that the spear had missed its mark and flown into a shelving unit containing large silver mixing bowls, causing it to fall over. Pauline had dived to the floor, and now sat watching the bowls bounce and clatter. And there, Trapuka next noticed that even the trouble-maker had turned in that same direction, which clinched the theory of the missed mark. The hero's lucky day, but he better not press it. For instance, why was he taking two steps back toward where the spear must have landed? Trapuka selected another and reloaded.

The telephone tapped against the wall at the end of its cord.

In a moment, Trapuka located the mental defective, getting to his feet among the mixing bowls, wheezing, hyperventilating, asymmetrical hands covering clownish face. He must have tripped in his blind escape, which now he resumed, moving off behind the kitchen, where he'd come from. The trouble-maker slowly revolved, as if performing a further aggression by showing Trapuka how the spear shaft stuck out from the left side of his belly, how the blood came out over his hands, and how it had already ruined his ridiculous yellow tie. The force of impact must have spun him. He stepped ponderously toward the punch bowl and the unconscious woman. Several people in the room screamed, then stifled themselves in deference to the man's own loud groans. The trouble-maker's face was gray; his lips were sucked far in between his teeth. He knelt at the punch bowl and, before Trapuka could reanimate his muscles, grabbed *Titus* by the tail, yanked her out of the water, staining it red, held her up. She bucked free of his hand, fine little soldier, and plopped back in; but he retrieved her and held her up with both hands this time. His lips needed two tries as well before they succeeded in staying put outside his teeth, allowing him to whisper, "Call an ambulance for Miss Sarles and myself, you coward, or I'll kill this fish."

There was a pause. Trapuka scratched his scalp brusquely, then heard a quiet voice, the voice of his gangly sentinel, standing in the doorway. It struck him that she could easily have jumped him at any time in the last few minutes. She said, "Get his access card and we can do your job together."

"Sure, sure, whatever," said the bleeding man. "But first—"

"Yes, operator," said Pauline into the telephone. "I need you to connect me—"

"Hey!" Trapuka shouted. "Pauline, if you don't hang up this instant, I will shoot this man, I promise you that. You should know by now I'm serious." And he brought the point to within two feet of the sticky tie. Pauline hung up.

"Let her," the man coughed, then achieved a series of quick breaths, which equipped him to say, "If this fish dies . . . his cells will die within minutes, making them . . . impossible to . . . replicate."

"Actually, that's untrue, Mr. Garvey," said the sentinel from the door.

"Shut up, you'll be dealt with." The man ran out of breath, slammed *Titus* onto the floor, where she flopped, and then he placed one knee firmly on her head and bore down. She convulsed. "I'll crush her."

"No you won't," said Trapuka.

"Call."

"Let her up."

"Call."

Titus fought, with startling resources.

Trapuka yelled his loudest, "You are an ignorant man . . ."

The knee bore down further.

"LET HER UP!"

"Fuck you!"

The spear entered the man's chest, pitching him backward.

Trapuka took *Titus* up carefully and examined her head, partially caved in. He lowered her into the bloody bath. Her gills still worked. Her fins paddled. He sat on the floor and hugged himself, barely registering the cries from the room.

Pauline came forward and tried the man's pulse. Then she dragged him by the armpits to the wall, helped him to sit up against it. Deftly avoiding the shafts of the spears, she removed her scarf and lay it on top of his head so that it draped down over his face, covering all but the mouth. The tongue stuck partway out.

Then she marched to where Trapuka sat, looked down at him with her arms dangling at her sides. Her brown hair, now free, crowded her face in salted clumps, not washed since her scuba dive. Her eyes would not focus, so she gave up the effort to see him, for which he was grateful. Instead, she walked toward the door.

"Give me an hour," Trapuka said. "Please, Pauline. Then I will turn myself in. If police storm this place, someone else might get shot. Pauline?"

Her footsteps trailed off down the corridor.

Trapuka's chest shuddered as he breathed. "I wish, people," he said, "that that had not happened. Obviously that's my wish." He did not know what to do. In the punch bowl, the fish didn't stir; in fact, she'd sunk out of view. He felt that under the circumstances, an extension of his lecture was inappropriate, and then he saw that no, everybody in his audience was wide awake at last, paying him an almost reverent attention. In response, he cleared his throat. "Would you like to hear one more episode in the case history?" He would respect whatever the group decided, but when many of them crisply nodded, he warmed to their desire for distraction from the casualty, to make the best of a difficult situation. "But I'll have to make it quick, you understand." In the doorway, the sentinel motioned her encouragement, and suddenly, he didn't care if the authorities did descend before he was able to finish. He would not allow himself to look at the man who wore Pauline's scarf. The sentinel asked him softly if she might lend comfort to "Miss Sarles." Trapuka consented, watching the woman come and sit on the floor behind her colleague, rubbing circles on her back, hunching down and humming into her ear.

"Well, this concerns events in 1997, the year in which our fish swam, so to speak, with a limp . . ."

A packet held lime-green pellets that Henry sprinkled onto the floor of the bathtub. The hermit crab ignored them for almost two days, and then began picking them up with the smaller of its two claws, placing them into its mouth, flappy mouthparts munching sideways. Henry laughed at how dainty it was; it never dropped a single pellet. When he teased it with the end of a toothpick, it swiped with both claws, blocking this from its face or trying to grab the wood and succeeding, like an expert. Even though he was alone, Henry looked around inside the bathroom and covered his face with his hands, embarrassed at how much he loved the crab.

Once, he brought some peanuts in and removed them from their shells before the crab's very eyes, which stood tall on their stalks—to give it the idea you could leave a shell. But little bursts of smoke came up when he popped them with his thumbnail, and he worried that this could ruin everything. For five days, Henry ate all his own food, too, here in the bathroom, so he wouldn't miss the event. Maybe the crab would know how to make the switch like lightning; maybe this was the reason it moved so slowly the rest of the time. Therefore, whenever he had to leave the room, to let his mother or father or Nicole use it, or else to take a short nap in his soft bed, he always brought the larger shell with him.

He slept with it in his fist and once he woke shrieking when the family cat tried to nose apart two of his fingers.

On the sixth day of the vigil, Henry's twelve-year-old sister Nicole returned home sore after field hockey practice and, without thinking twice, drew herself a scalding bath. Henry had just stepped outside to find some good mossy rocks for the tub, and when he heard the water running dropped them on the living room floor. His sister screamed when he broke the lock on the door and saw her naked at the mirror. Then she remembered, glanced through the steam at the floating shell, and became furious with Henry, calling him a selfish asshole. He couldn't think of anything to say.

Outside, the crab spilled easily from the shell, twice as long as he'd imagined and so limp that it could be handled only by fingertips. The back end—which Henry had wondered about a great deal—was nothing more than long red legs; it was impossible to tell whether they used to naturally curl with the wall of their shell, because now they flopped every whichway, like Henry's arm after he'd been sleeping on it.

His father told Henry he was sorry, then went back inside; and his mother, who was twenty-three years younger than his father and didn't like the man very much, yelled at him upstairs with the window open, saying he was an idiot for trying to be a father by giving an animal that would certainly die. Downstairs in the bathroom, Nicole soaked her muscles and sang, ". . . that's why I fell for . . . the leader of the pack!!"

Outside, Henry dug a hole with his hands where he'd found the mossy rocks. He stretched the crab, pink body, red legs, along his dirty palm. He thought for a minute, crying, letting wind blow, and whispered, "You *are* an expert." He buried it in the hole, but not naked; he fit it first into the other, larger shell, jiggling so the body would settle into the spiral, out of sight.

Zingman sat down on the couch with a steaming plateful of spaghetti on his lap, a can of beer in his hand, chuckling again at the image of those julienne beet slices—all over the place! He plunged his fork into the pasta.

Yes, you could say what you liked about this fellow, and certainly he wasn't tack-sharp in every department; still, the elf knew horror, and Zingman counted himself fortunate indeed to have discovered what must be a true rarity in the grand tapestry of the human race, an idiot savant of the macabre.

He'd first met his friend five years ago, at a local high school auditorium, having just delivered a reading from A Toast for Grief Among the Infants—Chapter Three, the flaying scene, with the iodine and the high winds. Afterward, this tiny man with one huge hand had stormed up and pumped Zingman's hand nonstop, for minutes, with that huge hand.

Initially, he'd appeared a mere dope, afflicted perhaps with too little oxygen at birth, not quite five feet tall with a round face deeply pink, except for olive-green eyes that seemed sorry ahead of time. And yet, something came through the hyperbolic handshake, something authentic that was only confirmed by the man's singular brand of metamorphic critique.

"It made me feel like a big black horse, hanging upside-down way up in the air. My legs were kicking the air!" Zingman had taken Mr. Ruthbar's name and number, and then, during his next dip in confidence, had invited him over to the house, introduced him to Andy, who left the boys to their fun. Acolyte became oracle, listening to endless prose without fatigue and then delivering concrete messages from the primal unconscious. "Mr. Z.," he might say, "that one made me feel like a frog at the bottom of a pond, and my foot was stuck under a rock, I pulled and pulled, and my elbow came apart!" Or: "I was a good little boy getting tripped by invisible snakes. I fell down and they started kissing me some and squeezing me some, and I couldn't tell which one they meant!" And dozens more, yet never anything like "A fish in a bowl."

After Andy died, Mr. Ruthbar became, for a while, the only person Zingman could stand to be around, and not, anymore, because of the visceral praise. They watched movies together, or played cards. He resisted all other social overtures, including and especially those from grief groups, until the dreaded, sunny day arrived when he had to vacate his and Andy's house, when Patrick Tenzer materialized beside him, kept his knees from buckling, and wrapped the round mirror in movers' padding.

Up till then, the battle for Ross Zingman had been especially fierce. SORW had yet to entirely accept defeat, even today, staging insidious head-huntings, such as laudatory articles about him in their official newsletter, "The Mourning Sentinel."

He set his clean plate and empty can down on the coffee table and stretched out on the couch, just to rest his eyes.

"Ross Zingman, Ross ZINGman?"

She had shown up at the front door of the house one afternoon not four months after Andy's death, posing as an admirer of his work.

"The same."

"Well, I just cannot believe I have finally found you, YOU, 'The Sultan of Strange'."

He invited her inside. He hadn't had such a visitor for a while, not since *Tales from Ugliville* came out in paperback.

She introduced herself as Candace and took a spot on his couch.

During the breathless spiel that followed, while he sat stiffly on a wooden chair, he stared not into her painfully forthright face but at her creamy, sinewy wrist, tensing and releasing, tensing and releasing, the hand tightening at times, cupped over the knee, the top knee of her crossed legs, legs sheathed in ultra-white slacks.

". . . and then I bet I was one of the first to fall in love with Wombdwellers, though naturally the film failed to do justice to your vision."

"Claire Danes held up her own, I thought."

"Yes, she did a commendable job with what they gave her. But the script . . . I noticed you weren't responsible for that."

"It didn't seem to me that—"

"Hey, you don't have to explain, I know. That book is right up there with *The Body Snatchers* any day, don't you doubt it, and I personally believe you do quick gore shots better than Jack Finney; I mean, restraint isn't everything."

"Finney didn't understand that."

"And then—hello!—you had to go and kill me all over again with *A Toast for Grief* . . . , didn't you?"

"Well, it was just a thing I couldn't seem to—"

"I mean, forget it, that one went way under my skin, Mister. How am I ever supposed to get rid of the image of a row of three-year-olds who've all hanged themselves? And they are The Olde Ones! Answer is I can't, and—the truth?—don't want to."

Oh, the woman had done her homework. Her creamy wrist kept tensing and releasing as she went on to offer a plausible assessment of the Jungian elements in Zingman's first novel, *Smell Something?*

Upstairs, he was surprised. This wasn't sex, not really; this was clear thinking. While she kissed his forehead, testing it with her tongue—discovering there, it seemed, certain indispensable salts—and then as she landed her lips in his bald spot, chattering there, something quiet, something dire, all he could do was to consider his own faults. When she removed her shirt and hugged his whole head to her like a harvest, Zingman sniffed her freckled, duplicitous clavicles, sensing already some ulterior motive. Only days later did he connect the dots, when she called, drunk, to confess that her husband had recently met a horrible death, and that she would give him all the details for use in his next book, provided he attend her SORW group, which had "absolutely saved my life." He hung up on her.

And up in his and Andy's bed, he had not gone through with intercourse. This upset the woman, but even her upset was somehow suspicious, as she continued pressing against him, now with her pants off. He became sick to his stomach; her movements were a mimicry of passion, the sounds she made, stagey.

Andy's, though—how easily they issue from her throat, how free of calculation, whereas his he almost always needs to manufacture, at least to some degree, to cloak the silence that comes with heavy concentration. If she happens to offer her ear before his mouth, he'll be stricken with genuine stage fright, like a fifth-grader presented with a live microphone, his big chance—"Hello? This thing on?" So he keeps silent. But that doesn't seem to bother her, remarkably, and to thank her, tacitly, he's developed a style of caring for her body that does not suffer from self-consciousness, from the racket. Perhaps it's less a style than a tone; its gift is every bit as solemn as it is sexual. Serendipity sees that it not detract from but complement Andy's more celebratory approach, deepen it. He contributes the belief, through his hands, that ministering to a naked body at such times is never without its share of pity, like caring for a poor wounded thing, not because of any specific wound but because of its having to be a body at all. His belief is the shadow side of the body electric, Andy's stronghold. The belief comes from all the way inside himself, as natural to him as the sounds she makes, and it produces melancholy, not sadness—rich, not hollow. Of course, all this is before her body obliges, before she finds herself locked in the same little cell with her cancer, and at his worst moments, after that, Zingman conceives the distinct possibility that although his belief is woven into how he loves her, it may also have always contained a background plea—that flesh be proven clay.

At the last, when in an instant Andy sheds his grave insistence, reclaiming joy, when her muscles are volted by him, and he, agreeing for the sake of argeement, turns himself into a crackling, carefree creature, she'll let out her final hermetic syllables into his ear, oddly precise, meant for a man who deserves them, who speaks the language. Not that he merely hears her syllables; no, she every time *finds* his ear, this particular port—dropping off a keenly personal message, as though at the plain round receiving window of an outpost, a stone rampart that possesses no door. Though she never has a clue, her syllables return him to pity, but this time pity for himself. He suspects this, that he is a tomb in which her meanings go to die.

When it came time for the slender state operative to stiffen and let out her own wordlike rasps, Candace's message was definitive—"This is me, ME, not HER, make no mistake."

Obvious fool, you should have held that fish over your heart.

"Had to be the hero, didn't he? And look at him now," Harriet whispered into Pepper's ear, rubbing circles on her back. Sometimes, the patient would moan, suggesting a return to the world. For more than an hour, she'd knelt by the stricken girl.

But Harriet didn't "look at him now," she'd quit. Unless he had taken up a new attitude—*unlikely*—Garvey's tongue stuck out beneath the scarf, pushy as ego yet punched full of teeth marks, nice, *same as I gave him once upon a time.*

Harriet kissed Pepper secretly on one of the waxy ridges of her ear, then sat up straight, stretched her neck and back, her arms, wiggled her fingers. Remarkably, the murderer hadn't fled; here he lingered, lecturing, pacing with his spear gun, face shining, telling everyone about his pet's historic refusal to be caught and studied, as if it were not lying even now at his feet in a bowl of blood. "Hey, he loves her with his whole heart, see?" she whispered, hunching again to Pepper's receptive ear. "Where can't the love of a good man take a girl?"

And the audience, proving that any state of affairs may be declared a fresh norm and embraced, had abandoned their clever hand signals to her long ago, their winks and their head gestures, urging her to attack from behind, had soon settled in again like dazed mice.

"Don't you think he's kind of quaint, though?" she whispered, resuming the gentle circles between Pepper's shoulder blades. "A relic of twentieth-century romanticism, when zoology used to bow before species purity, otherwise known as happenstance? But seriously, where's the police already?" Pepper's moaning had steadily evolved. Now it took up more space inside her, made her smack her lips like a child, squirm uncomfortably. "Darling, take it easy." Harriet passed a hand over Pepper's forehead. Have I never called a person "darling" before? My mother rubbed my back this way, and called me "darling." "Well, look, you're much too warm."

She reached and freed the top four buttons of Pepper's lab coat, then the top three of the blue-and-white floral blouse beneath. "There now." She fanned her open chest.

"What's this?" Embarrassed, but wishing she could put on her frog glasses without drawing attention, Harriet squinted at it anyway—on the side of the left breast, just above the bra-line, stood a small brown birthmark the approximate size and color of an old penny but shaped like a teardrop.

She tore herself away and glanced up to find that Butterfield glared at her from his seat across the room, his mouth hanging open.

"Oh, now," she whispered, "we just won't let him get to us, will we?"

That's it, my brother. Mom would tell me not to let him get to me, and then, for a brief time—and Mom never knew this—I was "darling" to him. Dougy was four years older, and equipped with a belittling manner and a clobbering temper. In fact, he invented these, long before Robert Jenwaugh. The more she sought his favor, the more she could forget about it. By the time she was eight, she'd given up and learned to be invisible to the boy, which was certainly the wisest course. Yet, that's when he started to come around. She was often sick, allergy-prone, receiving ear infections from swimming in the lake. She'd wear her flannel pajamas sometimes for days on end. The weakness and the outfit apparently moved Dougy; he'd come into her room and read to her, stumblingly, from school assignments, or from special requests—*Doctor Doolittle,* an illustrated *Frankenstein.* When she was happy and his eyes were sore, he'd put the book aside and rub her back—never in nice circles, like Mom, but then again his hand was bigger—and smooth down her hair, climb in bed next to her and hold her, rock her a little, especially if she was running a fever, and sometimes—or was it just once?—he'd sing that "little darlin'" song into her ear. Harriet hadn't been able to believe her great fortune. His chin tickled her neck each time. "Watch out you don't get sick," she'd say.

Pepper began gulping for breath, her eyelids fluttering, she cleared Harriet away with her arms and sat up, face bright red. "I need water!"

The gunman stopped talking. "Yes, somebody please get Miss . . . Sarles a glass of water." He swept his arm over the room like a kindly host.

Pepper toed her shoes loose and kicked them high into the air. She peeled her socks off, too, and stood up, wobbly, stepped vaguely in the direction of the punch bowl, as though she hoped to wade there. She reminded Harriet of a toddler at the beach; but when she spotted the scarved executive against the blue tiles of the wall, she aged quickly, sagging under the weight of the universe. She wheeled around in a circle, then another, arriving at the punch bowl anyway, where she jackknifed and released a plume the color of her spinach salad. It splashed into the water, making an almost pleasant sound.

The fish kicked back once, scrappy, then sank away again into the horrible soup. Harriet stood, but Pepper was already trotting in a wide arc to the doorway, eluding the dumbfounded killer. Harriet bee-lined to head her off, stood in the doorway, snapped her fingers. But the poor creature was elsewhere; blue eyes glassy with concussion, shirtfront flapping open, she mumbled in sing-song like a young girl again, inventing something silly on the fly . . ."oh, waxlips, waxlips, that's my favorite kind of lips, 'cause you can practice kissing them . . . but"—giggle, hand over mouth, side-stepping Harriet—"but they sure don't feel like wax . . . waxlips, oh, waxlips . . ." And she was on her way down the hall.

Harriet followed without thinking twice, but the spear gun halted her.

"Would you, really, sir?"

"Only with regret. She'll soon recover, I promise you. It's the specimen that concerns me." Voices around the room began to sound out, even to converse with one another; the man leaned close and spoke low, urgently huddling with her. "All right, obviously I have to go. I'm asking you to take her to the sink and rinse her off, and then . . . listen"—he leaned even closer, and Harriet could smell his sour breath, see the swollen veins running through his eye-whites—". . . we don't know each other, but you can tell I'm sincere, can't you?" She nodded zealously, because that's what one does when one huddles. "Yes, and I can feel a common outlook between us, a sort of pull. Will you preserve some of her cells, try to replicate them, grow more of her?"

"It's a long shot."

"But you told him that—"

"It's a matter of getting to the right equipment."

"We'll find that access card you mentioned."

"Yes, but still . . ."

He made two exhausted blinks. "My plan is to find a place in this city to put my other specimen that's out in the van, where she can survive a little longer. Then I'll need to get in touch with you, if I may. Tell me your name?"

Hard beams of abomination hit her from every angle as she labored through the room with the punch bowl. Whole spinach leaves floated on the dark surface, fragments of carrot bobbed. The hair-netted lady stepped aside, allowing Harriet to do her work at the deep chrome sink, pouring out the mess, then rubbing slatey scales clean with her fingers under a soft tepid waterfall, and feeling an odd peace wash over her own body, too, while out in the room, men swore at the killer, who searched through Garvey's wallet.

She found herself admiring this animal and the reluctant give of its ancient, oceangoing flesh. "If a man must lose his mind over a natural species, you are a fine choice." She lifted open a gill, searching for any strum of life inside.

"They think we're very rare, you and I," she whispered, flipping her over, checking the other gill. "And maybe we are, we're both swimmers, and at least we're not ubiquitous, like metal crosses inside drains, like that one." She tilted the fish, pointed an eye to see down the drain, but she knew she was only teasing herself. This fish was very dead, brain caved in by Garvey's knee, like Robert Jenwaugh's on Harriet's wrists, which turned black and blue. *That reminds me, my earache's all gone.*

And Pepper's brain, faring any better?

I wish I'd massaged your temples, darling. Don't go far. I'll chase you down and snap my fingers, make you focus your eyes, and tell you a bit of my own history with men, beginning oh long before strangulation. You're not the only one with a dramatic history.

She'd begin the history with her brother, why not? The period during which Douglas Corrigan treated his little sister with extreme tenderness lasted just two or three months. He was in the sixth grade, Harriet in the second, and while at school he'd march around ignoring her in the hallways. But at home, now, he'd bring her clear soup and saltine crackers when she was under the weather, and he'd hold her from behind, rocking her. She wouldn't say a word, even if the rocking made her nausea a little bit worse, made her sweat into her flannel pajamas. By the end, he'd given up on reading aloud to her, only wanted to hold her like this on her bed.

On his last two visits, Dougy held her tighter and pressed against her so that she couldn't breathe very well, while he was breathing better than ever . . . he's breathing for me. On the final visit, she had no idea it was going to be final. She got her courage together and asked him, "Not so tight, 'kay?" But he must not have heard, because she was squeaking, and he rocked her like that, like she weighed nothing, until he seemed to choke, then froze. He was alive, breathing, but he lay behind her a whole minute, frozen, with his huge hands hooked over her shoulders, on either side of her neck. And then, he got up and left her room.

After that, he never came back, or spoke to her, or looked at her, and—whenever she got close enough to sniff him—his cells gave off a musky opinion that she did not exist.

Click. Click. Click. Click. Zingman woke to that faithful duck-step nearing in the hallway, the jingling of Mr. Ruthbar's many keys. He sprang off the couch and got to the door just in time to pull the trick, opening up the instant before the man could knock. This normally made Mr. Ruthbar double over with laughter, but not tonight. He'd obviously run most of the way; his face was redder than ever, chest heaving.

"Missed the bus?" Zingman drew his shaky mainstay inside, arm across his shoulders, kicking the door shut behind them, and helped him across to the couch, sat him down, patted his back, easing him into a more promising relationship with oxygen.

"Ahoh, Mr. Z. . . I . . ."

"That's right, just deep breaths now. Let me get you something. What happened to put you in such a hurry? Try to relax. I mean, so you dropped a tray, or was it a bowl? I'm sure it's no big deal, everything got cleaned up. Or let me go in and speak to your . . . supervisor, if there's troub—"

"No, you can't go there!" Mr. Ruthbar's maximum hand clamped Zingman's shoulder. "I can't tell you, don't make me say it." He started gasping again, eyes trained on an absent scene, minimum hand out in the air, trying to cup the scene and hold it still but shaking it.

"No, okay, okay, nothing to worry about."

The man's two hands put aside their differences and rubbed his face together.

"Hey, new topic, then. I've got a story I'd like to read to you, if—Mr. Ru—"

He was undergoing some sort of fit, bouncing on his cushion, swiping and hissing like a cat, a cat who wore loud keys on his belt. And then Zingman noticed them emerging from beneath the collar of the blue-and-yellow-striped dress shirt, and now also from its unbuttoned cuffs and its breast pocket (which bulged with something solid) . . . those flies again, teensy, silent, and wild, zipping, spiralling up and out, spilling freely into the room.

"Oh, more!" said Mr. Ruthbar. "My fault, Mr. Z. My fault, my fault. I went back downstairs to do those chores like he told me but there's always more of them down there, more and more and more and . . . I hate them!"

He sprang up and began mashing them where they tapped against the nearest window, using both hands against the glass.

"Wait, that's not nec—Mr. Ruthbar, one of those panes is actually loose, as you can tell, so . . ."

Zingman coaxed him back to the couch and convinced him to lie down and close his eyes. No more flies came out, and those that had were bothering only with the window. Odd, how they wanted the dark outdoors, rather than the light bulbs.

He went for a glass of water, taking his plate and beer can into the kitchen. Jars still sat on the counter, and Zingman told himself to soon pour that frightening moldy sauce down the drain.

Mr. Ruthbar sat up and accepted the water gratefully, balanced the glass on his knee. "Oh, look," he said, reaching. "What's the matter with your face?" Zingman gently slapped the hand (XL) aside.

"I'm tender there. A maniac hit me tonight, can you believe it?"

Mr. Ruthbar sipped, sighed. "It's a bad, bad night. Oh yeah, I forgot." From his breast pocket he took a brownie, which immediately crumbled in his hand (S). "I got it DOWNSTAIRS. This is the last one. Mr. G. makes them for me, for energy, so I won't have to sleep so much, so I can help him more." He popped the dry pieces into his mouth. "Okay, last one gone. Mr. Z., I tried to get those wax lips to show you. He made them for me before, when I told him about your story."

"'Lip Service'?"

"Yeah, but I couldn't find them, and then I had to get out of there. I was crying too much. I didn't do any chores, Mr. G. asked me to."

Mr. Ruthbar lay back down and cried some more, then asked, "Read to me, please?" Zingman went to his desk and liberated "Tag" from beneath The Cost of Terror.

"All right, then, my innocent friend. Picture this, if you can . . . if . . . you . . . DARE." This introduction had the desired effect, as always. Mr. Ruthbar gave a start, seeming to think twice about being here, and somehow, at the same time, he settled gratefully in, staring up at the ceiling, black pupils dilating, green eyes cast upon the horizon of all that's unlikely and . . . inevitable.

Zingman tapped the tip of one of his guest's excellent black shoes. "Don't you want to take these off?" Mr. Ruthbar shook his head. This, too, was ritual. "Very well. . . . 'An ordinary Saturday afternoon, in a schoolyard. . . . Underway, one game of tag, but a particularly vicious one.'"

Mr. Ruthbar shuddered, perhaps with awful memories, but Zingman lived to make this weird body shudder.

"'Yes, let's look at it from above, shall we? It's like a dance—isn't it?—this art of very close evasion. The taunting lean-in-and-away. I believe you can almost hear a low drum beat in the background. There is a pinwheel of children revolving around whoever's IT. And now, let's peek through IT's own eyes for the moment . . . suppose this is none other than YOU, desperate not to be IT anymore. Sometimes, you spin slowly to keep watch on a particular child as she circles you, and sometimes you stand still, ready to lunge at any random elbow or shoulder or tempting arm flung toward you. They're nearly grazing you now—still, you do not strike.

"'Change views again. From directly above, you can see IT lunge. A moment of chaos, the dance dissolves. IT has brushed flesh or cloth or hair, freeing itself while imprisoning yet another poor soul.

"'SAFETY? Ha, good question! But ask yourself: "How long can I lean with my hand on the brick wall of a school building? Can I rest the bottom of my sneaker against this tree, through the dark and the rain, forever?"'"

Mr. Ruthbar covered his face with his major hand, then lay the other hand atop it.

"'Eventually, you know, most children grow up and leave this game far behind, find other games. But in this case, two boys do not; no, they never outgrow it, though grow they certainly do. Becoming strong and vigilant, expert in the ways of ambush and pursuit, down through their teenage years they exchange identities as hunter and hunted hundreds of times. They are famous in their home town, but only the performers understand it is much more than a performance, that at the instant of contact—that killing, new-born touch—a mighty voltage passes between them.

"'We can watch them going after each other in bold, lazy slow-motion, all the days of their youth, all the streets of their town—IT, waiting till FREE least suspects, then dashing out from hiding, chasing FREE for miles, or else perching, pained, on some tree branch, cramping with the ailment, then dropping onto that fluid body, bringing it down, turning it to IT, to a sort of stone. They mark these epic spots on countless sidewalk squares.

"'Comes time for them to leave home, to set out into the wide world. At the bus station they say good-bye, careful not to shake hands, of course, waving across a small distance. FREE has chosen the earlier bus, boards, then looks out through the window. They do not cry, for they know they will keep in touch, if you know what I mean . . ."

Zingman glanced to see that Mr. Ruthbar was only half awake, struggling valiantly after his long day. "'Over the years, as they wend from place to place, city to city, as people will, and sometimes venturing into this wilderness or that, they are never far from each other's hearts, though IT always begins missing FREE first, and FREE, cruel thing, becomes involved in social clubs, hobbies, and deep relationships. Imagine all the varied forms of disguise and discovery that pass between the two: a deadly skin-brush on a busy street in Phoenix, Arizona; a pitch-black capture in a tunnel beneath Chicago; tables suddenly turned by tackling, inside a great northwestern forest . . .

"'When each is thirty-two years of age, it happens that FREE is a ferryboat skipper, crossing back and forth between Nantucket Island and New Bedford, Massachusetts. IT has just completed a course in scuba diving. Well, one fine day, early in the morning . . .'"

Zingman looked at Mr. Ruthbar and sighed. Though he slept soundly, the man's hands had remained over his face, stacked in decreasing size, as one stacks books to keep them steady.

While reaching for a slice of toast with blackberry jam, Andy bumps the little model leopard off the table. Zingman wakes as it shatters on the floor. He sits up, sweaty, in the reclining lawn chair stationed beside the bed. It takes him a moment to figure out what happened. It's only a leopard skeleton, but it took him days to assemble. And now model bones lie everywhere.

"I could have handed you that toast."

"You were sleeping. I wasn't sure I could eat it."

Andy starts to whimper, and at first he doesn't get up. He's angry at her, after all. At least he doesn't recline. He sits straight and watches her, knowing how this would look to anyone else. How it looks to him. Part of the problem is that from the time she first collapses, four months ago in JCPenney, Zingman has no confidence in his worthiness for the task of being with her. Worse still, she hasn't seemed to suspect; she's released, in a quick spin, all past and pointed grievances, like letting go of her landscaping duties. She abundantly credits all his efforts instead, leans against him with her full weight, which shames him. Being drawn from so freely has made him brutal on himself.

It's mid-afternoon. He goes to wipe the sweat from his forehead, but his forearm is unsleeved, so it just slips.

Andy no longer has the strength to curl into a ball, as she did even as recently as last week. She lies flat on her back, under a violet sheet. She can't possibly sob, and her whimpering brings up no tears. She hardly perspires anymore, either, in this August heat, ninety degrees outside, hotter inside with the air conditioner turned off. At the moment, though, her face and neck show a faint sheen. Except for her papery lips, which she licks occasionally.

Zingman stands and approaches the bed. Her eyes are closed, as if to continue fighting with him. He touches her shoulder but she doesn't relent, and then he becomes aware of a novel, gnawing quality to his sadness. Under his socked feet, a few of the leopard bones crunch. He never got to glue together the stupid tail section, but of course this isn't it. It's as if he's nostalgic, but what for?

He stares at the sheen on her face and neck. "Oh," he says. He crosses to the window and switches on the air conditioner. "This all right?"

"Mm mm mm," she said, which means, 'I don't know'—the only sentence that can be represented by humming, though to recognize this is only to use his extra, nictating eyelids again, even now.

He watches the sheen slowly disappear, until all is dry but her upper lip and the hollow at the top of her breastbone. It takes just seconds to cool away the moisture now. His wife's body is drying up, and here he stands in rude good health. They've found they have to ration the use of this machine because it emits a high metallic shriek that Andy says grates on her bones.

And then, Zingman understands why he feels nostalgic. He rechecks the idea several times, but yes—it's her vomiting that he misses. Before her appetite faded out, two weeks ago, he'd make bland rice or protein fruit drinks and they'd eat together. When she couldn't keep it down, he'd help her, over the toilet, or with the silvery basin from the hospital, and he'd find himself freed entirely from self-doubt, holding back her hair and using the cold cloth as deftly as any ministering angel. Nor did this advantage come at Andy's expense, because she never felt stronger, more nearly her old self, never hungrier, than in the minutes following. In fact, the last time they made love was after such an episode, on the morning of July 31. If she hadn't insisted on brushing her teeth first, he wouldn't have cared.

Zingman reaches to pick a piece of crusty sleep from the corner of her eye, but her bluish lids snap open and she lifts her hand much more quickly than he knew she could—even if it is nearly weightless—and slaps his hand right out of the air.

"Nice try," she says. "You're IT." She's struck herself funny; sunken in their wells, her eyes do flicker. "You should see your face, Ross!" She laughs with force, which means choosing this particular exertion as the *only* exertion until sometime this evening. He laughs along with her, though less. They started this silly little game of tag in the period before the pancreatic cancer was pinpointed, nine weeks ago, when her symptoms terrified them both, when the comforts of an old childhood game seemed immense, when it first occurred to Andy that maybe now she might release her age-old grievances against him, when tagging her husband IT came to seem a comic and economical means of nullifying his racket. "Because in a sense," she explained that day, glad for a topic besides endless diagnoses, "you've been tagging me IT for years, haven't you?" They were outside, sitting on a bench in the hospital's courtyard, after blood tests. "You know, I've learned to stop worrying about it like I used to, and I'm happy we don't talk about it anymore, 'cause that got us nowhere. But being a mystery woman for these doctors has reminded me. I feel like they're encrypting me, which you do subtly. Amazingly, after six years, I believe I'm still a figure to be . . . for you to figure out, some shape-shifter from mythology that you tag with thoughts, to freeze me into one single shape so I won't slip away from you. Most recently, you turned me into Claire Danes!"

He opened a container of nonfat cherry yogurt, dipped the spoon in, handed it to her. "Oh? And who gave whom the lizard eyelids?" Shaking her head, Andy accepted the food. In the trees all around them, on this summer morning, birds were singing shrilly, boastfully; or was their noise pre-recorded, being piped into the courtyard? "Revere you? Truthfully, I barely even notice you anymore when you're not complaining," he said, tapping her elbow once as she took her first bite. She laughed, with the plastic spoon in her mouth.

Now, Andy's face draws together. "Ross." He hurries into the bathroom to prepare the syringe, his fingers moving skillfully, filling it halfway with morphine. His face in the round mirror is shining, but nonetheless, he'd better turn that air conditioner off.

His hand stings. He's IT.

She isn't dead.

"So our story has come to this, has it?" Zingman resumed, Mr. Ruthbar unmoving on the couch. "FREE lies gravely ill in a Clearwater, Florida, hospital, addressing an envelope to IT, hands it to an orderly. Meanwhile, in Albuquerque, New Mexico, IT is helped into a seat on a jet, and later that evening, here he stands, in the doorway of the hospital room. FREE cloudily awakes. Let's watch through FREE's failing eyes now, as IT moves across the white linoleum floor, using an aluminum walker.

"'Gently taking your hand in his own gnarled two, IT (suddenly FREE!) looks down upon you with genuine love, smiles, whispers, "You're IT . . ." Your eyes close.

"'Next day, home again, FREE receives the envelope from dear IT. A graceful concession, no doubt. He sits with the letter in his favorite chair, on the back porch, in the gorgeous slanting sunlight. With shaking hands, he manages to tear open the envelope. No letter inside! Instead, out pours a small shower of fingernail shavings, falling through the sunlight and onto the lap below.

"'Wheezing, he struggles to his feet. We flash to a boundless blue sky. A small propeller plane buzzes into view, banking prettily then leveling off. A door opens at mid-fuselage, a goggled figure empties a container, pulls the door shut again. The plane banks out of view, leaving us all alone in the silence, watching this falling cloud, and though it's black and fine, it also glitters in the sunlight, sinking toward the earth, where it will find SAFETY at last.'"

Zingman sighed again, neatened the stack of pages in a pile on the arm of the couch, and then looked. The hands had slid off the face. The oracle's eyes were nowhere to be seen, had been robbed from their sacred sites and spirited away, and the dark, red-rimmed mouth hung open, issuing long easy gusts from deep inside this Delphic cave.

He went into his bedroom and returned with the maroon mohair blanket that Andy had brought back to him from Ireland. Gripping the fringe at one side, he unfolded it in the air, and in the same motion let it settle over all of Mr. Ruthbar except head and feet. He unlaced the shoes but did not take them off; he drew the blanket down over the twin foot-points.

Lying in bed, then, Zingman pictured the cold field in Ohio where he and Andy's father had gone to scatter her ashes that next November, ahead of the first snows. She used to come here as a girl, to sit and think. They handed the tin canister back and forth, politely, until it was empty.

When he clicked on the tv, "Wombdwellers" was nearly finished. Here was the scene in which Lucas Haas is ascending the South Wall of the great labyrinthine monastery; somewhere inside, Claire Danes is barely alive, a shell of herself, but she's in labor, having already gotten rid of nineteen out of twenty-four festering fetuses. Lucas Haas knows none of this yet. His face is bathed in tears, and the tears are bathed in red sunset. He's simply trying to get back to his beloved, has been trying for weeks; he knows that his leaving her, the momentary wavering of his devotion, is what landed her in this fix to begin with. As he climbs, he's experiencing a vivid flashback to when he first glimpsed his future wife, in her reflective uniform, at dusk—the music soars—shepherding a group of school children across a treacherous intersection, in slow-motion. Nothing dwells inside her yet, growing.

Oddly enough, there wasn't a whole lot to see up here on the fourteenth floor, as Harriet had learned three years earlier while snooping, before being nabbed by Garvey. Weak greenish light came from wire-basketed bulbs above broad metal doors. The antiseptic, faintly cloying odor she recalled from her previous venture was masked today by the stink of the dead fish she carried in her arms.

Instead of knobs, these doors had slots beside them, but the bright red access card was firm between her teeth. *Still biting that man back.* Harriet made her way down the long, dim, after-hours corridor. Squinting, she checked each door for Garvey's name. What she hoped to accomplish once she found his door and passed through she wasn't precisely sure, but in a certain way nothing that had happened tonight surprised her; she'd always suspected something dramatic would finally occur for her, since she deserved it, and indeed she'd known what to do, now, at every step. Just as she'd acted instinctively twenty-three years ago, when the thing with Dougy continued to unfold. She'd tell Pepper all of this, too, of course, buying her a splendid breakfast at a fancy place; she'd even confess that in a sense she was grateful to her brother, "that's right, Pepper, grateful. For fueling my entire career."

After he cut her off, she heard nothing more from Dougy for three and a half years, nothing but requisite monosyllables in front of their parents. And then came the noises at night, through the particle board that separated their two bedrooms. She hated him; she vibrated with it, listening to him in there, calling out, "April Fisk!", "Roseanne, RoseAnne!", trying to stifle his voice, "Oh, how about it, Nancy Blake!" Girls, she figured, from his high school.

Yet there was something desperate and pained in his voice, and Harriet sensed an opportunity to strike back. She did some research. The thought of science had been steadily rising within her, anyway, and she believed it could be her ally. It was her instinct, already kicking in. At the library, she made her way through several biology textbooks, sitting off in a dim corner, and one called, *So We're Exploring Our Bodies—Boys.* Late at night on television, everybody else asleep, she found a rebroadcast documentary entitled, "Sex Among the Animals," which featured pairs of salmon and sloths and rhinos and chickens and praying manti, gazelle and toads, grizzlies and slugs, mounting and thrusting, subduing and ravishing and devouring each other, quickly and gradually. The male toads stayed locked atop their females for days and days; eagles intersected momentarily a thousand feet up. Sometimes, the photographer would zero in on the faces, faces of every description but each wearing a neutral expression—a kind of professional apathy.

One day, home "sick" from school, all alone, her parents at work, she stood on a stool and gouged a small hole in the particle board near the ceiling with a steak knife.

That night, Dougy left his bed lamp on, which gave the scene a fine yellow show-quality. Harriet could picture herself standing up there, ponytail lying quiet along her spine, left eye squeezed shut, right eye blinking through the thick lens of her first pair of frog glasses, and witnessing the act she would come to know all too well in her sorry career. The rosy toadstool of the penis, strangely in focus although his hand blurred upon it. Occasionally, the hand would slow way down and become visible, but still at work, forming the "okay" sign.

She improved her detached scientist's stance and stopped focusing on the penis, took in the whole body instead, trying to see how it compared with the driven physiques in "Sex Among the Animals." She decided that it really looked much more like that loose-limbed wooden figure she'd once played with at a doctor's office. Mounted on a pedestal, the figure's joints tied together with elastic that stretched taut, keeping the figure upright, until you pressed a button on the pedestal's underside, slackening him, more or less, at will, making him do a jerky dance. Dougy mercilessly marionetted himself, causing his upper half to rise off the mattress an inch, his head to flop back and forth, his legs to engage in a laughable frog-kick, his mouth to pop open and shut, emitting more of his helpless entreaties, like "Gina Conrad, please!" or "I like it when you do *that* to me."

The result of all this profound effort was four-and-one-half paltry pearly coughs landing on a tan, hairless belly. At the same time, the elastic connecting Dougy's bones tightened to its limit, seizing him up dangerously, nearly buckling him, like the wooden figure if you actually pulled *down* on the large button underneath the pedestal, gaining leverage with your fingernails along the sides between the button and what housed it.

Unlike that figure, though, Dougy snapped, dying back into a jumble of different-length pieces on the bed, the look on his face much softer and more appreciative than anyone's in "Sex Among the Animals." The trouble came later.

"JACOB C. GARVEY, Ph.D." Harriet snorted, inserting the key card, and the door slid open sideways with a tidy whoosh. This is what happens when Star Trek geeks grow up, get rich, and build their own companies. She stepped through—the door gliding shut behind her—and found the light switch. At first only a goose-neck lamp responded, shining dutifully down onto a cherrywood desktop; but soon, track-lighting flickered on above her.

This was no laboratory but a disappointing office, immaculate and standard, furnished with desk, sleek ivory telephone, a cheerful potted marigold at which Harriet sneered. From her angle she could see also the black-felt backs of propped picture frames leaning toward her and the hind end of his computer monitor.

The walls held no fewer than seven prints of Monet's "Haystack" series.

Harriet took a step on shag carpeting, more bleached than white, wall-to-wall. An attache case, matte-finish leather, came to view standing on the desk's farthest corner—so "The Hawk" was here before swooping down for his last supper?

Sitting at the desk, fish in lap, she discovered that the picture frames contained a generic family, in which the father of the two girls and one boy, the husband of that fun-loving beauty, was a specimen on whose tongue Harriet might not have bitten down quite so hard.

The top drawer was empty except for a small digital clock, lying face-up and showing 4:15 am. *Late! . . . But for exactly what?* On a hunch, she stood, gave the fish the chair, raised the attache case high over her head, and brought it crashing, hinges-first, onto the polished wood. It broke open, disgorging itself of pounds of top-secret . . . wallpaper catalogues. She'd knocked the whole phone unit off onto the carpet, so she kneeled and found that the launched and landed receiver gave off no sound. And then, like a match struck low in a room where you'd thought you were alone, something caught Harriet's eye. In front of a slatted wall vent the size of a playing card down by the floor. *Come'ere, you gnats do get around.* She crawled toward the phenomenon.

This carpet was so darn plush, Harriet so hungry, the hour so advanced, the fish so smelly, the office so boring, and these insects, finally, so fickle, most interested only in the fish, streaming toward it, that she sat up and lost her temper—swatted her forearm to punish those remaining. Immediately curious, she withdrew from her breast pocket her frog glasses, held one lens midway between her eye and the field of inquiry—the plunder against her white sleeve—so that it acted as a conventional magnifying glass. She took a moment to focus, and then thought she was flashing onto a memory from some nature footage of long ago, broken birds on a clean sandy beach; but no, she was really here, and so were they—birds killed and wounded, some flapping in an attempt to rise again. Judging by the sharpness of the dark wings, vivid against the fabric, she guessed these were raptors, mainly hawks—red-shouldered? gos? Cooper's? rough-legged? So tricky to tell them apart even under the best of circumstances—and perhaps those there, the littlest, those could be falcons. Harriet moved her lens several millimeters, up toward the elbow, till she came across something calm, perched, wings folded, on a single one of her arm hairs—bending it low—that poked through a pore in the cotton weave. Buff-brown plumage, pale, heart-shaped face—this one she knew from way back, a stunned encounter inside an abandoned warehouse in summertime. The common barn owl.

Like two benign pins inserted correctly into the inner corners of Harriet's eyes, she felt the happy prick of tears starting, then their run down each side of her nose, raindrops down glass, that delaying trip.

She blew on the owl, watched it swivel its head to face the wind, then lift off.

Lying down to rest, drifting off to sleep, she envisioned the territory of her earache now as a hunting-ground where these creatures had sought out cliffed dwellings, nested in thickets of cilia—raising young?—and had soared, swooped, struck at all manner of indigenous prey with lethal, microscopic talons, gouging her and causing her flesh to swell and blister so audibly, for weeks. To say nothing of her oversensitive nasal tissues.

So this is why they leave me but always come back. They're returning to roost.

The first thing Zingman noticed when he re-entered the living room just before dawn were balls of dust swirling in a low, unambitious tornado in the middle of the unswept floor. And the room was cold. Here and there, a lone fly wandered, still looking for the exit. The couch was empty, Mr. Ruthbar's blanket tossed to the floor. The loose windowpane was missing.

He stepped up to it, braving the pre-winter chill, which alerted his face to the pain it thought it had slept off. He sniffed the hollow world, heard a slight sprinkle, and then saw that, despite the breeze in here, the rain outside fell straight down. Three stories below lay the windowpane in mown grass—cracked though still square, glowing dully in the lights of his building's lobby. Raindrops struck it in the quiet, like mistaken music.

Around the corner at the Townsend Street Diner, the early birds had already arrived. They greeted him warmly—he rarely went a day without breakfasting here—but an extra element stood up from the very back booth, a skinny, unfamiliar man in a dapper beige raincoat, holding a notebook. "Aw, c'mon," said the waitress. "At least let him have his coffee, first." The man sat down again.

She met Zingman at his booth, the fifth from the front.

"Thanks, Monica. Who's that?"

"Some reporter from the paper." She filled his mug. "Wants to hear what you've been up to lately. 'Cause of the movie on tv last night."

"I should've known that would bring them out of the woodwork."

"What's her name, that actress? Anyway, the changes she went through, being pregnant for so long." Monica shivered. "Was that make-up? Hey, stupid question! Coffee and scrambled?"

"'Nother stupid question!"

"Whatja do to your face and ear? *That's* not make-up."

"Idiot slapped me."

"Jesus."

Alone, Zingman sipped his coffee, though it offended his lips (still swollen and smarting halfway across). To escape, he watched the dawn arrive in reflection. Running the length of the wall near the ceiling was a row of blue-tinted mirrors, circles no larger than sandwich plates; by positioning himself in this booth and tilting his head just so against the vinyl seatback, he could look into the third circle from the front, attaining a view out through the broad front window.

The sprinkle had ceased and sunlight now seethed into this round rendition of the world, a light—strange, yes it could be called strange—that seemed somehow more like water, filling everything, than had the rain.

At the center of the mirror were parked cars, and in front of them, close, a red bench. And before *this*, a brown paper bag lay on its side, shimmering in the breeze as though deciding whether or not to stand; but too soon, a bare foot crushed it. The foot belonged to a striking blonde woman who had stumbled into the picture and now fell seated onto the bench. She hugged around herself a white doctor's jacket. She plunged her head between her knees and threw up, the dark puddle collecting between her naked feet. Being reflected lent both the act and the puddle a certain classy, vintage quality. Even those slow-descending strings, like beads, now following the original gush seemed a precious series of whole notes after a rich crescendo—a faint reprise, sunstruck. And the puddle, how patiently it sat there on the concrete, right between those delicate feet.

As if responding to a call, the doctor abruptly stood, looked around her, then slanted off stage. Zingman wanted to jump up and pursue this vision, but, loyal to the mirror, he was also enticed by a second player who entered the scene now from the other side—a squirrel, stepping cautiously toward the puddle, flat-footed, tense, thick airy tail shining. One inch from the crimped shoreline, the animal abruptly relaxed, gazing into the distance.

He did too, and though he knows he's wishing more than seeing, Andy appears inside the circle—asleep in her yellow terrycloth robe, sprawled out on the floor of the pantry off the kitchen, long hair wound and pinned up in a ventilating bun (her hair has not fallen out because she's chosen against chemo). It's the same pantry that she painted last spring, deep ocean green, a semi-gloss, and it turns out to be the coolest place in the house, in the middle of this beastly August. It's not till next week that he'll buy the air conditioner, for the upstairs bedroom.

Zingman is sitting next to her, and he's intently busy with something, hunch-backed and cross-legged. Oh, he remembers; he's working to assemble the model leopard skeleton, 1/50th scale, piece by piece. They bought it just days ago in the gift shop at the city zoo, their last outing. The gift shop had had little else left, and certainly not the heart-stopping great blue shark, far too popular. But he felt he must get his hands on something for himself, something to put together, though he didn't understand why. He chose at random, quickly, because Andy had rushed back to the car, feeling awful.

One of their first dates occurred here at this zoo, seven years earlier, darting around together, exploring, she astonished and childlike, sporting for the first time her particular brand of steady fun, then lingering at the huge window of the Seaquarium. It is here, peering into this foreign realm, that Zingman finally confessed he's a writer who tries to invent other worlds, though he said "fantasy," not "horror." She puts her arm over his shoulders in the flickery undersea light. He felt as if they are someplace remote, though it was only a short concrete tunnel near crowds and hard sunshine.

This morning, marooned in the present, after everything, poised here in the fifth booth from the front at the Townsend Street Diner, Zingman noted that at some point good old Monica had slipped him his plate of scrambled eggs. He salted and peppered them, ate a large forkful, drank some more coffee. Good soul, she must also have kept that reporter at bay. She might have told him, "Listen, take pity—he can't even chase after the sick yet intriguing doctor woman because he's crippled by his recent past; his new story leans on history too much, so it put the idiot savant right to sleep. Go and type *that* up if you need a scoop so bad."

Taking a second bite of eggs, he consulted again the round mirror above him, saw himself place a hand on Andy's upper back, try to shake her awake, then return to work on the model, hunching over it where it stands on the deep ocean green. The rib cage is nearly done, hanging from the spine, whose vertebrae he's finally linked up. He's never been more diligent, though he has saved the tiny annoying tail bones for last and never, in fact, does get around to finishing them.

Watching himself, Zingman recognized something for the first time, that he worked on the model to be like Andy. She was building something too; she was building death, maybe no more intricate than this damned leopard. He finished his coffee, his eggs. He shook his head and smiled up at that unsuspecting guy, knowing the endless hours of mistakes and restarts it will take him to set the ninety-four pieces, blowing to dry the dizzying glue.

On the floor of the pantry, Andy laughs every time she wakes up and takes a look at his lack of progress. "That poor cat," she says one time. Another: "Give me the diagram," but she falls asleep over the sheet of paper.

And look, there they are again, on another day, long before Andy got sick. She's lying back on a patch of moss in Skoonlet Valley Nature Preserve, where they like to hike. He joins her, collapsing on the soft growth. They're beside a wide brook and have forgotten to pack a lunch. He puts his ear on her stomach, listens to its repertoire. Boy-oy-oy-oy-OYOYOooo-o-o-o-o. When she laughs, she tosses her head back and forth, each cheek making contact with the moss. Eeeeeeeeeeeeebipbipbipbip, goes her stomach, and then it makes another sound, an antique creaking, as though leather-built.

Elsewhere in the Preserve, another day, they've come upon a waterfall. It has a rock platform behind its crashing torrent. After they fight through, they crawl onto the platform, drenched, and find furthermore a little room. Inside, they cannot hear each other at all, unless they shout. For some reason, this tickles them to no end. Laughing, they make exaggerated faces and pantomime emotions.

Zingman turned from the mirror and looked directly out into the world through the diner's plate-glass window. The squirrel still stood by the puddle, which he could now tell was dark green. He felt cold and wished he could shiver—like the waitress had—just for the sheer normalcy of living that this would imply, but he had no room left inside. He was dense with memory. He couldn't breathe. He was cold the way a stone is cold, and suddenly he knew he'd remain this cold, exactly, throughout a future filled with hollow days.

But what finally released him, to throw his money down, to run out the door and chase after the barefoot doctor, was the squirrel. Its tail shone, shone, then flicked once.

"You're IT!"

Blinking awake, Harriet saw the red runt leaning over her, offering his outlandish hand, as though this same hand hadn't just lowered a blow onto her shoulder. He'd changed from his polyester kitchen top into a wrinkled dress shirt.

"I tagged you!"

The keys on his belt ring rummaged with his excitement. She sat up and breathed. "Right. That would make me IT, all right." The room was alive with gnats, thickest about the fish on the chair. She tried to disperse them with her hands, but they were too hungry. No hungrier than I.

"I called the elevator for us."

"Where?"

He pointed. One of Monet's "Haystack" paintings was on the shag carpet, leaning against the wall, and where it had been was a little window, wire netting embedded in its glass.

She heard a chugging and chirring, getting louder, and in ten seconds the window filled with light; the runt stepped over and pushed lightly on the beige, seamless wall. A narrow elevator door popped open, demonstrating seams after all. Harriet got to her feet.

"Can you help me, downstairs?"

"Why not? Got food down there?" Harriet picked up the specimen by the tail, slapped it against her thigh.

"That fish again? Not allowed downstairs. Mr. G. keeps his place or-ga-nized."

"Nope, fish comes with me. It's my new . . . hobby."

Inside the tiny room—going down!—the red runt seemed bashful, standing so close to a woman, though it was hard to tell for sure because he used his extensive filtering hand over nose and mouth. Harriet found that the fish, held out in front of her belly, effectively kept the gnats from her face. "We'll be there in two minutes," he said, muffled. "Got chores to do."

Three walls were covered with drab gray indoor-outdoor carpeting; the fourth side was open to the shaft, showing a zipping parade of pipes and clumps of wire, but no further doors.

"Listen, how is it you've been granted this access?"

"He lets me go anywhere I want."

"Does he?"

"Yeah, I work hard and I don't tell the secrets."

"Mm." The parade was thinning out, uniform metal walls passing, with here and there a region of rivets. "Aren't there other floors?"

"Nu-uh, just the bottom."

In a while, their craft clunked heavily home; the runt swung open the door, and Harriet had two perceptions.

First, a tremendous mortifying odor, piercing her nasal congestion—a particularly punishing blend of the organic and the synthetic, as if someone had dumped a bushel of fresh manure into a tank of rotten blood, and then somebody else had snuck up with a dainty atomizer, spraying cloud after cloud of sickly sweet, alcohol-based cologne.

Second, a hillside of micro-birds, casting a shadow, avalanching in.

"Ohhhhhhh, always MORE!" The runt took a deep breath, held it, and ran out with his arms thrown up, calling, "Be right back!"

Harriet lunged for the door, pulled it shut, and fit herself into a far corner, tossing the fish away. Curling on her side, like Pepper, and, it occurred to her, very much like herself as a ten-year-old, trying to rise above disgust while listening to her brother at night, through the particle board. Soon after she began peeking into Dougy's room, she'd undertaken, like any good researcher, to tape record and catalogue his sounds. She might have let him off the hook at this point if he'd accepted his birthday present with any grace. She made the mistake of feeling a little sorry for him after all her spying, so she'd given him "AMAZING LIVE SEA MONKEYS—ABSOLUTELY GUARANTEED TO GROW . . . JUST ADD WATER AND THEY COME TO LIFE!" They did come to life and they did grow, but not into the grinning aquatic folks pictured on the box—driving automobiles, playing tennis, attending parties. Instead, they were tiny brine shrimp. Even so, Dougy had kept them, in a fish bowl, and she'd espied him checking on them occasionally, on his bureau, and believed that although he never thanked her, he might be glad.

But one day soon, she rode with her mother to pick him up after basketball practice, not caring, just reading a book in the backseat. He approached the car with his gang of buddies, and before getting in, he said, "Hey, there she is, one who gave me those piece-of-shit bugs I was telling you guys about." He led them in a chorus of braying laughter.

"Yeah, she wants to turn me into a total science *freak* like she is!" The boys said, "I know it" and "That'll be the day, Doug!"

As it happened, in one of those coincidences that point a person in the right direction, the book she was reading in the backseat was James D. Watson's *The Double Helix,* given to her by her teacher, Mr. Bradley. It chronicles Watson's discovery, with Francis Crick, of the structure of the DNA molecule, and, though of course she understood none of the chemistry involved, she'd found it to be a readable saga whose sheer implications rocked her—the promise of embracing all of life with the mind, whereas she'd always felt, before nature, as frustrated as an amnesiac before her very own family.

It was late in the book, page 157, that Watson revealed his

true colors, confiding to the reader that he and Crick had finally managed to "give Rosy the boot." She got to page 157 that night after dinner, in her bed.

Harriet threw the book across the room and cried, and her mother climbed the stairs, sympathizing, rubbing her temples. The very next day she bought her a wonderful beginner's microscope. Now she could feast her eyes on the frenetic fringed denizens of a drop of pond water, and see how thick sheets of roast beef seemed to wrap each strand of light brown hair that she pulled from her head and stretched taut beneath the lens.

That evening, she broke her long-held silence toward her brother with a sharp rap on the particle board, which brought a halt to husky professions of love for a certain Naomi. She then tiptoed out into the hall and crouched by his bedroom door, cleared her throat and said, under the crack, "Ah HA."

Nothing from the room.

Harriet drew a blank, got nervous and scurried back to her bed, curled there for a long while in the cozy tranquility that comes after a formidable opponent has been neatly tipped off the brink of a cliff. Besides the incident at the car, Dougy had not tormented her outright, unless one counted stony neglect; but she knew from *The Double Helix* that this was only because a man doesn't have to fight in order to achieve victory in this world.

She got up and returned her lips to the crack beneath his door. "I must inform you," she whispered, "that I've been making tapes of you and I will be handing copies around to female members of your school whose names, I think, have been on your mind . . . unless . . ."

In the morning, early, a Saturday, she walked the young man, who looked pale, out to the empty softball field behind their house, pressed PLAY, and let him hear a particularly heartfelt example of himself.

Dougy bent, scooped up several small rocks, and began heaving them all the way from centerfield to the home-plate backstop on the fly. Harriet explained what she wanted him to do, then left him alone to think. She watched from her window for most of the afternoon—a tiny yellow-shirted boy lingering and wandering in the outfield, hurling rocks, making quite an impressive carpet of them at the backstop.

The runt busted in, tripping over a raised lip of carpet but keeping his balance. He wore green mosquito netting over his head, cinched at the neck with his small hand. In his spacious hand he carried some netting for her too, and a black-rubber bucket by its arched silver handle. The bucket contained a jumbo red spatula; several combs and brushes; three lidless jars of cold cream; and a brown paper bag of squirming, rustling somethings.

Through his veil, he croaked, "We got to do chores!"

Harriet stood and received the netting, placed it over her head, and inhaled gingerly. She gagged, then exploded coughing, understanding why the runt had croaked his words—one could not breathe freely here, or else esophagus would turn aviary.

After, she let herself be led humbly off, eyes shut, into the world's most populous flock, keeping hold of a little twist of shirt between the runt's shoulder blades. With her left elbow, she clamped the fish to her chest, right over her heart, while that hand noosed the bottom of the netting about her neck. Harriet was undone but also honored to know that her body was being buffeted every moment, if impalpably, by a million pair of perfectly formed wings.

The runt halted before an ordinary door, with keyhole and knob, which he unlocked with a mere metal key. She released his shirt, opened her eyes. "C'mon, hurry! You're letting them in!" She hopped over the threshold, and he locked the door again.

They were in a well-lit room, surrounded by a splendid array of sparrow-sized raptors, perched on genuine brown branches that extended from antiseptic white walls, maybe twenty or thirty bouncing, shuffling their wings angrily, tossing their sharp heads and crying out as though ready to hit the warpath; their cries, however, were dainty peeps. She laughed, which felt good. Some opened their wings, stretching them, brandishing them, then folded them again, repeatedly, reminding her of men, crack soldiers, assembling and disassembling their firearms. "Oh . . . please!"

"No, shut up!" said the runt, startling Harriet. He glared at her, his face completely different now, suddenly brash, like the birds', not dopey, not granting its own weakness. He snatched from her head the netting she'd forgotten she wore; his was already off, stuffed into the black bucket, where hers went. "Here, dump these out," he said, handing her the paper bag, "then follow me. We've got so much work to do." He marched away, bucket brushing his thigh with every swing of his arm, opened another door, and disappeared into the next bright room.

Harriet stood still, listening to the bag crinkling beneath her hand, looking down at the dented skull of the fish, into the dulled green eye. The runt thrust his head back in: "I said dump 'em!"

When she obeyed, the contents tumbled onto scuffed blue linoleum—flesh-tone, and more than merely flesh-tone, actual human bodies, two or three inches long. They lay in a heap, then the heap unbuilt itself as the bodies twisted, got their bearings, crawled off in all directions. Harriet jammed her glasses on, but barely had time to confirm what she hadn't wanted to believe—that these were naked female bodies, and, for some reason, headless—before the clear-eyed throng descended on them from above. She stepped back, but leaned forward, noting in the blurry fray that beaks were dabbed with blood, that swatches of flesh were being torn loose and tossed away over narrow downy shoulders in preference for vital organs. The victims kicked stringbean legs and flailed impossible spaghetti arms. Of course, they did not scream, nor did the birds comically peep anymore; the only sound was a moist, devoted feeding, innocent as drizzle.

Naturally, Harriet's stomach did not turn at this, because the stomach of a scientist does not turn.

She whirled, though, yanked by a huge hand on her upper arm—"LAZY BONES!"—so that the fish came loose, smacked onto the floor. Three raptors flew to investigate.

"Let go of me!" She freed herself from the runt, but before she could bend to reach it, he booted the fish into the other room, scattering the raptors, and then escorted her that way roughly, slamming the door to the first room behind them. When she tried for the fish again, he shoved her down, landing her painfully on her butt.

"You got to do what I say now . . . sad lady. We're not in the cafeteria." He took one of the lidless jars of cold cream from his bucket, pushed it at her; shocked, she simply accepted it, like a bite of spinach from Pepper. "Time to moisturize. I got to go check all the projects, flip the cakes (ooo I HATE those CAKES!), feed those giants in the big room . . . always getting on me and scratching me up, and Mr. G never lets me fight back . . ." The runt, standing over her, started to cry, then became infuriated with himself, sort of growled. He began to stomp on the fish with his strong shoes, alternating, making things clatter inside the bucket. Harriet couldn't move; he was like her brother Dougy, destroying her tape recorder, eventually, with his stomping feet. "BUT MR . . . G.'S . . . NOT . . . AROUND . . . ANY . . . MORE . . . HE . . . GOT . . . KILLED . . . SO . . . I . . . CAN . . . DO . . . WHAT . . . EVER . . . I . . . WANT!!!!" Worn out, he glared at Harriet, as though daring her to contradict, then stalked off down a hallway, keys jingling, and turned a corner.

Silence, finally. She seemed to be sitting at a museum exhibit; *focus, now, Harriet, study—find the point of fascination.* Everywhere stood compositions of flesh, like sculptural installations for a dream factory conjured by Mr. Jacob C. Garvey; each was housed within a pedestalled Lucite cube—shining antipode to her own black cube of threatened unconsciousness. She shaded her eyes as from a sunburst, found it easier, just yet, to study one humble punted fish, over there in the corner. She coughed in sympathy, throat still ticklish from earlier birds. She blinked to see, perched on a stiff little fin, an eagle the size of a cough drop. She clinked the cold cream jar on the floor several times half-heartedly, at which the eagle didn't scare.

The Lucite cubes, all about, were purposefully partial, missing top and front panes; each represented a single rationed glimpse into the limitless topography of the female anatomy. *Trouble getting dates, Jack? Need this daily floor show, do we?*

Nearest to Harriet was an upper back, only this, as if formed from ivory, with not the merest semblance of shoulders, no arms to the side, only the first quarter or third of the back itself extending from just above the scapulae down approximately—she adjusted her frog glasses—to the thirteenth vertebra, the spine so straight and delicate it made her eyes sting as had the barn owl.

This whole creation ended, top and bottom, abruptly, level across as though cropped, but much too cleanly to believe, not wounded; traveling downward, she noted—and this she found oddly touching—the earliest suggestion of an inward taper, left and right, the pure anticipation of a phantom waist.

She set down the jar of cold cream and hugged herself, then hugged herself tighter, aware of her head, light as a cinder, singed from within by hawks, owls, and intellectual affront.

Looking to the next-nearest cube, however, answered at least one question, that of sentience, because the tiny eagle now braked and fluttered to a careful landing on the smooth ridge of a hipbone, and just here the skin twitched, like horseflesh harried by a fly. And then it was still, this entire pelvis-and-onset-of-thigh, inclusive of pubic wisps but ceasing shy of any more. In fact, as Harriet made bold to sweep her vision around the entire showroom, she concluded that nowhere did Garvey permit that which most frightens men. Instead, all was sliced and offered up like rational conic sections. Breasts, yes, and well-posed legs; and over there a foot, pointed elegantly (its big toe providing the eagle's newest post); classy shoulders; necks; jaw-lines; even long chestnut hair from the back of a head (just the back), spilling from its cube, trailing halfway to the floor. But never once the allowance of genitalia, to say nothing—*coward*—of a face!

"Oooooh, I really hate those CAKES!"

The red runt re-entered the room, tossing the hairbrush, which clacked on the floor near her. "Do that one, too," he said, pointing past her toward the long spilling hair. He held delicately between index finger and thumb of his mini-hand an oversized pair—*yes, Pepper, I remember your "waxlips"*—of bright red lips, just the loop of them, no teeth or bolstering flesh of mouth, but full anyway and demurely pursed.

"Mr. G. made these for me. Five more grew last night!" He raised this pair to his face, lay upon them a protracted and squeaky smooch, eyes kindling above, and when he took them away he was ruby-smeared to three times the dimensions of his own slit-like mouth.

Out of his pocket he drew a tube of lipstick, with which he conscientiously retouched his pet. When finished, he lowered tube and looping lips into the black bucket.

"Hey, you didn't moisturize! You're in trouble!"

Harriet cringed, but his mood had apparently improved thanks to the kiss. "Okay," he huffed, "guess I better show you." Like a peevish five-year-old, he snatched the jar of cold cream from the floor by her knee, gave the fish another quick mash with his shoe, and stamped across the room to a cube containing one medium-sized breast mounted on a metal frame. The runt set down the bucket and began to apply the cream liberally with the hand that could best address the whole at once and, with the detail hand, to make sure the tiny lumps of the aureole and the burgundy nipple itself got sufficient attention. Harriet found herself recalling with a genuine start and tinge of shame that she too had a body; she felt her own breast gently, not aroused, just recalling some of its grim history. Her nipples were of another type, though. Oh, she'd been informed, by Robert Jenwaugh, that they made "a decent berry"; but until cold or touch caused them to scoot and gather inward, they were only lumps, dispersed, nothing he wished to see.

"Mr. G. taught me how to do this."

"Mmmmmm hmmmmm, I'll bet he did."

The runt dwelt on the task, and when he turned to her like a teacher, she nodded at the helpful demonstration and noticed in secret that his penis tensed the fabric on either side of his zipper.

Finished, the breast stood thickly spackled. "Got to go now!" he said, tossing her the cold cream and grabbing up his bucket, clicking urgently down the hallway, calling over his shoulder, "Be back soon, you start working!"

Did I place myself under a curse by what I did to Dougy? Oh, she was anything but superstitious; she meant that she may have felt less deserving of such treatment, less accepting, if she'd stopped with that first sober observation.

Her brother's first ransom payment appeared in a black plastic film canister outside her door. She rushed with it down to the basement, her first laboratory, where her microscope was all set, its highest-power (220x) having been rotated and clicked into place, a clean clear glass slide mounted on the platform under steadying silver clips. She switched on the 150-watt light bulb above her head, opened the canister, sniffed (stale boiled beets), and smeared some of the gray paste with a Q-tip very thinly over the slide.

No, the stomach of the scientist does not turn, even at ten years of age.

She took off her glasses, adjusted the small concave mirror under the platform to throw light up through the hole beneath the sample, held her breath, and looked into the scope.

She thumbed the focus-wheel on the side, first in large arcs that sent her this way and that past a perfect picture, then in feathery taps.

Harriet giggled, back then and right now, couldn't help it. Cream-cheese-and-poppy-seed cake frosting, seeds locked in place—giggled at the whole idea of Nature's erecting a lumbering egocentric baboon like Dougy who smelled bad and used words wrong, and then expertly packing all of this—not to mention of course the reeking dull futures of generations to come—like a hundred thousand Slinkies, as pictured in *The Double Helix,* inside each of those poppy seeds.

Her brother's heavy feet crossed the floor over her head, going toward breakfast, and then wished his father and mother Oh good morning in the sweetest tones possible for his lately broken voice, just as though he had never ever groaned, "Open up, Natalie!"

But the ransom payment had been left too long in lethal room temperature. So that afternoon, Harried found her subject in town playing basketball, walked right up to him in the middle of a heavy-breathing, grinning-in-the-sun pack of boys, the sort of pack who could never frighten her again, now that the power of science had revealed the secret of their grunting manhood: four-and-a-half paltry pearly coughs filled with poppy seeds.

Shirtless, glistening, hands on hips, sweat-darkened hair stuck in prongs across his forehead, Dougy looked down at her. She handed him the rinsed-out canister and said, "They were stone dead."

His face was stiff and empty, like the faces in "Sex Among the Animals." He did not take the canister from her, so she turned and tossed it back over her shoulder, heard it land and roll along blacktop. Without looking, she called out, "I want warm."

She heard predictable laughter at whatever joke Dougy had thought up, then the basketball bouncing again, hitting the iron rim and chain nets in the distance behind her. She took a delighted walk, the last pure one of her life, cutting through the electrical May breeze and inhaling the charge, discovering that when you breathe through your nose all the way to the last one-third of the lungs' capacity (something you rarely do), you can tug an entirely new set of scents from an atmosphere stingy with its secrets even in springtime.

At every step, Harriet wanted to fall over and sink into the grass of lawns, and several times she went ahead and did so, fitting her eyes carefully in through the blades until she had introduced herself to a realm where sunlight is white instead of yellow and where she understood all at once that the soil is a ceiling—trying to keep us satisfied with ourselves by holding a much more complicated, more exact and trickier, world down.

Next day, Dougy did deliver another canister to her door. In the basement, she poured the astonishingly fluid contents into a bowl. Organisms swam in water, visible without magnification. She blinked until it hit her—the sea monkeys, returned. Harriet held her head up over the bowl, one hand on each side, massaging her temples and staring at these impostors. She was beginning to become interested, despite herself, when the basement door crashed open.

She didn't budge.

He stomped down the stairs and across the concrete very slowly until he was two feet from her. "They're shit and so are you," he said, then he hurled her small tape recorder with both hands onto the floor, where it seemed to explode. For good measure, he stamped it into even smaller pieces, and when the tape popped out, he cracked it with his sneaker heel.

She didn't look up at him, not ever.

"You little fucking robot pervert, you'll never see jizz again. Any more pervert tricks and you're dead."

He went away. The sea monkeys swam and swam in their red ceramic bowl, in perfect squares, drawing each side of these squares with a true-line gradualness that can imply great weight.

Harriet did not cry. Instead, she removed one monkey gently with tweezers and put him on a microscope slide, where he was pinned secure by the water his body had brought with it. The elongated organs were vivid and startling within the transparent tube of him; they would demand much study.

Ravenous, Harriet stood, brush in hand, with every intention of tending to the gorgeous hair over there in the corner; after all, winning the runt's approval might lead her more quickly to a fridge. But a glance in passing at a breast he hadn't "moisturized" stopped her dead. This one was larger, and had the benefit of being mounted, not on a metal frame, but quite naturally on its own portion of upper torso, half a rib cage, which itself was mounted on a metal frame. The air of animacy was potent; this rib cage's quiescent failure to respire struck Harriet more than would have any sudden inhalation. But what had stopped her was something else. Plainly visible on the side of the breast—that penny- colored, teardrop birthmark she'd seen on Pepper up in the cafeteria.

"I see. He's used you as his prototype." She spoke at first to the breast alone, and then, to all assembled in the room, still mute but abruptly intimate, said, "Some boyfriend, huh, kid? Takes you away from yourself, cuts you up in pieces. But I know exactly how you feel." She drew a deep breath, trying a grin. "I thought you were a blonde."

Harriet swept the fish, battered ally, off the floor, and charged down the hallway, ready to take control. She opened and slammed three doors—a dark supply closet; a messy little office with charts and graphs on the wall, notebooks on the desk (read those later); a roomful of steel vats belching clouds of the gnat-sized, with their stench of decay and cologne (enough already). Until the moment she opened the fourth door and saw what the runt was doing, she felt every bit as ferocious as on the afternoon she'd tracked her brother down at the basketball court.

She found him sitting against the far wall of a little room, fingering what could only be one of the "cakes," eyes closed, and cooing to it, "Uhmmmmooomuhmuhmuhmuh," smiling, kissing it repeatedly and pressing it lovingly to his flushed cheek.

Here, just inside the door, was an entire table of them, a table lipped around its top to support a shallow bath of liquid made up, no doubt, of simple sugars and various bio- agents that stimulate cell division. The jumbo red-plastic spatula sat beneath one, mid-chore, and since the reveler remained unaware of her, she tossed the fish out onto the hall floor, took the spatula's handle, and quietly lifted the specimen—a round, soft creation, typical of Mr. Garvey's refined sensibilities, a pudendal mound richly furred with kinky black hair, and again, with no hint of genitalia. She replaced it in its bath.

Squinting across the room, Harriet now noticed that frantic dots had risen off the cake and clashed before the runt's shut lids. *These cakes are a favorite roosting-ground, I suppose. Most likely, those dots are swamp-dwellers . . . the osprey? the kite?* An expression of limitless peace had spread over his baby face.

Then he started to cry. "Mr. G.," he whimpered, "what'm I s'posedta do now?" He slipped his pubic plaything upright beneath his chin, cupped it carefully like the seat of a violin; it doubled inward thickly. "Mmmmmuhmuhm." He picked up another from a short stack beside him, opened his mouth, and inserted the object part-way, suckling: "Aaaaaahmuhmuhmuhuhaaaaaahmahmahmahmahmahmuh."

Harriet withdrew, pulling the door nearly to. She sat down in the hallway and crossed her legs, sighing beside the fish. I thought he HATED those cakes—*well, that never stops a man, does it? Usually helps him, in fact. More importantly, I'm starving.*

"Hey, where did you two come from?" she whispered. A pair of the headless women crawled toward her, making good time, one a little faster than the other, along the dull blue linoleum, their four breasts trembling beneath them, each like a drop hanging off the end of a spout.

The leading one now veered, it seemed at random, on a line that took her to the wall; she moved briskly along its base for three feet, reached the door frame, then slipped through the crack into the room where the runt still softly moaned. The other one kept coming till she bumped into the fish, just above the tail, backed up, bumped it, backed up, bumped it, like a determined bug. *Stop thinking "she."* When it had backed up yet again, Harriet took the organism in her hand, gripped it around its waist, felt it hoist itself higher, felt the ill-set gel of its hips slide up through the top of her easy fist so that only its slim legs remained trapped, kicking like a good swimmer's. She shook it back down, held on tighter.

From the room—"NOW I CAN DO WHATEVER I WANT TO!"

The skin wasn't firm and supple, as she'd expected, but grainy and seemed ready to come loose like overboiled chicken flesh. Harriet wanted to reject this body, not because of this flesh—*stomach of a scientist* . . . No, what repelled her repelled her mind—

how this project could move the way it did, attempting to free itself, prying and shoving so nimbly with flyspeck hands at her enfolding fingers, changing tactics minutely, cleverly, breasts jouncing—*there's the birthmark, all right, a fine point*—yet managing all the while so thoroughly to lack a head.

Harriet noticed that it possessed not even a vestigial neck, that its shoulders simply ran across flat from tip to tip, collarbones joined in front. She lay it supine across her palm, pillorying its ankles with her thumb, denying any sit-up with a fingertip on each shoulder.

She'd met a young man in the summer after sophomore year in college, and she'd lost her virginity to him. She didn't much like Greg—skinny, long hair like a greasy fan waving out behind his neck—but let him take her out for lobster and beer, and later, in his bed, when she told him that she found it difficult to breathe with him on top, Greg explained that the rib cages of women are designed for this, to be collapsible, that she should relax and let it happen.

Harriet took another deep breath, removed her fingertips from the shoulders, and with her pinky depressed this rib cage right between the breasts, and indeed the sternum gave way, alarmingly, although she guessed that not having to contend with functioning lungs brought this lucky lady much closer to Greg's ideal.

"Sorry, Pepper." After she lifted her pinky, a dimple remained at the center of the chest; this didn't appear to concern the victim, however, who only sat up and continued its impressively varied efforts at extrication.

"How do you work? What's your principle? Give me a little hint?" This is all Harriet had ever wanted to know about life itself, as a matter of fact, right from the beginning.

She stood the creation on the floor, where it swayed rather endearingly for a moment before toppling forward and crawling again. Snatching it back up, Harriet replaced the body on her palm and poked the dimple deeper—"This hurt?"—then drew it down, making a slow trench to the bottom of the abdomen, halting just before the black pinhead tuft.

Harriet crawled, herself, to the edge of the doorway, peeking. The runt didn't see her; he was attending too avidly to his own little friend—squeezing and massaging her, rocking and jiggling her, jollying her, rubbing her between her legs. "There-there-there-there," he sang to her sweetly. But she'd begun to slough, leaving smears of herself—not like boiled chicken anymore but like liverwurst—on his hands and face; even so, when he rubbed her between her legs, she seemed to enjoy it, approving of this partner, if unreflectively, and actually pitching in with her hips, riding his squat index finger like a fiend.

I see we've come equipped with a good, healthy sexual appetite—so important for a young woman these days.

The runt unzipped his pants and placed the teeny flirt on his slender penis, which she embraced and straddled with devotion, continuing to ride, and faster.

Why am I not surprised? Through her mind flashed an absurd temptation to make that old shame-on-you gesture toward him, index finger flinting across index finger.

Large hand covered his face, small covered back of large. His breathing seemed a powerful thank you to such an empathetic lover who understood just what he needed in his hour of grief, but when he ejaculated low onto his striped dress shirt—runt squeaked; Harriet yawned—his gratitude suddenly deserted him—*imagine that*—and with his little hand he simply reached down and squeezed so that she started to ooze between his fingers, which must have made him angry because he then peeled off her remains and flung them at the wall near him, where they stuck midway up, a gluey confusion of parts with only one leg still recognizable, not entirely wrecked, wispy, pointing up and off to one side like an antenna—still twitching, at the knee, in time to the recent effort.

Harriet's stomach turned.

Probably our eyes are real bright, thought Zingman, and that's why.

He and the barefoot woman paused to look at self-important rhinos already filthy at 8:30 am; a bison, whose tremendous head contained not a trace of humor; a gentle-pretending pair of mountain gorillas, picking mites from one another as in the kindest of endearments; angry, pacing leopards (complete with tails!) and cheetahs spot-lit by warm October sun. They passed through a swarm of elementary school children on a field trip, hopping, yelling, clapping. In front of the muddy pen that contained giant South American hogs, she tossed her head back and laughed. Her first words: "The Pig Trough!"

This relationship was really going quite smoothly, he had to say; although she hadn't yet looked directly into his face, they were together, like dumbstruck children. But when he began to notice zoo-goers doing double-takes, tapping others on their backs and slyly cocking their heads thisaway—one couple openly sneered; a first- or second-grade girl stuck out her tongue—that's when he decided it was because of their eyes, his and hers, how bright they must be, and that this case was no different from any sudden manifestation of the transcendent in the midst of the everyday—it allured, it rankled.

Zingman had found her wandering just a block from the diner, and wordlessly he'd led her here to the city zoo. It turned into a spectacular morning, like spring; she'd accompanied him without question, apparently craving direction. Maybe she wasn't a doctor at all. He wanted to hug her gently and whisper, What's the matter?

He knew better, of course, than to believe this was Andy with him again, or even some version of her, but he didn't mind letting his bones hum, either, with the same vibration.

Nor was he alone, as became clear when the beasts, too, began to swing snouts and beaks and muzzles toward her, this or that pair of eyes seeking her from behind bars or glass. She'd stop at each enclosure, lean close, trying to identify what she recognized in there, rubbing the top of her head and moaning quietly, stepping from side to side on her tender feet, every angle proving too feeble, somehow, whether this creature was delicate or great, whether or not it continued to pursue her with its own eyes.

Zingman waited patiently behind her every time she conducted this maneuver. He watched those simple, inspiring, white-jacketed shoulders of hers, his eyes actually smarting in the glare, and her blondeness, too, until he learned to focus near the roots, where the hair was brown.

He took her silent curiosity before the cages to bode thunderously well for him, because he recognized that he, too, in the months since Andy, had been sitting back on his haunches—like those lemurs, there, hunched and stunned—waiting to be rediscovered.

Once, he lost the woman briefly in the crowd when that reporter from the diner approached and stuck out his hand. "Mr. Zingman, I'm William Stennhouse, III." Zingman didn't shake. "I share your professional interest in odd events, but lack your talent to invent them. Last night's replay of your film begs the question, what's Ross Zingman been up to?"

Zingman turned and hurried away. At the screened gazebo housing birds of prey she suddenly began to speak, and rapidly, though still without looking at his face. Her voice was breathy, as though feigning immaturity.

"Oh, boy, now *that's* what they're s'posed to look like. Not itsy-bitsy, like those ones Jack showed me in the house."

She cocked her head and giggled, eyelids half shut. "Making me find their little eggs in his pockets! Like grains of rice. And what were you doing with those tweezers that night, sneaky boy? I pretended to be asleep. But I felt them on me, 'course I did, dopey. They were nipping my skin all over, under my shirt, even my lips, and other places, then I heard a jar opening, tweezers rattling inside." She turned to him, eager for answers, but noticed his swollen ear and cheek, clucked her tongue. "Oh, Jack, that man did hurt you, but not as bad as I thought. Hurt me, too, look." She rubbed the top of her head with two fingers. "Do me a favor?"

"Anything," he said.

"Show me those crazy waxlips again?"

In a perfect world, that would be some sort of roundabout praise for "Lip Service," his story. Quite a trick, since in *this* world it hadn't been published.

She looked into his eyes. He swallowed a dry bubble. Wildly, he thought he might lean and kiss her. Behind him, he heard a distant splash. She pointed that way, over his shoulder. "Oh, I just love those!" He turned and followed her, slowly, watching her shiny feet trot toward "The Dolphin Corral," where aqua paint curled and chipped off the low, curving cement wall, and where water puddled the asphalt.

Here it was again, coming back to him—the kissing triangle, an iron law of nature. Even before meeting Andy, Zingman had realized through hard experience that a first kiss will occur only if three distinct elements fit into place: the two must be having fun; their mouths must be near enough; there must be quiet between them. Usually, one or two of the points of this triangle will pop naturally into being, but this of course provides no real enclosure, nothing for the two of you to hide inside; you're still merely part of the world. If you are having fun and not talking, you will probably be separated by a distance that only an excruciating stretch or lean or broad jump could bridge. Or else your faces will be close enough, without doubt, but for reasons with their source far off in the dimmest, windiest corner of the cosmos, one of you will have taken on the role of chatterbox. ("You know, the first time I saw that old show 'Flipper' when I was a kid, I thought I'd missed the episode where he gets shot in the top of the head . . . Hey, I'm famished. Take me to that booth? I never get to eat hot dogs anymore . . .") If there be quiet, however, and nearness, then fun becomes a mere lament because this poised condition will enjoy its highest concentration for an instant only, one whose very nature it is to slide downward and away, like a descending trombone note. There is, then, a sour, prepossessing sense of urgency, felt by you both, which is certainly no fun.

In the end, the kiss will either be a geometrical miracle of staggering proportions or else the defaulted outcome of a mock-heroic confession, in which one of you (usually *you*) must take the other by the shoulders and say emphatically, "Listen—I've been trying to kiss you for hours now." And then either the deed will be slackly done or else the other, thinking quickly, will come out with, "All right, but I've got to warn you, I have this cold sore, here on my lip." Whereupon the reply, again, will not miss a beat: "Oh, yes, I know that." And the two of you will nod, secure in having reached this plateau of understanding.

"At least now you can drink again."

"Oh, Ross."

Ocracoke Island, North Carolina, August, 2001. He and Andy lie on their backs inside a shivering tent. Half a bottle of wine is corked and angled next to Zingman's shoulder, his arms stiff by his side. A level-three hurricane is bearing down on the Island, bullhorns urging evacuation. The storm will end up skipping this coast entirely, though, veering north, striking New England two days later.

Andy is exhausted. One bare arm is slung across her eyes, leaving her lips alone to carry the day, though by now she's nearly emptied of talk; and her eyes, Zingman knows, have resigned from straining to see him clearly.

"It's been two years."

"Almost," he says, hearing the wind outside the tent, sniffing the implausible tang of storm. "Next month. And in the beginning we weren't completely focused."

"Seems like that's always your response, Ross."

"And we've had several close calls."

"There's part two of the response. It's your focus I question overall."

"That's all you ever seem to say, Andy."

"Right."

The theme of their entire vacation has been hush; words would jinx; a test should wait till they return home. Though he'd never suggest this to her, it does seem to him that her bleeding, this morning, might have been provoked by the sharp plunge in the barometric pressure.

"People. We strongly recommend that you clear the area within the hour." A bullhorn blares from the grassy ridge above the beach. It's the stern voice of a female official. "The causeway will be closing down. Repeat . . ."

Their days have been filled with swimming separately, taking long silent walks together through polished stones, foam, zipping crabs and sandpipers. The campground is nearly deserted before the approaching gale.

Nights have been thick with tension; merely finding the one angle into each other's arms has become an elaborate production, leaving them both drawn and bewildered. It's reminded Zingman of the earliest, most delicate phase of their courtship, when each move seemed to put the planet at risk.

Suspense has continued between them, sometimes minor or ignored, but adapting itself. This morning's event ended suspense, and increased it.

For his part, here on Ocracoke, Zingman has begun work on a new novel, having great fun with an idea for the first time in many months. Up on the deck of the cafe, he has clacked away on his laptop—but only for the agreed-upon hour after lunch, while Andy naps. She's been hurt that he won't tell her about it, but he couldn't, and now, especially, he can't. He meant it as a good faith narrative. The book is going to be called *Wombdwellers: A Pre-Natal Nightmare.* Its central character is a woman who, temporarily rejected by her true love (later to be overplayed by Lucas Haas), falls into an anonymous one-night stand. She becomes abundantly pregnant with five fetuses; an attempted abortion does not succeed, the fetuses refusing to release, on the contrary only growing in number and determination. The woman "wished she'd never learned and internalized, so young, that age-old injunction to be fruitful and multiply."

Inside the tent, though it's early afternoon, the daylight has suffered a steady wane, so that Andy's skin glows waxily, as in eerie twilight. The sheer vinyl walls collapse and belly outward, snapping, the wind smelling ever riskier, and opportune, producing a low, steady moan that gives Zingman a thrill at the center of his bones. He reaches out to touch Andy's hand. She chooses right now to leap up and start gathering her things, to heed the advice of the fading bullhorn, and so he follows suit, bracing for a future that may yet prove generous, for a hurricane false alarm.

Today, at the zoo, the kissing triangle expanded into (at least) an octagon. While they sat beside each other, chewed hot dogs, and witnessed otters sliding again and again and again down a long, dingy ramp, Zingman passed on to another facet known as "questioning the existence of the goal." All of his tactics, the subtle angling smiles and skin-brush coups, were now not merely landing short of their mark but were not landing at all, sailing off instead into a fine irrelevancy. It was as if he were coming suddenly to realize that things had changed since he'd been away, that others, anymore, no longer participated in just this specific game of hunting intimate contact, this game which had once, he thought he remembered, been quite widespread. (An otter executed a grand belly-flop into the pool.) If he were to continue in this delusion, he'd risk being regarded as old clowns are regarded, if they insist on performing, with that substantial nostalgia reserved only for the sincerest of hold-outs.

At the duck pond, Zingman took the woman's hand. The school children were down here, too, playing on grass singed yellow already by forgotten September frosts, while up the hill their teachers joked in a cluster.

Zingman had walked with her right to the edge, and they'd sat together within arms' length of the brown-and-sparkly-green ducks who swam, taking sharp little lefts and rights, as Barefoot reached out for them. They quacked and she quacked. Then they quacked some more, decidedly, as if to put a stop to any further imitations. It was during all of this that Zingman took her hand, and she let him do so without so much as a nick in her steady smile at the ducks. She said, "My feet are cold," so he lent her his own sneakers (keeping his socks for dignity), and then her hand was his again immediately after she'd laced them up, as though this had been the fundamental state of things throughout time up until the lending of the sneakers.

A coach's whistle blew; the children ran off.

No longer hedged in, she stood and moved ten feet to the left, squatted beside a small cove where three more ducks seemed to be asleep, bobbing. Zingman joined her and asked if she knew what ducks dreamt. On this, she had no opinion. He was just concocting something to say that would earn him a measure of devotion when one of the ducks, greener than the other two, with his eyes shut, quacked, but softly, softly, as if he'd failed to say this to someone who was long gone. So Zingman explained that ducks tend to dream about the past more than human beings do, because they possess a keener sense of missed opportunity. She leaned and placed the tip of her left index finger on the sleeping duck's forehead. He promptly turned and tore himself loose from the water, splashing them both with pounding wings. Zingman was very dispirited, though he did laugh along with her while she wiped drops of pond water from his face with the pulse-spot on her jacket-sleeve.

Never thought my ship would come in at a man's messy office.

Besides a collection of what appeared to be Garvey's research notebooks, revealing methods Harriet could make her own, there was a little cubical refrigerator housing pre-packaged rice 'n' bean burritos. When she'd discovered these, minutes ago, Harriet's stomach had quickly settled, and she devoured most of them. To drink? Nothing but a pretty amber bottle of Courvoisier brandy, nearly full. Pouring some into a snifter clouded by the dead man's fingerprints, peering at Pepper's struggling body—which she had planted to the navel in the dirt of a dry, skeletal potted marigold, on the desk—she commented, "When in Rome," and raised the glass.

Now, sipping the last dimensional drops of this first drink, she took a seat and dug into the research notebooks, gradually orienting herself to his shorthand. Every now and then, she'd reach to hold Pepper's hands between thumbs and forefingers, stop their pounding on the hardened soil, conveying calm; but relaxation was not in her nature, and she'd return to the pounding. "What's your principle?" Harriet would ask again, returning to the notebooks. "And no, I haven't forgotten about you," she'd reassure the stinking fish, who lay among the clutter on the back corner of the desk.

At one point, the red runt had the nerve to barge in. "What're you doing in here?" But he'd lost his earlier bravado.

"I'm busy." She didn't turn to look at him, after what she'd witnessed. She rocked in Garvey's comfy swivel chair, flipped a notebook page.

"I'm kind of sleepy," she heard him say.

"I'll bet."

"But there's no more brownies. Mr. G. makes them for me, for energy."

"Hmmm."

"Keeps me awake."

"Mm."

"I can hear those giants in the big room. Can you hear them?"

"Nope."

"Screaming. Like they do." No, quiet, except for a tapping produced by him, behind her. She pictured his leg bent back, toe of one shoe pecking floor. "When they're hungry. Guess I better go feed 'em."

"Yeah, why don't you do that."

"Yeah." He left, shutting the door cautiously, opening it again. "I'm hungry, too."

"Well, there's some food left, after you're finished with . . . that 'chore'."

"'Kay." Pause. "Those giants always hurt me." Pause. "Don't go in *there,* okay?" He pointed to a metal door she'd found locked. Then he withdrew again, leaving the hallway door open this time, tromping off in his noisy shoes.

Harriet found a notebook labeled "Desiccation and Rehydration," and after ten or fifteen minutes she recognized that what Garvey was talking about, the experiments he'd already done in this realm, amounted to no more than a very sophisticated version of the case of the spadefoot toad.

During her junior year in college—shortly after Greg, the man who took her breath away—she'd read about the miraculous capacity, in certain species, for suspended animation. The spadefoot toad, for instance, will remain dormant for extended periods in the form of dried eggs that are blown about the Southwestern deserts, awaiting a significant rainfall. Then, they will hatch and grow, flopping about in shallow puddles, males calling to females.

Unless mating takes place within a week, it will not occur at all. Females bearing fertilized eggs proceed to gorge themselves on primitive blue-green algae, which itself may have drifted windborne in the desert as spores for fifty years before landing in this water and resuming their life cycle. If a toad can consume enough, her eggs will mature and be laid before the puddles dry up, tadpoles emerging years or decades hence, hundreds of miles away, with the next heavy rain.

The spadefoot also feeds on *Artemia salina*, a.k.a. "fairy shrimp," a.k.a. "brine shrimp," a.k.a. "AMAZING LIVE SEA MONKEYS . . . Just add water and the fun begins! They swim, play, and grow up to 3/4" long and live up to a year or MORE. They even produce dozens of adorable BABIES!"

Yes they did, they certainly did! For a while, after the incident in the basement, Harriet was a dedicated keeper of Artemia salina, running an impressive zoo down there, and witnessing many times, beneath her beginner's microscope lens, the sudden and consistently baffling genesis brought about merely by pinching a medicine dropper's rubber bulb, wetting the powder she'd tapped from a paper packet.

When to think, she used to be thrilled by so much less—feeling first at age six, in her gut, that intricate crisis of joy just from checking to discover that the avocado pit she'd propped with toothpicks down inside a glass of water only the day before had already sent out visible root hairs!

She poured another snifterful of the fine brandy and smiled at her excitable self—*and here I still am, amazed at what can be achieved by simply adding water.* She thought she heard a ringing in her ears, where the birds dwelt. It's no wonder, these rich fumes would affect any colony of raptors—they're blaring drunk!

Reading notebook pages, she continued to gain respect for the experiments logged in "Desiccation and Rehydration." It seemed the man had found a way not just to clone an organism from an adult cell—no great feat, after all, since "Dolly" the sheep back in '97—but to preserve the resultant germ cell in a dry, suspended state, and then to grow it, not slowly within an animal womb, but rapidly in a nutritious liquid matrix, in basins and vats, as had the sea monkeys themselves, in their occasional puddles, since seven million years before first being packaged and sold, "Absolutely guaranteed to grow!"

No, it was different, this ringing in her ears, located elsewhere than her ache, and equal on both sides of her head. She held her breath to listen; well, not a ringing, exactly, it was something feebler—a sort of thin, thin tone, hard to follow; she briefly cupped her ears and it broke up, garbling. Harriet pictured a line drawn through space on its way into her head, a pure signal seeking a home, but warped in the narrows of her semicircular canals.

"Or is it a signal coming from me?" she asked Pepper's body, which had finally extracted itself from the dirt and now clung rather lasciviously to the stalk of the deceased marigold. "If so, what's my point? A message to myself, a mental note, so to speak? I know, I know—'the world is always listening for its own long definition . . .' But that's a ton of pressure!

"Well, of course massive funding doesn't hurt. The guy must have one hell of an amino acid sequencer around here someplace, far beyond anything we've yet seen, eh, Pep—Pepper, pay attention." She glanced at the locked metal door—got to get me those runt keys. Other notebooks no doubt contained clarification on exactly how Garvey was able, in his cloning, to bypass a central nervous system, to select for certain traits—"traits like, oh, an extra dash of libido." She tried to pry Pepper's body off the tall, brittle stranger, but it wouldn't come lose, humping with every fibre, reminding Harriet—*was this his model?*—of the exploits of the male praying mantis, who will persist in the sex act long after his mate has gnawed off his head.

When she was close to identifying the sound in her own head, a pretty fluttering in the air arrived to distract her. Harriet craned to identify *it*, instead, circling and circling her; it dipped to light on the fish's lower jaw, which jutted off at an angle from the upper, displaying sawteeth.

"Hello, again"—the tiny eagle from the showroom; it folded its wings and stared up at her. "What's this you've brought me?" Clamped crosswise in its beak was the twitching leg. It moved less often now, and weakly, like a foggy afterthought. Nauseated, she peered more closely. Ankle bone having been runt-snapped beneath skin, the foot flapped, each time, half an instant behind the twitch—an afterthought of an afterthought.

"Goddamn it! Goddamn it!" She swept the bird away with her hand; gone was her brandied good cheer. "I see, all right?" The bird came down again on the rim of the flower pot. "I know!" Behind it, Pepper's body was furious, unable to find fulfillment. The eagle stared at her and stared at her, its eyes pitying planets the size of sand grains. "What am I missing?" She finished her drink in two great gulps, then hurled the snifter at the locked metal door, where it shattered. "That I'm right at home here, 'smy destiny, 've been headed here all my life, is that it? Blink, why don't you?" It shifted the leg to get a tighter grip. Harriet reached into her mouth and with her index finger scraped at the back of her tongue, then viewed the gray roll of paste she'd brought out under the nail—easily one hundred cells. "Pieces of me." She trowelled them out with her thumbnail, smeared them over the exposed page of "Desiccation and Rehydration," partially obscuring a formula she only partially understood. "Beats the petri dishes upstairs," she said, and took another sample, gouging deeper this time. The pain was wonderful. She went to a later spot in the notebook and painted these new cells across the words "be careful not" in a sentence concerning proper storage of enzymes. In a minute, the paper began to absorb the saliva, rendering the smear lumpier, blatant with protoplasm.

"Hey," she said. "Are you thinking what I'm thinking?"

Merely by hopping up and soaring off, the eagle concurred.

Harriet stood, unsteady, and bumped out of the office, set off on a mission before she quite realized that she was in pursuit of none other than the long sound.

Lunging along the elbowed corridor, almost there, she thought again of Henrietta Lacks, cervix overrun by cancer, then hoarded by the men of science, dished out planet-wide for their leisurely use; the sound at the end of the hall was filled with anguish, and she envisioned Henrietta trying to sleep on a slim hospital bed in Baltimore, lying on her side, too exhausted to scream anymore, and borne on a flying carpet of morphine, separated from twenty-six pounds of tumor and trying to get comfortable around what is left in her, smacking her lips together softly as an infant will . . . and Harriet pictured also Rosalind Franklin—"Rosy"—stepping along an early summer sidewalk in a beige raincoat, Cambridge, England, freshly "booted" from her lab—1953, soon after Henrietta died, fifty-three years ago—and now entering a leafy park for its quiet, finding instead two brown dogs fighting to the death, which she observes with interest, leaning against a tree . . . and Harriet stepped at last into the vaulted chamber where "those giants" were enormous raptors watching her from trapeze perches, and she noticed, to her left, the red runt—even redder now, slashed across abdomen, chest, forehead—kneeling, knees slipping on a bloody, white-feather-decorated floor, arms planted deep inside a scarlet-streaked meringue of ruff, throttling a snowy owl no slighter than himself, whose extended wings embraced him but, as though already spoken for, incompletely, hooked beak gagged ajar, now past sound, and lemony, silver-flecked eyes, terribly circular, appealing directly up to her.

They reached the Seaquarium over concrete dotted with lime, orange, and raspberry sherbet that had dripped from children's cones, suffering from this out-of-season sun.

Fortunately, though, these children now occupied the upper of two decks, an outdoor grandstand, where tricks were performed at feeding time. Zingman and the woman ducked inside, she in his big floppy sneakers, he helping her to negotiate the descending steps, to the lower level, a square tunnel, one wall of which was made of glass that revealed the dim green world of the fishes. Firmly planted grass, leathery and prodigious, rose swaying from the sandy floor, and blades of sun slanted from above, shimmering high, dying in the lower gloom.

The last time he'd gazed upon this seascape, Andy was having her last strong day.

"Look," said the woman, as a great slate-gray manta ray swept past them, right to left, wings flapping elaborately, as though overacting its part; in its way, a well-formed school of small silver fellows glinted as they banked to avoid him. And here came a pair of groupers, massive; one of them held something soft and tattered between thick, pessimistic lips. Only when it waved right before his face could Zingman tell it was a lost sugar cone.

He laughed quietly, as one does in church. He tried to point out the cone to his new friend, but she was glued to the glass, and the fish faded anyway into bending dusk.

In the ceiling directly over their heads, a speaker began to crackle. "The Sea . . ."—came a silky, reverent male voice—"our ancient home, our oldest frontier. What else on Earth is so barren yet so bountiful, so chaotic and destructive yet so reassuring, what else grips us like the sea, at once so strange and so . . . hauntingly familiar?"

This tape recording was a new feature. Something in the cadence of the voice favored Rod Serling's.

"Covering more than sixty-eight percent of our globe and remaining, even to this day, ninety-eight percent unexplored, playing host to ten times more undiscovered species than exist on land . . . the sea, always out there while we toil here on land. And yet, how many of us pay her a second thought?"

He glanced to his left and received a jolt, because yes, he'd let himself casually expect to see Andy standing there, like before, when it was August and ninety-two degrees outside, even hotter in this tunnel, and she'd pressed her face against this same cool window. It was nineteen days before she died, and she could stay only minutes, leaning here, palms flat against the glass on either side of her face.

"Doesn't it look like they're all waiting?" she'd said. "For some kind of big surprise?" Her drawn face, in this marine light, appeared to him drawn in the other sense, like a bungled caricature, an attempt to capture her essential aspect. Then, another cartoon—the parrot fish, brightly mottled box of a creature, outlandishly whiskered—rushed up and tapped on the other side, just opposite Andy's nose, causing her to say, "Huh." Zingman had touched her chocolate hair, not in a bun today but hanging free, the one thing about her body that hadn't given up any bulk; in truth, it had gained, and so helped to quilt the razor frankness, under his hand, of her spine and shoulder blades. "Oh, Ross," she'd said, "doesn't it look like that? Everyone's holding their breath."

"Jack," said today's unrecognizable voice. "I don't know what it is, but I have a strange feeling about this place."

"You too?"

"Like we're in danger. My head hurts, here."

Zingman bumped aside her fingers and rubbed lightly "here," right on top; she hissed backward through her teeth.

A shark long as a limousine slid by; one gelid eye judged Zingman and found him lacking.

"My poor little Flipper," he said.

Then she let her breath back out—"You're not Jack."

"No. I'm Ross."

"Pepper Sarles. I've been so fuzzy, you must think I—"

"Glad to meet you, Pepper." They shook hands.

"Thank you for helping me."

"Well, you've had some sort of trauma."

"Oh boy, you're not kidding."

From outdoors up in the grandstand rose the sharp shouts of the children. One girl called out, "Hey, Mister, whatcha got there?" Then, quieter, "Yeah, it's pretty I guess."

Zingman put his arm around this woman's waist and pulled her to him; she resisted only because, he decided, she was listening to the girl's voice—"You gonna make them do tricks now?" He leaned over and kissed her gently on the temple, whispering, "You're IT." The manta ray returned, passing them by, gravely flapping.

Pepper's mouth popped open, sucking air, and she clutched him like a sprung trap. Zingman looked where she pointed, and there, drifting slowly downward just beyond the window—a gray fish, not distinctive, not large. Still, she backed away, her hand over her mouth, pushing him off her, pointing. Pitched onto its side, forked tail at four o'clock, nose at ten, the fish had ceased to sink—fins strumming, gills fanning. And then, for a rousing moment, it made a spasmodic attempt to swim.

In the ceiling, the speaker crackled once more. "The sea . . . our ancient home, our oldest frontier . . ." Out in the grandstand, escalating pandemonium.

"Maybe you're overreacting?" Zingman suggested. This was all playing havoc with the kissing triangle.

"What else on Earth is so barren yet so bountiful, so chaotic and destructive yet so reassuring . . ."

"No, that's the one!" Pepper yelled. Her back met the wall with force and she stood stiff. "It's following me!"

"Listen, I like to think I have a hardy imagination too, but shouldn't you stop to consider—"

Her pointing hand fell limp and she slid to the floor, moaning. Her other hand stroked the top of her head, too hard, making Zingman grit his teeth for her.

He was just about to go and sit beside her when she pointed again. The shark re-entered the picture, missiling in from nowhere and taking up the fish in one proficient gulp, puffing out a single plume of smoky blood, then cruising on.

"Wow," said Zingman.

"Covering more than sixty-eight percent of our globe . . ."

"Uh-oh, Mister," said the same girl, topside. "Guess what happened."

"Sir," said a man. "Sir, I'm afraid you can't go in there. And we're going to have to ask you to put down that weapon. Sir, you may not—"

Splash!

Children cheered, yelled many things, like, "Yeah-yeah, you go show that bully," and, "Go and kill him!", and, "This is the best zoooo!"

Seated against the wall, Pepper began to hyperventilate. Inside the water, up high—a wild-haired frogman in face mask and flippers, puny compared to the shark, and in his hands something resembling a bayonet. He kicked himself frantically downward, driving the shark to loop back toward the window.

Zingman tried to help her up, planning to hustle her outside, remove her from the spectacle, but she made herself infinitely weighty, suddenly sobbing into her hands. He looked just in time to see the shark approach from an angle, the wild-haired man bearing down on it from behind. He cocked his weapon and a spear—not a bullet—crossed smartly over top of the broad head and struck the glass squarely.

A crack began to wander both up and down from the point of impact, slow and simple at first and then rapidly branching off in all directions, quite lovely, Zingman had to admit, especially when, for an instant—he blinked; look at this, Andy was right—the entire window stood crazed, dazzling, a thousand hair-thin fractures holding the sunlight as though electrified.

That salt sure was going to sting his ear.

"How many of us—"

"On the table is a motion to welcome our newest member, Mr. Ard, Mr. . . . let me see, where did I put—"

"Paul."

"Yes, Paul Ard . . . into the Buckley Street Branch."

"Seconded."

"Thank you, Gloria. And congratulations, Paul. You may not realize it right away, but you have found a home here with us." The woman in charge, Steffi, nodded crisply at him, smiling and gazing deep into his eyes. If every muscle in his back and neck weren't wrenched and his scalp multiply wounded from a botched experiment in shaving earlier this afternoon, if he weren't a fugitive from justice, seeking immediate refuge, Trapuka might have stood and kicked that simper off her face for her. "We've all been through what you're going through," she continued, leaning toward him slightly on her metal folding chair, placing her hand on his knee. She had gray, searching eyes. "You poor, poor thing. Not that any of us have had exactly your same experience"—she squeezed his knee quickly then removed her hand—"I'm not saying that, you understand. I only mean losing someone so close."

"No, I understand, Steffi. I count myself lucky to have found you all." He looked around the drab room at the twenty or so faces, some wearing meaningless smug expressions, the rest more honest, at least, radiating hollow need. 'You idiots,' he wanted to shout, 'you're aching to find your own *Titus*, each of you!' One lovely woman in the corner, though, needed nothing; he glanced at her, then away. He said, "Your poster in the grocery store was extremely eye-catching."

"Yes, well, we've got Gwendolyn to thank there. She does all our graphic work." A pasty lady of about sixty in a lavender dress lifted a Styrofoam cup; soft applause came from the others. A large chrome coffee-maker gurgled on a card table.

"I happened to be looking rather desperately just then—was it only this morning?—for a place to . . . hide out for a while, from a world that will never begin to understand."

"No, they sure don't," said a man with an unlit cigarette in his mouth. "They look at you like you just dropped off Jupiter, am I right?"

"You are. And as I was standing there, I came out of my fog long enough to realize that today's Saturday, meeting day."

"Welcome to good ole 'Widows' Luck,' as we like to call it," Steffi said. "That's how we last, how we make it through our days."

"You see, Paul," said the same man, taking the cigarette out of his mouth and sliding it into the breast pocket of his button-up shirt. "We believe there are certain . . . oh, compensations for our great loss, given to us by whoever runs things up there, if you know how to look for them."

"Thank you, Benjamin."

"Who was it," said Benjamin, "who came up with the name 'Widows' Luck' in the first place?"

"Guilty," said the lovely woman in the corner. "Hi, Paul, I'm Candace. And it's not just Widows' Luck but Widowers', too." She grinned broadly, red lipstick glossing.

"Which brings us back"—Steffi winked—"to one of the many advantages of our organization. We're co-ed!"

"Advantages?" said Trapuka.

"Well. Over . . . the alternative."

A shrunken-headed old man in another corner spat carefully into his coffee cup. He looked to the woman sitting beside him, two-thirds his age, who scowled off into space, skinny arms folded across her large chest.

"Wallowers!" she said.

He said, "Cornhuskers!"

"Oh, now," Candace chided them, "they're just men, trying to get through their days and nights. The poor guys, Tenzer, and that Zingman. They just happen to have a slightly different philosophy than ours, one that forgot about FUN!"

"We at SORW, on the other hand," Steffi added, "recognize that we are simple pilgrims, marching along a very rough and winding road. But that doesn't mean we have to pity ourselves, do you see? We believe we deserve to . . . soften the road as much as we possibly can, and even learn to dance on it, Paul."

Trapuka's back spasmed in two distinct places at once, between shoulder blades and down by his left kidney. "Dancing pilgrims," he said.

"That's exactly right, and well put. In fact, we hold actual dances pretty frequently, joining together with the other branches throughout the city, and beyond."

"That," said Trapuka, "is a stroke of genius." He tried shifting in his hard chair, sloping his back more favorably, but this only torqued his ruined neck muscles.

"'Stroke of genius,' I don't know, but I'm glad you approve! It does seem the natural thing to us. Oh, but look at you, you're in such great pain, still, Paul. Can you tell us, how long has it been?"

Trapuka kept quiet, thinking about marine toxins, invisible, swirling, attacking only her, only her.

"I know, it's extremely difficult. Louise, over here, for instance, is only seven weeks into life without her Charles."

"It's true," said Louise, standing and crossing to the coffeemaker, filling her cup. "At first I couldn't say a word, but once I got rolling," she said, resuming her seat, "you couldn't shut me up."

Laughter. "And believe me, we tried," said Steffi. "We feel that talking is helpful up to a point, but then it's important to—"

"I lost her today," Trapuka said.

People gasped, reached for one another's hands.

"Oh, you fresh pilgrim," said Steffi, leaning toward him again, hand only hovering, this time, above his knee. "We've never gotten to anyone so early."

"Actually, to be a little more precise, I should say she was essentially gone three days ago, way up north, in the ocean, though I battled to keep her going."

"A drowning, then a coma?"

Trapuka nodded.

"Yes, sometimes the most heroic efforts of modern medicine are absolutely powerless, aren't they? And I know it feels just like you were fighting the fight, right there beside her every moment. Let me get you in touch with Edward Weidner in our Niven Park Branch, who's doing so well now. Dorothy was swept out to sea last summer, an excellent swimmer, too, even won trophies in college.

"But back to you, Paul. I'll never cease to be amazed at all the personal rituals we get into when tragedy strikes us. Like, somehow it felt right for you to shave your head? Widows' Luck wasn't kind to you in that case, eh? Could've used a professional, it looks like!"

He laughed along with them all; this did feel better, he had to admit, than being stuck with a cafeteria full of cretins or being chased by frantic zoo personnel, *chased,* until they were distracted by the coughing couple who emerged from the concrete tunnel. He'd tangled with them briefly before the water calmed and let his flippers do their work. Not till they emerged did Trapuka recognize the man, whose ear was still red from last night.

"Yes, an electric razor would have been more intelligent, I'll agree." He patted his scalp, wincing; the pain from the many small cuts was real enough, but he exaggerated his reaction, which brought enthusiastic laughter. He was getting the swing of it, gaining group allegiance now through subtler means. "Evidently, I got a bit careless," he confessed sheepishly.

A woman who hadn't removed her green overcoat raised a finger and tried, "Excuse me, but don't you mean hairless?" which worked well. She took off her coat.

"Humor," announced a man in a very clean charcoal sweater, with circles under his eyes so dark they appeared almost silver, "becomes priceless."

"Amen to that, Arthur," said Steffi. "So, Paul, we'll getcha some bandages for those nicks. Lucky we're at a YMCA, first aid kits every ten feet! Ooop, there's our luck again."

Trapuka thought this might be the moment for him to make his proposal, so he took a breath and opened his mouth.

"Okay, we need to turn to today's agenda." Steffi consulted a clipboard on her lap. "Which, first, to firm up plans for our Halloween party this coming Tuesday . . ." While she spoke about refreshments and collected suggestions for games and group activities, Trapuka rose and crossed to the coffee-maker, concentrated on pouring himself a cup, his movements severely bounded. His hand shook; coffee slapped twice onto the polished cement floor, causing Candace to gaze up at him with startling pity. He managed an awkward bow in her direction, and then, reaching the safety of his chair, he was able to sip.

". . . and remember, folks, this year we're combining with the Atkins Court Branch, but don't expect me to do all the legwork again. Rose, I'm thinking of your uncle."

"Right . . . he said he could lend us costumes from his shop. I'll call him. This'll be fun."

"That's the idea! Paul, now I know you'll probably not wish to participate much this time around, just lie low and take in the festivities, but to fill you in real quick, see, Halloween is an important holiday to us. The dead are coming out to play, to dance with us, and we try to make them welcome, enjoy their company . . ."

"Kind of run wild with them," said Benjamin, removing the cigarette from his breast pocket once again, tapping it upright on his palm. "Focus not on missing them but taking them back into our lives, for just one night. Make everything into one big joke, give ourselves a break."

"Hey, and speaking of, you know, spooky, funny stuff," Candace burst in, "anybody catch that movie on tv last night, Zingman's 'Wombdwellers'?"

"Oh boy," said the woman who had said "Wallowers!", "was that a piece of trash!"

"I know, I know! That's what I mean by 'funny'."

"Though I personally felt . . ." said Benjamin, sticking the cigarette back between his lips, ruminating.

"Of course, Zingman can't be blamed for the script," said Candace. "Though, to tell you the truth," she added out of the side of her mouth, "his novel's not much better."

"You're somewhat acquainted with that man, we could say," said Steffi. "And weren't you a fan?"

"Let's say I've changed my mind."

"Paul, Candace won't mind my filling you in at this point, to bring you up to speed." Candace nodded to Steffi, smiling with fortitude hard-won. "In the summer of '02, her husband Keith was unfortunately ambushed and cut apart behind the state fairgrounds."

"Didn't I read about that?" asked Trapuka. "Wasn't he—"

Candace stood up. "Yes, it was well-covered in the papers, especially by Stennhouse, whose investigation helped find the men responsible." She crossed to Trapuka and stepped behind him, began massaging his shoulder muscles, which he assumed she found dreadfully rocklike, though she didn't make an issue of it. Normally, he'd have squirmed in decline of any such gesture, but this one introduced him to his fatigue, put him on hold. He kept picturing the murdered man in the cafeteria, how eventually he'd started to lean provokingly to his left, until Trapuka eased him down to pull the wallet, and he saw *Titus* through the jiggling water, devoured in replay again and again. (He had made a strategic error, dropping her there.) To distract himself he recalled accounts Jonna had read to him four years ago—probably to imply that life is short—about the man hacked to pieces and then somehow fed into the gears of several of the rides at the fair."

"And it's true," said Candace, going deeper with her thumbs, "what was written, but that's not the half of it. Which is why I was drawn to Ross Zingman in the first place, thought he might understand in some ridiculous way, give me a little help, in exchange for which, I figured he might want to hear the inside. . . ." She discontinued the massage. "Well, it doesn't matter now, I suppose, does it?"

The coffee-maker breathed wetly.

"Weh," said Trapuka, then licked his lips. "Well, it's interesting you should say what you said, before, Benjamin, about taking the dead into our lives, because it reminds me I have a little problem I wanted to discuss with the group."

"Yes, Paul?" Steffi asked.

"All right, now I am sure what I'm about to request goes far beyond the usual scope of your activity, but I must tell you all, because I . . . feel that I can trust you . . ."

He pretended to cry a bit. Steffi and Candace pretended to blink back tears of their own, which tempted him to laugh. "I cannot even begin to . . . uh, to grieve for her, because those who have possession of her . . . body . . . are, are refusing to release it."

"Paul," said Steffi, "I don't understand, who has kept your dear wife, and—"

But Benjamin leapt to his feet, pulling from the front pocket of his pants a book of matches. "It doesn't matter! Whatever the explanation, you can tell us on the way. C'mon, people, this is what we do, we take action, don't sit around wringing our hands like some others, we make things happen, am I right? This is an outrage."

Everyone stood up, grabbed their jackets and coats. Benjamin lit his cigarette and led the charge out the door.

Harriet wanted to eat the fish, though it stank worse than ever and though her stomach was full of beans. She understood that her desire for the animal meant something better than any straightforward dining, that they were two legendary swimmers, hounded by man, finally brought together. After first plucking off its six fins—daintily, lady-like; they offered little resistance, crispy—she took a deep breath and advanced into a full, vigorous dismantling. She recited the steps as she performed them. "We begin by placing three fingers deep inside gills; pull back firmly until gills spread and scaled skin tears away from skull. You will feel pang of guilt until you remember that its captor is to blame; she's in your hands now. Set her free. Expose skull by brute force; notice eye remains in socket, like frosted glass. Poke index finger into notch at side of skull, at back of jawbone, just where women in certain situations may experience nagging earache. Now poke finger further in; exert leverage, savor crack of cranium; work it; make room for other fingers. Reach through and massage brain, as Mother wished to do with yours sometimes. Feel it's glad."

Holding the brain, then, on a tripod of fingers in front of her glasses and her nose, Harriet said, "The world is always listening, so think straight." She decided it resembled a tasty paté, its delicate convolutions sculpted by some antic epicurean. She licked her lips; it was much smaller than a walnut, much larger than a pea. But she did not pop it into her mouth.

Her plan had begun to germinate the very instant that, armed with the runt's keyring, Harriet first breached the industrial-strength door and barged into this small interior room. The machines, chirring companionably, stole her heart; she'd only ever heard rumors of their existence, this newest generation of sequencers and synthesizers. The Pig Trough sported the squat ancestors, workhorses from the '80s and '90s designed for simpler organisms like microbes, while these knew what to do with human DNA. They towered sleekly toward the low ceiling.

Obviously, Garvey had not intended to linger long up there in the cafeteria; he was in the middle of something. Jars of solution were lined up on the shiny platform at the base of the sequencer, and in the wall between the two machines, a large blue screen was churning with data.

So no, she didn't pop the brain; it was a pill too powerful for that. She needed its cells, their DNA, to blend with samples she'd already collected from her own body and introduced into Garvey's powerful machines, which were hard at work sequencing or "reading" her genetic makeup and would soon proceed to synthesizing more of it. *Since ordinary make-up has failed me, Mother, let's finally admit.* In a giggly mood, she watched her distorted reflection in the many rectangular chrome panels of the amino acid sequencer, portions of herself shifting kaleidoscopically while she swayed back and forth—her stringy hair burnished fuller, flashing out from a tall mosaic head; her breasts, one up there, one way down here, looking bulged and clowny; her legs (as she backed away) stretching like rubber; as she leaned in close, the twin shields of her cheekbones grew apart but looked softer, more inviting. *So maybe PORTIONS of me are the answer after all, show me off to my best advantage. Don't you think that's ironic?*

To her right, shelves of jars. She went and read their labels. Most were unfamiliar to her, save for references to them in Garvey's notebooks. Occasionally, she'd recognize a chemical symbol or name from her graduate school days of studying salt and pH levels in the seminiferous tubules of the testes, on one level of course just an elongated grinning private joke, giving the lie to Dougy's assurance that she'd "never see jizz again."

Vice President in Charge of Enzymes—yes, despite that ostensible office up on the fourteenth floor, Garvey's company title was no false front. He turned out to have a world-class library here of this rare and powerful class of protein molecules that catalyze all metabolic chemical reactions. Human beings have been isolating and extracting enzymes from yeasts and bacteria for centuries, starting with those that cause beer and wine to ferment. One of Harriet's insights, too, had been that their potential role in bioengineering had been chronically underexplored. A different enzyme or combination of enzymes is responsible for each particular reaction, for any change that may take place within an organism. It was clear to her that the agents in these jars—born and refined in the darknesses of ancient bloodstreams and simple cells millennia before a scientist first blinked an eye—that these were Garvey's "haystack hunters" every bit as much as the gleaming technology in this room. These machines could only analyze and synthesize DNA molecules, not make them self-replicate, grow complex, fly, crawl. Not intercept the normal differentiation processes involved in the maturation of a human body, such that cloning a woman could be accomplished piecemeal, yielding only a thigh, say, or a marked breast. Garvey's innovation was to introduce these catalysts right away, and varieties that human cells have never tasted, as perhaps those that allow a praying mantis to operate so proficiently without his head.

Harriet picked out three standbys from her graduate school days—KLENOW; GENTID; ALACTRONASE—and then stepped up to the monitor screen in the wall. Since at this point she still possessed her frog glasses, she was able to watch with some fundamental comprehension as columns of numbers scrolled upward beside columns of letters, scrolling down. These letters were T,C,G, and A, no others, representing the essential nucleotide molecules that compose DNA—Thymine, Cytosine, Guanine, and Adenine. Even though her recent bout of brandy drinking had left her with a headache, she ran the same film in her head that she'd been running since childhood, since she learned that all living forms arise from only those four bases, in their endless combinations—combinations not merely of the nucleotides themselves, in strands of four, but of all the possible juxtapositions of those strands with one another. As a fifth-grader, Harriet had been astonished and just a bit hurt to find out that the whole abundant epic of organic nature comes down to a shockingly straightforward premise—strands, chains, sequences, and proteins. In the nucleus of every cell stands DNA's famed double helix which, for all its splendor, is much like a palace stuffed with rope—strands of chromosomes containing thready genes carrying information (like varying gauges of fiber) in that same clubby alphabet, T, C, G, A. And then, wily infiltrators known as RNA and transfer-RNA storm the palace and unwind the self-satisfied rope coils, unravel the codes, lay them out into useful, democratic blueprints—to be shared, shared, dispersed like liberation leaflets, like spores on the wind. To the factories! Factories where proteins are manufactured out of chains of amino acids, proteins that take the revolution from there, do all the heavy lifting; they are, in other words, as she'd learned to intone piously along with other wide-eyed nerdlings, "the building blocks of life."

Wide-eyed today once again, Harriet gazed at the screen of scrolling characters, her stomach percolating with the eight amino acids supplied by beans and rice. She held the three jars of fluid up to the ceiling lights—a dark blue, a clear, a rose—trusted friends of hers whose worksite was none other than the seminiferous tubules of the testes. During one thirteen-month period of her research into the initial phases of spermatogenesis, she'd employed these three almost daily, because they help form an environment within the germinal epithelium favorable to the production of spermatozoa.

She was just starting to speculate upon why Garvey might

possess KLENOW, GENTID, ALACTRONASE—*what business do you have in BALLS? That's MY territory, said so yourself. Planning to celebrate your own sperm, sir, grow them like bouncing baby polliwogs big enough to hug?*—when she was interrupted by the slinking return of the red runt, who'd no doubt been wandering the corridors in his thick owled daze. Still bleeding from several wounds, he flopped onto the cot on the other side of the room, but not before tossing her a plastic first aid kit he'd located—gauze strips and a spool of white medical tape. "Oh, hello! I was just going to mix you up a nice refreshing cocktail, after your hard day!" She held the jars up like a spokesmodel.

"Brownies, please."

"Right, brownies, hmmmm. Okay, here's a deal. I'll make you some if you try this drink first. Does Mr. G. have a coffee cup, or—What are you doing?"

The runt slid open a drawer beside the cot and lifted out a smudged beige telephone unit, much more worn and ordinary than the phone on the cherrywood desk upstairs. While he dialed and slurred a message for a "Mr. Z."—". . . but I forget what's that street called, next one that's Bigelow Street, okay? Okay, I'll go wait for you there . . ."—Harriet found a chipped maroon mug down inside a sink in the corner, rinsed it out, and then carefully poured in a drop of the GENTID, the dark blue color. These were highly concentrated solutions, plenty for this first experiment even if she filled the mug the rest of the way with water, which she did. But when she turned around, the runt was slumping, eyes glassy. She took the phone from his huge, flaccid hand and hung it up, set the unit back in the drawer.

Then she shook him awake and helped him to sit up.

"Brownies?"

"Soon. Here, drink this; it'll help you sleep."

"But I gotta go meet Mr. Z."

"I understand . . ."

He gulped it down, made a sour face, and lay on his side.

For the next two hours, while the runt was out cold, Harriet underwent a crash course in the technology now available to her. Given what she already knew, her learning curve was quite steep, as she became passably conversant with the programs Garvey had been running.

"Are you aware," Harriet asked the runt at one point, "of the Human Genome Project, undertaken during the 1990s by the Lawrence Berkeley Laboratory at the University of California?" He slept peacefully on the cot in his torn bloody shirt. She sat at the keypad before the sequencer, punching in commands culled from Garvey's notebooks.

"The U.S. government commissioned the project while I was still in high school. Naturally, I followed it in the journals. The idea was to map the entire human genome." She glanced over at the runt's blank face, those twitching eyelids. "Sorry, a bit of jargon there, no reason to be intimidated. 'Genome' only means the aggregate of all our chromosomes with their six billion genes, a few more or less than the norm in your case, little man, no offense. Well, anyway, it took nine years, but the effort was a complete success. Without this work, whose results are loaded into these machines here, our boy would probably be home right now with dirty magazines . . . 'course, he'd still be alive to enjoy them."

She talked him through the necessary phases, hoping he would wake up when she needed his help—soon—but that he would not wake up any earlier, as when she had to remove very personal cells from herself, from parts Garvey had steered clear of, and add them to those samples she'd already scraped off, applied to slides treated with biofixative, and introduced, hand in pre-mounted glove, incubator-style, into the machine's sterile vacuum chamber. All superfluous protoplasm would be separated out by centrifuge and flushed as waste, leaving nothing but Harriet's own dubious double helices.

On the monitor in the wall, she watched herself translate into swiftly rising, falling columns of numbers and letters, amounting to a sky-high haystack with maybe a few promising needles buried inside. "Hmmm, I look much better in that form, don't you think? You could say I'm 'stacked'." She read herself, timeless, happy.

Sometimes, just to clear her head, she'd roll around the room in Garvey's desk chair, its casters squeaking. Twice, she nearly mushed a Pepper crawling across the floor. And once, she knocked open the door into a walk-in closet, which led her to discover basins, shallow basins on further shelves. She hadn't had time to examine them well—because the runt was beginning to make sounds approaching consciousness—but they contained embryonic farms, endless studies of Pepper, fixed in transparent gel. One had seemed at first like budding beans, limas, two rows of eight—but instead, she suddenly realized, they were delicate feminine chins, shaping themselves admirably. Or, perhaps it was not too much to hope that they would in due course turn into whole faces in the dim lighting of this adventurous closet, perishable faces full of force, confirming a new courage in the dead scientist.

For the tireless sequencer there was nothing but work, work, work—breaking her cells down into a fine substrate of information; "and when that's finished," she told her partner in crime, who expelled little huffs, as of amazement, "the synthesizer will take over, reversing the process, going from pure information to living tissue. Or, more accurately," she said, sailing past the runt's cot, "to the encapsulated potential for living tissue. Like mold spores," digging in her heels to halt herself before eviscerated fish rotting on a counter. "Or," she continued, but now addressing the fish, poking at the soggy contents of its stomach sack, separating its drab organs, arraying them across the countertop, "in the case of aquatic life, take for example those dried airborne bundles of spadefoot toad and fairy shrimp that last for decades in the desert, dead and alive at once, blown everywhere together in the same dust clouds until rains release them and toad feeds on shrimp, its traveling companion. Shrimp may escape this fate only by volunteering to be packaged as 'AMAZING LIVE SEA MONKEYS—ABSOLUTELY GUARANTEED TO GROW!'"

She mused upon which fish cells to introduce into the sequencer, where her own had been at play for hours, thereupon to step back and let the machine entwine them as it may . . . building our bundle, our spore. Our tiny tablet . . . if taken orally not a cure-all, maybe, but a cure-me, a cure-me.

"Because, you understand," she shared with the runt, carrying fish parts, safely, on foot, across the lab, "we have lots in common, this creature and I. We've suffered similar fates, now we can ride the wind together."

The runt sat up, sneezed three times in a row.

"Having a little allergic reaction to the beverage? Well, but the real question is, has it reached its destination through your bloodstream? Only one way to find out. But first, let's try to slip you into something more comfortable."

When she'd pressed the last tab of medical tape down onto his shoulder, securing a length of gauze, said, "There, that's nice," she got down on her hands and knees and peered beneath the cot. Indeed, several Peppers had congregated there, fetching up against the wall, and she took one. Holding it up to the runt, she said, "Now I know this may sound a little strange, but I need you to do what you did before. I'll leave the room, of course."

He stared at her, then made a grab for the telephone drawer.

"Patrick, you're sure now?"

But on Pepper's behalf, Zingman accepted the startling offer with gratitude—Estelle Tenzer's kimono, printed with those lime-green willow trees and brown swallows. Where it had hung on the wall, like a tapestry all the Cobhouse years, a pale clean shadow remained.

Zingman spread the garment across Pepper's shoulders, draped it over the battered white jacket, salt-shrunk by the inrushing sea; he cinched the black ribbon around her waist and helped her limp to the couch.

"Now tell me again, Ross," Tenzer said, "more slowly this time. At the zoo? Why are you barefoot?"

"Well, no, I saw her first near my place. It was obvious she was in some sort of distress. But look at me, knight in armor—damsel gets shot at, nearly devoured by a shark . . ." Pepper coughed. "Least I had footwear to lend her," he said, pointing to the sneakers. Pepper shuddered and lay down. Zingman expected the retired doctor to take an interest in a thorough check-up. Instead, Tenzer's eyelids twitched and his back teeth ground, like the creak of an old boat, causing Zingman to turn and see Ronald Gilbeau and Nick Mezzanotte waiting patiently in straight-backed chairs, dressed formally like last night, with new haircuts, close shaves, and laps still conspicuously free of corn. He'd forgotten about the emergency meeting for this disgruntled committee of two, had brought Pepper here (by swift cab) only because she was for a while having genuine difficulty catching her breath.

"Gentlemen . . ." said Zingman.

They nodded, would not look up at him. Pepper beginning to relax on the cushions, he and Tenzer took seats across the room from them.

"All right, so now he's here." Tenzer's voice was weak with spite.

Mezzanotte began uncertainly, "Well. All right, you see, it's been for a . . . a few weeks that we've felt, I mean, it's . . ." He pulled up short, pressed two fingers to his eyebrow, as if he felt it twitching and thought it might be noticeable. His wife Bethany had delayed too long being seen for her aches, until one day while she ran down a staircase her fibula snapped, brittled by bone marrow cancer.

"Listen," said Gilbeau, whose Marion had fallen asleep at the wheel one Wednesday night, not far from home, "we probably shouldn't have made this feel so adversarial. We just didn't know the best way to get your attention, Patrick. We're still pretty new here, and you didn't seem to take our suggestions seriously, when we made them."

"The Cobhouse was formed in order for men to feel safe giving voice to every aspect of their grief, not to go on field trips like other groups."

"Now see, you're getting defensive," said Mezzanotte. "We're not proposing anything radical, it's just that we feel sort of . . . confined. All this sitting and talking, reading poetry aloud. We agree it definitely has its place . . . even peeling the corn, that's been pretty good. We're just saying why couldn't we . . . expand sometimes?"

"I have a good idea where you could expand all the time." Tenzer was actually trembling in his faded green cardigan. Zingman had never seen him so upset, had always known he took the group format personally, but not this personally. "And that's down the street at SORW."

"Oh, my God," said Gilbeau. "This is. . . . Ross, could you tell him, please, not to insult our intelligence?" To avoid shedding tears, Gilbeau blinked, turned to look at the couch. When this wasn't brief, Zingman and Tenzer looked as well. Then Mezzanotte. The young woman was asleep, she whose name had returned to her only moments before the deluge, then eluded her again when requested by that reporter, William Sten-something. Now she had pulled her knees in tight to her chest, and her face, down-turned, half-visible, seemed swept clear of everything but a kind of dim effortless bravery.

When Zingman checked, the Grievance Committee was, like her, breathing gently.

Zingman tried to listen, with a large heart. What had happened first, even before the tunnel filled with surprisingly warm water, was that the shark came through sideways and blocked out all the light.

"So maybe we've found out there's no place for us," said Mezzanotte, rubbing the top of his head like a grim good sport, "don't know, could be there's no middle ground. We sure tried out that other option, and quickly rejected it. But we never imagined . . . well, it's okay, it's fine."

Tenzer stood and stepped to a bookshelf set into one wall, slid out the dog-eared Rilke volume familiar to the Cobhouse. He flipped pages until he found what he wanted. "'Even lamenting grief purely decides to take form, serves as a Thing . . . —and blissfully escapes far beyond the violin . . .' That's all I've tried to do here, to provide a form for us, give us something to hold onto, to touch while we . . ."

While Tenzer kept talking, even righteously shared further passages from the "Ninth" of Rilke's "Dueno Elegies," Zingman watched Pepper, her arms and legs twitching quietly under the folds of the kimono. Next to him in bed, Andy used to relax and become still, then jitter her way into sleep, so cautiously, as though pretending. Pepper yawned, then gave a little whimper.

In had poured the entire ocean, also unreal, and Zingman had had no choice but to forget about the shark—who thrashed away somewhere beneath him—and search for Pepper, haul her heavy body up and keep her screaming mouth screaming inside the roar of air quickly shallowing toward the ceiling. Her feet kicked, useless, in his big sneakers. Briefly, the wild-haired man fell in with them, churning, and they all converged in a momentary embrace, sputtering within foam. Then Zingman heard him start to breathe like someone still in full control. The two men shoved apart, swam their separate ways, Zingman sidestroking toward the exit with Pepper's head safe on his hip, except that every time a little fish knocked against one of his stocking feet, he'd think, of-course-shark.

"Ross?" said Tenzer, this prematurely, permanently old man, sitting hunched, poetry book splayed open, face-down over his knee. "Ross, please."

"I seem to remember another part of that poem, where Rilke speaks about 'The sufferings, then. And, above all, the heaviness, and the long experience of love—just what is wholly unsayable . . . they are better as they are: unsayable.'"

Apparently, mouth seeking oxygen, Tenzer hadn't felt so betrayed since being Caesar in a previous incarnation. And Zingman had never, in his memory, felt so glad to hear a knock on a door, or to respond.

In fell Matthew Glennon, dressed for January, shutting the front door behind himself against the sheer size of the outdoors. Zingman escorted him to the vacated chair, then helped him off with his puffy burnt-orange coat, dark woolen hat and scarf. Of course, the man was soaking; the day had warmed since melting the zoo children's treats. He was flushed and panting, reminiscent of Mr. Ruthbar, who had fled why, and where?

Sympathetically, Gilbeau and Mezzanotte removed their suit jackets. Unlike last night, the Grievance Committee now seemed only too captivated by this wandering soul, who tried to smooth down his sparse hair, got sweat on his hands, wiped them on his corduroys. But he wasn't crying anymore; instead, his face was solid with anger.

Tenzer closed the Rilke book, tapped its spine against his pursed lips, looking at Matthew Glennon distantly as though reappraising the worthiness of death.

"How far have you come on foot?" asked Mezzanotte.

Lost in the whole world, the rookie widower called for corn. Gilbeau leapt to gather several ears from last night's table, sidelined since the meeting, and then the men watched those green husks fly off. Now the anger could move to his hands; his face relaxed. Eyes unfocused, he didn't even notice Pepper. "I've been walking since about dawn, when it was a lot cooler, and Sheila'd always make sure I bundled up enough. I found myself in this neighborhood, saw all your cars parked outside. At the house, I took the car keys out of the bowl but then I didn't trust myself to drive, and also, where I was headed there aren't any roads." He finished denuding his second cob of corn, results strewn around him on the rug, then started in briskly on the third, as though he resented the very idea of layers. "But I wasn't able to get there, I turned back. Mnot sure how I got myself here."

"From where?" said Zingman.

"A spot inside the state park."

"Skoonlet Valley?"

"That's right, in the Nature Preserve."

"Andy and I used to hike there, too, all the time."

"Sheila and I never did. I wish. I wish it was that simple for me, Ross, to go back there to feel close."

"Actually," said Zingman, "I've never been back since."

"Everything's so, it's so complicated for me, and my head can't keep it all at the same time, or else I'd try to—Wait, who is she, exactly?"

Pepper had caught his eye by turning over in her sleep. The kimono stuck beneath her and twisted, so that she had to yank it free. She sighed, muttered, "Butterfield, you know I can't. He's waiting for me, down in the parking lot."

"It's a woman I just met, found her wandering at dawn. She's been injured and I've been . . . keeping her with me, under my wing sort of, until she feels better."

"Weird thing, dawn for both of us. She's lost?"

"I suppose you could say that, her memory's not . . ." But Matthew Glennon's face halted Zingman, having regrouped its bitter forces.

"Sheila was lost, in Virginia. It seems like she was. You know she'd gone off her itinerary, for some reason. In a town called Tarboro, when she was supposed to be in Greenville for a meeting with a distributor."

Gilbeau handed him another ear of corn, which he accepted automatically. Tenzer stood up and returned the poetry book to its slot on the shelf, then stayed there, leaning, calmer than before.

"I mean, Tarboro? A nothing little place. And meanwhile"—Matthew Glennon idly stood the ear of corn down on the carpet by his chair, released it, timber—"where am I?" There was a long silence. Zingman said, "Skoonlet Valley?"

Matthew Glennon nodded tinily, very astonished. "Neither of us were where we should've been. See how confusing it is? But . . . I went there on purpose, and we've got no idea how she ended up in Tarboro. And she had something done to her, but I did something. I did something."

Nothing happened until the leader of the Cobhouse crossed to the sofa and knelt down beside Pepper. He drew a deep breath and held it, then absorbed himself in taking the patient's pulse, leaning in close to listen to her breathing. Zingman thought, he'll fetch his stethoscope if necessary.

Mezzanotte finally asked, "So why do you want to go back?"

"I don't want to, I have to. It was a . . . I can't tell you right now, but it's the only way I'm going to start to understand."

"Would it help if we went with you?"

"Might. Might. Not the whole way, though. Maybe just walk me close?"

Tenzer pretended he hadn't heard. He'd found the wound at the top of Pepper's head, tried gently to clear aside the hair, though it was still matted despite the salt-water rinse. Zingman realized that the water had not stung his ear, after all.

Nobody spoke for a while, until Pepper whimpered and sat up, blinked at the four unfamiliar faces, and Zingman's, also unfamiliar? She saw what she was wearing and started removing the kimono roughly, making Tenzer reach to assist her.

"Listen," she said. "I don't mean to be rude, but I've got to get back to where I work, Archimedean Products. Figure some stuff out."

Zingman stood. "The Colossus!"

"What?"

"I'm sorry, nothing, noth—just an exciting connection for me."

She stood up, too, uncertainly but seeming steadied by the broad soles of Zingman's sneakers, taking swipes at smoothing her jacket and impossible hair.

"But . . . so you're starting to remember things?"

She smiled, touched his shoulder. "Yes, and people, too. I do remember you, Mr. Ross Zingman. At the zoo, that was wild."

"I'm Matthew Glennon." Honor was vivid in his voice. "We might have passed each other this morning, in our travels."

Pepper shook his hand, respectfully. "Well, I don't know, Matthew. The earlier you go today, the less I can remember. I'm Pepper. And thank you, sir," she said to Tenzer, who was neatly folding the kimono, "for the rest on your couch." She looked around the room, at the drawn window shade, pregnant with blocked sunlight, then spotted the front door through the entranceway.

"Now hold on there, Pepper," said Zingman. "I'll take you over. Just let me get us a ride." He stepped to the wall, took the phone off its bracket, extended its antenna, and dialed information. "May I, Patrick? And you'll let me know if you guys decide to go to the Valley before next session?" Tenzer looked extremely weary, acquiescing in every direction, his wife's kimono now a neat package before him on his palms.

Turning back to Pepper, Zingman said, "I happen to know somebody with a fancy purple sportscar, someone who owes me a favor. Yes, I'd like the number for an Oliver F. Griffith, please. Junior?"

"No, no, no, I can't!" The runt had drunk two more mugsful—each one with extra ingredients, more in keeping with the final goals—in exchange for three more calls to Mr. Z., and now he felt he'd reached his limit.

But the experiment had been a rousing success. His objections had risen during its course, but she'd held the telephone hostage and exerted a newfound degree of sheer physical prowess over him, especially in his downcast state.

Her victories, several and distinct, were evidenced by the mangled bodies of three tiny females, stuck to three spots on the walls, where they remained, restless. One had even alit on a large enzyme jar marked "BELLA BELLA," nearly toppling it.

They'd embraced their task with characteristic elan, after Harriet curtsied politely, as promised, away into the walk-in closet, phone in hands, studying the budding forms in the basins until she heard tell it was time to peek. While waiting, she'd bite the inside of her lips, which brought the relaxing taste of blood.

The human body is both the most sophisticated machine conceivable and alarmingly simplistic, by turns. Her tracking method was no more than that used by plumbers to confirm, without excavating streets, the soundness of linkages beneath a congested city district, who will pump dyed water into the main, then simply check to see if it flows out the faucets of all systems down the line. Thus, that first time, she'd rejoiced at the pale blue tint of the runt's seminal fluid, though holding her applause.

Harriet had given him a minute to tidy up, using surplus gauze left thoughtfully on the cot. She'd allowed another frantic call to that friend or case manager—"are you home, are you HOME? . . . sorry I wasn't out there by the street, I couldn't wake up, can you come back, please? . . . I wish you could get me down here, but . . ."—while she prepared the next mixture, this time adding a single dash of the compound that the synthesizer had begun to squeeze out, an amber syrup adrip into a pipette. The bundles it held came fully equipped, of course, with their own enzymes for growth and nutrition. GENTID and ALACTRONASE were only the delivery system; they'd bond with the compound, she hoped, and become a "vector," ferrying it directly to the one site in the body where they knew to go. The reason the color of the GENTID came through visibly at all, albeit faintly, was that the runt had swallowed perhaps two million percent the amount required to catalyze his intimate reactions, and this same superfluity had swamped his seminiferous tubules and flooded from there into the winding antechamber of the vas deferens, leaving no room for such feeble creatures as sperm.

Several of the chemicals named in "Desiccation and Rehydration"—which she'd found and added—were said to possess powerful evaporative properties, but Harriet's unlikely postmortem confidence in the mind of Mr. Jack Garvey was born out only when the runt's second donation actually evinced an impressive viscosity, startling the runt himself, pointing toward a state, Harriet adjudged, of desert dryblow. One more weepy phone call—"home yet? home yet?"—meant a newly proportioned synthesis down the hatch. The third and final result had Harriet hopping up and down behind the closet door. He took this opportunity to bolt from the room, out through the messy office—hyperventilating, spooked and clicking away down the corridor.

Granting his servitude, she took time out of her busy schedule to locate the vaunted brownie mix—microwaveable—at the back of a high cupboard, where a miniature hand could not reach it. In a bowl, she added water to the chocolately dust, stirring the aroma to life and smiling fondly—*everything's coming up desiccation and rehydration today.* Not making use of the worker productivity boosters that Garvey had stashed alongside the package—St. John's wort, ginseng, Chinese ephedra—she patiently collected several ounces of her improved compound, as it dripped from the pipette at the front of the synthesizer, before folding this into the batter and cooking the entire triumph, in a tin, for three minutes and forty-five seconds.

"Shh!" Trapuka crouched in the minibus; had he been spotted? Police and the curious were swarming everywhere, but he focused on a shocking trio that stood just outside the building, not fifty meters away: Eugene Lash, Pauline Ard . . . and Ellie Trapuka herself. She looked small and out of place in the bright afternoon light, wrapped in the glossy yellow slicker he'd bought her two summers ago; he'd gotten the size wrong, and it still seemed like a tent on her. He'd meant to remedy that situation. A recent haircut only served to make her head look smaller, the coat more ridiculous, but she'd worn it anyway, today, although no rain impended. Trapuka wanted to give her something much better, something alive and fascinating, like a hermit crab. Why had he waited so long? Pauline slung her arm across Ellie's shoulders, and his daughter's head rested against her immediately, against a maroon sweater of Jonna's, which he hadn't seen in years. His wife was no doubt lurking around here somewhere, believing the worst about him. She couldn't bear to face him even before last night. The two girls were somber, withheld, each biting her lip. But Eugene's hands flew; he babbled before a rapt little audience of men and women with notebooks. A man took his picture.

"Just over by that curb, if you would?" Trapuka pointed to the back of the lot, nearest the building, and that's where Steffi parked the brand new twelve-seater minibus with "SORW WHEELS" crisply stenciled on the side, white on maroon.

"'Archimedean Products, Incorporated'?" said Benjamin from the rearmost seat, smoking beside an open window. "What kind of company would keep your—"

So this was Eugene's gratitude for being invited into Trapuka's home last Thanksgiving, for meeting Ellie, to return there and commandeer the girl, thrust her into this regrettable mix.

Three squad cars stood empty on the grass nearby. He crouched even lower—hunkering atop the annoying bulkhead of the motor for the wheelchair lift—and scanned the grounds. At the far corner of the building, officers and a work crew were arrayed around some huge, droning machine. At least construction projects were moving ahead as scheduled, and the law was interested, perhaps even tiring of his case already; the boy and Pauline had certainly given their statements, permitting procedures to grind forward.

"Um, hey, Paul?" said Steffi, poking him gently in the ribs. "What's the plan here?"

Trapuka thought.

"And why're ya hiding like this? Don't forget that you have every right to . . . Paul?"

He stroked the cool plastic contour of the bulkhead, placed his foot on the platform that could be raised and lowered to street-level: skewed priorities and Federal mandates, when there's nobody handicapped here. The money for this single contraption could fund many years of expeditions. He found a latch and worked it, lifted a hinged panel in the bulkhead, felt canvas and metal down inside. "What's this in here?"

"A spare," said Steffi. "You unfold it. In case someone needs a rest."

"There's a blanket in here, too."

"Yes. What're you doing?"

"Unlacing my boots."

"I can see that."

Jammed into a sadistic backseat compartment, nauseated by sudden changes of course—Pepper, up front, acting the ambivalent navigator—had never been Zingman's vision, although he'd had his eye on Oliver's deep purple Mitsubishi Vector ever since that first class meeting, when the condensed powerhouse had aced to a stop in front of the YMCA building, delivering man and manuscript to "Advanced Horror!"

But on the phone, less than an hour ago, he'd said only, "I hoped we could get beyond last night . . ." Oliver had sent back a brooding silence. "And listen, something is going on that I want you to be a part of, an unfolding mystery you can help me decipher." He'd answered with the information that today was Saturday, a day he always pledged himself to his desk, to his novel. "Well, think of it as on-the-job training for the writer of dark speculative fiction." Oliver had cleared his throat, agreeing flatly, because it so happened he was on a short break, following a strong morning's stint.

Zingman wished they'd arrive at the scene of his latest humiliation, the Colossus's parking lot, because besides the nausea, he also wished he hadn't invited Vivian along; she lived right on the way, though, and last night she'd been so earnest. She fit herself in beside him, somehow comfortable, even snugly venturesome, and her monologue had conspired with the whining rpm's to mask the interchanges, likely revealing, up front. After being introduced to Pepper and waving good-bye to her husband, forlorn on the porch, Vivian had apologized for missing "Wombdwellers"—post-class elation, last night, had led quickly to exhaustion—and then she recalled something drastic and looked at him afresh, gauging his health, producing an article torn from the afternoon newspaper about the accident at the Seaquarium. "And I can tell, she must be your 'unidentified female companion.' Now I know her name!" Vivian read the whole purple piece aloud, with performative emphasis—

> VALUABLE SHARK, OTHERS, PERISH IN SEAQUARIUM SPILL
> At approximately 8:35 this morning, the glass containing wall through which 'Seaquarium' visitors may view the marine life was shattered, causing twenty thousand gallons of. . . . None other than well-known local author Ross Zingman, whose books of horror and the unexpected used to thrill readers nationwide, until certain nebulous 'personal troubles' apparently emptied his pen. Only moments earlier, this reporter had caught up to the reclusive and surly writer, seeking an interview on the occasion of the re-airing of his. . . . only to be summarily rebuffed. He hurried off to join his mysterious lady friend on their Hot Date with Disaster . . . What is this blocked bard trying to hide, we must ask. Was this entire sorry incident perhaps nothing more

> than a stunt designed to return him to the public eye, to rescue a career that is struggling to remain afloat . . ."

—and Zingman guessed he ought to have sat down to a friendly coffee with Stennhouse at the diner. Vivian next wondered if, to take his mind off his trouble, he might like to hear the gist of what she'd written already today, to learn what had befallen Gladys, her central character in *The Cost of Terror* (she called it, "The Cost"). "Though I must warn you, it isn't cheery." Zingman cautioned that often writers fear losing their impetus by sharing work too soon, but she didn't feel that way at all.

When they pulled into the lot, an enticing buzz of official activity turned him into a skilled contortionist; thus—after Pepper hopped from her seat, saying, "follow me," and trotted off across the broad lawn in a pair of sandals belonging to Tenzer's daughter Mathilda, heading toward a massive, squash-colored truck, parked and apparently drilling into the earth at the base of the Colossus—Zingman leveraged himself out in phases and shook his legs, newly weighted with old sneakers, restoring circulation. He watched Pepper recede, which naturally put him in mind of further categories of Eros; she was striking despite her scientist's jacket having been so badly grayed at the zoo; he saw her arrive at the drill—maybe forty yards away—and station herself in the midst of a group of policemen and engineer-types, far burlier than he, who monitored the operation.

"No flies on her," said Vivian, coming up beside him, the aqua beads of her necklace clacking softly. The men seemed concerned for Pepper's safety, set her up with goggles and a hard hat, though they weren't wearing any themselves. She shouted a question; a policeman cupped his hand over his mouth; she leaned her ear into the cup. Obviously, she was feeling better; it was almost as though Zingman didn't know her anymore. He laughed at himself, at his mind's readiness to sail out past persuasive gravity, and so he told himself to stop. He'd given her a slip of paper with his phone number and address, a least little thing to do, like an ordinary man attracted to an ordinary woman, no shapely tricks, no grand perspectives.

Oliver stayed at the wheel, gunning his engine, frozen in the festivity of probing for a flaw in the works. Zingman led Vivian along the walkway toward the great knot of people by the front entrance, asking one another questions, appealing to authorities. With each step, the sound of the industrial drill further overcame that of the Mitsubishi Vector.

Edgewise, Zingman had been able to hear stray segments of the frontseat conversation, as Pepper directed the driver via last-second hunches, short-cuts through alleyways and grocery store parking lots, and Oliver had found his voice, asking her details about her work, being, he said, quite a science buff himself. The next segment he caught, they were on to pigs, and microbes, and something about it struck Oliver very funny, and Zingman recalled her laughing at the giant South American hogs this morning. But Vivian was now in the middle of relating an encounter between Gladys and Gladys's new doctor at the institute, fascinated by her case, a disagreement—"'Blindness is not a lifestyle choice, Mrs. Tull!'"—that turned into an outright fracas over the issue of day passes, and Zingman gave up trying to listen for Pepper's profession, being, himself, anyway, no science buff.

When Oliver caught up with them on the walkway, he only glowered in response to Zingman's greeting nod; all three kept walking. "And where did our young Miss Sarles go?"

So now she had a last name? Zingman pointed. "We'd only have to compete."

"I'd leave that part to you," Oliver scoffed.

Zingman said, "Why do you suppose they're drilling like that?"

Oliver stopped and placed his hands on his hips. He wore a black turtleneck and a thin leather jacket, brown. The breeze had no hair to play through on his head, so it batted at his face, making him frown. "It would appear," he said, "that they are preparing to descend into the shaft. Note the basket connected to the winch, how it hangs near the hole. Or perhaps they are lowering other materials, for some purpose."

"All right," Zingman said, "a good start, but now, my friend—what purpose? As Mr. Clive Barker has urged us, 'Imagine more! Imagine harder!'"

Vivian nodded firmly.

Oliver swung around to Zingman, face alarmingly broad and unimpressed. "I am in no mood," he said, "for your games. I think I'll take my own way for a while." And back he surged along the cement walk in the direction of the lot, then paused and turned, tossing his car keys underhand. Zingman grabbed them out of the air. "I will ask you two to wait for me in the car after your foray, so that I won't have to hunt for you. I must get back to my desk by three o'clock sharp." The man surveyed for a promising route, then left the cement and strode over grass toward the side of the building, busting through a prim hedge.

"Well," said Vivian. "Well, my, my."

"Who invented him, Bram Stoker? Anyway, Vivian, back to our story. What purpose?"

"Yes," she said, "'meet mystery with mastery.' Okay, they might be digging for a . . . a lost child . . ."

"What happened?"

"Fell down a cistern, days ago."

"Why?"

"Foolish, foolish."

"More, Vivian."

"Playing, all this good weather. Dropped her doll in."

"What's the girl's name?"

"Name's Rachel."

"Doll's name?"

"Um, Lady . . . Lady Postman."

"Now you're cooking."

The drill caught their attention by rising to another gear, shrieking for ten seconds, then falling silent. And now all the human voices, suddenly exposed, the many pitches and colors and concerns, sounded remarkably sweet and thoughtful, even the men at the drill, who were shouting, their ears probably whining still. A cruiser had pulled up tight to the great machine, and Pepper sat in the front seat, speaking with a policeman. The workers extracted the drill bit—thick and gunmetal gray, threaded with a bold spiral—from the ground. "Ooo, poor Rachel," Vivian cooed.

"Or," said Zingman, "a different story might relate to the microbes, that she was mentioning in the car, and even to the pigs, somehow."

"I didn't hear that."

"But it would take time to extrapolate . . ."

"Or we could ask her for more details."

"Vivian, no, now," he said, taking the liberty of putting a hand lightly on the shoulder pad of her tulip-red blouse. "Now, you don't know it, but you're walking a fine line. See, science is conservative, in its basic conception. It traffics in the literal, pure facts."

"I know you've probably thought this through, Mr. Zingman, but I must admit I'm curious."

"Me too, me too, but there are many ways to fill that space. I'm just saying I strongly doubt anything we could learn conventionally would hold a candle to what we could make up by ourselves. In the right hands, fiction is far stranger than truth. We'll have to find a fruitful starting place. For instance, I've had a feeling that this building here is malevolent in some way. At night, I've experienced distant eye contact through the windows with the shadowy figures who work inside, and—"

She nodded, then, as if regretfully, waved past him.

"Excuse me, officers," she called to the two who quickly approached up the walkway, startling Zingman. "Could you tell us what exactly's going on here?"

Zingman sighed. "Hey, no, you guys are much too busy—"

A blurt of siren from the cruiser near the idle drill turned everybody's head. Behind the windshield, Pepper was covering her mouth contritely, laughing; Zingman believed he could almost make out her eyes, wide—woops!

The officers laughed too; the taller said, "*That* one."

"So you've met," Zingman muttered.

"Ma'am," said the shorter, "yes, we are in a hurry, but we can tell you there's been a murder, and—"

"Yes! I saw about it in the paper. It happened here?" "It did, and we have reason to believe the assailant may still be on the premises." Zingman studied the hat of the tall officer; its scuffed brim needed a polish. His eyes were a fine blue and openly rolled because of his partner's running mouth. "Security system indicates some significant activity way down below, so we're going to blast our way in there."

"From underground?" she asked. "No access from inside?"

The taller officer removed his walky-talky from his belt, depressed a button on its side, and turned away to speak. A staticky voice answered him.

"Well, this is a strategy matter, ma'am. Situation like this, you want to counteract expectations."

"Oh, the element of surprise!"

"We should sign you up! Now, we have located a single elevator shaft and have placed men at the top, to block an escape . . ."

"And because . . . what if that shaft is booby-trapped?" Vivian glanced proudly at Zingman.

"Ma'am, don't tell me, you're a member of a S.W.A.T. team, correct?"

"Oh, hardly!"

"Steve, ten minutes," said the taller officer. "We'd better man our position."

"'Man your position.' You actually say that."

"It's been a real pleasure, ma'am. You're going to have to maintain a safe distance now. See, we're stringing rope over there, to keep back the public and the press."

The Law jogged off toward the drill.

"Let's go get a good spot for the explosion." She set off toward the main entrance, where the ropes were going up. "This is so exciting! They say that, Mr. Zingman."

"I heard."

He dragged his feet, entitling this brief episode, "Stolen Thunder." And then, it got even worse; up ahead, standing at the outskirts of the gathering crowd—William Stennhouse III, shifting his weight from foot to foot, scribbling into his notebook.

Zingman braked. "Vivian, uh!" She turned. "I can't . . . there's someone I'd rather not. . . . How about you meet us afterward, back at the car? I'll try and find our unhappy friend."

She was torn, but followed her heart.

Zingman cut through the hedge Oliver had cut through, and he didn't have to hunt for long. There he stood before a statue—a life-sized brass sculpture, greening with age, of a man in a toga, mounted high on a cubic pedestal.

"Archimedes," said Oliver, though without looking to Zingman. He pulled the collar of his black turtleneck more snugly up beneath his chin, beneath his great sallow face, and pointed to a plaque, also greenish, reading, "'405-324 B.C.' He was a Greek mathematician and the father of modern science, a proto-physicist."

"Uh huh."

"In fact, he was the gentleman who cried 'Eureka!' while sitting in the bathtub."

"Be . . . cause," Zingman held out tentatively, "he saw the water rise as his body . . . lowered?"

"Not really. In this moment he recognized that volume could be measured by the displacement of a fluid." Oliver took a walk around the base of the pedestal, head tilted back, wringing his hands. "Another of his discoveries also has to do with displacement, but in this case displacement of a solid through space. He learned that one may cause a great weight to shift if one applies pressure to it with a lever poised atop a fulcrum . . ."

Zingman noticed that the man was actually choking up, breathing oddly and straining to keep his face composed, as though he felt some quirky vast affinity for this statue, for a ton of quiet metal. Had someone somehow tagged him "IT"?

". . . a fulcrum is a point of support placed so as to maximize leverage . . . also known as the Archimedean Point . . . where everything . . ." He breathed again, more successfully. "Where everything is possible."

Zingman moved as close as he dared, but Oliver backed away, pretending to gain a better angle on Archimedes, like Pepper's upon the beasts, reaching up and brushing the bottom of the pleated toga, sighing heavily.

"Coincidentally," said Zingman, "I was just talking to Vivian about finding just such a point in writing a story, where you can start your imag—"

"No." Oliver's head pivoted so gradually toward him that he listened despite himself for a series of bony clicks. "A great weight is shifted, I said."

Zingman swallowed. "I'm . . . yeah, sorry?" He made a mental note never again to forget the teacher/student boundary. "So, what's that he's holding there, in his left hand? Looks like a tiny staircase? Or, a giant rotini! Sure he was Greek, not Italian?"

Oliver started moving again, but swore under his breath before condescending to instruct the teacher. "You are looking at the double helix, a molecule of deoxyribonucleic acid, the structure behind all living forms. Miss Sarles and her colleagues—"

"Can that be who I think it is," a woman shouted, "Mr. Ross Zingman?"

From off behind the Colossus, they marched this way along the edge of a sparse grouping of pine trees, maybe twelve people led by none other than . . . yes, what was her name? Two years ago, after Andy died, she'd accosted Zingman wherever she could find him, everywhere except his own home—*that* she left to Candace.

"Steffi West?"

Pleased beyond measure, the woman nodded, pushing one of her charges—a feeble, bald, blanketed widower with his head in his hands—through the grass in a flimsy wheelchair. She arrived, SORW filling in behind her.

"And you," he said, pointing to the back of the group where a straggler swung her arms languorously; he checked her wrists for creaminess, and there it was. "'Candace,' is it?"

Not knowing how else to lash out, he formed exaggerated quotation marks with his fingers, which only made everybody laugh, everybody but the bald man sitting hopeless before him and the bald man standing hateful beside him.

She grinned. "Oh, you're right, it's an alias. And if yours is a pen name, are you keeping it? I notice they're showing your old stuff on tv, but I've been waiting and waiting for your next new publication, checking the bookstores every day . . ."

"Really now," said Steffi West, "let's not. Show some compassion for this gentleman here. We're here on a mission of mercy." She squeezed the handles of his chair. "Paul . . . has been unable to recover his beloved from somewhere inside this building." Zingman began to believe her, trying it on for size, picturing the silhouettes up in the windows, carrying an old woman from room to room. SORW cozied in tighter. "And although he cannot bring himself to look at these . . . people around here, some of whom are employees, we have circled this entire building twice and found no way in that isn't guarded."

Zingman felt like being decent. "Oliver Griffith, this is Steffi West." But he wouldn't acknowledge her, staring down instead at the old widower—a great weight? "Oliver, maybe you have a theory to help in this mystery?"

"Or maybe," said a man smoking a cigarette at the left flank, "we should ask what you're doing here? You and your . . . silent friend there. Maybe there's a theory in that."

"What?"

"No telling," someone huffed. "Cornhuskers."

"Oh, I get it. Right, that's right. You've caught me, I do have her, she's in this, in this crypt here." He patted the granite, readying for a run with this good lark, until Oliver slapped his shoulder, quite hard.

"Sir," Oliver said to the man in the chair, whose body had further sagged, showing a scalp that bore tiny criss- crossing Band-Aids. "Sir, let me apologize for Mr. Zingman, he . . ."

A bullhorn in the distance barked cautions to the public.

"Mr. Creepy rides again!" sang Candace.

"No, I didn't mean to belittle what this man is—" The brass plaque on the side of the pedestal sprang open on a hinge, banged back against the stone. People exclaimed and backpedalled, some diving to the ground. Zingman grabbed onto Oliver. Oliver grabbed onto him. They stared into the black chamber. Oliver pushed him away but leaned in again, grazing Zingman with fingertips when an object flew out, landing and bouncing until they could see it was a small cardboard box, having spilled most of its contents onto the grass—dark brownies, crumbly. A SORW member shrieked and Zingman looked to see two familiar hands, first big, then little, appear over the bottom of the hatchway, gripping. They executed a chin-up. "Mr. Z., you came."

Mr. Ruthbar's face and neck were swollen, had gashes and abrasions, several still bleeding. "You're . . . hurt."

"I waited till I could hear your voice out there."

"Author sure is well-connected," said Candace, sitting on the ground.

Mr. Ruthbar's eyes were bloodshot and teary. "I kept calling you from downstairs but you didn't answer. I thought you stayed asleep all day."

Zingman stepped up to him. "No, I went out to breakfast and then things . . . started to happen."

"I didn't know if I said it good enough, how to get here."

"You left . . . directions on my machine. No, no, they were . . . perfect. I found you, didn't I?"

"Keeps in touch with all sorts of people . . ."

"Candace!" said Steffi in a stage-whisper.

". . . can't return my phonecalls."

"You came," said Mr. Ruthbar.

"That's right, of course I did. Now let's get you out of there." Zingman reached for his friend, but Mr. Ruthbar's pea-green eyes flared and shot back and forth.

"Waitwait, I was out before," he said, breathless. "I'ws standing by the street waiting for you. But all those policemen started coming and I got back in here. They started digging, so I climbed back down the ladder, all the way down to tell her they're coming."

"Tell who?"

"That lady, who made the brownies, and who . . ." He tried to catch his breath. "She's hiding in the drain right now. Where I showed her my hiding place."

"What? Okay, okay, c'mon out and we can—"

"Mr. Z., I'm scared. I . . . think they're looking for me . . . 'cause of what I did down there. They're digging for me." Mr. Ruthbar almost caught his breath but stumbled into a few coughs. "But the lady made me do it . . . she wouldn't stop . . ."

Zingman patted the cold little hand, and he would have let the man babble until he was all ready to be hoisted out of the pedestal if it hadn't happened—the blast, a great remote snarl from away and below, followed immediately by a sprightly explosion of applause from the crowd out front. Some of those behind him ran in that direction, but Zingman's attention stayed on Mr. Ruthbar, who spooked him, though, by letting out a childlike whoop. "Oh, feel that!"

"Feel what?"

"All the air! Feels good on my cuts, woooo!" His wispy hair stood straight on end, as though he were at the top of a smoke stack. Then, his face fell again. "Uh-oh."

"Now what?"

"I can hear them, they're coming up. Pull me out!"

Zingman caused much pain by contact with chest wounds; the man's shirt was in tatters; gauze strips had been applied to his chest, sloppily, and they were now crusty and coming off. By the time Mr. Ruthbar sat beside Zingman on the grass, the smoke stack had begun belching its waste. So here was where the flies had come from. And soon bats zipped out through the hatch and into the sky. No, they were birds. They got larger—sparrow-size, pigeon-size, then the size of the ducks at the zoo this morning. He felt a pang that Pepper wasn't here to witness the spectacle. And now the birds were getting outlandish. Several would clog together at the opening like Stooges in a doorway, hawks and owls, perching briefly and pounding their wings—some holding scraps of meat or sticks of bone in beaks so sharp he felt they disagreed with everything he'd ever thought of—before battling free with zero grace and then taking to the air with infinite grace, with almost laughable care, establishing flight as though spreading thick frosting with their wingtips over the top of an uncooled cake.

"Pretty, pretty," said Vivian, coming up behind them, her face rosy from excitement. "No wonder you weren't at the car. At least the police have flushed something interesting, because so far no killer, nope. Oliver was absolutely right about them lowering men down the hole in that basket. After the explosion, down they went, maybe half a dozen so far. Oliver missed that, too. I saw him running through the pine trees over there, chasing another bald man. Well, hello there."

Zingman turned and saw that not only had the ambulatory members of SORW, ever fun-loving, run to check the explosion, but the wheelchair was empty. "Oh, Vivian, yes, this is my good friend, Mr. Ruthbar."

They shook hands; he used his big, which gave her the shivers. "Sure you're not the killer, hmmm?"

He didn't laugh. "No, but I saw him. He killed Mr. G. He had a fish."

"Oh my. Have you talked to the police?"

"No!"

"He needs medical attention, I'm afraid, Vivian. Help me walk him to the car?" Zingman stood, cupping one of Mr. Ruthbar's elbows in his hand, though the trip for medical attention might have to compete with a sunset spent high on a hill with the widowers. Before Zingman left Tenzer's house, the Grievance Committee had been lobbying to storm Skoonlet Valley first thing in the morning, while Matthew Glennon, paling, now wary of what he'd wished for, preferred a calmer overview beforehand, from a ridge he knew.

"I could interview you on the way, Mr. Ruthbar, if you'd be willing," Vivian said, cradling the other elbow, and they lifted him to his feet. "I'd convey the information to officer Matthews . . ."

"Hmmm, I hadn't caught his name," said Zingman. "Might give you a badge!"

"Not very likely," she laughed. Zingman gathered the brownies back into their box and handed it to Mr. Ruthbar, then the three departed, Mr. Ruthbar limping, the roughness of the hedge, as they crossed through, making him hiss. They progressed toward the purple sportscar, out beneath the warm sun that had emerged without warning as if to announce its declining, Zingman jingling the keys softly in his pocket.

"She took away my keys," said Mr. Ruthbar.

"That doesn't sound fair. So, Vivian, Oliver ran into the woods?"

"Looked to me like he was after someone, but I couldn't tell. I don't know."

"Well, we can't just wait around, if he's off doing something crazy. One of us should find Pepper and try—"

"That won't be necessary. She found me and said we should go on without her, said she'll call you later."

"Thank you."

All right, Zingman had plenty on his mind besides Pepper, just plenty. There was the delicious task of knitting all of these bizarre events together into a single tale, for example. This current Mr. Ruthbar—racked and ruined here beside him, starting to tremble—was connected somehow to the slap twenty-four hours ago, to that fish-smelling van, and to the advent of the barefoot woman early this morning . . . and yes, even to her stopping before the Giant South American Hogs, tossing her head back to laugh: "The Pig Trough!" The net of story contained as well the paralyzed fish, so much shark bait, which had terrified Pepper, and the wild-haired man—"It's him again!"—who shot out the glass. But to find and follow the thread, Zingman would never take the direct route of brazen objectivity; no, you sneak up on truth from an off-angle, and follow the clues, and while you are at it, something else discovers you, and springs. When he was a boy, "The Twilight Zone" was like this for him, like a breath that blows out, one by one, your heart's fondest beliefs like a grove of birthday candles.

Hey, that was not half bad, Zingman thought; even as he stepped conservatively along the walkway, his ankles and the tops of his feet tingled in a wild swirling dust storm of possibility. He'd first experienced this swirl—the "zing" in his ankles which he'd always supposed was the secret meaning of his name—when he'd seen Rod Serling emerge dolefully from the shadows, to one side of the could-be-anywhere small-town stage setting, and regard him, the viewer, with heavy head slightly cocked to the left—dark, overstuffed eyebrows, with a grave regretful concern that said, "I only wish it were not so, my defenseless comrade, but the world is indeed a far stranger place than you will ever know." Oh, Zingman knew all right, nor was he defenseless. He vowed to make up rival stories of his own; even then, he felt his ankles beginning to sing the stories out. Eyes sixteen inches from the television screen, he'd witness the tales taking shape—say, a doll who, when you pull her string, chirps, "My name is Talky Tina and I don't like you. . . . My name is Talky Tina . . . and I think I hate you . . . My name is Talky Tina . . . and I'm going to kill you"; or, "submitted for your approval," an old stopwatch that when punched suspends the motion of the world, and if dropped and shattered locks its owner forever in a hellish limbo; or, a rescue mission to the moon to discover what happened to the previous mission, beaming back pictures to Houston, on the huge screen, as they come upon the construction site where the previous mission was supposed to be building a colony, but look, they seem to have used the materials, the steel girders and the guy wires, to make something else, but what is it, what? Well, it looks like, but how can it be . . . a . . . a mouse trap! And there, looming over the landing craft . . . the mouse! Or—

"No, YOU!" Looking up, Mr. Ruthbar ripped loose from Zingman's supportive hold and dashed onto the grass, scrambled in a circle as though evasively—"should have KILLED you!"—then collapsed into a ball. A tremendous white bird dove, shrieking, out of the partly cloudy sky and, seeming larger than its victim, clubbed at his head with bulky wings, bounced up and down on his back, talons pushing, trying to dig into flesh. Zingman couldn't move, but by the time he told himself to move, Vivian had already arrived at the scene and begun lashing the creature—it was an owl—again and again with her necklace, which she held looped in her hand. The aqua beads must have stung even this broad cushioned skull, because the creature muscled itself back where it came from, rising, tilting into the sun, where Zingman lost sight.

When he knelt beside his friend on the turf, Mr. Ruthbar was heaving for breath and huffing the words, "I was going to . . . I had the chance to . . ."

"I'm sure you did," said Vivian.

Even this episode he'd figure into the story, later, but what struck him at the moment was the way Mr. Ruthbar had clutched his box to his chest through the whole event, and how he clutched it still, which suggested to Zingman—who had not eaten since the rubbery hot dog at the zoo—that these could be just the tastiest chocolate brownies in the world.

"Oh? Then it may also interest you to learn," said Trapuka, "that if you pulled absolutely smooth the craggy surface of our earth, making of it a true sphere, the oceans would stand at a uniform depth of more than 8,000 feet." The man held aside for him a whiplike branch.

The two had been walking briskly for more than an hour along a narrow creek, sometimes through forest, sometimes across open fields, south of the city; and they had recently entered a valley with high ridges on either side.

Mr. Griffith said, "That"—tossing his head—"that is perfectly astonishing." He'd given up trying to persuade Trapuka to stop and rest, seemed satisfied, finally, with this onward march, indeed growing hardier on a diet of facts about the sea, with *Titus* only tossed in lightly on the side.

At first, when this tall enthusiastic man had chased him into the brush and few trees behind the firm, then nearly tripped over him where he sat lacing up his boots (they'd been stashed behind him in the wheelchair), Trapuka had had to place him in an immediate headlock. He'd coughed and insisted he was no threat. "Do you know why all these police are here?" Trapuka had asked.

"No."

"You've heard nothing of . . . irregularities?"

Trapuka had released the man, who tried to look composed,

straightening his shirt and leather jacket, rubbing his own neck. "But I can find out for you, sir. I would have made inquiries, but somebody was bothering me, and . . . no, I'm quite a curious person, which is why I couldn't help following you when you jumped up and started to run, Mr. . . ."

"Doctor Trapuka." They'd shaken hands. "Listen, I need to get somewhere in a hurry, and if you have the time and the . . . the curiosity, would you be willing to . . . lend a hand?" Trapuka had leaned and picked up the wheelchair blanket, which he'd carried along in case he had to sleep outside.

"Yes!" The man's outburst had startled Trapuka; had he been yearning for such an invitation?

"Let's go, then . . . um, this way. I can tell you that you are entering a sort of . . . unusual situation, Mr. . . ."

"Griffith, Oliver," he'd said, struggling to keep up, already winded, tripping on a tree root but not falling. The two had passed into thicker woods, pursued the sound of flowing water. Evidently, Archimedean Products had been built on the southern edge of the city, abutting protected land. He'd felt fortunate, even as a branchful of pine needles swatted Trapuka's scalp.

"Well, the sad fact is, Mr. Griffith . . ." Only as he formed the words had he recognized their truth: "I'm searching for my daughter, Ellie . . ." Earlier, peeking through his fingers from the wheelchair, he'd glimpsed her being hustled into the Subaru station wagon by Jonna, who seemed beside herself. Eugene helped Pauline into the backseat, slid in next to her.

"So then," said Mr. Griffith, "your girl is camping somewhere around here, in the refuge?"

And then, it had happened once again; Trapuka had enlightened himself and this new assistant simultaneously. "Let me clarify," he said. "You see, it's a safe place I want to find, a place to bring her. We haven't gotten the chance to speak recently, she and I."

"A depth of 8,000 feet?" Oliver repeated, now, in this sharp valley. The men had come upon a small pond, fed by the creek they'd followed for miles. "Do you mean to tell me, Doctor, that this calculation does not require us to factor out all or any of the major mountain ranges?"

"Yes, Mr. Griffith, I'm afraid I do." Dusk was beginning to gather, although the sky overhead was clear, lit well by an unseen sunset beyond the ridge. He folded the blanket neatly and set it on a rock. "The Pacific Trenches alone cancel out the Andes, the Alps, and the Rockies put together—I mean of course the Marianas, the Tonga, and the Philippines Trenches, each of which plunges more than seven miles below the surface of the sea and extends more than two thousand miles along its floor."

Mr. Griffith shuddered and sucked in a breath so loud it might be his last before he was transported into an abyss. "That," he said again, shaking his head, "that's just amazing to me."

The pond was covered with green algae. Trapuka squatted down on the stony, muddy bank, and Oliver squatted beside him. Trapuka said, "You know, come to think of it," swishing his hand back and forth on the pond, fingers spread, to clear a spot. "I'm hungry."

"Lucky you!" Mr. Griffith jumped to his feet and made an inclusive gesture with his arms. "Because look around—this whole area is rich in flora, and I just happen to know a thing or two about edible plants and mushrooms. I took a class last year, with field trips, but I never dreamed it would become relevant so soon. I keep meaning to get outside more, but I have this, well, this novel underway, at home, which I'm trying to finish up and send . . . well, anyway"—he clapped his hands—"let me, as they say on the trail, rustle you up a meal! Which is only fair, I'd say, considering all the information you've given me." And he was off taking inventory of what grew on nearby logs and tree trunks, what clung to boulders.

Trapuka stood, tempted to put an end to this respite in the interest of gaining more distance upon civilization before darkness concluded its take-over. But he saw that the man was too far into his task, already finding samples, and he lost strength. He turned back to the pond, and with the toe of his right boot he enlarged the window in the algae. He breathed deeply through his nose and was surprised to feel the quick return of an ancient sensation, surprised because he'd been wedded for so long to maritime pleasures, had nearly forgotten about the earth, how he'd begun his evolution on land, or beside shallow land-locked bodies of water like this one, only later learning to scuba dive in the town pool, before slipping into the sea.

He bent to watch, on the bottom of this pond, a pale crayfish scuttle backward away from his hand. He got on his knees and leaned further down, peering through the algae window, a ragged circle slowly closing in toward its center. How cunning, the tail, and its overlapping panels of armor—how it so efficiently scooped several times per second, making momentum out of so little. Numberless scuba dives by now had distanced him from such freshwater miniatures, and he smiled upon this crustacean in its indignant surge, wishing he could introduce it to its tremendous cousin, the lobster.

The window finished healing over with a soundless draw of suction, and Trapuka stared for a moment down at the primitive floating plants, at the carpet of diminutive blooms, furred stalks, twining tendrils—so busily repetitive yet so terribly unthinking—and tried to fathom how a person could become passionate about such things, while behind him, one such whistled a chipper tune, procuring dinner.

Trapuka sat down squarely on the bank, learning his fatigue all over again, gazing out across the entire green sheet—twenty meters wide, forty meters broad—filled with nothing but the same, the mindless same. He began to feel queasy (and to envision frantic bloodhounds employing their intelligence here in this forest, and then a prison cell, patiently replicating itself into endless copies with him inside each one, sitting like "The Thinker" . . . and the copies were the days . . .) until he recalled that underneath this algae in front of him, everywhere, solid creatures had intentions, knew how to accomplish ends and defend and to fortify themselves, could adjust to circumstances. He pictured the man in the cafeteria pitching backward when the second spear hit him, one who had misread circumstances; the expression on his face betrayed zero comprehension of natural law.

Trapuka switched to the fresh memory of the hard, narrow crayfish body in its flight through fine silt, how it made a roiling trail like the dust kicked up by his van on dirt roads in summer. Sometimes, Ellie would ride with him, and he'd play along as she pretended they were far from home on an expedition. This morning, after escaping the zoo, he'd parked the van on a random cul-de-sac, Ayrdale Crescent. Could he persuade this zealous amateur botanist—approaching from behind, breathless, probably laden with specimens to show off—to retrieve it for him? Trapuka would first have to feign interest in the world of woodland fungus.

"I know, Doctor, it's difficult to pull your eyes away—the algae peaks just now, in late October. That russet tinge you've picked out most people wouldn't even notice." Mr. Griffith sat down with a hiss that indicated sore muscles.

"Did you know that the lichens are actually not one but two organisms, living symbiotically?"

"I did not," said Trapuka, smiling and turning around, feeling somehow that his case had abruptly improved. But he was startled to see that in the hand held before him was not a cornucopia but rather a single clump of moss, out of which projected delicate pink mushrooms, standing tall, with tiny domed heads, admittedly appealing.

"These I found on a rotten log. They are very rare in this region, and, despite their appearance, quite deadly. The smallest poison mushrooms on the continent, as I remember. Oh, don't look so worried, Doctor Trapuka, I've put together an excellent salad for us, when you're ready; "but this species here is called 'Mephisto's wand,' and I should have brought my magnifying glass, damn. Can you see down inside the moss, all those thready runners that connect the stems?" Instead of looking and against a wave of nausea, Trapuka stood, and so did Mr. Griffith. "It's getting too dark anyway, but this is how they spread, sending out runners, and there's almost no limit. In fact," said Mr. Griffith, "the largest single living organism ever discovered was a fungus." Smallest fatal mushrooms in one hand, he leaned down and placed the other on Trapuka's shoulder, which embarrassed him but charmed him, too. Its warmth, sinking even through his windbreaker, told Trapuka that a chill had come into the air, and he thought of the nearby blanket.

"Okay, suppertime, Doctor, right this way, to the corner table." His laugh was higher than expected, from such a large man. "And remind me to stop boring you!" They approached a large boulder beside a tilting tree; a shallow depression in the stone was filled with plant matter. "I found lots of mint and marsh marigolds and a pungent variety of flower known as 'genie's tongue.' The rest are large mushrooms, perfectly safe, and wholesome—they'll remind you of meat." They knelt, and Trapuka rubbed his hands together, lamenting that his Coleman lantern sat in the van on Ayrdale Crescent. This jumble of bleak indigenous growths made his mouth water as if they were a bowl of cheese ravioli and a glass of wine. This image fled when he took his first, musky bite.

"In western Minnesota, that's where they found it. And it's still alive. It covers three hundred acres and grows underground, all lacy and bound together by runners, like tentacles. It's seven hundred years old, and it continues to enlarge, inch by inch. Frightening, wouldn't you say?"

"Frightening?"

"Well, to me. When I was young, the first horror stories I tried to write were inspired by . . . by the idea of tentacles in the sea."

"Oh, yes."

"Stinging tentacles, and long arms with suction cups that grab hold of a swimmer. I'd heard about a boy in Hawaii who was nearly killed by one of those Portuguese man-of-war jellyfish. Apparently the top of that creature was—"

"The 'bell,' you mean." Trapuka grew tired of kneeling and sat down, cross-legged; Mr. Griffith followed suit.

"That's what it's called? So, the bell was bigger than a beach umbrella."

"Doubtful. They rarely exceed eighteen inches across." "Another myth destroyed!" The man laughed again, and again Trapuka was surprised, ate a red flower.

"And from time to time the bell will convulse with a muscular action so that it sinks into the water to wet its surface. I have seen this, off of Monterey."

"I would pay money to see that, for certain. So anyway, this boy was paralyzed for three days, sick for weeks. I brought him into my earliest writings, made him the hero, described his ongoing battles against the jellyfish, tales of high terror, or so I thought, until Peter Benchly's *JAWS!* came out, just as I was picking up steam. I was . . . well, shamed into silence."

Dusk had established itself firmly in the past five or ten minutes, but something about how Mr. Griffith now cleared his throat—as though getting ready to say something, perhaps, emotional—brought down the final curtain on day.

"Certainly," Trapuka quickly put in, chewing a bitter stem, "tentacles are very common in the ocean, though most are nontoxic, merely appendages for the taking of nourishment." Mr. Griffith laughed, this time quietly, and held out his hand, patting Trapuka's knee, then leaving the hand there. "But those of Physalia, or man-of-war, yes, they can stretch to more than one hundred feet and have claimed their share of careless human beings over the centuries, who were not so lucky as your Hawaiian boy."

A wind was picking up; Trapuka turned his head and shoulders, looked back wistfully at the lidded pond, which showed no ripples. Mr. Griffith withdrew his hand, sighing once.

"Physalia has a constant companion," Trapuka continued, fumbling in the stone bowl and selecting a spongy bulb of some sort, feeling suddenly very thirsty. "It is a type of small fish that is only to be found swimming beneath this host, having adapted a protective coloration in the form of vertical bands the same brilliant blue as the hanging tentacles. This causes predators to swim the other way."

"Of course, wouldn't you?"

"The fish spends its whole life among these tentacles, in spite of the huge threat."

"Threat?" Mr. Griffith said. "But it must be immune to the toxin."

"One would assume so, given eons of co-evolution, but as it turns out, not so, not so. In laboratory aquaria, if forced up against a tentacle, it will not survive."

"Isn't that," said Mr. Griffith, tossing his head once again and releasing all of his breath, "just something? Think of it."

Far below, Skoonlet Valley looked like a trough full of night, except for the glinting. Ponds were strung together along the valley floor by a single little river that Zingman remembered well from hikes with Andy. Some of these ponds were only dark blots, small and choked with weeds; but some were larger, stretched out, and still held daylight on their surfaces, shining as though in tribute to it, or then coarsened by night's wind, pushing through.

The Cobhouse men had witnessed one sunset already, driving in their short processional; but they'd forced a new sunrise by climbing the steep hill after Matthew Glennon, who wheezed, Sheila's blue terry cloth bathrobe draped over his forearm and sweeping the brown and yellow grass behind him the entire way. Cresting the ridgetop in shorts and t-shirts, sweaters and jackets tied around their waists, the sun struck their faces too hard, maybe a little resentful of reprise.

Zingman had been late meeting everybody at Tenzer's house, once he finally gave up on Pepper (Honorary Crime-Fighter, Learning to Use a Walky-Talky) and Oliver (AWOL) and drove the Vector, proudly, to drop Vivian off, and once he called his machine and learned the sunset plan, all the while tending to an agitated, shivering Mr. Ruthbar, whose breathing had not regained any steady rhythm since the attack from the heavens, and who now sat slumped in the sportscar, which was parked down beside the road, its engine running, heater blasting even though the air temperature must be above sixty. Patrick Tenzer had looked him over and diagnosed anxiety, given him several outdated tranquilizers from the early days of his widowerhood.

All took seats overlooking the Valley, except Zingman, who started to pace behind the group. "Glad we get a sunset up here," said Gilbeau, quietly, eyelids lowered to gather warmth. A garish orange scarf was loosely tied around his bare upper arm. In their laps, the men held things—a plaid diary; a pile of German sheet music; a pair of sneakers with clean white socks tucked inside; a little gold-framed painting of a ship stuck in fog. Simon Reese wore Theresa's straw hat and stood a tall, cobalt-blue bottle on his knee. Zingman hadn't brought along anything of Andy's; he hadn't been home since dawn. Stanley Keillor lifted Jessie's riding crop to his face, sniffed at the worn leather handle, and this prompted Matthew Glennon, still out of breath, sweating, to drape the bathrobe across his shoulders and soft-saw it back and forth over his neck.

"Well, naturally it is lovely up here, naturally," said Tenzer, who had brought nothing of Estelle's, only three ears of Indian corn that lay untouched in the grass beside him.

Matthew Glennon said, "I just really have to thank everybody for going along with this, on such short notice."

Pacing, Zingman smiled down at them all but felt a certain unaccustomed removal from the thick processes of grief, which alarmed him, but again, the alarm was remote; mostly, he was pleased, because instead of grieving his mind was up to what it always used to do, playing, inventing, making proposals and connections. He gazed again into the Valley, trying to locate on the opposite slope the strong waterfall that he and Andy had stumbled upon that afternoon. Over the years, they must have explored every last trailway in the Preserve, but they'd had to clear their own path to reach the crashing sound, and he didn't remember where. That early day, after their time inside the stone room behind the falls, their throats were sore for days, from shouting. They never succeeded in finding the place again; nor could Zingman spot it now, even through trees that had lost most of their leaves. But he spotted a pair of tiny upright figures beside one of the dark little ponds. It was not possible to read details, like gender; and unlike the crisp silhouettes in the windows of the Colossus, these two looked hypothetical, their outlines, and even their centers, a flimsy guess, as if proving that objects disappear only by softening the brain.

"I'll tell you," said Simon Reese, "all this reminds me so much of Theresa." He plucked at the brim of her straw hat. "See those wild flowers over there? Well, they aren't a great example, since they're faded out like that. They can die, for all I care. Personally, I hate flowers. But Theresa would make me hike places exactly like this. She's here, I'll bet she'd drag me down that path into the Valley, even now, at night." Men laughed low. "And wouldn't you think some of that would have rubbed off on me, eventually?" The sun was half. "She might as well have picked another guy. Thank God there's Anthony, who turned ten last month and has been keeping his own garden for three summers. You should have seen the pumpkin that boy managed to grow last . . ."

Talk continued, but Zingman decided to save his attention for any revelations about Sheila Glennon. Not that he was impatient with talk of dead wives, or could ever lose interest in the constant cringe and stretch of these Cobhouse souls—it nourished him, always. But darkness was creeping quickly up the Valley wall, would soon threaten their feet, urging them home, and Zingman had promised himself to start commanding into place the details of the story while he paced, while he commanded this view of Skoonlet Valley.

All right, find the starting point—the wild-haired man in the Seaquarium, why not? Pepper knew him and feared him. "Let us suppose for the moment that he and this 'Jack' she referred to were in fact one and the same," Zingman murmured, not loud enough to interfere with Reese's talking about his boy Anthony, who'd won a horticulture prize at the 4-H. "But she stopped calling me

Jack around the time he showed up. They began as lovers, and he gradually went insane, going at her skin with tweezers in the middle of the night . . . just what was he putting into those jars of his? . . . and finally attempting to drown her. Or no, not insane, that's no good. Something is happening that's drawn them both into its expanding web. Yes, that's better. Something that also includes those giant South American Hogs and a behind-the-scenes 'Pig Trough.' What's the connection? What's the connection?"

He needed a break. The racket had been shamed out of town for so long, its synapses had gotten muffled. He felt frightened, and deserving, to choose this practice over that of loyal grief.

Now Reese was onto an African violet that Theresa had brought back to life. Zingman stopped pacing right behind Matthew Glennon, who craned his neck to look up at him, awkwardly, trying to grin. "She pulled off all the brown leaves," said Reese, "until only little green ones were left. Anthony was three or four at the time, and she said to him, 'See? This is called pinching it back. Now all the energy can flow where it's most needed.' Soon after she died, when he was six, Anthony came running up to me one night, and I've never seen him happier, eureka! Give you one guess, guys, to what he said."

"'We can pinch back Mom,'" said Gilbeau.

Zingman reached down and touched the top of Glennon's balding head lightly with the heel of his hand. Like magic, the man seemed able to breathe again, and deeply.

"Okay, the connection," Zingman mouthed, resuming his back-and-forth trip. The sun was no more than a manageable fire behind the trees on the ridge opposite. "Wait! In the front seat with Oliver, she went on and on about pigs . . . and microbes . . . that's it, she's sick. No wonder she threw up, poor thing, and probably she'd gotten extremely dizzy at some point, had fallen and hit her head there on top, where it still hurt, though that's not the usual place to hit your head. And her eyes, at the zoo, were bright with fever, not infatuation. Humbling, yes, but an enticing lead. A ravaging illness, it must be, to cause temporary amnesia. Best that we did not kiss. Insidious, too—giving rise to fits of high spirit and excessive sociability, like this afternoon at the drill. A bi-polar illness. And thus, did I read her laughter wrong in front of the hogs? It was not light-hearted, it was hysterical, because . . . they are the carriers. The bug has come from South America, and it is festering, multiplying rapidly inside their trough—where they breathe, where they snort, where they shove their snouts down in and root around inside rotting garbage. Maybe Pepper works with them. And so of course she was the first to contract the disease. But I'll bet she didn't suspect, at first, given a generally sunny disposition. Somehow, Jack did, knew he'd lose her soon, and that's exactly what drove him gradually insane."

Zingman's ankles stung with inspiration. He'd forgotten how it felt, having gone years without, since Andy's first symptom—a sudden cold sweat in JCPenney, which caused her to plunk down in a bin of socks.

"Oh, in the beginning, I'm sure he tried subtle methods of studying and identifying the bug, hoping to contain the outbreak. Why panic zoo personnel or the wider public? So he tried to collect the bug from Pepper's skin, at night, without upsetting her—he does possess an ounce of sympathy, after all. But he failed, failed miserably, growing more and more desperate as the plague spread, more . . . wild-haired. Come to think of it, those spider monkeys looked rather slack-jawed, too. And the others, how they stared at Pepper from their enclosures, their dying-chambers—as if they knew also. And how she stared back soberly at them, accepting her due of blame. But by no means did she deserve what befell her at the Seaquarium, uh-uh. To be confronted, on purpose, with that pitiable fish, a creature in its final throes, overwhelmed by the very demons that infested her, perhaps bodying forth her own impending fate. He expected this sight to knock her off her feet. Further—he expected that shark to take its bite- sized treat, and that the sight would say to her, 'You, too, shall be swallowed!' And so it had, oh, it had. She was in no condition to flee, then, when he shattered the crystal dike. How positively diabolical—do away with the only person who has a chance to put the pieces together and tell the world that this scourge began here, under his watch, and that it could have ended here, if not for his failure to contain it. You had it all figured out, didn't you? Stamp out the story and create a spectacular diversion all at once—then run far from the scene, try to save yourself. The one thing you never counted on, though, was me! Think of it, my wild-haired friend—your plan might have worked but for me . . . or if that brute in the parking lot last night had taken me out of your way, had been fiercer, had landed a stronger blow to my head . . . if he'd possessed a fraction of your resolve."

Zingman rubbed the side of his face, his ear; they hurt again, mildly, reawakened by a stiff twilight wind rearing out of Skoonlet Valley. For this wind the Cobhouse men stood, whereas the sun's unceremonious departure they'd ignored, going on and on, speaking, he presumed, about their wives. But as everybody now pulled on their additional clothing, leaned down to pick up their mementos from the grass, Gilbeau had the floor, and his topic was not death, after all, but exercise. "I'll bet we could all use it. I mean, doesn't this Valley just reach up and grab you by the lapels?"

"Shit, Ron, you sound just like my wife!" Reese laughed. "I thought I'd outlived that kind of little pep talk."

Tenzer laughed, as well, picking up the third ear of Indian corn, the first two shucked while Zingman was plotting. Keillor said, "No, I think he's right," running in place to keep warm, slapping his thigh with the riding crop. "Tomorrow's Sunday, and they say the weather's going to hold."

Certainly, much remained to be woven into the story—an apparently successful murder inside the Colossus; Mr. Ruthbar's adventures underground, whatever they were; a kamikaze episode . . ."well, of course the disease would scramble the brain of a bird, even a mammoth once-noble bird, causing it to dive at random, or to mistake man for rodent . . ." Zingman had no jacket, no sweater, but he was cooking nonetheless, pacing faster, glorying for now in this sweet, sweet sensation, being returned to him after so long. He was never nearly this clear, till tonight, quite how tired he'd become of supporting absence. There was absolutely nothing like this instead, making a story, a mere telling that does nothing less than push back the darkness—"and the more you write, the more you see just what must come next, and the more you cut your way, holding a torch. Granted—"

"Ross, shhhh." It was Tenzer, attempting to intercept him along the path he'd worn in the grass. "Matthew is trying to get our attention." Zingman simply held up a finger and stepped around the man, thinking: granted, you discard infinite possibilities in order to blaze your one trail, narrowing your options severely with each step, but the secret is—this emancipates you as well, this tightening that loosens, opening shapes inside you.

But now, a shape had formed outside that glared in the near darkness, demanding he stop to encounter it; five men stood frozen in a rough semi-circle, with Matthew Glennon in the lee of it, sheltered from increased wind, arms crossed before him like a Roman centurion, hair buffeting sparsely. Zingman adopted a timid angle upon the emotional scene until he checked to find that the precipitating event hadn't really passed him by, that his inner ear had stored it moments ago—"I know what you're doing and honestly, I find it a little insulting."

The man shuffled his feet, in the present, and continued. "You're trying to be kind, I guess, but you're putting words in my mouth, like why I want us to go down there is because of the Valley's natural beauty or something." Matthew Glennon rubbed his eyes with the heels of his hands. "Well, I guess that was part of why they chose it for the party. My friend, Bruce Reardon. I'm sure none of you . . . Sheila couldn't stand the guy. I used to know him where I went to school. Anyway, he was throwing this bachelor party for someone, happened to fall the week she was in Virginia, and they all thought it would be, you know, cool to have this enormous bonfire in the middle of the night, in the farthest part of the Preserve, or the deepest, you know, where the rangers would leave 'em alone. Not your typical bachelor party, but in other ways, it was typical. Sheila found out about it and we had a couple fights. I got so angry at her for not trusting me. I shouldn't have gone, even though I didn't know what was going to happen, and no way to predict what was—to predict Virginia, I still, I knew I should've never gone." He gazed into the dark breeze, into the hugeness of the Valley, giving Zingman, who looked also, a little squeeze in his chest. The glinting ponds were no more, and so he knew he didn't need to search to be sure the two upright figures by the small pond had finished their vanishing, but he searched anyway. Voice shaking but less than last night, Matthew Glennon continued, "I'll probably never be able to find that spot again . . ."—Zingman thought, waterfall, cave behind waterfall, Andy shouting over the roar, giving up and making ridiculous hand signals—". . . even with the big fire pit they left. This wind reminds me of things I heard from the police. From what I can tell, when I was there, getting drunk, was when Sheila was . . . getting off course down in Virginia, ending up in Tarboro. They found her in a field, close to her rental car, some stupid Ford she picked up at the airport. I saw it, looking brand new, with no dents. They suspect foul play, but one thing I can't stop thinking about, they mentioned in passing. That night there was a windstorm, not widespread, just this weird local blow, not any big system that showed up on radar. Lots of trees came down on houses and power lines in Tarboro and Kells, but not on Sheila. All she had was a blunt trauma to the left temple. Amazing how I've learned to blurt that out. I'm . . . I think I'll leave this here overnight," he said, tossing something formless to the ground that waited two beats before remembering itself as Sheila's bathrobe. "So I'll be sure to come back tomorrow morning with you guys. I'm sorry I snapped at you before, you're my life line right now. Can you take me down in from up here? It's the way I should go in, because it's not the way I went in before, think I've got to approach the whole thing from a different angle, you know?"

Tenzer laid his three hefty ears of Indian corn on top of the robe, and the men started picking their way back down the hill to their cars. At one point, Matthew Glennon, short of breath from the exertion of descending without light and of trying to cry without being heard, began to panic, and while Keillor talked the man through, Zingman hurried to the Vector. When he opened its door, he found that Mr. Ruthbar was asleep, snoring featherily on his side, having eked himself into the rear compartment, legs bent awkwardly upward, sturdy shoes wedged between the driver's seat and the driver's window.

"Yes, and take those lemmings, for another example," said Mr. Griffith, "whose methods of populations control—plunging off of cliffs—are forever being interpreted as an existential choice."

"It is crass!"

"Exactly."

The two men reclined on a bed of moss, laughing in the darkness. The blanket barely covered them, if they lay close. The stars were out, but in their uniformity and frozenness they had never done much for Trapuka. Tonight, he felt almost free of his troubles. He remembered his and Jonna's courtship days, that back then, he'd allowed himself to be impressed by stars, and that the moon was always shining.

"What about those chimpanzees, with their American Sign Language!" trumpeted Mr. Griffith.

"You mean Koko, and her gregarious descendants?"

"Yes, please try to teach hand signals to wrens and see how far you get; naturally the chimps are chatty and clever with their human trainers . . ."

"They're from our own damn phylum!"

Trapuka and Mr. Griffith fell quiet and listened to the wind crashing smoothly through the pines, to the cry of a high bird, shrill, which Mr. Griffith identified as an owl, a nocturnal hunter. Every now and then, since they'd finished their chewy meal and lain down, this man would let his arm flop onto Trapuka's full belly and remain there for a minute, on top of the blanket. Trapuka told himself that yes, this was likely some sort of mild sexual gesture, but that indeed it was harmless enough—comparable perhaps to male courtship rituals play-acted by most large mammals the year before coming into first rut.

"I'm sleepy, Doctor Trapuka." The arm did not flop this time, thank goodness. "We're lost, aren't we? Don't answer that, I'll speak for myself. I must tell you, this is just what I needed. I've been a little . . . oh, lost and depressed myself lately. It's about my career, as well as my personal life, to be frank. And then last night, at class, I received quite a blow. But never mind about that. When I saw you in that wheelchair, you seemed . . . maybe . . . weighed down. And now I know you were, and are, by this whole *Titus* situation. Now . . . this may sound funny . . ." Trapuka held his breath. "But you wouldn't happen to know any good bedtime stories, would you?"

Trapuka exhaled. "Well, as it happens, my daughter, Ellie, often enjoys hearing examples from my work. One in particular has been known to help her to sleep. It concerns the difference between *Titus* and her undistinguished cousin, the tuna."

Mr. Griffith hummed by saying the word, "Hum."

"I was once charged with the bleak task of counting deceased octopi and sponges on the ocean floor off Jamaica. The oceans there were already being compromised by industry in 1993. I dangled at twelve fathoms beneath the hull of a research vessel, sitting inside the Henderson Bell—that dank dinosaur—and eating my lunch in the middle of a ten-hour shift. Well, suddenly, I found myself buffeted at the heart of perhaps twenty thousand tuna! Not that they ever once struck the Bell or even brushed the structure on their way past—no, that would have been a surprise, and I was to learn that only *Titus* is the specialist in surprise. So, there I was, watching through the thick glass of my portal. I always tell Ellie to picture my face, looking out. Her mother once bought glass baubles to hang on our Christmas tree that reminded me of that antiquated bathysphere, so I tell Ellie that I felt like I was inside one of those glass balls, shaking in the breeze of an opened door. For—"

"Oh, that's pretty, Doctor Trapuka," the man whispered, fading out.

"Thank you. For fully nine minutes, I watched the school of massive tuna entering the Bell's fluorescence from one side, travelling at probably thirty-five knots, and then instantly dividing. Their four-foot bodies were adept as minnows'. They'd flash past my portal before merging again on the other side of the sphere, without a single wrinkle in the routine. Eventually, I became dizzy and backed away from the spectacle, holding my head in my hands. When the Bell was finally still again and the last proficient tail had left me far behind, I regained my appetite and took a bite of my sandwich, remembering only as I tasted it that it was filled with none other than tuna salad!"

Once, Ellie had laughed here.

Trapuka shivered and lay down, curled up like the woman whose head he'd had to strike, fixed the blanket carefully over himself. He didn't go ahead to relate how he'd devoured that tuna sandwich, and a second one, in a sort of jubilant celebration of his own fish, never systematically caught by man. Mr. Griffith whispered something, but Trapuka didn't listen, calmed by his own thoughts, amused even tonight by the tuna's blunt predictability—which allows them to be netted by the millions, year after year, in the selfsame locations, that place them so readily between slices of bread.

"Anyway, remind me to tell you about my novel, tomorrow, okay. Doctor?" Trapuka pretended to be asleep, breathing level. "I'm calling it, *A Modest Rebate from the Grave,* and it concerns"—elaborately, Mr. Griffith yawned—"another failed marriage and a dreadful misuse of technology . . ." The wind had eased, leaving a wide space around them; this seemed a moment for the owl to cry out again, but it didn't. "Goodnight, Doctor."

"Have I got a bedtime story for you, my good man, that is . . . if . . . you . . . DARE!" But no, tonight the poor man couldn't dare. "No, thank you, Mr. Z." His face was puffier, even, than Zingman's used to be, and Patrick Tenzer's anxiety pills had made him dopey and suspicious, though he'd asked to be brought here as they soared along after sunset inside the borrowed purple bullet; Zingman chided, "Oh, but how can I trust you? Last night you broke my window and ran away from home!" The man, though, was too brittle to jest.

Mr. Ruthbar now lay beneath the covers in Zingman's bed, blanket gripped in both hands, breathing with a grim deliberation, eyes fixed at some point on the opposite wall. Two minutes ago, Zingman had stood him before the bathroom's round mirror—the same one Tenzer had once wrapped in padding—and tried to show him to himself. "Will you please tell me what happened to you down there? Did that 'lady' make these cuts, or—" But he'd only started to weep dryly, knees buckling; Zingman had wetted a washcloth and conducted him into the bedroom, helped him out of the ruined shirt and crusty gauze bandages—shoddy care!—and blotted him gently with the cool cloth. The formal shoes and the pants had come off; Zingman turned his back.

In bed, it seemed his friend had to concentrate in order to live. "But listen, this story concerns a dreadful disease that came to our country from far down south, and a beauty who, through no fault of her—"

"'No,' I said."

"All right, we can postpone it. You'll be fine in the morning. You've just been through some kind of harrowing experience which we will get to the bottom of over breakfast, after you get yourself a night's sleep. I'll be right outside that door if you need me." Zingman stood up from the side of the bed, bent to switch off the reading lamp; during the last instant before darkness, the olive green eyes remained wide and fixed, unblinking.

Invisible, he said, "Mr. Z.," then took four breaths of equal size and weight. "I can feel my heart." Heavy breaths. "And I can see it, too . . ."

"Yes, and what's it look like, Mr. Ruthbar, can you describe it to me?" But the little king of vivid analogies wasn't playing right now; he had turned his full attention to his fractious pump, so Zingman decided to leave the two of them alone to work things out.

The living room was a chilly, breezy place, but he couldn't spot any remaining flies from Archimedes' pedestal hatch; they'd all left via the missing pane of glass, which he didn't even consider trying to fix, except to chuckle at a quick vision of himself plugging the hole with the pulpy pages of A Modest Rebate from the Grave, by Oliver F. Griffith, Jr., First North American Serial Rights. . . . "Hey, cereal, wish I had some."

Ravenous, Zingman stepped into the kitchen, flicked on the light; he smacked his forehead, noticing the five old jars of spaghetti sauce on the counter—"Do I dare?" Unscrewing the first jar and peeking inside, he found that those dots of mold had proliferated horribly—a pox upon his house . . . thanks, no doubt, and by some circuitous means, to the seething food trough of the South American hogs! The growth had even leapt off the sauce and now dappled the jar's inner walls and adhered like bright decals to the underside of the lid, salmon and yellow, with some kind of stark blistery white streaking through. And then, indeed, a fly dove straight inside, and Zingman trapped it, the last one, ha-HA.

Returning to the living room, he espied Mr. Ruthbar's precious box sitting battered on the table by the front door; fifteen minutes before, he'd pried it gently from its owner's arms and set it here. "But he makes them for me . . ."

Sitting on the sofa, Zingman lifted the lid and consumed three of the arid gray brownies immediately, nearly choking but too busy to go for water. In this he felt like a child, and because here he was, ready to go to bed at 8:45. Somehow, he'd grown up, for real, only the night Andy'd taken her last breath; and not since then had he lived a day so full and without burden that he could play the boy again.

Halfway through the fourth treat, he realized that not only were these not the tastiest brownies in the world; they must be among the worst. By the sixth, he'd pinpointed a similarity—detergent cakes, like those pretty pink round crumblies his mother used to drop into the washing machine when he was young. He'd never actually bitten into one, of course, but he'd sneaked a sniff, touched them to his lips, trying to resist, to convince himself that they would be very bad to eat. Nibbling on a seventh, he guessed that it did possess, after all, an evasive sort of chocolatey aftertaste, if you could get there. No sweetness, however, no, no—like those blocks of pointless "baker's chocolate" he'd discovered with such initial triumph in a cabinet.

After turning out all the lights, he stretched, stomach hurting, on the couch beneath a single flannel sheet but zipped into a bulky coat, bought on sale, with Andy's advice, in that glorious spring of 2003, her last healthy one, Zingman noticed the tiny red light across the room, blinking emphatically—four messages. Two or three would be from Mr. Ruthbar, trying to explain how to locate and rescue him, but could one represent Pepper's voice, sorry to have lost him? Better not to check, so the idea could be a portal into sleep. He breathed air that stole in from the vast, readable evening, that kicked into the corners of the room and slapped at his healing face—"Not to worry, handsome . . ."—and although this air did contain the rigid splintery scents of sleet and snow advancing inevitably toward the city, it also made the lenient pledge of one more soft day, at least, to come. He tried to anticipate the descent into Skoonlet Valley early in the morning, what Matthew Glennon might find down in there, but instead Zingman found that he was replaying sunny moments at the zoo with Pepper, nostalgic for this time before they had names.

Knocking? 1:34, by the digital clock on the wall. Silence. "Hello?" Zingman said, "Pepper?" It didn't come out a solid word. "I'm sorry," she said. He got up, wrapped in sheet and winter coat, now unzipped. At the door, she cried, but concisely, awkward, looking, aside from her wine-red sweater, all washed out in the hallway lights, her blonde hair messy and seeming severe, almost artificial. At the couch, she apologized again, at length, and Zingman let himself imagine, to poke his mind awake, that she was referring to his sudden exposure to the South American Plague. "Listen, let me turn on some lights, fix a cup—"

"No, please, I'm awful. I want you to go back to bed. My goodness, I mean . . . if I could just lie down here, I won't bother you. I—Jeez, you sure do keep it chilly in here." Zingman pointed out the missing pane, then transferred the sheet onto her; in the dark, he snuck off his coat, tossed it to one side. "At my place, I couldn't sleep, everything's been way too crazy, can't understand any of it. Guys from work keep on calling, trying to comfort me, but they don't get it. I don't want to be reminded of that place. Makes me feel totally stumped and sick. This has been the worst day of my—except for your kindness to me, of course. Suddenly, I remembered I had your piece of paper in my pocket, but I couldn't use the phone number, because nothing's worse than hearing the phone ring in the middle of the night. Even this isn't worse . . ."

She was talking loud. From behind the door, Mr. Ruthbar moaned. Zingman said, "That's my friend, in the bedroom."

"You're . . . not alone." She hushed. "What an idiot I am. I never even—"

"No, actually, I was sleeping out here, so he could have the bed. He's sick. You . . . almost met him today. I'll tell you about him, you'll be interested, I think."

They sat awkwardly side by side for a while. Zingman retrieved his coat from the floor and offered it to Pepper.

"You were wearing that. Boy, what a good friend, to camp out in the wind. Now put it back on. I've got my sweater, and we can share this thing." She held out an edge of sheet. "I said, 'Put it back on,' Ross."

She bundled him herself, and something in the sound of the long zipper, going up, taught him an instant appreciation—he lacked the urge to tell this woman about Andy and her death, didn't feel made of that anymore, and so he hardly recognized himself. He could see Pepper only as shady contours by the light from the streets, far below; and then he was enclosed with her under flannel.

"We almost drowned today," she whispered, pulling the sheet over their heads.

"I know. You're going to be okay."

"I'm glad I came. I've got to tell you, I was really going out of my mind. I've started having flashbacks to Jack being killed, even though I wasn't conscious for that. The man had knocked me out, same one we saw in the fish tank later, if you can believe that. Don't ask me, I don't understand any of it, though I seem to remember opening a bag and seeing that fish inside. I've tried to find my friend Harriet, she could help put things in order, but naturally she's not around. Nothing's in the right place anymore.

"Yesterday, I felt completely connected to my life; well, my job was stupid, but that was about to change. And I didn't think I was with Jack for the long haul, but it's just . . . the fact that he's gone makes it feel kind of like I was, because he's dead for the long haul, you know?"

"I—Yes, I do know." He was disappointed in himself for shivering.

"So has anybody ever—"

"Once, pretty long time ago."

"Hmmmm. Want to talk about it?"

"Actually, not so much."

"Then I'll put a lid on myself, too. And we won't talk about our work. I don't even know what you do! But I'm sure there'll be time for that, let's just keep it simple, that's what I want, why I came over, to take a break from all the—I'm so used to understanding the world, it's what I'm trained for, what I've always been good at, seeing through to the mechanisms behind phenomena." Pepper gave him a hug. "Hey, you're shaking, come here." She hugged him harder, and why was he disappointed in himself? "You strike me as just a very normal, good-hearted guy, exactly what the doctor ordered for me right now. Maybe you too? Don't worry," Pepper said, drawing him down to lie next to her, both balancing on the narrow cushions. "I'm not mistaking you for him. I'm clear who's who. Can we just sleep, is there room? Can you relax if I rub your back? I'm not trying to be weird here, just trying not to think. And the last thing I want to say about Jack is, he was into creepy things, things I was trying to understand, and my fascination was real, but now what's real is, I want to forget." She forcibly slowed her breathing. "Those cops I was playing with at Archimedean, they were trying to tell me what was found underground, to get information out of me about Jack." Zingman rubbed her back in recompense, because she was shivering, too. "To the point I finally put my hands over my ears and got in my car."

A bit slimmer and farther spaced, these rungs—Harriet started up the ladder, eyes firmly shut, frog glasses lost during the melee underground—*than those leading up to the statue of Archimedes. Perhaps eighteen as opposed to sixteen inches apart . . . ummmmm, or nineteen. And damp, kind of slippery. But certainly, the total distance will be less than a third of the distance up to Archimedes.*

She was cold but kept reminding herself to go slowly so that the five jars in the plastic bag tied to her belt would not clink together and attract attention. Already, a dog was barking rapidly somewhere below. With progress, though, pale rose arrived on her eyelids, and warmth quiet-clapped both cheeks—she had topped through the layer of ground fog, emerging into sunshine. The rungs became drier; her hands could relax. Her neck ached from many hours inside her ridiculous hiding place during the police ransack.

It was dawn. Harriet climbed—one hand up, opposite foot; other foot, opposite hand. The dog had circled in closer, barking still, but Harriet wasn't worried. She slit open her eyes and there above her was the great curving belly of the water tank, glaring a hurtful silver. She squinted, hunting right away for some sort of obvious access to the interior. She pictured an inviting, open funnel up on top, although she knew better, which was why she'd brought along her new toy, her triumphant find—a little something left behind by the marauders, one of their fancy entry tools, an aluminum pry bar, nearly weightless, that must have fallen from one of their crowded belts and never been missed because by then no doors were locked anymore. Harriet held it clamped under her left armpit.

Now, at this height, the ladder was enclosed by a long vertical basket, like a rib cage made of bright metal staves. She saw she was striped by shadows that slid down as she approached her goal—a balcony that ran around the tank's entire midsection, skirted by a low railing. When she got there, she would rest awhile in sunlight magnified by paint.

The dog stopped barking and began to nuzzle, to snuffle, a sound so precisely audible at sixty feet below that it was as if she'd grown a new ear on the ground.

"Hey! Hey!" she shouted into the fog. "Go home!" At the base of this ladder, which was attached to one of the water tank's enormous stanchions, she'd had to set down her basin of developing forms amid leggy weeds; she'd carried this basin all the way up that first ladder to Archimedes, and then on foot as she stole through the darkness, seeking this tower that she'd passed so many times on her way to work. Her car was out of the question—a decrepit '99 Nissan—because the authorities still had the parking lot secured (a blue light revolved) and she'd certainly been fingered as an accomplice many times over by her good friends from the cafeteria.

"You, hey!" She could hear an affronted growling, then the snap of jaws. But she forgot all about that low problem when a faraway siren came and went like slang tossed off.

When she gained the balcony, she circled to the north side of the tank to survey the city's southern skyline. Like a raptor, she was far-sighted without glasses. There was the Goodall Insurance Tower to the left and, slightly shorter, the jade-green Rand Building—both rising radiant out of the fog. But here, she shivered within the tank's shadow. She relocated on the south side. *Mmmmmmm.* Hand on forehead, visoring her eyes, she could see rural land, fields and farms where the fog had burned off in patches, hills and forests—with still some green among the expanse of brown, like points of tenacious mold in a bed of simple sugars. To bring this green, she breathed deeply through her nose, but only whiffed the paint baking behind her head. The ground beneath her remained hidden by fog, but she knew the dog was long gone, probably under his own home porch gnawing on what he'd found.

Harriet returned to her task. Another ladder proceeded onward to the top, laid flush against the metal and looking like a scale model of a ladder, curving up and out of sight. Hardly room for feet. *Are children sent up there?* She took off her shoes and socks. Refitting the pry bar under her arm and checking to be sure that the plastic bag with its historic contents was still tightly knotted to her belt, she addressed this ladder. If Robert Jenwaugh had ever examined her toes, he would no doubt have pronounced them simian, if he'd known the word, and then executed one of his trademark shudders of disgust. Harriet hopped on board and clutched rungs with prehensile digits high and low, reducing the pain in low by letting her hands pull most of her weight.

Ascending, she remembered how that man used to shudder, as well, following orgasm. "Oh, it's like belching after a good meal?" she asked once. He'd already started refusing intercourse; when she'd help him with her hand, she'd slow at the end, to make him weak, to make him suffer, to make him glance over at her, resembling affection, and then, the pomp and circumstance—again with the guttural cries of worship at the blessed event! She'd squeeze him in her fingers. *Pare it down to its essence and we find it meagre, underproportioned—a cricket trapped in a closed hand.*

The five jars clinked in their bag. Harriet had trouble catching her breath as she continued cresting the tank; the black cube threatened at the center of her brain. *But of course you're only teasing. I can't faint here, in the sky.* (Only when she'd re-entered the world and the sun rose did she sit to rest on a bench near the water tower, and by squinting through one eye, by pressing with her index finger on the side of this eye to improve it slightly—an old trick—did she make out in the basin certain long bones, not yet dressed in flesh. And when she stepped up to the ladder, wondering whether to carry her up—*you weigh almost nothing, a woman can't survive on spinach salad!*—she suddenly recognized Pepper's arm in twelve excellent albeit skeletal copies, the left arm, judging by the position of thumb and fingers—*frog glasses, who needs 'em?*—the very same one she'd clapped across Harriet's shoulders in the cafeteria line, alienating Butterfield's bunch. The arms were stirring now inside their gel, as if waving her off, too, but probably, in truth, only offended by all this jostling, this bright sunlight. "You'll prefer it here in the fog, in the shade here," Harriet had said, setting the basin down safely among leggy weeds.)

It seemed to take forever for gravity to change jobs, to go from trying to peel her off the side to pressing her down onto the flattening top. Thankfully, the ladder continued for a while past necessity, out of kindness, as the surface finished levelling, as it started to drag and bounce obnoxiously her five breakable jars. In her gut, an electric ball was spinning, and she recognized it immediately. This same ball had come to her when she was just ten years old, in the YWCA swimming pool; and speaking of orgasms, it accompanied, it caused, Harriet's own first.

She was alone, was late leaving the pool after the lesson, and the other students, even the instructor, were already in the locker room. Her mother would arrive any moment to pick her up, and the Y was going to close, shut its doors! They might turn off all the lights with an echoing bang, right away! Everyone had forgotten about her. The way she'd lost track of time was by pogo-sticking herself up out of the water and back down to the floor of the pool, crouching and erupting, again and again, at the eight-foot depth, pushing just her head and shoulders into the warm chlorine-heavy air and swallowing a big gulp of it before dropping down again. She was very dizzy by the time she swam to the edge of the pool; her head seemed full of water. In fact, she had contracted a major ear infection, initiating a sensitivity that continued to this day.

Now she reached the final rung of the kindly little ladder, and was on her own. She pulled past it, pushed off with her feet and then simply, unbelievably, kept on, summitting the last ten feet over blank silver. She took the pry bar in her hand and held it sideways in her fist, as if it might somehow help her make this crossing, like those great balancing poles used by highwire walkers. She stretched out her arms and her legs, for maximum contact. The electric ball sent tongues to her feet and hands.

She had stayed behind in the pool for no reason other than to dare herself. Oh, she was extremely late, only getting later, hiding her face just above the blue surface, against the wall, holding onto the tiled brink with just the tips of her fingers, taking in little mouthfuls of water and spitting them out fast, like a frightened creature instead of a smart young scientist. She felt strange; the ball of electricity spun itself lower, until it rested quiet, shrunken, just beneath her navel. Her shoulders trembled, and her arms trembled, too, tense with the effort that was concentrated in her fingertips, but below her rib cage her entire body felt paralyzed, or else transformed into silk.

Her legs drifted free, like the long stems of the water lilies she'd seen in the pond behind the softball field. Except her feet weren't rooted, though they wanted to be. She only found out she was panting because she heard the sound bounce back to her from the tiny glossy tiles. Even then it was not loud, it was only distinct, and part of her wondered whether one should be so intimate with oneself. Nothing but water touched her, yet it seemed that her perilous lateness had immobilized her body and was embracing her hips and thighs and privates (where the ball of electricity had ended up, smaller still) along with the water, squeezing her now with an impossible type of malignant tenderness that she could not well live without.

Oddly, she'd failed, for years, to quite associate what occurred this day in the pool with what Dougy went ahead and started doing to himself in his room the following summer. Or not so oddly—it was utterly different. The ball of electricity next diminished to a hush, the opposite of an explosion ("Naomi!"), and moreover she was thinking of nobody; the silent pressure of her lateness, enormous and doubling by the second, and the ceaseless hurried modesty of her panting, tight-throated within this pressure, the sound hitting her as if from someone else but no one in particular—these were plenty, plenty.

When the moment arrived, she didn't breathe. Not then but later, thinking back, she envisioned a membrane inside of her belling inward further and further, as when one afternoon at a birthday party she had pulled taut against her lips the skin of a burst balloon and sucked on it to produce a bubble that filled her mouth, made breathing obsolete; disappointment rode inside that bubble, even at the party, and definitely at the pool, because it could not hold. She understood. And she understood the same today, creeping toward the apex of an elevated egg, earth widespread around her, understood a thing or two about organic life on this planet. That whereas the male orgasm is a direct punch, a little punch, a cricket working steelspring hind legs to escape the fist, the female's, while not a yielding to this punch, must be allowed as a repeated honest *consideration* of yielding, as the hand will wonder about setting the cricket free. And then it will tighten again until the next sad request.

She arrived, gasping. There was neither funnel nor hatch here at the center; but there was a rusty bolt the size of a modest birthday cake, which very soon she'd attack with her invincible police tool, pry it loose, remove whatever cap or piping it imprisoned, and then simply empty all five jars of her syrupy compound into the water beneath her.

Water tanks like these were not yet entirely obsolete. Harriet had heard that they were no longer used, in modern cities and suburbs, as a regular source of drinking water but only as backups. So, if the main reservoir were somehow to become contaminated by a virus such as anthrax, risking public health, authorities would switch off that flow immediately and activate the numerous local towers, impose a strict rationing for the hours or days it took to ascertain the hoax. This particular tower would supply just a few surrounding neighborhoods, neighborhoods housing, however, hundreds of men, dozens of whom, for sure, were horny and unloved.

While waiting for the sun to come up, Harriet had found a pay phone at a gas station and put in the call to the Department of Natural Resources, had left a message that would be played before long to a high-ranking official, interrupting his breakfast.

To gather back some strength, Harriet curled up around the bolt, knees tucked like Pepper's in the cafeteria, like her own in the hiding place, down where the runt had shown her, inside a drain. While she'd hid, there was rude stomping on the floor above her, policemen's bulk pushing into the washroom. "Jesus, Murphy, smells worse in here than my wife's snatch!"

Earlier, shortly before the explosion and the raid, the runt had returned breathless to Garvey's inner lab; he'd tried to convince her to come with him up an emergency ladder which, he told her, led to the surface; from how, in his urgency, he mimed the climbing, she deduced that he himself had taken this route once already. He said that outside of the statue he'd seen policemen digging into the ground. "They're coming to GET you, and ME TOO."

"So why did you come all the way back down here to warn me, after what I've put you through?"

He started to cry, looking at the cot against the wall. "Because," he said, regaining his composure and smoothing with his littler palm the shiny chrome of the amino acid sequencer before him. "'Cause if you're here working, they'll get mad and break everything with axes. They'll make you tell 'em about what I did. If nobody's here and the lights're off, they won't touch the machines." He hiccoughed. "Mr. G. calls them 'haystack hunters'."

"To hunt for needles?"

The runt shrugged.

Harriet hugged him stiffly yet with sincerity for a full half minute, patting his back, then said, "Guess what I found?" She retrieved a cardboard box from the counter beside the sequencer.

"Some extra brownies he made for you!" He accepted the box and opened it, stared down at the ugly confections, attempting to believe in them.

"I feel sick," he said, and no, he didn't look so good, face blanched—apart from paths of dried blood—and unsteady on his feet. *Minor side effects already? Hey, a girl can't cover all the bases in one night.* He smiled weakly, brought the cardboard box in against his chest.

"Listen, I'm sorry, but I can't go up the ladder with you quite yet, I want to make more of my compound, but maybe if you'd give me another couple hours I could get—"

"No, they're almost here!"

"Oh, now I seriously doubt that those pol—"

"Then you gotta hide!" That was when he took her arm and led her—Harriet playing along, the short trip down the hall to the washroom—while back in the lab her machines kept humming for her.

After obediently peering inside the drain bed, then replacing the grille, she'd said, "Well, sure, but I doubt those guys will actually be able to reach us this far down by digging, or tunneling, or whatever you say they're doing." She'd laughed, kindly. "I promise you, though, if they do break in, I'll vacate the lab and dive right on in here."

She didn't laugh twenty-five minutes later. The red runt had fled for good, when the explosion set off an instant hurricane among the billion birds. Even the tiniest raptors who'd found her in the inner lab—those once so fascinating who'd faded to a background phenomenon during the past fifteen hours of brainstorming and trials—began to swarm at the concussion, searching for an exit. It jabbed her eardrums, this wave of compressed air, and she'd cried out. And then she'd panicked. Somewhere in the dash to consolidate her winnings, to bottle and cork the compound, she'd lost her frog glasses, and so she careened into several wrong turns before pinpointing the washroom.

The men weren't far, running, banging doors, knocking things over—"All right, we know you're in here, Trapuka, it's the end of the line, Professor Henry Trapuka, we know all about you, better come out before we start shooting." Harriet had just torn off the grille and postured herself for a dive, when a thought struck her—*won't I be lonesome down there?*

But then, racing back to this closet just ahead of the invaders, gasping, Harriet could grab only one at random and carry it like a restaurant tray—the five jars of compound cradled in her other arm—to her appointed crawlspace.

No, she realized, diving in wouldn't do at all—she had a basinful of life to consider now, though she hadn't even peeked to identify just what sprouts of Pepper she had here.

Love is blind, and the police are loud. She'd bent down and gingerly placed it in the bed, then followed, feet-first, crouching, lying on her side, tucking, reaching up to fit the grille into place with her fingers.

With every gouge and twist, the bolt coughed out flakes of rust, but Harriet could find no gap to dig into, couldn't gain a hold, exercise leverage. The sun, however, had well established itself, and now angled upward and upward, hoping to part her from her judgment. She only kept hacking away at the seam that joined bolt to tank, and sweating. She'd catch herself believing she was battling for water rather than for distant access to water. Occasionally, she heard distant raptor cries and checked the sky in vain, eyes aching with light, then returned to work. She wondered what she must look like from half a mile high, sprawled here and so diligent. *Yes, diligent as a headless hunk of bait, that's me—ready for you . . . come on down, I want to see your breathtaking dive and to feel your long dagger beak plunging between my shoulder blades, cracking me apart.*

She checked to find that all her labor had produced no more than a sort of extremely hypothetical notch. Swirling winds made her feel precarious and were beginning to carry sound up to her, strangely amplified by this vast curve of metal leading to her ear, car doors and residential doors opening and slamming, scraps of voice—"if you're gonna help me"; "s'posed to rain?"; "didn't mean that." She heard the reluctant gears of a passing truck and thought at first that this came from valves and flywheels down inside the tank itself, that years-dormant mechanisms were groaning into action because a sleepy somebody at the Department of Natural Resources had panicked and flipped a switch.

She laughed at herself, then realized that any moment now just such a thing might well occur, and that although people around her seemed to be only embarking upon their Sundays—to churches, to lakes and ball fields—rather than listening for suspicious noises from above, she'd soon need to abandon this particular method of dissemination.

She laid her pry bar down with a click, then palmed in turn each of the five jars through their thin plastic caul. With her other hand, she patted the top of the bolt almost affectionately. Whereas her very recent experience underground had served to assure her that for every ambitious proposal there exists a specific catalyst, this foe here possessed one very recalcitrant trait—it was not organic.

Harriet had fit herself in the nick of time down inside the cool, dripping drainage bed beneath the washroom—a large shower stall for rinsing containers and instruments, for the thorough disposal of materials. Although it was she who'd stared all her life into drains, it took the red runt to show her this most helpful version. "I stayed in here one time," he said, "when Mr. G. got really mad at me." She had knelt and lifted a grille twice the diameter of a dinner plate, exposing not only no cross but no vertical pipe either—only this concrete bed, or catch basin, circular, cramped, with many holes running around its base. Foul odors plumed out, rare enzymes from Garvey's extensive collection, and the decayed results of failed or short-lived organic creations. She'd replaced the grille, even amusing herself by overdoing it, wiggling her fingers through the slats dramatically till the last second, like Orson Wells's at the end of "The Third Man," when he's about to rise out of the Paris sewers, the difference being that here she was going *in*, and also that she—proudly melded with Rosalind and dear Henrietta Lacks—was The First Woman, like Eve if Eve had had, in addition to womb and naked mate, advanced training in biogeneration theory and practice.

"Jesus, Murphy, smells worse in here than my wife's snatch!"

"I know, but it beats that other room; fuckin' guy musta chopped up half the women in town, and . . . and *cleaned* 'em!"

"Glad he didn't get that blonde one, up top."

"Yeah, I'd take her on top!"

A walky-talky sparked to life, a man saying, "What the hell are these? Jenkins, are you seeing these, too?"

The speaker went dead for ten seconds, then came on again. "Oh, yeah, you can? Well, I've never been to those kind of stores, like you. But these things feel awful Goddamn real. They're moving. Get over here!"

You'll never ever find me. And at that, her men marched off toward their troubled colleague. And she'd laughed once, hysterically. It echoed around her, probably audible through unseen ducts. But they're after a man—a woman's laugh might not even register in their ears. Afterward, she'd saddened—damp, chilly, and forcibly hunchbacked, her knees up, havening the basin against her belly, the jars, too, in the free space she made for them. Every once in a while, she'd stretch against the curving musty walls as much as they would allow. The five jars rolled around, never still, clinking as she breathed, never finished finding themselves new spots. She could have stood them upright, except she found comfort in this stupid game of theirs, in the annoyance of it.

An hour passed, she'd guessed, and policemen still tromped up and down the halls, shouting and using their walky-talkys. Now and then, things crashed—the "haystack hunters"? She heard the elevator machinery rumbling, muffled and far. Once, she edged the grille aside and poked her head out, but just then a flashlight beam cut across the doorway. "Close one, Pepper," she whispered, back down.

After maybe two hours, most men had quit the premises, but not all. She stood the jars upright and tried to sleep.

When she woke, it was quiet. *TOO quiet, as they say.* She envisioned officers stationed everywhere—"The Shhh Squad"—in wait for this man Trapuka to emerge from hiding, but she was in too much pain to care.

With jars and basin, Harriet had walked like an extremely old lady along the hall and into Garvey's office, where torn notebook pages and dirt from the potted geranium covered the floor. And where is the sexy marigold itself? Taken in for analysis? She saw glass from the shattered brandy snifter, and she feared to check the inner lab; when she did, she flashed onto her long-ago tape recorder hitting the basement floor, how it seemed to explode. She saw Dougy's sneaker heel crushing her cassette.

The room was a spectacular ruin. *What were they searching for? Their own needle in a haystack . . . but with pitchforks!*

Harriet didn't even catalogue the casualties singly; her brain refused to dwell on meaningless hardware, carcasses of the most sophisticated recombinant DNA technology in the world. Machines capable of synthesizing life itself now lay strewn about in pieces.

She focused only on what didn't fit even with this chaos, trying for some relief. Squinting, with finger onto eye, she located cigarette butts; candy wrappers; three empty plastic bags (to seal evidence?); the peeled husks of Polaroid snapshots, curled here and there; and then her eyes had fallen on the pry bar, oddly cute among the rubble.

Harriet reached the bar high over her head, now, and swung it down with all her might, missed the bolt and clanged hard against the silver metal.

For the first time, she sat up, dizzy, holding her breath; she imagined her mistake ringing throughout the neighborhood, into people's bedrooms, buzzing on their eardrums. She strained to see down over the side of the tank to the streets and sidewalks below, the nearest of which were occluded—packed with early walkers, frozen in place, heads cocked? She'd be invisible, too, of course, but they'd suppose her instinctively; and they'd spy a raptor, point as one at its black shape, wheeling directly above, and then somebody would know the right whistle to use to draw him down upon her. Or else they'd call the cops.

Harriet quickly sprawled down again, embracing the tank.

She'd eaten nothing for maybe twenty hours, since sparing that snowy owl, since twisting the master keys violently off of the runt's belt.

Back to work on the huge bolt, vowing prudence, she held the bar firmly in her left hand, attempting once more to insert its sharp blade where it belonged, pressing the heel of her right hand against its flared butt end.

A sharp, distant clang of metal from somewhere in the neighborhood brought him awake, and Zingman found he was hard, as though the clang had woken *that* up first. He kissed Pepper carefully, and she laughed—"sh-sh-sh"—then reconsidered and kissed him back. Then they were hugging, too, and before a quick advance in attitude, it flitted through Zingman's mind that he was still only acting the guide, conducting this woman out of her shaded wandering, even solacing a sickly creature, because she seemed supremely in her element now.

But who was rescuing whom? Pepper unzipped his down coat, helped him off it and with his t-shirt; the spots she kissed on his chest were precise, as though pre-selected. The flannel sheet had slipped to the floor, but he wasn't cold. Then, she unzipped more and took him, just like that, in her hand, and helped him, resumed kissing his lips. Zingman wasn't able to free himself into the moment—"IT"—and peeked to check that her eyes were still closed; otherwise, he'd have had to put a stop to all this, because even he couldn't look at his penis. It made him remarkably sad, suddenly, this allowing himself to be exposed and held by a stranger, at any moment to be seen; but, trying to remember how to be a man, or at least a sport, he began to touch her breast, remote through cable-knit sweater.

Andy is sleeping calmly in bed, on her back, when Zingman sneaks up and leans, lowers his ear to her chest, hoping to be purified by the heartbeat, to catch a frank core of what he's loved, and to dash this elaborate paranoia about distance. Instead, he sinks into embarrassment at the heart's naked go. It has the thoughtless honesty of a thing at hard work. He pulls his ear away and then replaces it, keeps listening, not because he knows, already, that in three days she will be gone, but only in order not to be cowardly; he's waiting for his embarrassment to fade like a tricky mood. Yet the muscle slugs away at the ridges of his cartilage, his eavesdropping seeming to brighten, to fill his mind with the garish picture of the bare gray cluster in the intimacy and optimism of its campaign. If Andy were to wake up right this moment and see his face, she'd say nothing; all she's ever accused him of, all that she's lately chanced to forgive, would be written there.

Kindly Pepper was still laboring on his behalf, and Zingman's heart pounded proudly, also much too honestly, in a new breeze from outdoors. Some pages of *The Cost of Terror* riffled from their pile on the desk, skittered across the floor.

Mr. Ruthbar moaned in the other room, just once, loudly, like a warning. Or like another kind of warning, much too late—you never deserved her, living.

PUFF! PUFF!

PUFF!

At first, Zingman thought: Fog must have rolled in from outside. But then, he fumbled to cover Pepper's eyes with his hand because it was he himself who—like a bag of flour with a pinhole on top, set down firmly on a counter—sent forth a powdery cloud, faintly blue, high toward the ceiling, where . . .

Puff. puff, puffuf

. . . some remained floating, circling in the wind, the rest drifting gently back upon them. It was like a cloud of ash.

Zingman held his breath, grabbed the sheet from the floor to hide himself.

Pepper sat up straight, blinking within the cloud. "Yeah," she said, standing, hurrying out of range. "Yeah, just my luck."

When the front door slammed, more fright carried from the bedroom; and from nowhere, flies leapt into the hanging fallout, seemed to dance in it wildly, as though they'd been awaiting only this.

"'Chuh doing up there, Corrigan? You lose something?"

Harriet recognized the voice, far off somewhere, but it took some time, awkwardly periscoping, to spot its source. From this distance, Pepper looked no larger than her laboratory counterpart, except that she owned a head (shading her eyes) and she did not crawl (standing near a curb, astride a bicycle, which leaned between her legs). She wore shorts and a summery peach top, down through whose scooped neck Harriet could pick out the birthmark; somehow, she was more surprised about this than about seeing the woman at all.

"Steady there, don't fall off!" Pepper's hands were cupped around her mouth; she squinted. "But for God's sake, get down from that thing. I knew you were a little eccentric, Corrigan, but I need a regular friend right now . . ."

"'Harriet.' Take—"

"What?"

Harriet yelled, "It'll take me a couple minutes!"

At the foot of the bottom ladder, Pepper was holding the basin by one corner, letting the last of the gel drip onto the grass. "What's this?" She put her hand on her stomach and made a face, her skin flushed from riding.

"Oh. It's just some—You know, I was—It's empty because . . ."

"Please, don't tell me." Pepper dropped it and shook her hand out like a rag. "Believe me, I've given up on curiosity cold turkey. Don't even care what *those* are." She pointed to the bag of jars swinging from Harriet's belt loop. "And plus, it smells a little like Jack." She turned and righted her bicycle. "I've been pedalling since about dawn, trying to beat the woozies. Long shower didn't work, I needed to sweat. Seems like you need something yourself, badly."

"Yeah, I was up late, working."

"Guess we've all got our favorite coping strategies. Mine are running out. Listen, I know your car's . . . unavailable still, back at the lot, so here. Climb aboard, my apartment's not too far." She held the bike steady, patted the seat. When Harriet hesitated, she gave her a playful shove on the shoulder; the bag of jars tinkled, sounding like assent. "I used to be good at this, when I was twelve!"

"Ten whole years ago?"

"You flatter me, don't you, sunflower? Now I've got to warn you," Pepper said, helping Harriet aboard, "my place's a mess, but you obviously need an emergency nap." Harriet looked into Pepper's eyes, noticed their red rims, adjusted herself on the too-small seat. "Tell me later about your project, if I'm up to it?"

Harriet nodded. "Or else I'll show you."

"Fair enough," said Pepper, then slid sideways over the slanting bar, pushed forward on the handlebars, stepping forward, too, Harriet lifting her feet so they wouldn't drag, until the burdened bike wobbled through the grass and onto the sidewalk. Pepper leapt on the pedals with her fancy teal sneakers, and plunged them. The jars strongly agreed with the entire turn of events, though Harriet was suspicious, somehow. She glanced over her shoulder and waved goodbye to the victorious tower and its dubious reward, the pry bar. At the first intersection, Pepper took the mini ramp off the sidewalk and accelerated to street speed; Harriet grabbed hold of the seat and felt her face bend into an inane grin.

"'Sa snap, Corrigan, like it was just yesterday." The wind yanked the voice away. Pepper's back and shoulders bobbed up and down an inch from Harriet's front; sometimes they brushed against her, especially if Harriet leaned forward slightly. Blurrily, she stared through blonde to sense dark roots, sure enough. She also perceived sweat glistening on the back of the neck, sniffed at it, instituted a program of inhaling through nose, exhaling through mouth onto neck, onto tiny hairs she could only, poor eyes unaided, imagine.

"I'm dying of thirst! Oh, get this, I heard on the radio some know-nothing claims to have put anthrax into our water supply."

"Yeah?"

"Even though we know it only comes in the form of airborne spores."

"The idiot." They laughed, and when Pepper dodged through traffic, Harriet had no choice but to be thrown to the pavement under the wheels of a sport utility vehicle, or else to steady herself by clutching onto Pepper's rib cage, both sides. This time it was whole, and breathing; but as in the Showroom, it seemed on display, though functioning, going home.

Pepper's apartment was stacked with books and cardboard boxes; colorful clothing lay strewn on the living room floor—truly chaotic, not at all the sort of orderly "mess" people usually mean when they warn you.

"I just moved in two weeks ago, Corrigan, please don't judge. Okay, three. But I've been out almost every night, with the boys, or with Jack. Guess now I'll have time to get a handle on things. Sorry, more black humor. Water!"

At the sink, Pepper filled and downed a large glass, filled it again. "Mmmmm, anthrax in the morning."

"You've got a message." Harriet pointed to the machine on the counter.

Pepper drank some, pressed the glass to her forehead. "That'll be Butterfield, he's been checking in nonstop, telling me not to sleep with my concussion, wants to come over and observe me."

She drained the rest of the water—pale throat gulping, Harriet squinting at it—and refilled the glass, handed it over.

Harriet drank while Pepper swept several glossy issues of "Nucleus" off a chair, offering it.

"I think I'm too tired to sit, but may I. . . ?" She poised her index finger over the answering machine.

"Be my guest."

"I want to hear how the other half lives." And to know the enemy at his weaker moment.

Pepper's recorded voice jumped out: "Receptor site activated, begin transfer of protein code immediately."

"Cute."

"Guilty."

"Pepper? Hi, it's Ross. Zing—Oh, it's me. Um, listen, I feel . . . uh, pretty, well, really mortified, actually. That's never happened to me before . . ."

Harriet glanced at Pepper, who shrugged, held up her hand, signaling goose-egg. "'Ut can I tell ya? I'm just an overwhelming specimen! They tend to go up in smoke."

"Anyway, so I've got kind of a strange invitation, to help us put the . . . past behind us. I'm going on a hike with some friends, if you're up for an advent—Down into this valley, Skoonlet, it's called Skoonlet Valley Nature Preserve. Was hoping I might catch you, I can't stand to leave it like that, and thought—All right, if you get this message before six-thirty, or say seven, I'll be at the Townsend Street Diner with my friend who was in the other room, getting some food into him. I'll wait for you there." "Big fat chance," Pepper laughed, not the "sh-sh-sh" but a new, shriller sound. "Too late now, anyway. Hey, where are my manners? Of course you're too tired to sit down, that's why you're here—it's a damn tautology, n'est pas?" Harriet nodded, suddenly sick with nerves both because of the phone message—*a different league is a different league, not mine*—and because of this re-emphasized narrowness of the visit; *I'm here only because I possess a valid exhaustion.* "Now quit stalling and get unconscious!"

Pepper showed her into the bedroom, insisted she wouldn't need the bed herself, had errands to run, people to call, no, not that hiker, friends from California. "And I've got a memorial service to help plan."

"I can help, too."

"I'll accept . . . I can take those, if you'd like."

"Nice try," said Harriet, freeing the bag and stashing it beneath a pillow. "Top secret!"

In the adjoining bathroom, Harriet held herself upright and awake just long enough to poke through the advanced beauty products on the shelves, a foreign realm, though reminiscent of her mother's. Applying pressure once again to her right eyeball, she could read the large print, such as "Melinda Jean—Blonde Tone #7" on an oddly ugly brown tube. She enjoyed recognizing the French word "lilas" on a slender blue-frosted bottle of perfume; after removing its silver cap, nearly weightless, with her index finger on top of the delicate plunger, she depressed twice—tap, tap—so that two clouds emerged. She stepped through them, as her mother had shown her once. When she located the "Oil of Olay," she broke out laughing. "You didn't moisturize," the angry red runt had said, after knocking her to the floor. "Guess I better show you."

"All right in there?" said Pepper, knocking softly.

"Morning, Doctor," said Mr. Griffith, blocking the sun, hands full of gray-green forage. "Or should I say, Dan'l Boon!"

"Ha. Just when I thought you'd left me to fend for myself," Trapuka said, sitting up.

"Oh, not to worry about that." He deposited the harvest on the moss, where Trapuka's head had made an impression. "You can start in. I'll be right back with more."

He turned and stepped away, bombing Trapuka with too much light. "Well, not so fast, could you? I mean, if you'd sit down first, Mr. Griffith. Please. I've got a huge favor to ask of you."

"Nope," said Monica, pouring coffee. "Order of the city, no water today, till we get the All Clear. This we brewed up last night, and it tastes it."

"What's the problem?" said Zingman, wishing he could scratch his body, ugly and itching with the dusty substance. He hadn't had time to wash, with Mr. Ruthbar in crisis.

"They say anthrax."

"Boy, hey." Before this morning, he'd have been only too pleased to tie this scare into the South American Plague. Now, though, he was horrified most literally by what had occurred on the couch, his storytelling brain frozen up again, his heart even skipping beats.

"Whatsa matter with your friend? Can he move?"

"Just needs a good breakfast, I'm pretty sure, Monica." The man was ghostly and still, eyes locked open, one fist on either side of his plate. "Had a traumatic day, yesterday."

"Hmmmm. Did he drink some of the bad water? Is he . . . breathing?" She bent down. "Are ya?"

"Yeah, but to keep breathing he says he has to concentrate hard."

"He's not breathing on me, then," said the waitress, backing up, laughing. "I'll put a rush on this." She flashed her green pad, turned and marched toward the kitchen.

Zingman swallowed half his coffee, then resumed scratching, sneakily, frantically—torso and arms and neck and head. Before he could run to the shower, Mr. Ruthbar had stumbled from the bedroom complaining that "My heart kept stopping all night, all night. Had to make it start." It being too early to visit Tenzer for more pills, they'd defaulted to the breakfast cure. Zingman had stalled—"Nothing like pancakes and eggs to put you back together, I always say"—while fighting into his clothes underneath the flannel sheet. And then he hurried his friend into socks, shoes, pants, and lent him a fresh shirt, drew it gingerly over the long fresh-dried scabs.

"Remember the last time we ate here? Lunch?" he said now, still scratching, getting not a flicker of response. "We were in this same booth, and I sat you over here with me and showed you how to look at that mirror up there." Nothing.

The round portal still featured the sidewalk bench, outside.

It was empty—on the sidewalk in front of it, a dark stain.

"And remember, you told me a dream you had where my wife Andy was a raccoon?"

Mr. Ruthbar nodded briskly for a moment, his eyes pointing at Zingman's lips, then returning to space. Zingman was able to take one normal breath. Yesterday at the hour, he'd saved himself, barely, from a fate of stone, and now this man was petrifying on the same seat.

"And you remember we just couldn't figure that one out, could we? Till it hit me, the last time you saw her she had dark circles under her—oooo." Zingman's heart faltered, seemed to quit and, for no good reason, to start up again. The next time, he gasped and experienced a dreadful rush of cold nonexistence into his chest, as though he'd never deserved to exist in the first place; but all he could do was touch his sternum lightly with his eight fingertips.

Mr. Ruthbar focused on him, telling him silently to concentrate, so Zingman envisioned the feeble bulb of muscle, asked it to remember itself. Of course, he'd had palpitations before, but those had felt like a brief regrouping, whereas now it had lost its authority.

Mr. Ruthbar had stopped looking at him again, had returned to his own survival, breathing in quick bursts, eyes closed.

"Well," said Zingman, "maybe this coffee is even worse than she said. It's after seven and we're supposed to meet at Tenzer's house. We can get him to listen to our hearts."

He stood and pulled on Mr. Ruthbar's upper arm.

"Zingman, you're always cutting out on me lately!"

"I'm sorry, Monica. Could you maybe wrap those up? Here's the money."

"So what do I tell him?"

"William Stennhouse III," said the reporter, long-stepping from the back of the diner. "I write 'The Off Beat'. I hope you are recovered from yesterday, sir, my readers have expressed concern. Would you mind if I did some follow-up?"

This time, Zingman came closer to shaking the man's hand than at the zoo, but at the last second reached for Mr. Ruthbar's instead, both sizes, yanked him to his feet, and fled. Monica caught them at the door with two Styrofoam containers.

"Common arrhythmia, it sounds like," said Tenzer, ninety minutes later. "Usually nothing, Ross."

"But why, and why *both* of us?" They were negotiating a particularly tricky section of trail, steeply descending into Skoonlet Valley along a classically sun-dappled pathway. Gilbeau, Mezzanotte, and Reese were leading the way. Matthew Glennon straggled, as though he'd changed his mind, and Stanley Keillor kept him company. "I mean, why does he say he has to concentrate so hard?" Mr. Ruthbar had stumbled between them the whole way, like a blank-eyed zombie, his shoes woefully inapt, occasionally tripping on a root and needing to be steadied, or else stopping to lean against a tree, little hand on trunk, cocking his head as if listening intently, eyes screwed shut, dutifully giving himself to the new job of perpetuating his life. "And I know what he means now. Three times already today I've had the same sensations myself."

The trail flattened out. They had reached the edge of the Valley floor. Soon, Zingman expected, they'd emerge gloriously from chilly shade; the fancy dappling effect had ceased, the sun having set behind the ridge. "All right. So, you're saying it feels as if . . ."

"Like I'm suddenly placed in charge of vital operations."

"Uh huh. Well, most likely it just seems that way, you know. There are lots of illusions when something organic but minor gets spiralled by the mind. But of course, on the other hand, it makes me think of the autonomic nervous system."

"The what?"

"Those functions of the central nervous system that run autonomously, primarily heartbeat and respiration. Though our breathing can switch back and forth, voluntary, involuntary. Did the two of you ingest anything together?"

"Just the brownies. He brought these wretched brownies last night. I think he'd eaten some before."

"Right, that could be helpful. We might be able to—"

"Except I kind of finished them off."

"Ah, hmmm. Well, it sounds like an allergic reaction, not acute, after this long, but exacerbated by anxiety. I've brought these tranquilizers, just say the word."

Zingman had been debating for more than a mile whether to inform the doctor about the episode on the sofa. If his symptoms got any worse, he decided, he'd certainly have no choice. The coating beneath his clothes had stopped itching, dampened by sweat; but the idea of it, lying pasty and quiet all over his skin, began to bother him a lot.

Finally, pine trees thinned and sunshine re-entered the world. Up ahead, Simon Reese, Gilbeau and Mezzanotte were sitting on rocks, passing around a gallon jug of water. Stanley Keillor swatted flies with Jessie's riding crop.

"Look at what I found," said Simon Reese as Zingman pulled up, with Mr. Ruthbar. He held in his fingers a long bulky grasshopper. "Poor guy shouldn't've lasted past summer, but this weird weather . . ." The insect seemed to have been charred by longevity—terribly crisp and brown all over, the tips of its folded wings blackened, as were two blunt horns at the top of its head; the tail, sticking out beyond the wingtips, was bloated, starting to burst at the seams, curling. At the other end, the mouth spat out a ball of ooze, like oil, which slid down Reese's thumbnail to his cuticle. He threw the grasshopper up high, but it didn't deploy its wings until too late, and then they only scraped at the air.

It bounced in the dirt, then came to rest on its back.

"That's exactly how I feel most of the time," said Tenzer, pushing the straps off his shoulders, lowering his backpack to the ground. "Like I've lived too long, outstayed my welcome."

"Put her there," said Zingman, shaking Tenzer's hand, making the man laugh and feeling good about it. The others laughed, too, except Mr. Ruthbar, who had taken up another listening post nearby, bent at the waist, hand against a tree trunk.

"But right now, this cadaver's famished," Zingman said, pointing to the backpack. Tenzer unzipped it and withdrew the Styrofoam containers from the diner. "Thanks, Patrick, and for carrying them."

"Certainly. How's your nervous system right now?"

"Nothing some coagulated sausage won't cure." But before he could find a rock of his own and get settled, could consider how to persuade the patient to take some nourishment, a sound arose off to his left, ahead. "Stanley?" A large something was dragging itself along stones and roots. Just then, Keillor and Matthew Glennon arrived at the rear, short of breath. The dragging sound kept building until Zingman could make out through ferns and tree trunks a sort of wrinkled yellow presence, low to the ground, sliding forward, forward, like a giant's rain coat.

"Can't leave me alone, huh?"

"Oliver Griffith?" The man had stepped out from behind a fat tree and now stood in the middle of the path, a rope in his hand, face shining, dripping, black turtleneck drenched.

"Funny thing, Professor, I couldn't seem to locate my car in the parking lot, which has made my task more difficult."

"I'm . . . we couldn't find you, so I've been taking care of your car. What're you doing here, and what's that?"

"None of your business, sir, I'm afraid. Let's just say it's a mission of mercy, and leave it at that. I'll have my keys now."

Zingman threw them. Oliver caught them and stuffed them into his pants pocket, resumed hauling his load, leaning against the weight. "And don't follow me! You've done enough to hold me back already. I've finally found a true teacher, and friend." The giant's rain coat—rubberized, canary yellow, mud-smeared, voluminous—crossed in its own direction, perpendicular to the pathway.

"Don't you even want to know where it's parked?"

"I want nothing more from you!"

The rain coat vanished, and its rasp eventually faded.

"Students," Zingman said, appealing to his friends, who were nonplussed. "They'll break your heart."

Half an hour later, the Cobhouse party reached an impasse at the edge of a dense marsh that smelled heavily spoiled; floating patches of algae looked like illness; a few skeletal trees poked high out of the sullen waters. Zingman said, "We've wandered straight into a Gothic novel, friends! What can we expect now?"

"Hounds?" said Mezzanotte.

"Ummm, lightning?" Gilbeau added.

"And you're probably looking for 'The Walking Dead,'" proffered Mezzanotte.

"Especially if they mingle with the flesh of the living."

"Red glowing eyes, yes?" said Tenzer.

"Fog, don't forget," Reese laughed, "some thick fog."

"I'd settle for a Port-O-Potty," said Matthew Glennon, all shaky.

Everybody laughed, except for Mr. Ruthbar. While they moved off in search of a lunch site, Zingman stayed behind and watched the man, bent, hands on thighs, seeming pained at the sight of a harmless brown hawk that sat in the sunlight at the top of one of the dead trees. Zingman recognized in himself a pang of impatience at the delay, even aggravation, but the pang burst into another event in his chest, doubling him over and focusing his mind with a silent shout, "Think! Think!" As soon as he was able, he shuffled over to Mr. Ruthbar and laid his hands on his shoulders, and together they breathed and tried to think their hearts into tune, tried to be geniuses.

They succeeded, and the hawk flew away.

"I saved you some breakfast."

"Good, Mr. Z."

Reese located a sort of beachhead, grassy with lots of light, where the marsh had changed into a broad, healthier pond. The Cobhouse broke out their thermoses and their sandwiches. They were quiet, enjoying the late morning air. They had brought the same objects as last night. Keillor pressed the riding crop back into service, to keep the flying bugs away from his tuna and swiss grinder. Reese removed Theresa's straw hat from his head and hung it at a funny angle on a bush, stood the cobalt bottle tall on a rock, shining as though lit from within; he bit into an apple. Matthew Glennon spread Sheila's terry bathrobe out on some pine needles to warm, checking first to make sure there was no dirt or dew.

Zingman carefully scanned the pondside for birds of prey, told Mr. Ruthbar, "Coast is clear," led him to a private shady spot down by the sparkly water. He put his own breakfast down and opened the other container, cut the short stack of pancakes into pieces with a plastic fork kindly tucked in by Monica. Mr. Ruthbar took the fork and began to eat.

The itching was back, with a vengeance. While looking along the muddy bank for a place to wade in, Zingman came across Patrick Tenzer, like a hiding forest spirit behind a tree. But unlike a forest spirit, the man had just peed.

When he emerged, shards of shadow and shards of sun vied for dominance of his face.

"Matty got up with me today, Ross, before dawn, and we had peanut butter toast. Our daughter."

"I know who she is, Patrick."

"I know you do. She usually sleeps till noon on weekends. But then, we always stay home together on weekends. I'm there whenever she pries herself out of bed. I'd told her I was leaving at six-thirty, so this morning, she was already in the kitchen when I came downstairs, in her huge puffy slippers. We didn't talk, just made the toast, had orange juice, and sat down at the table. Finally, she looked over and said, 'It still surprises me.'"

But Zingman didn't feel up to grief talk right at the moment. He knew he should sit down with Tenzer. "Just a sec, Patrick. I'm sorry." He tore off his shirt, shoes and socks and charged into the pond, sinking past the ankles in cold mud. When the water slipped up over his waist, he knelt in and paddled deeper, immersed himself head and all. Then thrashed.

Stretched out inside the grounded rubber launch, head resting upon its soft bow, Trapuka finally had the chance to tease apart the elements of his discomfort. He was extremely light-headed, and his lips were in great pain. Also, perspiration had gotten underneath the Band-Aids on his scalp, stinging each of the many nicks. He reached up and tore the crossed strips off, one by one. Mr. Griffith, lying beside him, made too much of this. "Oooo, ouch. How about if I do that for you? That way, you won't know exactly when it's coming."

"No, thank you, Mr. Griffith."

He'd never before inflated the launch without the electric pump, and for the past three hours he and this massive, highly motivated assistant had been at work almost without a break, taking turns breathing into the valve stem. At last, now, the little vessel had attained its proper shape but was still slack, far from seaworthy.

A peculiar thing had occurred earlier. Mr. Griffith abruptly discontinued the procedure, but instead of relinquishing the stem he'd placed his thumb over it. Then, the man had leaned against the partially inflated side tube and lifted his thumb, causing a major breach and laughing about it. He'd prevented Trapuka from intervening, and moreover, had demanded a kiss. When Trapuka shouted, "Yes!", the small black plastic stopper went into the valve. On hands and knees, smiling, Mr. Griffith had crawled very close.

Trapuka shut his eyes and reminded himself that Jacques Cousteau had lost a son, Philippe, to the arctic ocean; Pavel Sucek, three brides to the unendurable tedium of life in Fretil Province, Sumatra, where the alabaster hornspinner performed her confounding slow-motion dances. A fourth wife, Olena, possessed the necessary patience, but had stepped on a poisonous toad and succumbed within hours.

When the man's breath, heavy with fungus, fell on Trapuka's face and his lips bore in, Trapuka had experienced once again, as on the Grand Manan III, the delicate webwork of muscles around his right eye, twitching, and had brought to mind further instances of zoological sacrifice, by Armando LaPolombara, for instance, in pursuit of his cave-dwelling apes. Before too long, the kiss was over with and Mr. Griffith was snickering. "My Dear Lord, I don't recommend you set up any kissing booths anytime soon!"

"It's only . . . my lips are extremely sore, from our work."

"Yeah."

That was an hour ago. Now the man was sitting up straight in the floor of the launch, gazing down at Trapuka, at his scalp and the few remaining Band-Aids, with a pitying expression. "I mean, I always prefer someone else to yank them off, always. I don't know, I guess I'm kind of a baby in that way. I close my eyes and tell 'em not to count one-two-three or anything but just to surprise me. You know? Yup, sure did a number on yourself there. I'll have to teach you the fine art of shaving your head. There is an art to it, contrary to popular opinion." He pulled his turtleneck off over his head, revealing a torso whiter than any fish's belly, and stretched mightily, yawning. Trapuka sat up, wanting to stretch as well but refraining. He explained to himself that, after all, homosexuality was not, in a significant sense, at odds with nature. It had been long demonstrated that in any given population of organisms, at least ten percent simply do not participate in the breeding process, sometimes for no discernable reason; and while they may not engage in sexual behavior with members of their own gender, whatever else they do amounts to the same, with regard to species perpetuation.

"Don't think too much, there, Doctor," said Mr. Griffith, snapping his fingers in Trapuka's face, at a respectful distance. "You're liable to fall asleep. I know it's nearly November, and this stagnant pond's a little disgusting, but I'm feeling like a dip. Are you? It's either that or a nap, I'm afraid, before we finish blowing this boy up . . ." He stood. "Oh, forgot. Here you go, as per request." He removed Trapuka's miniature tape recorder from his front pocket, handed it down. Then he stepped out of the launch, began to unbuckle his belt. "So?"

"I'll stay here and keep at it, for now. But let me know how the water is."

"Suit yourself!" Mr. Griffith did not remove his underwear, for which Trapuka was grateful.

When he'd waded out waist-deep, Trapuka called, "Oh, by the way, Mr. Griffith? Sorry, but I wonder, did you see any sort of bulletin board with a map of this park, or . . ."

"In fact I did notice a sign pointing to a ranger station a couple miles that way," he said, attempting to clear algae with his hands, preparatory to plunging in. "They probably have maps there."

"We're less than ten kilometers from the harbor, and I'd just—"

"'Kilometers,' listen to you!"

"I'd like to get a look at how these streams go, where they join together. And I'd gladly go to the station myself, except as I explained, my ex-wife is on the warpath and . . ."

"Hey, no problemo. You hide out here. But you realize this will cost you." He beamed. "Two kisses this time, at least." He barely made a splash, backstroked to the center of the pond, cutting a swathe in the algae and gazing up at the blue sky.

A telephone blasted by Harriet's ear. She had no idea where she was or, really, who. All she knew was, there went the damn phone again, and she tried pushing her head under the pillow, but something blocked her way with more noise. Oh, jars in the bag—that's who. It was, judging by the window, mid-afternoon. In the next room, an answering machine kicked in. "Receptor site activated"—*and that's where*—"begin transfer of protein code immediately."

"Pepper, it's me again, me Ross. Thought I might catch you, uh, and just wanted to let you know the offer's still good because we're still in the Valley. Actually, right now I'm at a friend's house, getting blankets and things, but I'm going back. Standing here trying to convince his daughter here to come along . . ."—girl's laughter—". . . get outa the house on such a beautiful day. But anyway, we're leaving, so you'd have to find your way to the ranger station at the front entrance, right off Route 7. We sort of stumbled on it by finding an easier trail out than we took in. It's weird, we've just been poking around and taking naps, talking, I've been in swimming . . . the point is, some of us have decided to stay over, roast marshmallows, like that." The girl's voice behind him chimed, "'Sk her 'bout my sandals."

The front door unlocked and Harriet heard Pepper step into the apartment, stop to listen, a floorboard squeaking.

". . . so, I thought you might want to join us, just for the hell of it, you know? We've located our site on the map—it's just called "Pond #10"—and the trail's pretty well-marked, 'bout a twenty-, twenty-five-minute hike in there. We've got plenty of blankets, and there's no call for rain. But it'll be dark in a couple hours, so this is all probably pointless, unless you get home soon and. . . . Or you could come for breakfast tomorrow! You're not back to work already, I hope. My friend Simon is bringing skillets and eggs and bacon and those packets of freeze-dried oatmeal left over from . . . his wife used to camp a lot. I'll let you go, well, I mean—you know. I was sort of . . . thinking there might be a message from you . . . but you're probably in no shape, not even counting what happened this morning. Maybe I've got some kind of . . . I'll get checked. Hey, I haven't even asked how you're feeling today. For myself, I'm feeling like a jerk! Well, maybe you'll forgive me, and maybe I'll see you. Bye."

Pepper resumed stepping across the floor, put something down on a table—*a grocery bag, from how it crinkles*—and then Harriet heard her approach the bedroom door and turn the knob. "You awake?" she whispered through the crack.

"Come in, yes."

Pepper stood by the bed. "Did you catch all that?"

"It droned on forever before you got here." Pepper laughed but her face looked drawn in the slanting window light. Harriet sat up, patted the side of the bed, and Pepper smiled, noticing who had borrowed one of her t-shirts. She drew in a deep breath that hitched in the middle. "Oh, Harriet, I've been—"

"Poor darling, sit." Harriet patted the bed again, this time with results.

"I'm having terrible flashbacks. That man put two spears into him, and Jack died right there in the cafeteria. I remember the whole thing, even though I was apparently out cold.

"At the company, this afternoon, I met his sister Catherine. I never knew he had a sister, much less here in town. His parents are flying in today. There's a funeral scheduled for Tuesday, day after tomorrow. On Halloween, Harriet, isn't that strange?"

Harriet held out her arms, but Pepper kept talking. "We were going to go to this company party. You?" Harriet shook her head and gave a little laugh. "Well, Jack insisted, wanted us to be completely incognito, dress up as praying mantises. Manti? Don't ask me; his idea."

Harriet re-offered her arms, emphatically, and Pepper fell between them, crying.

"I ran away from him, that much I'm sure of. I didn't even try to see if—"

"No, Pepper, there wasn't anything to be done." With her right hand, she smoothed and smoothed the peach fabric between the shoulder blades. She felt along the spinal column, casually. "It was all over by the time you came to."

Pepper lifted her head. "Are you sure?" She pierced Harriet's eyes, the liquid standing on Pepper's seeming somehow to enhance their focus like the softest lenses.

"Yes, I swear."

Pepper laid her head back down under Harriet's chin for a moment, and she held onto this head with her right hand, pressing the base of her neck, saying "Darling" again, worrying that once had been enough. No trace of "lilas" scent remained. With her left hand, she palmed the area on top where the butt of the spear gun had struck, then moved that arm down, to join the hug. Pepper snuffled once sharply and sat up straight, shuddered as though her brief collapse had been a spoof, and cleared the tears aside with the sides of her index fingers. She squeezed Harriet's elbow thanks, wetting it, and sighed the sort of sigh that declares control regained.

"Listen," she said. "I didn't want to tell you this before, you were so tired. But the police . . ."

"I figured. Where . . ."

"They interviewed me yesterday at the company, and some more today. I told them of course that I hadn't seen hide nor hair of you, and that you were an innocent bystander, but some of our co-workers have jumped to ridiculous conclusions . . ."

"I was only trying to appear to cooperate in order to minimize—"

"That's exactly what I said. Anyway, they'd like you to help them, well, y'know, identify the murderer. I can't believe I'm saying these words."

"They don't have enough witnesses?"

"They're thinking he may have said things to you that could—"

"He didn't, no. I wish he had. I can't go into custody, I have too much to do."

"I wouldn't try going home, then. I cruised by there on my bike—personnel coughed up the address; Bob Leverett's a pushover for these eyes—but naturally the cops've got your building slammed. Then I just rode around, thinking you might be wandering. I knew you didn't have your car, it's still in the lot. And by the way, I wheedled this from one of the cops—they took a t-shirt out of your backseat and let their dogs sniff it. Creepy stuff, I know. Nobody I asked at the company seemed to know who your friends around here were, are, so . . . And then, after an hour or more I suddenly hear this banging, and I look up. As they say, imagine my surprise!"

"Mine too!"

Pepper's eyes had refilled, and Harriet reached to assist; no tears fell out, though, so she was left feeling embarrassed. "Aw, shit, Harriet!" Pepper saved the day by grabbing Harriet's hands out of the air, pumping them up and down like a playground friend's. "What a couple of days, huh? C'mon, get up, I went shopping. I'm cooking us my famous stuffed eggplant. And while I do, we will not talk about Friday night. And you, young lady, will go ahead and explain to me what exactly . . ."—she let go one of her hands, plunged it under the pillow—"what these are for." She stood and danced the plastic bag of jars about, backing out of the room, luring Harriet from the bed, making her grab for her pants, draped over the headboard. "Or else, no wine. Plus," she said, wagging a finger, slipping from the room, "I'll have to sic the police on ya!"

"Pepper?" Harriet got decent, then slapped barefoot into the kitchen. Do you happen to have any . . . oh, boy."

"These? Yeah, well, I got a deal."

Eight potted marigolds sat along a shelf beneath the window. Pepper threw open the door to a back staircase, revealing bags of garbage collected at the top. She grabbed an armful of pots, five the first trip, three the second, and pitched them down the stairs, where they shattered. Shutting the door with contrasting delicacy, she turned back to Harriet, brushing her hands against one another. "There. Now what were you wondering?"

"Um, just if you had any bread tins. I seem to have been baking lately." She took a very deep breath. "Relaxes me."

Pepper stooped and slid open the large drawer beneath the oven, crashed through options with maximum volume and some glee. Harriet glanced on the counter, where today's city newspaper bore the headline:

NEW BRUNSWICKITE, PROTEGE
IDENTIFY KILLER, CITE MOTIVES

A color photograph showed a skinny young man, grinning, holding proudly before him with one hand a framed drawing of the same fish whose brain Harriet had held, whose chromosomes were now laced through her own in the five jars Pepper had plunked down on the kitchen table. Her stomach heaved a little, seeing the drawing. Get me—*it's like catching a spouse nude in a magazine.* Standing beside this young man, in the photo, was the bedraggled girl from the cafeteria, frowning and leaning subtly, as if trying to pull away from his arm, slung across her shoulders. The article was labeled "The Off Beat" and began, "What is being dubbed the marine bio murder swam a bit closer to authorities' nets late Saturday when two acquaintances of the alleged killer stepped forward, furnishing vital—"

"Hey!" Pepper ripped the paper away. "Now didn't I say no murder stuff?" She folded it tightly and slapped it back down on the counter, exposing part of another headline— Harriet's ploy imprinting itself upon the face of the world:

NTHRAX SCARE
ORCES SHUTDO
F DISTRICT F
RESERVOIR

But claimed by another:

alse alarm!
oss Zingman
trikes again
nother stunt
t public exp

"You're in luck, see?" Pepper waved three medium-sized tins. "And there's yeast or whatever around the corner at the store." She walked toward the brown bag on the opposite counter. "You planning to bribe the officers with fresh steaming loaves?"

"Only if they're single."

"Oh HO, listen to that. Well, you might be wearing my perfume . . ."—she winked over her shoulder, removing a jug of dark red wine and two shamefully smooth-skinned eggplants from the brown bag—"but I guess I'll be taking some lessons from you, too, sweets!"

The wink, the "sweets," the dinner plans, all gathered in the wrong place, at the center of her brain. The black cube emerged from wherever it hid, and Harriet steadied herself, hand on counter. But this time, the cube stopped growing early, because an invisible finger tapped it from above, three times—a suggestion. *Keep improvising, Harriet, off the top of your head. That's the way to get to the bottom of things.*

Primatologist Armando LaPolombara, his body racked with advanced arthritis, found himself required, during the last five years of his life in the 1970s, to resort to outlandish means in order to carry on his studies of the rare and reclusive cave-dwelling apes of Madagascar. His helpers would affix him with elastic restraints to a backboard, rendering him as flat as possible, to counter the curvature of his spine that was driving his face down into his chest. And then, they would bind into his blasted hands with leather thongs a sixteen-millimeter film camera and a strong sulfur lamp. LaPolombara would next direct himself to be lowered into the winding rock chimney, to a depth of fifteen hundred meters, by means of a system of pulleys and a winch.

Mr. Griffith had persuaded Trapuka to enter the pond with him, after much protestation. The two sat in the mud, surrounded by clinging algae, in water whose warmth made Trapuka queasy. Mr. Griffith was naked. Trapuka was fully clothed, but minnows poked at him, palpable even through the fabric of his shirt and pants. Mr. Griffith held Trapuka's hand tenderly, his head leaning heavy on Trapuka's shoulder. Trapuka had finally ceased agreeing to kiss the man, had consented to the pond instead, after Mr. Griffith brought back from the ranger station not only the invaluable map of the Preserve, but somehow a soda and a loaf of homemade bread as well. This coup, he'd felt, entitled him to some reward. "Get this," he'd told Trapuka. "The woman who gave it to me asked if I was currently involved with a woman. I said no!"

Somewhere beneath the thick algae, Mr. Griffith touched himself, but in no frenzy, not, in fact, even discourteously. "Don't think I'm a sex maniac, please, Doctor," he said. "It's just been so long since I've had an adventure, or . . . clicked with a guy, that's all."

"No, please, Mr. Griffith, don't give it a second thought. I can assure you that there is nothing unnatural to this. The animal kingdom, we included, show a startling variety. And men have sacrificed much in order to understand it."

Suspended within the apes' domain, where the humidity and the cold did his condition no good, LaPolombara would hang in absolute darkness, not lighting his lamp until he heard the unmistakable sounds of the apes finally shuffling about him, approaching warily through their side corridors. But they no longer recognized him in his current condition (sometimes he bumped against the walls of the chimney), and when he'd illuminate them, suddenly, they would only retreat, or stare.

Trapuka and his assistant had eaten the loaf of bread immediately, an hour ago, as the sun dipped behind the ridgetop. It tasted a little bit like dirt, but with a shared can of Orange Crush it was better than wood rot and marsh marigolds.

Mr. Griffith took his hand from Trapuka's and wrapped his arm around Trapuka's back, pulling him closer.

Years before the advent of his arthritis, LaPolombara had become a master spelunker; in order to gain access to the apes' home environment, he had simply followed them, down and in. When careless, at times, crowding them, or stumbling into brooding chambers he hadn't known of, he'd received severe bites on his face and hands and forearms, which remained as breathtaking scars until his death, in Verona, in 1976. For nine years, from 1955 to 1964, he sat hunched for days on end in dripping nooks and grottoes of rock, or partially submerged in ice cold lakes half a mile below the earth's surface, earning their trust merely by his friendly presence, his excruciating patience, a method later made famous by Jane Goodall, who, although she always denied the fact, had learned it direct from LaPolombara himself, her third lover.

Mr. Griffith produced a high repeated sound in his throat; his head rolled onto Trapuka's back and became even heavier than before. Trapuka noticed that the moon had recently risen over the ridgetop, though he wished it had not.

The apes gave off a pungent, mustard-like scent when they courted, and during copulation itself they appeared bashful. Careful as ever, of course, to guard against any facile anthropomorphism, LaPolombara was forced to conclude (during year ten, when he was first allowed to respectfully witness the act) that this interpretation uniquely fit the evidence. No growling took place, no violence or domination, as is characteristic of other primates' coupling; indeed, so far did these observed pairs differ from expectation that the naturalist found it impossible to convince the world at large that he was telling the truth, that the male and female would engage in intercourse without embracing, without emitting a sound. His movie camera would have ruined the encounters, too loud, its lights too bright. Thus, until he finally succeeded in persuading them to show themselves above ground, his story went uncredited, including the claim that the male and female would, during the act, *cover their faces,* a gesture all the more remarkable in view of the fact that these creatures so perfectly suited to subterranean life had developed their intimate habits eons ago in pitch blackness.

Trapuka asked if he might sleep alone tonight. Mr. Griffith, dressed again, offered him the one blanket with an awkward bow, and then helped to push him in the rubber launch, now fully inflated, out into the pond. Only then, lying hidden on the nylon floor, did Trapuka peel off his slimy clothing. He spread his shirt and pants out to dry, then floated, trying to calm himself. Now and then, his heart would race, and slip out of sync, which told him that perhaps his ears had registered at low level the baying of distant bloodhounds. Covered, shivering, Trapuka tried to focus his mind on the decisive morning to come. Twice, he called in a whisper for Mr. Griffith to stop his singing.

"Well, guys, I've decided to call it quits," said Matthew Glennon, poking bright orange logs around with the end of a charred stick. "I know I'll never find the place, but we're close enough." This brought an end to a mute, pensive period during which nobody was sure how to treat him. "The bachelor party started after dark, like this, and by the time I arrived most of the guys were drunk already, including my friend, Bruce Reardon. The groom hadn't gotten there yet. He was being led on the path, blindfolded."

Gilbeau and Mezzanotte reclined, heads on pillows, stomachs full, listening to the fire's crackle, and now and then a small, specific splash from somewhere out in the dark pond, and watching the rising moon, as though they owned these treasures, as indeed they did, in a sense—the spoils of their world-restoring crusade. They'd consolidated their gains by going home, earlier, and returning with supplies, including blankets and sleeping bags enough for eight, although only five were spending the night and the night they were spending was much too warm for all this bedding, much less a fire.

Zingman paced out the circle of light, again and again, because each time he tried to sit down and rest, he'd become intimately aware of his heart jarring loose from its moorings; he found he could concentrate better thanks to the rhythm of his steps.

Dinner had consisted of hot dogs turned on a spit (well, a coat hanger) and roasted corn donated by a contrite Patrick Tenzer, who'd stayed home with his daughter; Mathilda was not exactly the camping type. And it was a school night, after all, meaning that Simon Reese, too, was with his son, Anthony, the green thumb, although the boy had donated to the cause—Grievance swinging by to pick it up—his mildewed pup tent. This afternoon, while Matthew Glennon had wandered, alone by choice, in search of the bachelors' bonfire pit, and during the others' foray into civilization, Mr. Ruthbar had remained on-site, sitting cross-legged, manning the fort, manning his heartbeat. Zingman had given him two tranquilizers, doctor's orders, but timed it wrong, his friend conking out just two bites into his first hot dog. Now he breathed evenly, down inside the pup tent, where Zingman had tucked him.

"Bruce's got all these pretty disgusting buddies, and naturally I wasn't too happy to see them dancing around this ridiculous fire." Matthew Glennon had ceased adjusting the logs and now sat on the hard earth, declining the pillow offered by Gilbeau, eating another hot dog, on a bun but uncooked. "I was worried about the fire, that it would get out of control, but Bruce came up and slapped me on the back and put a huge drink in my hand in one of those massive plastic cups you get for filling up your car. I was still feeling angry with Sheila, so I gulped it half down and talked with Bruce about stupid shit. When I'd dropped her off at the airport she didn't even kiss me, just because I wouldn't promise not to go to the party. I said, 'What do you think's going to happen, Sheila? You know me a lot better than those guys know me, it's not like I'm cut from the same cloth, and it doesn't mean I agree . . . bla bla bla.' She slammed the car door and didn't need any help with her bags, so I just drove away. The bonfire was so outrageous, it really made you sweat. Pretty soon after I finished that first drink, the groom arrived and Bruce ripped the blindfold off him. And then the girls rushed on shore. I couldn't believe it—they'd been waiting out on the pond, in a boat!"

Occasionally, an ash lifted from the flames, slowing Zingman's step, disappearing over his head, and he recalled being young in his front yard, in summertime, and seeing such patches—wrinkly, whitening, crumbling at their edges—slide through the air beyond his reach, having travelled from the next neighborhood, or maybe the next after that, from some barrel fire, burning leaves, burning trash. In the right mood, he would chase it for a while down the street. Oh, they were *wily*, every time, turning a corner between houses, skimming slate shingles.

Thanks to these sportive ashes, he let himself begin to consider what had happened this morning. Probably, he'd have been inclined to calm himself by pronouncing the event clinching proof that his earlier story had pointed truly—that the South American hogs had indeed carried a plague to the zoo, which Pepper had contracted, and which she'd then expressed into Zingman during all their derring-do, or else passed modestly during their night of breathing together on the couch, scrambling his bloodstream, swiftly infesting his fluids with too much foreign matter—if only the resulting cloud didn't fit the thesis quite so snugly. Instead, he leaned away from that solid house of cards, his attention required elsewhere, by the trembling structure of historical fact.

The cloud was more distinctive than disease, it was moral fallout, a long time coming. Seven separate plunges into the pond today, even naked, hadn't washed him clean of what clung to his skin; fresh clothes lent by Tenzer didn't hide the truth. A rumbling heart made sure to remind him, and though he'd downed more than a liter of water, his mortification spoke up also in how it burned him to pee.

"I always had this kind of pet theory about bachelor parties, that the reason they, y'know, emphasize the *flesh* aspect so much, really stick it in your face, is just so guys can kind of get grossed out and see it's not the point, even though they'd never admit that. I actually tried explaining this theory to Sheila." The fire had died down, so Matthew Glennon was up and adding more wood from the stack he'd gathered in the afternoon. "Big mistake." He sat back down to watch the new logs catch. "The girls—there were three of them—pretended to be too shy to take off their robes, so the guys worked on the bonfire till it was roaring. I thought for sure we were going to start a forest fire, burn everything to a crisp."

Zingman flashed onto the desiccated grasshopper that Simon Reese had picked up at sunrise, obviously living far past its season, looking like a horror monster spitting its last liquid onto Reese's thumb. Andy had dried up in her August bed, stopped making vomit, making urine, making tears, and then sweat, till even her unbothered pump ran dry, because he couldn't listen to it without embarrassment, until she made only ashes to drift onto a field in Ohio. Odd, how drying and burning can begin with their opposites, a cold sweat.

It covers Andy as she emerges from a changing room at JCPenney, her face gone gray. (The mint-green sundress is soaked through, so even though she doesn't like it, they have to go ahead and buy it anyway.) "Ross, I'm not sure what's . . ." She sits down hard in a binful of multi-colored socks, which seems placed there kindly from time immemorial. Of course, he throws down the pair of false-leather gloves he's been sniffing at and rushes to her, helps her to sit more securely, though the edge of the bin bites into her thighs. Her brown bangs are pasted to her forehead, and she is looking not at him but almost, maybe at his ear, afraid, her cheeks luffing. "Don't overbreathe, okay, just concentrate." She holds onto him unusually, one hand pressed to his sternum, the other to his back, as though trying his shape in a new way, and remembering Andy's bottomless dark eyes, that day, more than two years later, Zingman will mark a similarity to Mr. Ruthbar's green ones, charged with duty, locked in, the sudden high duty of infinite inwardness. The same must go, Zingman will realize, for his own eyes.

"Okay, can we please have a little help here?" Zingman hears the panic in his own voice, and when a store clerk responds, he certainly feels glad for the practical support the boy is able to provide, but most of the relief comes from having someone else to talk to, other eyes to face.

Lest he forget any such thing, gloss over his complicity, at her deathbed, in Andy's becoming ashes—the enormous harm of his inexact, nictating presence—he now understands that he was obliged to stage, this dawn, his own horror scene, his dusty surprise, to frighten the woman on the couch, and drive her away.

"Underneath their robes, of course the girls were in these skimpy sequined bikinis, and I hardly looked. The groom was on top of the world, his name's Pete. Bruce brought me another drink, but he was too distracted and drunk to notice me pouring out most of it. I stood off to one side. The girls had brought a boom box, for some type of routine, but the guys wanted to go swimming first and waved hundred dollar bills in front of them and stripped down to their underpants. Two of the girls agreed, but one of them got mad and put her robe back on."

"Shit!" Mezzanotte whispered, "who's that? Shhh."

Maybe thirty feet off through the trees, twigs were snapping. The Cobhouse held its breath until Zingman heard a giggle, then Pepper's voice. "Yes, I think you're quite correct, Doctor Corrigan." She sounded very tipsy. "I entirely agree. But will you kindly remind me, what is our current topic?"

"Don't worry," Zingman said. "I know what that is, I invited her."

"You what?" said Matthew Glennon.

"I must say, Doctor Sarles, that that is an excellent question." This was the voice of an unknown woman, slurring as well, certain words punched out because she was stumbling along. Zingman took several steps through ferns in their direction and saw where a ludicrously slim flashlight beam bobbed, batteries failing. "Should we conduct an inquiry?"

"But we've no time for that!" said Pepper. "Look, the campfire approaches."

"Right you are, we'll have to proceed without the inquiry, then. There is much to accomplish."

"Yes, and you need my help in this . . . pressing matter?"

"I cannot do without it, I'm sure."

"Mmmm hmmm."

"So what do you say, Doctor Sarles, may I consult with you, for some reason?"

"Ouch!"

"What's the matter?"

"Thorns have my legs."

"You are caught. I will free you. Please give me our trusty torch."

Zingman located Mezzanotte's heavy-duty flashlight on its rock beside the pup tent, and switched it on. After a brief trip, he found Pepper, boldly lit in a pink shirt, propped with one hand against a larger woman, holding in the other a jug of wine, three-quarters empty. The larger woman stopped fumbling down in the brambles, straightened, appearing ashamed of her penlight. Without turning it off, she jammed it into her back pocket.

"Ross, hi," said Pepper, liberating herself with a mighty yank of the knee, nearly tipping over in the aftermath. "Hi, we've been walking forever, the ranger said the trail was clearly marked, but. Hey, got your message, but then we got a late start."

"Making some bread for ya," said the larger, displaying a battered grocery bag, happy. "All-natural ingredients, sir. But I'm afraid I must ask you a personal question, if—"

"Ross, this is my friend from work, Harriet Corrigan. Harriet, Ross Zingman."

The two nodded. Zingman said, "I'm being very rude, blinding you." He shone his beam at the rooty ground before them, moving it as they advanced toward him over roots.

"So," said the stranger. "I've heard a lot about you, am very impressed."

Pepper launched a blow at her shoulder, missing clumsily, and then she gave Zingman a quick, sheepish hug. "I'm sorry to barge in like this."

"No, I was expec—at least hoping you'd come, you know?"

They arrived at the fire; Zingman made introductions; everybody sat, and there was an awkward shifting on the dirt.

"Oh, have some wine," said Pepper. "There's . . . well, there's not plenty anymore, but you're welcome to it. We're done."

Gilbeau and Mezzanotte shook their heads, holding up palms, looking smug, as though still accepting full credit for everything.

"I'll say you are," said Zingman. "And I'm a little jealous, to be honest!" Pepper swung the jug to him. Its screw-cap must have been lost miles ago. He upended it and took three great gulps, then wiped his mouth with the back of his hand like a ruffian. Matthew Glennon stood, offered a clipped apology, and carried a blanket into the dark, toward the bank of the pond. Zingman would have to make it up to the man in the morning, but for the present, he meant to seize the opportunity to redeem himself for his prior insult. "I've got some catching up to do, I think. Ma'am, now what was that 'personal question' you had for me?" Zingman thought he could guess, and on whose behalf it was being asked. He twinkled at Pepper; she stretched her lips into a copy of a smile; he understood they were numb from wine.

"Actually, it's for everybody, everybody who . . . qualifies. See, I brought this home-made bread, but it's only for—"

"She completely refuses to tell me the reason for that!" Pepper burst out, causing Zingman to snort, then take another swig.

"But I haven't even said what, yet!"

"Or to divulge her super-secret ingredient."

"It's for men who do not happen to be romantically attached at the moment," said Harriet.

Zingman wowed himself by his recuperative powers. Pepper wowed him, too; just mix a little forgiveness with a little initiative—what a tonic. The Grievance Committee nodded at him, congratulated him with their sleepy faces, further earning their stripes by granting him center stage, demurring to answer the woman's flirtatious challenge.

"Romeo back there looked pretty disappointed."

"Thought I was going to wriggle into his sleeping bag, keep him warm."

"After his performance this morning?"

"No kidding. And after he guzzled the wine and told me an endless freaky story."

"What he was whispering to you?"

"Right. Christ, I'm dizzy. I should never've let you drag me all the way out here. I need to forget. I knew that, but I . . . forgot."

Harriet laughed till her belly smarted. *Oh, but my belly is smart.* "It just seemed to me that a swamp would be the ideal matrix for the experiment, Doctor Sarles."

"Yeah, okay. Shut up 'n' let me sleep."

She wrapped her arm around Pepper's waist from behind; they were spoons, on top of a blanket and beneath a blanket, far enough from the campfire that they didn't have to whisper, and where the night was turning chilly. Repeatedly, a cricket creased the air, sounding at once distant and snug within the ear canal.

"What did he whisper to you?"

"Oh . . ."

"Never mind."

"It's sad." The cricket had stopped. They pushed out the long suppressed breaths that are wine's last enjoyment.

"It was a story starring me," said Pepper.

"What was?"

"What he whispered to me. I couldn't make out a lot of it, I got stuff about hogs, but apparently's trying to pass off what happened this morning onto me, *me.*"

"Like you're kriptonite?"

"Right, something along those lines."

Harriet held her tightly, felt the bottom of her rib cage with her wrist. *I'd massage this for you if ribs liked such things.* "Well, my old boyfriend, Robert Jenwaugh, used to come up with ridiculous excuses for his own failings, like I was too special to fuck." *You I can talk to, soft little fireplug.* "That was before he turned downright mean."

"Yeah? We'll have to exchange war stories."

"I know it." The cricket took up again, insistently.

"So I guess you're sorry we came out here."

"We didn't have a choice, right?"

The phone had rung right in the middle of dinner—eggplant stuffed with tomatoes, onions, zucchini, and pesto; wine. Harriet, now dressed in a plum blouse and black jeans, jumped up to check the oven; the three loaves of bread were nearly ready to come out. Hanging up, Pepper had said that was the police, wanted to talk to her again about the suspected accomplice, whom she'd been seen with earlier in the day, on a bicycle. Officers Stilton and Murphy were on their way over. Pepper had had just enough to drink so that she agreed to escape. Harriet left a warm loaf outside the locked door, for the officers to fight over. *And Murphy, by the way, if you eat it, please aim clear of your dear wife's snatch.*

"We could've gone out to a nice, stupid horror movie, help you forget yours."

"I'm still seeing those spears sticking out of him."

"Me, too," said Harriet. She moved her arm from around Pepper's waist, bent it so it lay along her sternum, between her breasts. "I kept thinking, poor thing should have held that fish in front of his heart for protection."

"Oh, that fish." Pepper rested her own arm along Harriet's.

"If I never see it again it'll be too soon. What purpose did it serve for him to die?"

"None at all." *Unless you count allowing me to live.*

"You think Jack was a dim bulb."

"Ooop, forgot." Harriet took her arm away and reached into her back pocket, withdrew the flashlight they'd found in Pepper's glove compartment. They laughed at how feeble it was now, how you had to blink to trust the glow. They replaced their arms, and Harriet pressed the lens of the flashlight up under Pepper's chin, then switched it on and off, on and off.

"Jack? Well, my opinion of him has actually sort of . . . matured since everything started up."

"Harriet, I'm not as confident or blustery as I seem."

"No? I had no idea."

"Shut up. Tell me what's in the bread?"

"You'll see . . ."

"What do you mean?"

"You'll see . . ."

"I need a friend, not a bullshit artist. You're being as evasive as Jack. I told him, 'People always disappoint,' and he said he couldn't agree more, said that was why he got into genetic engineering at all, to gain some leverage. He actually said I was impossible to pin down, too, that getting to know me was like trying to find a needle in a haystack."

"But I won't disappoint you," Harriet said. "You'll see, pretty soon I'll be popping up everywhere you look." Harriet kissed Pepper once, for a long time, on the back of her neck. "Our friendship is absolutely guaranteed to grow."

"October 30th. 9:09 a.m. After brief period of extinction, Scombridae vagrantitus has re-emerged, as expected. Located feeding on plant life at perimeter of pond, she has been forced to radically adapt herself in order to engage and escape the genetic technicians upstream. She has prevailed, however, retaining many salient features, with the exception of . . ."

Trapuka shut off the tape recorder and leaned over the side of the rubber launch, worked to free it for the seventh time from another muddy bank where it had run aground. On his way again, he navigated a difficult bend and then rode into a relieving straightaway lined on both sides with pines. His clothing had dried poorly, clinging to him now like fungal matting. His boots were half submerged in water, which he'd poured onto the floor of the launch and stocked with as many of the specimens as he could find, even though, of course, fresh water ailed her.

Nor did he feel well, himself. During the night, he'd suffered extremely disconcerting cardiac symptoms in response to visions of police dogs swiftly approaching. Also, some blockage had made urination a thick and painful discharge, no doubt the result of consuming wild mushrooms and almost no liquid.

After laborious persuasion, Mr. Griffith had finally agreed to his role in Trapuka's plan and departed in search of his car, and Trapuka had made ready, equipped with the map of the Preserve, to pilot the launch along a series of narrow waterways that led from this pond down through the rest of the Valley, eventually widening to merge with the Skoonlet River, which flowed on, then, into the ocean harbor itself.

He had discovered her only forty minutes earlier, while Trapuka was just beginning his own journey to freedom. Thankfully, Mr. Griffith had left him in peace, and he was towing the launch by its rope around the curve of the bank to the place where the pond fed into its stream, a great swell of rotting algae built up ahead of the bow, significantly retarding his progress. Clearing it away angrily by the fistful, he began to feel subtle twitchings in his right hand. He ignored them for a while, assuming minnows. But the fit that his heart threw when he did look into his hand was the very same as had occurred that morning so long ago aboard "The Sebastian Quick" so many years ago, when he'd first encountered *Titus* on the other side of a glass porthole.

There, she was magnified, all of her features on bold display. Here, she was scarcely visible, newborn and off-design. He'd sat on the stony ground and watched her wiggle in his hand, seeming to grow perceptibly in just minutes. This urgency of regeneration, certainly unprecedented in the annals of biology, made Trapuka weep like a child—to see how she strove with all legendary genius to embody herself again, as though to prove him right, as though to repay him for his trust, for every drop of it.

Even in that first instant, when she was less than a millimeter long, he'd recognized a single fin paddling clear of its viscous coating. Rinsing the specimen revealed a desperate, misshapen gill opening and shutting, and a snout (though stunted and too small for him to make out any tooth-rows), and even the flat, unblinking eye, only a dot yet, but already telltale. And she was growing. Within twenty minutes, above this eye, Trapuka was able to confirm the distinctive bevelling of skull, as it began to show forth.

What hampered the entire project of recognition was the stubborn appearance of heterogenous traits such as skeletal outcroppings and bulging muscle groups, obscure shelves and wattles of tissue and non-fin appendages with articulable joints, processes not quite identifiable but betraying a mammalian influence. Here and there, as well, his examination was frustrated by leafy dark-green algae that seemed to have taken root in the very flesh, and by patches of brown fur.

Having no time to conduct a proper analysis, he'd gathered an armload of algae and set about plucking out perhaps three dozen individuals, introducing them onto the floor of the launch and dousing them with a temporary environment, then racing them off toward salt water.

At the end of the straightaway, now, the stream bore sharply left and the launch hove up onto a pebbly beach, causing a few moments of heavy turbulence around Trapuka's ankles. Titus fought these waves, but was badly buffeted.

"9:37 a.m. Estimate progress at less than two kilometers toward goal. Plan must function like Swiss watch. Can't give details here, clock is ticking. Problematic assistant has agreed to meet me, if possible, at mouth of river, with last delivery. In exchange, have promised him moon."

Mr. Ruthbar was back to normal and then some—marching around, chirping enthusiasms to those assembled, and stretching up his arms, laughing, as though in praise of the skies, as though the previous day had gone blank and here he'd found himself suddenly on safari. That blank day had, however, brought expanded bruising on face and throat, vivid lengthy scabs, and, more startling still—Zingman watching through the trees, lying on his stomach, chin on fist, inside a sleeping bag—the feet were bare, without their trademark black shoes. Zingman had woken to sounds of distant waterplay, making him, also, feel briefly enchanted until he recognized the women's voices in the pond and envisioned himself, last night, crawling away from the fire.

By the time he was finally up and stepping stiffly toward divine aromas, Mr. Ruthbar had vanished, probably off exploring. Gilbeau and Mezzanotte greeted Zingman with heads lowered in annoying, muted empathy—"G'morning"—while scrupulously reinventing the fire. "Fellas," he said, voice hoarse. Simon Reese, who'd recently arrived and set bacon frying in a pan, was busy cutting a loaf of bread into ragged slices with his Swiss army knife. "Ross! We won't tell the lady that made this, but she's no Theresa." He cocked Theresa's straw hat back on his head, to better expose his face to the sun, recently risen over the ridgetop. "My wife could've taught her how to bake bread. Didn't dare taste it. Thought

I'd make it into toast over the fire, then pile on this bacon and scramble up some eggs . . ."—he covered his mouth, shifted his eyes, even though the party in question wasn't near—". . . so we can choke it down without insulting her. I also brought some potatoes from my son Anthony's garden, and tinfoil. You wrap 'em up and chuck 'em in the fire, and they're done by lunchtime. Oh, and coffee in that thermos over there, when you're ready."

"You're a marvel, Simon," said Zingman. "Have you seen our newest?"

Mezzanotte looked up and said, "We found his blanket right next to the water, but he's not there anymore. Ronald had the idea he was skinny-dipping with the ladies"—Gilbeau laughed—"but frankly, we don't have the guts to look."

"No, I see. I owe him an apology. Maybe I'll take a look around, find my friend, too."

"He went that way," said Mezzanotte. "Talking about summer camp."

"Thanks, Nick."

"Breakfast in five!" said Reese.

"Okay, thanks, you guys, and I promise I'll do my share of work. I'll clean up."

"I've got witnesses," said Reese, cracking an eggshell one handed on the edge of the pan, sending yolk and whites into bacon grease, where they were frantic and at ease.

Not far away, Mr. Ruthbar squatted by the pond in semi-firm mud, washing his face with handfuls of water. "Mr. Z., hiya. Come 'ere, look. If I go like this they're the same size." Zingman squatted beside him, put his own hands under. Sure enough, sinking one hand deep—magnifying it—while keeping the other near the surface made all the difference, turning Zingman's aberrant, while it cured Mr. Ruthbar's.

"I woke up, I was so happy. Thought I wasn't going to."

"I know, you were scared. I feel better, too." Zingman scanned the glittering pond before him, and the weedy bank, opposite, but couldn't spot the skinny-dippers anywhere. Even their voices had faded away, for which he was grateful; maybe they had fallen in love, changed into an intertwining beast, and joined the elements.

"I heard your voice in my tent."

"Dreaming?"

"You were telling me one about a heart that ran away from home."

"I was."

"Yeah. I was at school again, and the big kids were yelling at me, calling me a retard, like they used to. All the other kids were having a good time."

"On the playground?"

"Uh huh."

"Playing tag?"

"I don't know. I was trying to get away from them and I saw it go bouncing by out on the street. I heard it going BOING BOING BOING."

Zingman smelled the air, warming up already, Indian Summer remaining in force. From out of sight, he heard an isolated feminine hoot. "What bouncing by?"

"The heart!"

"That ran away from home."

"Yeah! It was all dirty, I was running. If I could grab, the mean kids said they'd leave me alone, Mr. Z. I found a hole in the fence, I saw it bouncing through. I crawled through the hole and started running down the street." Mr. Ruthbar stood up, shook water from his hands, looked at them.

"'BOING,' really?"

"I almost caught it but I tripped. And they jumped on top of me, all those boys. They yelled at me, called me Wall-Ass."

Zingman put his arm over Mr. Ruthbar's shoulders. "That's your first name?"

"Wallace."

"You're one of the smartest people I know, Wallace."

He sighed, the kind that softly warbles. "Call me Mr. Ruthbar, okay? When those kids went to summer camp, they never said for me to come with them. I never slept in a tent before. I was telling your friends about that." He pointed back toward camp.

"Well, hey, go get yourself some breakfast, my friend." Zingman stood up. "I'm going for a short walk."

"Me, too!" But when Mr. Ruthbar stood, his knees gave way and Zingman had to hold him up until his brain could find its share of blood. "Wooo, Mr. Z."

"You take it easy, Mr. Ruthbar, you didn't have dinner last night. We'll walk later on."

"'Kay." He started back, weaving.

"Sure you can make it? Talk to Simon, he'll feed you."

Zingman discovered that the pond stretched farther than he'd thought, that it turned a sort of corner and continued, shining; unfortunately, in order to discover this, he first had to pass by the elemental creatures, who stood in the shallows on the opposite side, talking in low tones. He sneaked behind trees, and not only did they not see him and gain the satisfaction of believing him to be spying, but moreover, he was not spying, except to notice quickly that Pepper's friend, compared to Pepper, was terribly scrawny. He climbed up and over a modest ridge and now felt cleanly separated from the women and the campsite. A large dragonfly hung in place near his shoulder, sounding like a dry deck of cards being shuffled endlessly. His heart made an answering thrum. The dragonfly selected a fuzzy cattail down at the edge and thus instantly appeared there, alighting, wings proving neon blue in the sun.

Zingman kept walking for two minutes and then took a seat halfway up the steep bank, overlooking a fine stretch of water maybe thirty feet wide and one hundred feet long, extending as far as he could see—then turning perhaps another corner.

Directly below, sunlight filtered into general shadow. A sunken tree limb with branches rested on the pond's bottom; although it was eight or ten feet down and could have been lying there for years, it looked more distinct than any limb he'd seen before, not because its branches were glowing in the sun but because they were not; they looked stark and black. A small fish, though, couldn't avoid the sunlight, flicked its way among them.

The other end of the pond must have opened into further water, because an old man in a rowboat had come into view. A slight breeze seemed to be pushing the boat this way, but he hadn't noticed Zingman yet. He was too busy fishing.

"Mom and I used to live in the woods, after the divorce."

"You mentioned she was a glass-blower?"

Pepper laughed. A breeze swept across the water, making them shiver. Harriet hugged herself, but Pepper dipped to her shoulders, smiling as though to say, 'don't fool yourself, this is the only way to go.' "Yeah, well, she wanted to be. That was her master plan, but she couldn't do it by herself. Anyway, we had this pond in back, and my popularity soared in eleventh grade, once I could have swimming parties."

Harriet tried slowly bending her knees, but when the brown water reached her diaphragm she stood back up. It wasn't that it was so terribly cold as much as that she couldn't, somehow, believe she was naked in a pond. Pepper had flung herself so thoughtlessly in that she'd had no choice but to follow, to be seen by those blue eyes, although they did not, mercifully, linger and judge. And at least, now, Harriet was covered up past her belly button. After a night full of sisterly cuddling, and then this shock of immersion, she found she didn't feel sexual at all. Instead, she needed to study the situation, meaning not Pepper's body but the pond itself. Here was a case in which being far-sighted and without eye wear came in handy. Even before the body had sunk from view, she'd only gazed past it, focusing on the rushes and mud thirty feet away, on the shallows where a dull musty film lay on the water, and where colonies of thick algae reminded her of the healthiest of the petri dishes in her former life.

"You weren't always popular?"

"Oh, please."

Harriet thought this latest visitation of breeze might have passed, but no, not before a small shingle of Pepper's blonde hair suddenly hopped.

"C'mon, Corrigan, you look like a statue! Remember, this is good for us. It's our last chance at summer. If you're anything like me, you've let it just slip by." She gulped a major breath and disappeared beneath the surface, stayed away long enough for Harriet to nearly forget about her, or pretend to forget. She expected to see nothing in the shallows without her frog glasses, nothing valuable, nothing other than, perhaps, a frog. After all, who eats bread outdoors late at night? Should've made some sort of hot toddy mix, or cookies. Even if they did eat some, could a man weaken so soon, have they zero dignity? Even with Pepper hammered and sprawling ready (they think) not far off, and under cloak of darkness, could he lie back and set loose his cloud of admiration to drift onto the pond, like anthrax spores—*airborne, so I learn?*

The air hung still; sun warmed her back. A rock sat partially submerged at water's edge, wearing a skirt of gray-green algae that spread out flat around it. The upper half was dry, a jag of white quartz running through it. *That girl has lung capacity! Washing off her recent past. Not that anybody here is thinking about her. So, what did I notice over there? Is there a reason I'm staring at this particular rock?* She shut one eye and relaxed her self-embrace enough to reach up and lightly press the other eyeball, again, with her index finger. *Yes.*

In the algae, something. Or *on* the algae, just to the rock's left. It wasn't large, but it was playing. Or in pain. Or neither, but spinning, definitely spinning.

Harriet adjusted her feet on the squishy pond bottom, blinked, and increased the pressure on her eyeball.

Now she could see another, even smaller, right up against the side of the rock. This one was not spinning, but seemed to be trying to get a grip and climb. It kept sliding back down. It was approximately the same color as the algae, so Harriet thought it most likely a frog until she saw that now, on its newest attempt to climb, when it fell it left behind, stuck to the rock wall, a strand of hair exactly the boring color of her own.

Zero dignity.

Harriet felt she might start to cry, out of general sadness and general gratitude, but she found herself under water, upended, ankles clasped hard. Shrieking into murk and then sputtering at the surface, she kicked free, swam five healthy strokes toward the shallows, stood and coughed harshly. When her throat had calmed, she realized that she was all exposed and that Pepper was looking, crouched to spring again. "Doctor Sarles," she said, sitting down PLUNK! up to her neck such that she put on a fine collar of algae, "won't you at least listen to reason?"

But Doctor Sarles would not, vanishing again, a gentle swirl showing where her head had been. What with the gratitude, with a brilliant woman sliding invisibly toward her whom she was going to astonish in moments with a carefully off-hand revelation, and frankly, given that Harriet's mud seat was so soft and the water over here at the edge so much warmer, she became aware of a very specific sexual uplift. She took a deep breath, remembered staying too late in the YMCA pool that afternoon twenty-five years ago.

It seemed certain that Pepper would attack again, but Harriet didn't retreat; she prepared her legs, without folding them. When she only grazed past her, though nearing the bank and breaking gradually through the vegetation with a sustained outbreathing hiss, Harriet laughed and pushed back to join her and match her posture—stretched on her side, hidden beneath algae except for a shoulder, and a head propped on a hand.

"See there, I said I wouldn't disappoint you," Harriet said. Strung throughout Pepper's algae headdress, even squinting faulty eyes could notice flickers and twists, experimental, successful. *I guess I'm all in pieces over you. Eureka.*

Underneath the headdress, however, this woman's eyes did not flicker, weren't as bright and tricky as Harriet had hoped. But neither were they disappointed, even as she placed her hand up on Pepper's hip, slippery like in that corridor a thousand years ago, but nothing like boiled chicken skin or liverwurst, ready to slough off. And far from struggling, this time around, Pepper reached out, swishing water, and landed her palm in the small of Harriet's back.

"Corrigan, this is . . ."

"This is your birthmark, darling." Harriet moved her hand up and touched Pepper with her pinky in the memorized location. "This is your birthmark."

"Exactly. How do you know? You haven't dared look at me."

"Because I've never . . ."

"Me neither. Not since college, anyway. Told you, I'm trying to lose myself. Seems like we both are, today."

"Well." Harriet pressed the birthmark again.

"No, really, how did you know?"

"Lots of ways. You'll know everything in just a minute."

A hollow knocking brought Zingman out of meditation on Andy's Ohio childhood, distilled from all her telling. He pictured not individual events, but the running shape of it.

The old man's boat had gray paint chipped off its sides. He wasn't fishing at the moment, but rowing steadily this way, oar handles hitting against wood.

Soon Zingman would be forced to make his presence known. First, though, he looked back into the water and found that his eyes could take him further now, down past the branches into a spacious murky region beneath them, where drowned formations seemed to rise and recede simultaneously as he blinked. It was as though he were peering into the mouth of a cave, on the verge of recognition. But then the surface of the water jiggled, wiping the cave away.

"Hello there," said Zingman.

The old man started, lifting one oar blade out of the water, which caused the boat to twirl prettily around the trailing oar.

"I'm sorry, I thought you'd seen me, sir."

"No, it's—Hey, how're you doing, there? We hardly get folks this far back so late in the season." He swung the two dripping oar blades inside the boat, set them down. His face was shaded by the bill of a white baseball cap.

"Right, strange year."

"Something, huh?" While talking, the man picked up his fishing pole and checked a blue rubber worm on the hook, securing it. "Yeah, always seem to have this pond to myself in October. I could swear I heard talking, few minutes ago. A couple women." He pointed over the rise behind Zingman with the tip of the pole. "But then it stopped and I figured it was my imagination." He didn't cast but tossed the worm out a ways into the water, then slowly cranked the little handle on the reel with thumb and forefinger, making quiet clicks. When he was satisfied as to placement, he stopped cranking and tipped his cap. "Alexander. Been retired seven years, from cutting hair."

From the other part of the pond—a shout of overacted outrage. "Well, there, it's true, somebody's having a good old time," said Alexander. Zingman thought, then told himself not to gripe at Pepper when she came to breakfast, not to ruin his chances.

"I'm Ross. I'm a writer, I write books, but you've probably never heard of me. If I were smart, I ought to retire, too." The old man nodded up at him, smiling. "Zingman?" He shook his head but continued smiling and gently cranked the polished black handle three more times. The sun, over Zingman's left shoulder, fell amiably on the old man's whiskered face. Something tugged on the line, bobbing the pole, but when he reeled in, there was nothing but worm. This time, he cast, far, cranked, then sat still. Suddenly, he reached back into a cardboard Dewars Scotch box and took out a bright red can of soda, gestured that he'd toss it underhand. A silver wedding band shone on his finger.

"Oh, no thank you. So, does your wife ever come fishing with you?"

"Never did, then I lost Helen five and a half years ago."

"I'm sorry, Alexander." There was a long pause. The old man opened the soda and sipped. "Actually, I myself—"

"That's a big one." A shadow took the man's face, and then his body and his whole boat. The shadow left him and raced across the intervening water, across the sunken tree branches. It swept over Zingman, freezing his heart for an instant. "Got to be some kind of a record." The old man's vision dropped fast, and behind Zingman, before he could turn, the Cobhouse started screaming.

Harriet held her breath and drew down across Pepper's stomach, finding its other target—*"I hate those CAKES!"*—with infinite, almost laughable, respect. Instead of laughing, though, Pepper closed her eyes. Harriet forgot how to start breathing again until Pepper reminded her.

The earlier gratitude now ballooned painfully, and Harriet's eyes stung, tried to rinse themselves. They couldn't, so she blinked many times rapidly, resumed watching the face to check for what she was doing with her finger delicately and found out; the face was fuzzy until another blink brought it clear—firmly set as though pledged, mouth slightly open. Harriet understood that her own finger was much less astonished than she herself was.

As she kept respecting Pepper's brand new wishes, Harriet breathed deeply through her nose, pulling in the essence of pre-winter—an undramatic dying of plant cells, just drab, lazing. Meanwhile, everywhere in the headdress, knots of invented flesh twinkled.

When Pepper came, it was a subtle event. In the small of Harriet's back, she splayed and pressed her fingers, barely jiggling the water, then not. It was a rushed arrival at stillness, held, cooler than expected, producing less.

In a while, eyes still shut, she gave the same "shh-shh-shh" laugh as in the cafeteria line. "Hey, what's the idea, tickling me where I got hurt?" Pepper opened her eyes and sat up, began yanking algae out of her hair, searching through it. "And what are these?"

Harriet sat up, too, tilted her head and put on the best coy face of her life. "Oh? And whom do they remind you of?"

"Well, it's . . . seems like a mutation of some sort, 'sall messed up. Here's like a spine, almost, and underdeveloped limbs, maybe the bud of a tail? Is it one of those deformed frogs I've been reading about?" She dropped it into the water and selected another. "This one's weird, all covered with . . ."

"Long luxurious hair, natural brown?" Eyes shut, Harriet ran her fingers through her hair, finding it disgusting, humorous.

"No, wrinkly leaves, dark green . . ."

Harriet let out a massive whoop, which made Pepper shrink. "Pepper, Pepper, your salad, remember from before?"

"What?"

"No, listen, some of it must have gotten in through the gills. You know, when you lost it into that bowl on the floor, where the fish . . ."

"Shit, why are you talking about that fish? You're starting to really—"

"I used its cells, but this is so funny, you're going to love this. Some spinach cells—"

"You what? Funny?" She pulled more algae off her shoulder, picked through. "Here's a fin. Kind of practical joke are—"

"No. Here, I'll explain everything." Harriet giggled faintly, felt a nice breeze on her breasts.

"I'm gone."

"Hey."

She stood up and giant-stepped into deeper water.

"Pepper, hey."

She dove and disappeared for fifteen seconds. Harriet waded vaguely in that direction, covering herself partially with her arms. Pepper emerged in the middle of the pond, clean-headed, treading water.

"And don't follow me. I have to be alone. The funeral, for

God's sake. I don't know what game you're playing, but it's the wrong one. That—"

"No, let me tell you everything. You're going to love—"

"That fish is why Jack is killed. He's dead, get it?"

"I didn't mean . . . I meant aside from—"

"Oh, perfect." Pepper was looking straight up. "Like he's been watching us."

Harriet searched the sky and saw it, too—a raptor, circling, very high.

"I'm telling you, I can't do this. I feel like you're taking advantage of me." After several backstrokes, she said, her words nearly swallowed by the gray water, "Who the hell knows, maybe you *were* an accomplice."

This made Harriet suddenly want to tear Pepper apart, but the foolish little girl, having twirled over into a basic breaststroke, was approaching the opposite bank already, tucking her arms and kicking smoothly, hardly raising any wake as though to demonstrate the precision of her judgments. "He cleared the way," Harriet said in a level, indoor voice.

When the raptor tipped and began its breathtaking slide, plunging for the swimmer, Harriet lifted her hands to her mouth to yell a warning, but she whispered, "If it's an accomplice you see . . ."

The Cobsite looked like the merry aftermath of a pillow fight, a settling storm of soft white feathers, until Gilbeau, Mezzanotte, Simon Reese, and the scrawn (wrapped in a kelly green blanket) stood aside. Mr. Ruthbar was sprawled out on the ground beside the low-burning fire. Zingman knelt down and selected the larger hand, said, "Hey, you must be pretty tasty, like a rodent." But Mr. Ruthbar's eyes were closed. He had two fresh cuts, true as a razor's, on the left side of his face, so clean they hardly bled.

Mezzanotte said, "It was an owl, out of nowhere, came right for him, clobbered him, Ross."

The tone of the scrawn's voice was admiring. "It went for his throat."

"Absolutely unbelievable," said Gilbeau.

"We can't find any major wounds, other than those two," said Simon Reese, "but I wish Patrick was here. He does seem to be breathing okay. We pushed the thing off him pretty quick, with sticks from the fire. God, it was so huge. Poor guy was doing so great, wolfing down pieces of toast with eggs like they were going out of style, thanking us for taking him camping, and then BANG. Didn't see it coming. Thing seemed like one of those evil creatures . . ."

Zingman noticed that Mr. Ruthbar's eyes were twitching rhythmically beneath their lids.

"Not at all," said the scrawn. "That animal is merely seeking vengeance, preserving its interests."

"What do you mean?" said Zingman, looking up at her strained face—faintly smiling, though her eyes were red, teary—and envisioning the owl from the other night, feeling just a pang of jealousy that he hadn't dreamed up "vengeance" for his story, and wishing he hadn't gotten loose last night and blurted the story into the protagonist's ear. "Where's Pepper?"

"Oh, relax, will you? I sent her packing. We'll be spending our time together away from spying eyes. I saw you looking! Compared to that bird, you men are the real danger." She adjusted the blanket around her shoulders and took two steps backward. "Have a good time last night? At least one of you did, after consuming my bread." Zingman saw what remained of the loaf on the dirt next to a smattering of dropped scrambled egg, a twist of bacon; he picked it up and heaved it like a football out into the water. The scrawn muttered, "Glad to see the runt's found himself an appropriate circle of buddies." She rubbed roughly at her ear, scowling. "Ouch."

"I think he's coming to," said Mezzanotte.

The scrawn sped up her retreat, laughing. "I'd love to see his face when he wakes up to me! But I'm afraid it might really kill him." She turned around and swaggered back toward the pond, mumbling, "Whereas he should thank me for everything, for the brownies, for—"

"Those were from you? They were terrible."

"I'll have you know, sir," she said over her shoulder, "I take that quite personally." She ran into the water and swam away, blanket floating behind her like some grotesque parody of a corn husk. He was trying to concoct something to shout at her, something trenchant and so clever like, 'Yeah, that's right, go swim for your floating bread—fetch, fetch!' But the hand was squeezing Zingman back.

"I was sitting in my sandbox, the one I had back home." Mr. Ruthbar was blinking in amazement, more at the dream than at return of his personal foe. He couldn't catch his breath, so Zingman took out the bottle of tranquilizers and shook three into his palm, but Mr. Ruthbar didn't notice. "I was happy, 'cause Mommy and Daddy were alive again, I could see them in the kitchen, through the kitchen window. They waved at me, Mr. Z. I was going to get up and run inside, but I couldn't get up. I looked down at the sand, and these two things came up. They were like . . . metal points. One came up in that corner." He showed where with his lesser index finger. "The other . . ."

"In the opposite corner, rising out of the sand?"

"They stopped coming up when they were this high." Four inches.

"Kind of like the beak of that owl, maybe?"

"No, they were metal, I said. And then they started moving." He drew 'toward each other' in the air. "I got so scared, but I couldn't get up. I was stuck by them. They got closer and closer. I tried to get up. I yelled but my mom and dad just kept on smiling and waving."

"In the kitchen."

"Now they were upstairs, in my bedroom. But the two points were almost together, in front of me. I started crying, and then you and me were sitting on your couch, watching the sandbox on tv, and watching me in the sandbox. You put your arm around me and we saw the points hit each other. They made a click. Words came on the screen and you said, 'Wallace, can you read those words? You can't? Let me tell you why, it's because it's true you are a re-tard, Wall-ass.'"

Zingman glanced quickly at the three men's faces, feeling as though he ought to disavow his own dreamt words. "Oh, Mr.—"

"'Read it for me?' And you said, '"YOU'RE DEAD."'"

After a heavy silence, Zingman said, "Well, hey, this is what happens when you hang around too much with widowers." Mr. Ruthbar didn't laugh, or return Zingman's hug; instead, he began hurriedly chewing strips of floppy bacon, impatient with the pan in weak fire. "You get kind of morbid. Those aren't cooked," said Zingman. Reese, Gilbeau, and Mezzanotte made themselves busy cleaning up the campsite, and Zingman got the idea to go and find Mr. Ruthbar's socks and shoes. After lacing up, making loopy ears and tying, Mr. Ruthbar swallowed the three tranquilizers, one by one, then experienced a spike in poisonous nerve, pacing a three-stride circuit back and forth, green eyes scanning the skies.

"Everybody sit!" said Zingman. "You, too; I've got just the story, one that used to calm my wife down after a nightmare." Gilbeau had a handful of long white feathers, which he placed neatly on the dirt, then sat on them. Mr. Ruthbar laughed, with the others. "It's from a book called The Bat-Poet, by Randall Jarrell. That bacon's really not fully cooked, Mr. Ruthbar; you'll get, what's that . . . trichinosis? It'll kill you quick. Plenty of frightening things in this world . . . and the next. Of course, that's where I come in. And that's what this story's about. Okay, our main character is a bat whose best friend is a chipmunk, who always wants to hear the bat's poems. One night, the chipmunk asks him, 'Say me the one about the owl.' Naturally, the owl is their mortal enemy, and probably as much of a giant to all the woodland creatures as our owl is to us. Let's see how much I can remember.

"'Say me the one about the owl.'
"The bat recited to the chipmunk:

'A shadow is floating through the moonlight.
Its wings don't make a sound.
Its claws are long, its beak is bright.

'It calls and calls: all the air swells and heaves
And washes up and down like water.
The ear that listens to the owl believes
In death. The bat beneath the eaves,

'The mouse beside the stone are still as death—
The owl's air washes them like water.
The owl goes back and forth inside the night,
And the night holds its breath.'

"The chipmunk said: 'It makes me shiver. Why do I like it if it makes me shiver?'

"The bat said: 'I don't know. I see why the owl would like it, but I don't see why we like it.'"

Mr. Ruthbar said, frankly, "'Cause it's fun." The bacon was finally sizzling in the pan, though wearily, and he didn't reach.

"There you go," said Zingman. "That's the friend I know."

"Yeah," said Mezzanotte, "but shivering in a room with poetry and corn can get old, drain the life out of you."

"Oh, chills can do that, or they can stir your strength, if the wind is blowing just right."

The men were quiet, but the wind only worked pine trees so far away they might be an hypothesis.

Gilbeau said, "Feels less like wallowing when we're out here, more like facing up."

"I always figured I'd read The Bat-Poet for our kid one day," said Zingman. "And Grimms' Tales, of course. Andy would've had me arrested."

Soon, Alexander, the fisherman, scraped ashore in his rowboat, inquiring about the bird. He was properly impressed by the facts, and sat for a cup of coffee, sharing—"That monster reminds me . . ."—tall fish tales. Mr. Ruthbar's eyelids stuck lower each time he blinked. The two cuts on his face looked like they were ready to bleed, now that the owl had dived again in the telling, so Zingman helped him back to the pup tent, watched him crawl inside, sturdy shoes last to disappear.

When Alexander shoved off, Zingman told the men that he wanted to walk. This time, under the hot noon sun, he struck off in the other direction, to the broad marsh they'd first passed this morning. After several ill-fated inroads—including one which sent his left leg plunging to the thigh in spongy mud and nearly costing his sneaker—he accomplished a crossing by way of firm grassy hillocks and slippery logs. A small musty turtle slid off one and into grim water, as though consigning itself to decay. Further dragonflies swung close, assessing him and granting clearance, against their better judgment. He held his breath. Tight clouds of flies rose around him, reminiscent of Mr. Ruthbar's zealous imports. Having crossed, Zingman began to climb the valley wall, amid pine trees and boulders, finding no trail and trying unsuccessfully to recognize landmarks from when he and Andy had hiked in the vicinity years earlier. Instead, he only got tired. At one point, his feet slid on muddy leaves and he sat hard, holding to thin trees on either side the way that Andy had gripped the sides of the sock bin at JCPenney.

Zingman remained seated, to rest. From below came the faint sound of barking dogs. From up ahead—crashing water.

First, Trapuka saw the glossy yellow slicker, up on the dock. Then, Ellie's shut-down face and meagre resentful efforts to struggle out of Mr. Griffith's arms. The two stood in front of a low purple car, he, madly searching the river, she, steadfastly refusing to.

Mr. Griffith also kept looking behind him, at the street. Without paddles or its outboard motor, the launch was nearly impossible to maneuver against the flow of the river, but Trapuka had been leaning over and pulling his hands through the water, making for the bank, ever since he'd begun to smell salt.

"Ellie!" he shouted. "I'm down here."

"Doctor Trapuka, ahoy!" Mr. Griffith waved and started down the short wooden staircase, tugging Ellie by the wrist. She stared at Trapuka all the way.

He threw the rope. Mr. Griffith caught it, pulled it hand over hand, leaving Ellie free to flee if she wanted.

"Have I got a story for you. They weren't in any of the places you—Well, before that I had to hitchhike around the Preserve to find my car. I just kept cruising around between the police station and that hotel you said . . ."

Trapuka held out his hand but his daughter wouldn't take it, still smoldering at him. While Mr. Griffith continued explaining how he'd found them sitting at an outdoor cafe—"So I took the next table and just ordered some lunch, turkey club sandwich! I was so cool, like a spy. My life has definitely gotten a lot more exciting since you came along, my friend, as I think you know. So. Okay, now, your wife looks like sh—like hell. They were talking softly, so I edged my chair . . ."—Trapuka removed his boots and set them upright on the platform. He pointed to Ellie's little orange and white sneakers and then to the water sloshing inside the launch around his own socks. As if to prove she could stare and change at the same time, Ellie knelt to undo her laces, stood again, toed off her sneakers and stepped sideways into the oversized boots. She tried to land her hands squarely and angrily on her hips, but they kept slipping, what with the tent-like slicker. Even this particular awkwardness was damning, meaning, 'Everything you give me never fits.' Trapuka leaned over and tied them up for her.

". . . then your wife came back from the ladies' room sooner than I expected, and lucky you wrote that birthday note or this one would've been screaming, ruining the whole thing. Berry juice on birch bark, I still can't get over that. But anyway, I'm pretty sure your wife saw us getting into my car and peeling out. Kept expecting to see cops on my tail. And then I had Ellie here to contend with, started doubting my story, and, like, panicking." Joylessly, now, she let Trapuka help her into the launch, then perched on the narrow aluminum bench he'd taken out of its pouch, assembled and set up for her. "I said, 'How would I know it's your birthday?' 'That was two days ago,' she said. 'But look, it's your dad's handwriting.' Oooh, I can see this is going to be a bit of a squeeze here. Where are we headed, exactly? Any way we can get this water out of there?"

"Mr. Griffith, may I ask you for a few minutes alone with my daughter?"

"That is not a problem at all. God, I'm so thick-headed, like you should have to tell me. No, I'll just go sit in my car. Give me a shout, okay?"

"Will do. And Mr. Griffith?"

"Yes, sir."

"Thank you." They shook hands.

"Hey, you'll find ways . . ." His smile remained while he handed Trapuka back the coil of rope and watched him push off from the platform. He still hadn't turned to climb the stairs as the launch drifted out toward the heart of the river. Soon, he looked very quizzical.

"Leave the note in the car?"

Ellie sat hunched, trembling, eyes fixed on a shiny forty-foot vessel in full sail, tacking across the harbor two hundred meters away. She pulled her hood up over her ears. During the past few laborious hours, clouds had moved in to cover the sun, to drop the temperature depressingly and kick up a breeze. As a compensation, though, Trapuka had been able, in stages, to empty his bladder.

He cleared his throat and hand-paddled for a time, out past a rusted buoy that wobbled a warning of hidden rocks, for boats with hulls. The river was broadening, now fifty meters from bank to bank. "I guess you've probably heard some . . . distressing things about me. I want you to know that I intend to turn myself in to the authorities and face the consequences, try to explain what precisely went on in that cafeteria. But, Ellie?"

She'd started watching the clouds scudding high above, while gnawing on her lower lip.

"I wanted . . ." Trapuka shifted position to sit on top of the side tube, facing his daughter's delicate profile.

"I wanted first to take you on a small expedition, long overdue. I thought . . . you might think it was, well, I don't know . . . fun. You know, for your birthday."

"Yeah, like you're really spoiling me."

"I'd hoped for better weather . . ."

She kicked around angrily in his boots. "And anyway, I said it was two days ago. You never remember. I hate this water . . . there a leak, or—" She noticed that one of the survivors—green, brown, and gray in regions; raggedly oblong; and now about half the size of Ellie's hand—had attached itself to the top of the left boot. "Ew." She raised her leg and flicked

Titus off herself. "And I hate how you always bring such gross things home from the stupid ocean."

She glanced at him, which jabbed his heart, made it sound in his ears. "Your head looks ridiculous, you know. Your eye is twitching, too." And then she returned her attention to the sailboat, now cutting back across in front of them, nearer. They were being carried along briskly toward the harbor. It was much larger than Seal Cove on Grand Manan Island, and ringed, Trapuka could see already, by hotels and restaurants with large decks full of afternoon diners. But it was no industrial harbor. According to the map in his hip pocket, less than six hundred meters separated the mouth of the river from the wider mouth opening to the Atlantic.

"I caught sight of you yesterday, saw you were wearing this slicker, even though it was sunny. It made me feel good."

"It's not a slicker, it's a rain coat, and it doesn't fit."

"But see how you match the launch?"

"Great."

"Do you want to talk about what they're saying about me, Ellie?"

"No." She scratched her nose, blinked, coughed quietly, adjusted her hood. "They're coming to get you and take you away, not that you ever even. . . . What's there to talk about?"

"Well, then, would you like me to tell you a secret?"

"Whatever floats your little boat, Dad. Long as it's not about that fish."

"As a matter of fact, it does concern Titus, but not like you think. I know—"

"Oh, how 'bout the time you were down in that ball and all those tuna came at you? Hmmm, I wonder what kind of sandwich you had in your hand."

"I don't blame you for being mad at me. You can push me, but rest assured, I will not cancel our expedition. Now, I know that not much of interest to you has happened in the area of Titus in the past, it's been a rather subtle case, and it's difficult to have much patience. But not anymore, as I want to explain. . . . You see, everything has started changing. Haven't I always told you this time would come, that it would probably sneak up on us. . . . Well, the other day—"

"I like *horses,* Dad."

Trapuka had to swivel and paddle frantically, to gain safe distance from a flashy pleasure craft riding high in the water, back, apparently, to "O'REILLY'S DEEP-SEA FISHING" after a half-day cruise. Its seven clients stood behind a railing mounted with heavy-gauge poles and tackle, beaming and waving down to Trapuka and Ellie. Two men held their trophies aloft—northeastern rye muskies, common bottom feeders. The spreading wake arrived, rudely tossing the launch. Trapuka was out of breath, queasy. He took his seat again, his back toward the noble adventurers. The steady whine of the outboard made him sad. What would he have owed Mr. Griffith, yesterday, if he'd dragged the motor too? His feet were beginning to tire of being submerged, in socks. Overhead, the clouds continued to thicken, a cold front bringing wind. Ellie's hood blew off her head and she popped it back on.

"I'm aware that you do, and something struck me not too long ago, when I was thinking about you. Have you ever stopped to consider the peculiar case of the sea horse?"

"All the time."

"Truly, though, from its barrel chest upward, the resemblance is quite extraordinary. You have to admit it. Tell me, what other mammal possesses such a counterpart? Do you find, for instance, seacats?"

Ellie sighed. "Catfish."

"Ah, you fell into my trap! Unfortunately, those look nothing at all like felines, except perhaps for the whiskers. And the so-called 'dogfish' is an even more ludicrous example. Can you imagine a fish that looks just like a . . . mouse?" She didn't respond. "Or a big giraffe, or a pig?"

Ellie held herself still, then laughed hard. "Or a kangaroo!"

"Exactly. You see my point then. And I know you won't believe this, but the sea horse has been around millions of years longer than your land horse. So we really ought to ask ourselves the question the other way around: How is it that the land horse looks so much like the original horse?"

"Real tricky, Dad."

They entered the harbor, immediately losing momentum. Trapuka felt all of his strength returning.

"Hey, get us over to that restaurant, would you please? See it has a dock, okay. I haven't eaten like in days, and I have got to have a slice of pizza."

The roan, slinky hound was obviously astray on the mission. His colleagues—men and dogs—were running higher up the wall of the valley, shouting, baying, in the great spirit of murder. But he would quickly become the heroic center, would bring the others barrelling down here, if Harriet were not so well immersed at the margin of the swamp, if these rushes didn't form a sort of loose hut around her head. *Or if my clothes—my borrowed clothes—were in their little heap on THIS bank.* You have my scent, I hear.

She watched the hound pass on by, sniffing avidly through ferns and rocks, never pausing. She squinted—*yes, you're a he*—and before he got too far from where she lay in the water, she gave a sharp whistle. He cut back. Harriet tossed the loaf of bread she'd found floating. It was swollen and split into chunks when it landed, spooking the dog, whose wide ears pulled flat against the sides of his long skull. He stood still, front legs spread and planted firm, nostrils fingering the warm air; but he couldn't detect a molecule of Harriet, *because only my muddy eyes and muddy hair, and my rush-colored forehead, are above the water, smelling of swamp. This posture I got from Pepper. She's my accomplice, you know.* He then deigned to appraise the bread, which he judged extremely dull, although—for the heck of it—he licked up a swatch of wet crumbs and sprang forward, bounding away up the steep hill.

Harriet slid herself out of the rushes and into deeper water, where she could kneel on a surprisingly sandy floor. From here, the distance was enough for her to make out the campsite without squinting—three of the whiny divorced guys and one newly roused red runt, sitting around a dying fire. (She'd watched the tender-head traverse the swamp an hour ago, had quietly cheered when he nearly got sucked under, though probably she'd have had to go rescue him, an ugly episode.) The runt had his little hand on his chest—*still experiencing side-effects, I see; but you've got to admit it's for a good cause*—and the two scratches were bleeding in twin trails onto his cheek and neck; the older man beside him kept wiping him off, holding ice to his face from a dark blue cooler.

When the owl hit, Pepper had been hiding from them behind a tree, furiously dressing, unaware of the dive until the men screamed like babies. She took one look at Jack's magnificent snowy work of art and bolted, tripping because of a troublesome pant leg.

And sadly, darling, you remain unaware of a much grander magnificence, that of retaliation itself. I'd have explained everything to you. It would have taken all day, you'd want details, details, because that's just how you are. We'd have laughed and been thrilled with how things've turned out, and even proud of your boyfriend. How about a bit of show-and-tell at the funeral tomorrow? I could arrange that.

Harriet spotted her borrowed clothes and knew she'd have to stage a raid for them by nightfall. But for the present, it was right to be naked.

She resumed her acquaintance with the specimen in her hand, under water. They were bigger now, and still tended to stick to the security of the algae, although she'd bumped into a few milling about the rushes. One had nipped her on the foot, striking her funny.

Blind to specifics point-blank, she'd taken up a tactile approach, which had entailed the peculiar sensation of recognizing her own least favorite features and conceding that they'd gained something in the translation. Aside from the fact that she now possessed certain adorable fins and a vastly improved set of teeth—

that doesn't tickle!—Harriet had been gladdened by each of several hands she'd shaken between her massive fingerpads, by the arms and legs she'd massaged to quicken bloodflow, and naturally by her own stout back, discovered arching up like a prize inside a patch of spinach leaves. *And here I'd always thought I was kind of scrawny.*

She didn't have to brace for the startlement of head or face—she'd harvested no such cells for the bundle, adding only the root of a single hair plucked from her scalp, essentially the same hair she'd first inspected under the plastic microscope her mother had given her as a girl. *Does that make me as much a coward as Jack, in that regard? Well, a more charitable interpretation would be this, I've been relying for too long on having a good head on my shoulders, time to play to my weaknesses.*

But now, wary anyway, she was surprised to discern her breast and not feel pity. She gave it a companionable jiggle. Its nipple felt nonexistent until indeed it responded to stimulation, scooting and gathering into its old "decent berry"; its miniscule bravery nearly broke her heart.

Oh, this was true, the room behind the waterfall wasn't easy to enter. Zingman had also forgotten how this water generated its own wind, and the treacherous tip-toe along a narrow ledge high above welcoming jagged rocks, and finally the problem of bending one's body around a slanting rock pillar without coming in the way of the cascade, right there by one's shoulder.

But he hadn't forgotten the room itself; once inside, he found everything familiar, just as they'd left it—from the deafening noise, to the dim milky light, to the disorienting cleft ceiling, the smooth walls, and the fact that the limited confines somehow managed to feel dank and cozy at once.

He stooped, sat on his heels, closed his eyes to listen.

After knocking the leopard off the table, Andy never takes another bite of solid food, sips water only grudgingly, loses the ability to perspire. Their last real conversation takes place on a Tuesday morning, when she asks him out of the blue what he plans to write next. (Later that night, her kidneys will begin to fail, ahead of schedule, and by Friday noon, everything will rush to an end.)

"Are you crazy, Andrea Parker? My writing has been about the Dead, the Other Side, about Suffering and staring into the Abyss. Like I know what the hell I'm talking about, like there's anything titil—*What,* Andy?!"

She's been holding her hand up off the bed, five inches, a tremendous effort that nauseates him to witness. These hands used to make topiary.

"Turn that thing off, will you?"

Zingman crosses the room and smacks the button on the air conditioner. Their ears rest. Andy tries to scratch her knee, but he has to take over.

"Thanks."

"You're IT."

"Hmmm," she laughs gently. "When's my father coming today, early afternoon or late?"

"Early."

"I better get sleep."

Zingman stands up from his chair, checks her forehead, which is too cool. It flashes through his mind, once again, that he must be some sort of criminal, the kind of flash that won't be blinked away. His nausea sharpens when he sees that although he's touching her forehead he can't really touch it. Her forehead is stony, and he feels like his hand is writing her legend onto it. Is it too late, already, for her to tell him who he is? Is he actually going to run out of chances? Feeling once again the rich dark rot of accurate guilt spread like florets of mold, like feigned cancer, over the walls of his chest cavity, he blinks down at her closed eyes, the twin hills beneath the lids, wishes he could see the stitching motion of a dream, wishes he could lean down, at least, and listen to her heart.

"Ross, though?"

"You're still awake."

"Let's not . . ." She opens her eyes, which are precisely the brown he saw the first day, from fifty feet away. "Let's not fall into saying lines like in some good-bye scene."

"This is me you're talking to." She doesn't smile, maybe just because her lips have painful cracks.

"When it comes time, couple months, whatever, I don't want us to sound like . . . sound . . . Remember Mrs. Orleans?"

"Sure I do."

"That's the way."

Mrs. Orleans was an old woman they've heard about, the grandmother of a friend. Her entire extended family gathered around her deathbed for days while she lay unconscious, slipping away. 'We're here, Jennie, all of us, we're not going anywhere.' 'There's nothing to fear, Grandma.' 'We're *here* for you, please don't ever forget that?' 'We love you, Mom, and we're right *beside* you.' Five minutes before she died, Mrs. Orleans came to, looked around the room, and said, 'I know, and you're *annoying* me.'

"But," says Zingman, "what if we have . . ."

"What?" She seems to enjoy his awkwardness. "Any 'unresolved issues'?" She even manages the quotation marks with her whispery fingers, though her two hands remain far apart, on either side of her. "Yeah, I've got some. Let's get this out of the way, then. Early. I'll start."

Zingman pretends to brace himself, and he braces himself.

"Sorry about the leopard."

He laughs extra hard, feeling freed. "Forgiven. Next?"

She thinks for a full minute. "Good-bye, y'know?"

The waterfall smashed down from its high source, more and more and more. But standing, he noticed that, for the first time, he was not crying at this particular memory. His heart bucked, pivoted very wrongly, putting him in charge again, making him decide, each moment, whether to go forward.

Voting yes, emphatically, his ankle bones were back to their stinging. He brushed them thankfully with his fingers, thinking he must be on the verge of a great idea, something to develop and then to tell around the campfire tonight. But when he turned around and looked, it was no idea but a forest of diminutive mushrooms stemming from the rear wall of rock, like a display, surprising him first with their very existence and second with their care, like a treat—the earnestness of their many pale yellow domes.

When Zingman turned again toward the mouth of the cave, there was Andy herself, simply leaning, hands on knees, studying something on the floor of the cave, looking like she did the last time they were in this room together, slender but healthy, wearing her moss-green cardigan sweater and blue jeans, her face reddish from the climb, her dark brown hair wound into one hasty braid. He stands slowly, expecting her to vanish, but luckily she is too preoccupied. A stone tongue projects into the torrent, crossing first the weak interior splashes that accompany the falls, the tinkles that play, implying the entire phenomenon has been overrated in terms of danger. To get the thing she wants, Andy goes down on one knee, too close for comfort. He holds out his hand toward her, eight feet away, as though to convince himself he'll be sure to catch her if she slips. She reaches into the splashes and retrieves a flat pebble, then crawls rapidly backward.

This is the kind of place where talking is out of the question, so communication becomes gestural. One is boxed into melodrama. Last time they were here, they found their voices so thoroughly drowned out by the waterfall that they started lampooning the very act of speaking back and forth, making it a broad farce. Today, Andy stands in front of Zingman, showing him her pebble, which has flecks of mica in it but is not—in truth, like so many once you actually get them in your hand—beautiful. She curves her mouth downward like a sad clown's. He copies her, then raises his palms by his sides, to mean, "Ain't life just like that?" And then they give each other exaggerated nods.

Zingman takes a step toward his wife, ready to halt the game, but she halts him instead by aping scandal with her eyebrows, her jaw hinged open.

"Oh, c'mon!" he mouths, taking another absurd gradual step, as toward a person on a ledge, which it happens she is. "Okay, you're just making fun of the racket. That's not fair, come here." He holds out his arms. "I mean it, now."

Andy backs up, also in slow-motion, glancing behind her into the white thrash of catastrophe and then back at him, wearing an expression of outlandish horror, making sport of his chosen career, turning the tables.

Zingman gives up on trying to catch her and decides to peer more closely at her than he ever has before, at the Andy safe and sound, that is. It's difficult, he's still so used to her, even after twenty-five months apart. But there—he's clean forgotten that before the weight loss, her chin was shaped that way, underneath, that sort of half circle.

She tilts back her head, points to the area in question, and puts on a face of grandly dumbfounded surprise. And then her eyes, wide, holding their pose, begin to change. He steps closer and she allows it. Before he can touch her face with his fingers, a translucent film appears at the outer corners of her eyes and pulls across, retracts, pulls across, blinking sideways. For the first time in his life, he truly screams.

Zingman couldn't stop laughing all the way down the valley, a seizure that finally settled in the most intricate muscles of his abdomen, painting them present. In passing, he wondered where Andy had gotten off to. What had happened after her excellent trick? When did he leave that room, and why, why in all the world? But as he kept jogging and sliding toward marsh and pond and toward an eager audience, he couldn't generate any remorse at all. He had in his mind only Andy's silhouette, finger to chin, as if printed against the silver backdrop of the falls.

While hopping from hillock to hillock across the marsh, Zingman's eye happened upon a fresh relief—her arm twining up the base of a reed stalk like a pale sprout. He breathed, "I had a feeling I'd see something like that." It was almost not there, but his ankle bones sang otherwise, and so he gave it the exact wink it deserved.

"My friends," said the fool on the bank, waving his arms, "have I got a horror story for you. There's really only one, and you're the audience for it." The hapless band stood in the mud, looking out across the water, blowing on their hands because of a fast-approaching cold front.

Try being inside the pond. Harriet stayed low, peeking over the surface through rushes.

"What I mean is this. People are separated from what they want most, even when it seems they have it in hand. We can take heart in the fact that we're a prime example, we're in position to understand what others only suspect. We used to think we truly possessed our wives, merely because we loved them so much . . ."

I'm sure that's why they left. And you're a fine one to talk, Mister, speaking in such high tones when just last night you were beating off to images of a grieving drunk girl, and the night before that, when she needed to forget, you couldn't even get it up.

The red runt made Harriet laugh, how he cringed up into the sky. *Have you finally seen yourself, understand our owl retaliates only for good reason? And I don't just mean strangulation, though strangulation's pretty good already.*

". . . of a certain way to embrace the absence. If we treat this marshy pond as the gap that's been killing us, we can use it for practice, like an object for meditation . . ."

Preserve me! I've been disappointed, too, but I offer practical solutions, give the world "its own long definition," but not by giving empty speeches. Mom always said I was a budding genius, and look now, I'm budding everywhere.

". . . because you can train the eye to pick up details, like signals. To sort of peek over the brink and learn to play with our longing, to keep on longing but not to take it literally, which, granted, isn't easy, and which is . . ."

Which is to entirely miss the fact that your sacred gap happens to be occupied at the moment, boys, that it's the site of trouble requiring concrete action. If instead of holding forth you were holding what I am holding in my hand—nothing hypothetical but a real specimen whose strength is ebbing, whose muscles are losing tone, whose tendons are slackening, whose skin responds less and less to direct stimulus—you'd certainly freeze up and fall mute, wouldn't you?

"Or maybe, call this a pond stocked with desire?" While he invented the story—ankle bones wild with the best aching—Zingman could sense the heads nodding tentatively behind him. They might not be ready, might prefer the fire, but his bones said, "Tell it." If Matthew Glennon were here, so raw, Zingman would never venture this proposal, but when he'd gotten back to the Cobsite, Stanley Keillor had arrived with his riding crop and a good attitude, and Mr. Ruthbar was groggy but out of the tent. The Grievance Committee was revamping the fire against the quickly rising chill. He'd walked the party along the bank until the border between marsh and pond, where reeds and hillocks began to show, dead trees fallen and upright, rotting and dry, and the bank became lower and spongy, the air thicker, fetid, and sounding with the rasps of insects. Here, Zingman had turned and watched each of ten feet devise its own standpoint, on a stone or inches sunk in muck, even on a bending twig, making do.

He wasn't quite sure yet what he was suggesting; his concept was still taking shape, but his eyes were farther advanced. Soon, he hoped, the others would stop measuring his vague words and start using their eyes in the loose yet lasering manner, to see what he was seeing; it was like an Easter egg hunt designed especially for widowers, but with a catch—you could only look, not take. Surveying the marsh, he'd picked out four more manifestations like the one he'd spotted earlier twining up the base of the reed stalk. These four—oop, there was a fifth—seemed a bit more substantial than the inaugural arm and yet, with the exception of a clear finger hooking up over the edge of a lily pad, they were not so specific, were mere gestures of reunion sent from elsewhere, as unapproachable, as unavailable to the touch as Andy in the room behind the waterfall. Or even to grasp with the mind. For instance, that one—at fifteen feet, it may as well be fifteen miles away—was mostly submerged, paddling or kicking beside the mossy log, or no, say it was more in the manner of a creature with a tail, though trailing long dark hair, too, hair, not fur, but from its flanks, not from a head, and showing, on top, a flesh-tone length of smoothly feminine skin. Well, he wished it were straight flesh-tone (he could be fonder of it); but it was stippled the color of ash. So far, on the strength of his coups—and although teaching himself what extras are packed into every second glance—Zingman had wanted to perceive in these offerings much more than they were willing, at last, to give; he constantly caught himself stretching for sharp definition, for a higher kindred nature, the unashamed nod of family, and then he'd successfully pull back.

Harriet had noticed him noticing individuals throughout her swamp, her hatchery, and could tell from his inflated face that he believed them arrayed for his benefit, *which is not surprising, come to think of it, given that as already determined a man's orgasm is beyond precious to him, particularly when achieved through his own dependable devices. But the organisms that may, surprise, issue forth? No, he'll let the girl take care of those, especially when they're sick. They didn't inherit my brain, but these children got my black cube inside them.*

Even *with* her brain, Harriet couldn't decide between two leading explanations—that of a fatal flaw in the original bundle itself (probable, given the schedule of production), or that of climatological shift, though anyone can see they went downhill when the weather changed. The pond water was growing colder by the minute, and the Valley was already darkening again. Her stomach stabbed with hunger. She had to get herself dry and dressed right away, find the pile of borrowed clothing, plum blouse, black jeans—Pepper's sweet gesture. *Nobody has ever said "accomplice" and meant it less . . . and no man has ever had the nerve to stand before a swamp alluding to Hermes . . .*

". . . otherwise known as Mercury, he of winged feet, herald of the gods, who carried messages across to the realm of men."

"Like from Zeus," said Mezzanotte, "who threw lightning bolts."

"Yes," said Zingman, "and they strike us constantly, like when you, Nick, recall something about Bethany for the first time. I'd say the lightning is a form of Mercury's work."

"Right, one just 'struck' me this afternoon. I'll tell you back at the fire."

"I'm getting pretty cold, too," said Gilbeau.

"Or how about when we wake up in the morning," said Simon Reese, "and realize it's all still true."

Zingman nodded. "Well, sure, that's the lightning, also. The truth comes near, slams us, almost kills us, then withdraws out of range. Like Mercury flying messages over this gap, but often they're in strange code." He flirted with directing the men's attention to all his discoveries—he'd now achieved a sixth and a seventh, both nuances, wisps tangled in the complicated tendrils of the same leggy vine, even though light was fast draining from this theater—until, at the last moment, wisdom prevailed and he knew each would need to grow into his own glimpses, that this was not, after all, like a birders' collective but a job for a self.

"I wasn't planning on coming back," said Matthew Glennon,

closing in from the direction of the Cobsite, startling everybody less by his presence than by its tone; his t-shirt and jeans had been replaced by white dress shirt and solid maroon tie, navy blue blazer, and slacks to match. His brown shoes squished in the mud, threatening their shine; his face seemed vigorously scrubbed, revealing some fresh hope. "I thought I'd have to do without."

"Matthew, listen, let me apologize."

"Don't worry about it, Ross. I can understand, she's lovely, and I guess I'll be at your stage, one day. I just—"

"They're gone now." Zingman shook his hand. Of course Pepper had to go; forgiveness and initiative are from Andy's side, and one never runs out of chances, though they bend.

"At least it got me home, which was important. Gone, really? I could swear I saw a pile of clothes by the water."

"Can't be. You show me."

"Anyway, I had to tell you guys, at home there was a message from the Tarboro Police, saying they had a witness. I called them back and got a few tidbits. Someone saw Sheila that night. I threw some of her ratatouille into a pot—not the way she cooks it, but I lugged it over here. 'S on cooking now," he said, pointing back toward the fire. "Guess our luck's running out, huh?" He hugged himself, cast a glance to the clouds lowering from above. "Funny what new details do in your head, even if they don't make sense."

"Especially then," said Zingman, gesturing over the theater, thinking up words that might spark a virgin sighting. "That's when you've got to look at them askance, at an angle." But no, and he took his first steps away from the water.

Matthew Glennon walked beside Zingman toward the fire, the other five falling in behind, but he walked backward so that everyone could hear. "Sheila wasn't where she was supposed to be, but I've already told you that. She had a business meeting that night in Greenville, which is a tiny town, almost as small as Tarboro. She likes to go where her distributors live, you know, to their houses, when she can make time. But that's not the problem. I'm not jealous, she's not capable. . . . She'd driven almost twenty miles from Greenville, and remember how she was found in a field near her rental car? Well, now I find out it wasn't like I pictured. She didn't just get out and go into the field. She'd been away from the car, and she was trying to get *back*."

Harriet opened her hand to release the specimen she'd been gripping, as though freedom mattered to the stricken. She inhaled a chestful of air, ducked under, swam a long, secret way—a trick lately showcased by her skilled mentor—out of the rushes and into colder, deeper water, rose up quietly for another few breaths then ducked again. Soon, she stumbled into the "realm of men," her legs barely operational, anymore, on land. Her stomach still hurt from hunger, and she shivered violently, but she found her pile of clothes, got dressed and—after crouching to let a dapper pudge place a pot inside the fire, then clear out—climbed the slight incline. *Touching, really, that pudge all dolled up sadly like they do, divorced fellas putting their best feet forward—i.e., they're always on the make.*

At the fire, she recognized how cold she'd been. Clouds were descending in a block; it would be full dark in less than an hour. She glanced around for matches to take away with her but didn't dare extend her search to bags and backpacks, because she could hear the voices down the way—"askance, at an angle," he pontificated—and couldn't quite tell whether they were nearing. In her abdomen, the deep hollow pain called for attention. Within the radiant heat, still shaking, she leaned over the pot of stew and sniffed—*mainly eggplant, like Pepper's delicious creation.* She took hold of a long wooden spoon that was plunged into the stew and stirred, then lifted to her lips a large bite of vegetables and broth, blew on it, took it in her mouth and swallowed. Her stomach twisted—*ah, they can't cook to save their lives.* Her pain was lower, anyway, and she guessed it was, after all, her womb. *Odd, I've never been so aware of it before, not quite like this ache, different from cramps.*

The voices were certainly getting closer; the men were ready for their evening of gluttony and profound speeches, healthy displays of emotion, of keeping the fire strong and believing themselves the discoverers of heartsickness, of what it means to be thrown back on the self alone, just because their wives had left them, wising up. *But even still, they coddle you, giving you such martyred shape. See if Hermes warns you about* this.

She took out of the pocket of Pepper's jeans the remaining jar of compound. She'd hoped to preserve this one, but she placed her hand low against her womb, pressing in toward the deep and hollow pain, and she breathed, trying not to double over. The pain seemed to punish her most when she pictured herself sitting all night on the far bank of the pond, furious at Prometheus and his fire; then, it grew more lenient when she decided she might not, after all, not all night. She uncorked the jar and poured the contents into the pot, stirring well.

At pondside, she hurled the empty jar back toward the swamp, then disrobed and forced herself into the icy water again, sidestroking "askance, at an angle," her one bundle warming countlessly in the pot, her other bundle held high in the twilight.

"Daddy, I said, 'I'm *cold!*'"

"And I said, 'At least you're not hungry, are you?'"

Under thick evening clouds, it was all but completely dark now on the open ocean; their craft drifted in twenty-five-knot winds, on six-foot swells. Trapuka could still make out Ellie's miserable little shape, hunched and nauseated on its aluminum perch. He'd stationed her on the opposite side from where he sat, to balance the launch. Looking at her, he knew at least that she was dry inside her slicker—its tent-like quality proving beneficial, enveloping, under the circumstances—and her feet to be the same inside his boots. His own immersed and aching feet kept searching for and caressing *Titus,* while his ankles kept being struck by the large empty pizza box that slid on the water inside the launch. An earlier fight had seen him refuse to let Ellie toss it and a plastic root beer bottle over the side—"You know that marine pollution is the number one hazard facing the fishes, because I've explained that to you many times"—even though she'd had to use her own money, the last of it, at the restaurant, because his was wet, and his credit cards bore a wanted name. Twice already, a helicopter had buzzed overhead, sweeping a searchlight back and forth over the waves, narrowly missing its target.

"I'm only doing my best, Ellie. Expeditions are not always

comfortable. Here's one example I'm sure you haven't heard. When I was just starting out—"

"I-told-you-that-if-Mom-hadn't-paid-me-my-allowance-I-would-be-starving-right-now," Ellie said through clenched teeth, but taking pains to enunciate every word. "And-after-I-throw-up-I-will-be." She made herself calm down, deep-breathing. "Thanks a lot for naming me Tra-PUKE-a. Mom says we'll probably go back to her old name."

Trapuka thought that if he were alone, he'd throw himself into the sea with Titus. But without insults, he might not wish to die.

He watched his daughter's shape come briefly out of its hunch, reach for the pizza box, and fling it overboard, followed by the root beer bottle. "You crazy man!"

"Well, there goes our paddle."

Within the harbor, this afternoon, Trapuka had found it impossible to make any headway against the incoming tide, until Ellie, taking her time, and offering him only one slice, had finished off her pineapple and Canadian bacon pizza. Then, the stiff cardboard had proven just the tool to pull them over the threshold and out into countervailing Atlantic currents.

"I don't care! They're about to find us anyway, if I'm lucky. And then Mom's going to kill you before they even take you to jail."

Trapuka felt like slapping the girl, which frightened him. He too was shaking with cold, and was starving already, not to mention that he was being hunted down by men who knew where to look, tipped off by yet another back-stabbing assistant. He could not continue thinking along these lines, or he would have some sort of seizure. The muscles around his left eye, too, now, twitched, ever since the first helicopter pass. The twitching ran up beneath the eyebrow, and it felt precise as a coded language in there. But he couldn't concentrate, because his heart kept faltering, as it had all day long, more and more seriously. While she had still cared about him, Jonna used to badger him about getting his cholesterol level tested. And now Ellie wanted her to kill him. In prison, nobody would think to check his cholesterol. Could he request one test, perhaps, in lieu of a phone call? If it came out well, maybe he could survive his trial, and even gain the confidence necessary to represent himself. Perhaps it would become a celebrated trial, at which he'd be permitted or even encouraged to stand up and, with no time limit, to speak in his own defense, to expand and advocate for the voiceless, to enter, at least, certain coherent thoughts into the public record, thoughts which, had events not unfolded as they did, he might have labored the rest of his life without putting across so widely.

A rogue wave suddenly lifted them up and abandoned them to freefall. They slammed down, their spines compressing. The salty spray stung the cuts on his scalp, as it had for hours. They could easily capsize. He wondered whether Ellie understood how easily.

"Oh. Daddy, I'm—" She vomited pizza and root beer into Titus's temporary environment, restaging the insult from the cafeteria, though in this volume of water it would dissipate much more than in the glass bowl. He left his seat on the side tube and staggered over next to her. This change destabilized the craft badly, but Ellie was still being sick, so he pushed her hood off and gathered as much of her hair in his hands as he could, held it back away from her face, as he had seen Jonna do.

"That's okay," he said, "that's good now, Ellie. You'll feel better after." She sputtered and spat. The launch pitched severely to the left, then to the right. Afraid of going over, Trapuka grabbed the girl around the middle, tightly, but she only squirmed his arms loose impatiently, and she sputtered and spat some more, and gave a little shudder in the wind.

"I do feel better."

"See there. I'm sorry, but I really should get back, keep us balanced out."

"Okay."

He flipped her hood back up and returned to his seat. Far away, the slicing blade of the helicopter, approaching again.

Trapuka couldn't get a breath, but not because of the fear. His chest hurt, too, not because his heart was failing. It was the shudder she'd just given, the kind one might give at home, after one has made it through a brief harrowing experience and is free to comment upon it—"That was unpleasant!"—from a place of safety. Anybody who believes she can be allowed to drown will grab whatever is near, whatever floats or knows how to swim, and will never let go. Surprising himself, he started to cry, the muscles of his throat clenching shut, to prevent sound. When he'd tried to hold her, she was impatient.

Up ahead, the helicopter's searchlight beam looked professional, tilting this way and that over the dark ocean. When at last it struck and blinded them, the rotor and downwash making them scream, the nightmare didn't last long. No man with a gun was lowered on a rope ladder. Instead, the chopper merely leaned forward and raced off, leaving them in relative silence. Trapuka knew what this meant, of course, but he decided to pretend for these few minutes that he and his daughter had received a grant of mercy, that from above, the authorities had understood perfectly what their light so perfectly illuminated, what had just occurred down here.

"Ellie . . . thank you."

"What?!"

". . . which is why this witness lady noticed her in the first place, from her window, because Sheila was dressed in her nice business suit, pinstriped, just walking along a little road, leaning into the wind." Zingman sat close to the fire, part of the ring of men, and watched Matthew Glennon's face hop minimally in the light, his features nevertheless heavier than dance. At the far end, Mr. Ruthbar's eyes were slits, and he swayed like he could topple forward into the flames, but for this one—if not for "Tag"—he'd stay awake.

"That local windstorm I told you about had kicked up by then. The woman assumed Sheila knew where she was going, but I'm sure she'd gotten lost. Maybe she'd already gotten that hit to her head. When I saw her the next day, of course she was just under a sheet, so I never pictured her in that suit. I was with her when she bought it. Why she'd driven herself out there and left her car, I have no idea, 'cept it wasn't raining, no clouds, in fact, an attractive night. But seeing her in her suit is why I decided to put on some decent clothes, myself, coming back here. To honor her." Matthew Glennon re-centered the knot of his tie, took out a comb and, knowing this was useless, smiling, ran it through his hair.

"That makes sense, Matthew," said Mezzanotte, looking over at Gilbeau, then clearing his throat. "Makes me realize Ronald and I got dressed up not . . . not trying to be assholes." Zingman leaned and squeezed Gilbeau's upper arm briefly. A cold gust brought pops from the fire, set off remote sirens inside the logs. The pot was bubbling low, because each except one of those present had enjoyed several hearty helpings.

Soon, Patrick Tenzer arrived, beating pitch black by a nose, completing the group, lugging a peace offering, a grocery bag filled with snacks, and venturing the opinion that Mr. Ruthbar's new facial wounds really should have stitches. Zingman dished him up some ratatouille, which he accepted with a quick bow, recalling who the cook was, and then Zingman scraped out the last several wooden spoonfuls onto a paper plate, extending it pessimistically to Matthew Glennon who exhaled pointedly. "I said I can't." He reached into Tenzer's brown bag instead, selected a bag of mixed nuts and a granola bar. "There's plenty more at home, in the freezer, and maybe I'll figure out how to deserve it."

Sheila's details took a pause. Mathilda Tenzer was sullen, going to a friend's house, away from home overnight for the first time since Estelle; Anthony was home by himself but not allowed to invite more than two friends, not a party, no drinking. "'C'mon, Dad, next you'll say they've got to be from 4H!' Thinks he's in bargaining position now," Reese laughed, "because he lent us his moldy old tent."

"That reminds me," said Matthew Glennon, when he sensed he had the floor again, by tacit acclamation. "The reason I went to down there last night, to sleep next to the water, was one, I felt put off by what you did, Ross, as you know, and two, the big reason, I was so wishing I'd gone in that direction the night of the bachelor party. The guys who swam got all sobered up and cooled off. But me, oh no, I had to stage a little pout. I was angry at my friend Bruce and so I left the party to protest, and went off into the woods. And this girl, who'd been hired, her name was Mickyanne, she was pissed off at her two friends for breaking the contract in some ways, I don't know, so she came with me, taking two guys' drinks who were swimming—a giant plastic cup in each hand."

He made himself laugh a little as he held his hands like

Mickyanne's, made alternating moves to sip alcohol. "We fooled around, by this wide rock, like a wall."

"You didn't have sex, though?" said Gilbeau.

"No. But to me that doesn't really matter. Because while I was groping this girl my wife was trying to . . . well, grope her way back to the car, to safety. We both went astray, and neither of us made it home, almost but not quite.

"You know she lay there in the field all night, unconscious—I hope unconscious—and was still alive in the morning, and at the hospital for three hours. But by then her brain . . . there was too much blood in there. So I mean, if . . ."—legs crossed, he slapped his knees repeatedly—"if she'd made it back to the car and been able to drive somewhere. . . . And she was only forty or fifty feet from the car, they said. You know what else they said, would you like to know? It's very, very strange."

The wind had been steadily rising, invading their section of Valley with muscle, with intention, and Zingman knew he'd be drummed out of the profession if he were to add this detail to a story; he made a mental note to give up writing his own pale horror fiction and devote his life instead to the case of Sheila Glennon.

"They said that her death is being taken out of homicide investigation. It's being blamed on the *storm*. So many things were flying around. You've heard them say that before, you know, 'Five deaths are being blamed on that hurricane, or the tornado.' I can't believe that. I can't believe it."

"Well, maybe, maybe," Mr. Ruthbar piped, rubbing his forehead (with small), "maybe you could run 'n' chase your heart when it goes out in the water."

When the man looked around, suddenly wondering what he'd said, Zingman asked, "Were you dreaming again, Mr. Ruthbar?" He nodded and laughed at himself, at which point the Cobhouse got to have a solid laugh, including Sheila Glennon's husband. For the first time since being dragged from his house two days ago, Tenzer smoothed his pesky jowls with his thumbs.

Hearing echoes of agony along the stone corridors of the monastery, Lucas Haas runs; torches line the walls. He stumbles up and then down slippery, winding staircases, until the fifth tower yields a dank little room. Arrayed around their mother, on a bed of horse blankets, the twenty-three newborns strike wretched, frozen poses, not breathing, steam rising from their tiny bodies. In the flickering light, one can read disappointment written on their faces like a repeated emblem stamped on clean coins. Robed Brother Wilhelm releases Claire Danes's hand and recedes into the shadows, bowing to Lucas Haas, who approaches the apparently bloodless form of his beloved, sits, takes both her hands. "Melanie, look, I've found my way back to you." Tears streak down his face, each swifter than the last. His British accent is painful. "I never should have let you go, I know that now. But I love you, completely, and so you're free, free. This foul rot has been shed. Doesn't that prove we're free, as well? I have searched three countries for you, and as I neared, the beasts quit your body. Oh, Melanie." (It's not exactly the dialogue Zingman wrote, but beside him in the theater, Andy wouldn't know; she's never been able to finish reading *Wombdwellers.* She sits, hands to herself, breathing on a tight schedule. The rest of the audience whispers behind them, some giggling outright, and he's only too glad they don't know he's amongst them. Andy stopped having fun with the movie at the graphic delivery scene, twenty minutes ago, when the audience roused itself into a communal gagging fest.) Claire Danes opens her eyes, and they are narrow, wry; the actress's distinctive, potatoey brow now pleats with scorn. "You fool, Steven. Can't you count?" The camera zooms in on his bloodshot eyes as they scan the carnage. He whispers, "There's . . . one . . . more," and when he looks back at her, she is gone. As the lights come up, Andy is rubbing her temples for a bad headache; she won't look at him. When the audience has filed out and they are alone, she says, "If only they'd applauded, right?"

Mr. Ruthbar said goodnight and turned in. As the campfire died, Matthew Glennon requested several of Sheila's favorites songs.

The memorial service had been too stiff for these, for Jimmy Cliff's "Many Rivers to Cross," even for "Sweet Chariot." At Paul Simon's "Homeward Bound," Mr. Ruthbar joined in from the pup tent, in a voice suprisingly rich and low. "Hoh-ohmward bound . . . I wish I was . . ."

"Well, I had planned to wait until first light to reintroduce her," said Trapuka, catching up a sluggish individual. He'd scooped salt water to the matrix as soon as they'd left harbor, and since then much more salt water had added itself. The survivors had grown, each now filling one of his hands, and he'd gradually given up trying to understand their constantly emerging form. He'd been busy, yes, but more important, they had become lumpy, furred, weary but complicated; here again, as always, inexhaustible, *Titus* had dreamt up fresh ways to draw him along while giving his intelligence the dodge. "You know, so we could make sure we'd gained enough margin from land. Wouldn't want her washing ashore within hours, would we?"

"Nope."

Ellie had turned sulky since an initial blurt of enthusiasm, five minutes earlier, at the sight of a small flotilla of police boats, blue and red lights accenting the waves, sirens sounding plaintive in the gusts. The flotilla had closed half the distance.

"Now, I have a favor to ask you. I know you think these are . . . gross, and you haven't wanted to see them, or touch them. But I wonder if you could help me." He handed his first survivor gently overboard and rummaged at his feet for another, secured it, placed it into the ocean. After his third, Ellie picked up her first.

It started to seem so much like a game, in a little while, that when they heard the bullhorn crackling out its warning, "MAKE NO ATTEMPT TO FLEE!", they looked at each other through the brightening blue-red air and broke out laughing.

"As if!" Ellie shouted.

"I guess they found out about that pizza box!"

The warning repeated.

Soon they were tossing Titus high in all directions, over their shoulders, behind their backs, fancy, under their legs. Ellie balanced one on top of her head, exclaiming "Ewwwwwwww! Happy now?", but it toppled off into her lap because she couldn't hold still.

After two more, Trapuka said, "I think I'm out."

"Me too . . . oh, no, here's the last one, Daddy." Ellie held it up, but the boats had arrived, three of them, sirens falling silent. The nearest contained officers with rifles trained on the launch. On the deck of the farthest boat stood Pauline, grim-faced in Jonna's sweater, and beside her, his arm around her waist, Eugene in his black pea coat and Greek fisherman's cap, nodding and pointing for the benefit of a photographer, whose flashbulb went off. On his other side, a short stocky woman reached up and slapped his pointing hand. It was Mrs. Ard, Pauline's mother, staring and staring at Trapuka as though still knowing she was irresistible somehow, as though she'd not finished asking him questions on Grand Manan Island, questions having nothing to do with murder.

The middle-distance boat kept coming until it was the closest, a low vessel used for diving, for recovery efforts, with a platform at water level in the bow. This platform was obviously going to slide underneath the launch.

"Daddy."

He focused on Ellie, who, before she carefully two-handed *Titus* over the edge, gave it a peck.

Sli-ide through, sleeeeek Haaarry . . . eheht, goin' for to carry me hoooome . . .

No moon, or stars, no more Indian Summer left. Any hatchery has a delicate metabolism, and even cold water cools in the middle of the night . . .

But in the heart of the pond, she felt warm, breaststroking, frog-kicking across, making no sound, exhaling with each efficient sweep of her arms—from hands back to back before her, to scooped and tailing in beside her hips.

They are famously temperamental, hatcheries. Sli-ide through . . .

Harriet crawled out of the water, like our ancestors from the sea, when they were halfway between blue-green algae and Rosalind Franklin. A feathery snore led her to a piteous vertebrate, who'd laid his sleeping bag out right here within reach of the pond.

She peeled the bag and kissed his cheek, in deep darkness. On her bank, she'd waited for the death of their campfire.

"Sheila?"

"Shhh-shh-shh," said Harriet, like Pepper laughing.

She kissed the man's mouth, whoever he was, and climbed against him, rubbed his belly, pillowy beneath some sort of terry number—*ah, Mr. Pudge, I presume.* For two moments, he kissed back, then he sucked a breath and went rigid. "This isn't real," he whispered. "This is not real."

"Shhhhhhhhhh." And she let him stroke her wet hair.

Both inside the sleeping bag, he understood she had no clothes on, and so invented a way to put his disbelief between parentheses. Weeping was part of the method, apparently; but placing her weight on top of him, compressing his rib cage, helped to quell it.

I must say, he is the most appreciative lover I have yet come across during my long and distinguished career. And look at this, won't even hear of my hand, wants me whole.

"Sheila!" "Naomi!" "Open up, Gina Conrad!"

Out on the pond again, Harriet selected the backstroke, though windmilling one arm only. The other hand she used to cover herself, a loving lid.

"That's much better," she said quietly. "A reliable environment." Her legs kicked with vigor, agitating the surface. And this movement, she thought—knowing as she did that for an organism the very first order of business, after hatching, is to worry—must agitate her as well, inside, helping to carry the countless along to where they needed to go, saving them trouble, making them welcome.

"Sleep now," she said. "It's real."

Frigid morning brought trouble to the Cobsite—reports of heart symptoms, nightmares and great difficulty peeing, and then, fumbling efforts to locate the matches, dense white plumes from gasping mouths, the symptoms growing worse. Even the doctor, down on one knee, measuring out his breaths, agreed, "That's what it feels like, all right, Ross, like some compromise of the autonomic nervous system."

"Concentrate, Patrick," said Zingman, his arm around the man's shoulder, familiar with the alarm in his eyes. "Picture it pumping, it'll respond."

"We need to get ourselves to the hospital, for a toxicology screening."

Renouncing fire—matches vanished—they began to pack their equipment in a qualified panic, achieving a certain dexterous heroism until Gilbeau discovered Matthew Glennon's empty sleeping bag down close to the water. Nobody had seen the man, and Zingman couldn't bring himself to share the fact that he'd heard him calling out in the night for his wife. Everybody searched, along shore and in the woods, even while tending to the ruthless demands of self-circulation. Zingman and Mr. Ruthbar helped each other in amongst the trees. While they were among these trees, they separated and attempted again to relieve themselves. "Mr. Z., it hurts to! It hurt yesterday and the day before."

"I know it does, me too. Just keep trying, we're going to the hospital. For you it's long overdue." Zingman stared down at his intended target—a pitiful scarlet mushroom, curled and fading at the edges and pocked throughout with lesions that reminded him of the dots of mold on his spaghetti sauces. He noticed, too, that tiny flies were on the job again, this time gathering in upon the top of the mushroom, where his few painful drops—thick and stinking—had landed, steaming grandly. The flies cared for this as they had cared, so much, for his cloud of ash, if not firelight or ratatouille. He decided that after all it was a fair price to pay, that when the world finally turns strange again, some of what occurs will resist interpretation altogether, that mastery must occasionally bow down before mystery.

"Look!" Mr. Ruthbar shouted from behind his tree. "They're getting my pee! Stupid birds!"

Zingman whispered to himself, "A case in point."

Simon Reese shouted from a distance, from by the marsh. When Zingman and Mr. Ruthbar joined the others, Matthew Glennon was visible through gauzy hanging mist. He sat a distance out, cross-legged on a hillock, fully dressed down to well turned knot of tie, but with Sheila's blue robe hooded over his head, spreading down his back like a cape.

"Hey, Matthew," Tenzer called. "What's up, there?"

After two beats, the man pointed to a nearby foot sticking out of shallow water, smaller than a baby's and covered with frost.

"Oh, I thought . . ." said Mezzanotte, hand clapping to his chest. He and Gilbeau and Reese and Keillor and Tenzer all sat down nearly as one, smack into spongy earth, which, unlike yesterday, softly crunched with early ice. Matthew Glennon gestured in another direction, toward a brown rock that had a dark greenleafy arm slung across it, tapering to a leafless hand, lighter, closer to celery. Neither limb stirred.

Mr. Ruthbar remained standing, smiling wistfully into the mist.

Simon Reese chuckled tightly. "I think Theresa would come

back looking like that arm. She's joking with me about letting the garden go for so long."

"I mean, I thought I saw something yesterday, here," Mezzanotte continued, in hushed reverence, "but I didn't believe it. And all night, Bethany talked to me, like I was tuning her in."

Mr. Ruthbar echoed the reverence, hands to the side of his head, when he gasped, "Mr. G.?"

"It's funny, you know," Simon Reese said. "Ever since she died I've been looking everywhere, inch by inch, expecting to see her, or at least some sign from her. I've had my heart set on it."

"It's not Bethany exactly, I'm well aware," said Mezzanotte. "But it's not not her, either."

Gilbeau said, "It's like something, just . . . simple. Like they're stating kindness to us. A reward."

The next phenomenon that Matthew Glennon demonstrated was less akin, although it was obviously alive. It resembled not a returning wife so much as a fish, tangled in some kind of stringy plant back toward the pond, spasming like that poor creature in the Seaquarium just before being gulped. It could be easily distinguished from any such commonplace, however, by the unassuming fact that between two sharp fins, a round chalky breast was visible, trembling as if lodged there.

Simon Reese breathed, "That is the saddest thing I have ever seen."

"Sameness within difference," Zingman found himself answering, as if an answer were needed, as if his held water.

Matthew Glennon continued to draw attention to further instances, but now only by turning his head, and slowly, as though reluctant anymore to unveil his perceptions, especially since they were far subtler than those for which Zingman had congratulated himself yesterday evening.

When Tenzer said, "But I can't look anymore," he struggled for air. "My heart's . . . I can't get a rhythm going."

"He's right," said Zingman, recognizing the same in his own

chest, but having learned not to panic. "We shouldn't. Let's get back to camp and pull ourselves together."

Puffing, Gilbeau agreed, "It's too much too fast. Like staring at the sun."

The men rose and began walking where they'd been told.

"Come with us, Matthew?" At his name, he dropped his hand to his lap, where it joined the other hand, and he swiveled his head toward Zingman. "Look at you, your eyes are so bloodshot. Have you been up all night? Okay, just to let you know, we're heading back now, to cook up some breakfast. We'll make enough for you, but we won't force you. You can stay here."

The man turned back toward the far side of the marsh.

Before giving up, for now, Zingman shivered, because the leafy arm was no longer on its rock.

Unzipping and rezipping zippers, stirring the ashes in the fire pit, the group members succeeded in convincing each other wordlessly and without progress for six or seven minutes that they mostly just wanted to find oatmeal, until one by one they drifted again toward the water, where it was easier to tend to the heart.

"Peaceful," said Gilbeau, after a while.

The clouds were still gray and low, the air cold and motionless—where was the wind? The smooth surface of the pond, not shining, hinted at nothing, letting off thin swirls of mist like a cliche to hide the truth. Nobody sat down, but nobody went toward the marsh. Zingman kept picturing the vivid red in those eyes.

Perhaps ten minutes had gone by, perhaps twenty, when they heard the far-away voice. They held their breath, eyes fixed on the water, listening. It was the rapid voice of a woman, high-spirited, even joyous. It seemed she was explaining something. Zingman recalled Andy's syllables, left off at his ear during love. At this, his heart lurched and debated; he pushed it onward, which felt to him like what one does vainly within sex, late, after orgasm—the effort to keep the pulses going.

Suddenly, the voice located itself behind them. "All right, Pilgrims! Look alive, I think we've made it!"

A band of people in bright, startling Halloween costumes sashayed into camp. Quickly, Zingman and the others marched up to halt them at that limit.

Several witches bounced up and down, cackling. A hideous hunchback dragged one foot. Two tall green mummies thrust aloft wooden poles, each attached to one end of a long cloth banner reading, in gold script lettering, "NEW HOPE FOR THE DEAD!"

Patrick Tenzer said, "Hello, Steffi. How did you find us?"

Through the mouth slit of her Princess Diana mask, she answered, "We have our anonymous sources, you know that."

"Hey, that ranger at the station, Patrick," said Zingman. "The network of state government, don't forget." Despite this invasion and its timing, though, he found himself irresistibly gladdened by the presence of such traditional figures from the realm of horror, quite different from the mocking inflicted by the home decorations on Bigelow Street four days earlier, when the van had nearly struck him and strangeness began again to transfuse into the poor world. In fact, forgetting for a second who these people were, he could believe them beneficent emissaries sent to welcome him back into the craft. None of his Cobhouse fellows appeared capable of such charity; they were somber, husbanding their heartbeats, though Mr. Ruthbar did seem charmed by a certain pallid vampiress all in black who struck languid poses and bore fangs that kept slipping.

No doubt grinning underneath her mask, Steffi said, "Someone saw you men entering this Preserve two days ago and . . . and then it got so much colder, and frankly, we'd become concerned. Though we took it as a good sign you were out of doors, at least, stepping into the wide world." Her gray, searching eyes shone convincingly through their plastic holes. "But I must say that seeing you all enjoying this beautiful pond so much brings us 'new hope' for you. And since today also happens to be our big day, we decided to kick off our annual jamboree, come on down and spook you, cheer you up, tell you what happens to the souls of the dead on this night of all nights, gentlemen. Happy Halloween!" Steffi slipped her arm through Tenzer's and tried to spin him around, which Zingman admitted was humorous enough—"C'mon, let's put aside our differences and dance the dead in!"—as her glamorous sequined gown only began to swirl out before falling slack again. But he couldn't help laughing out loud when a man exquisitely disguised as the Headless Horseman lit a cigarette and took a lengthy drag through an aperture in his papier-mache neck.

Another tall reveller approached from the side. "I'm glad to see you're in a positive mood, at least, Mr. Zingman," he said in an unpracticed falsetto.

"Oh, yes," said Steffi. "Another reason for our visit, my friend . . . uh, Cleopatra, wanted to meet you."

His costume was hastily thrown together—jumbo tan beach towels meant for the flowing robes; three layers of mosquito netting for a facial veil; and draped over the shoulders, a child's dirty stuffed snake for an asp, red tongue lolling. "I wonder," continued Cleopatra's taut, straining voice, "whether I might have a short word with you, over there where we can talk. I am a huge admirer of your work, your mind, and so I wanted to get your take on some odd things that have been going on in our region these last couple of days."

"You are, are you?" said Zingman, holding out his hand, happier by the moment. The man shook it, briskly. "Well, now, it has been quite an unusual period here, hasn't it? Though I wasn't aware that so much of it had gotten around yet. Haven't been reading the newspaper. But Cleo, I think you'll have to lose that voice if we're going to—" As their hands parted, a little spiral notebook fell out from beneath the beach towels, slapped onto the dirt.

A pleasured squeak escaped the vampire.

Steffi pointed downrange, off into the marsh. "Look over there, everyone. We recognize that young man—tragic case, very young wife, baffling circumstances. Glenning. He almost came our way, we almost had him, and he doesn't seem too thrilled with the choice he made, either. I mean, sitting off in some swamp by himself. Pilgrims . . . to the rescue!"

"No!" Zingman yelled. "Show's over!" He herded SORW

fiercely away from the water, back onto the trail; several times, he had to shove. The Cobhouse flanked him, shoulders holding firm against covert flutters, skips, and, he knew, the sense that a sucking trapdoor had opened beneath their hearts.

"All right, all right, we're going," said Lady Di, lifting her royal arms. "But you've got it all wrong, preferring to dance with hopelessness. I mean, I wish you could see your own gloomy faces. You're clinging to your sorrow . . ."

"Oh, hey, Vampira," Zingman said. "Looks like your fangs're loose! Did somebody pull away from you too soon?"

Candace said, swirling away, "I dressed like this because this is how you see me. Sorry I thought you'd understand. My husband was chopped up like meat. You're a charlatan, and now the cops are coming for you. Are those dogs I hear?"

Steffi walked backward, SORW retreating behind her, and added, "Your masks of grief are much thicker than these masks we're wearing. Which is sure to keep your beloved wives at a distance, I'm afraid to say." The mummies' banner slumped between them. "I know it seems like some kind of heavy obligation, like work, to keep pulling for them, keep them going. I hope you'll learn it's not like that at all. Let the burden go. Throw it off, and then give us a call!"

As they were finally consumed by the forest, Zingman heard, "Wallowers!" and "Where's their corn now?" and then Vampira's voice, lisping—"Hey, Author . . . just read one of your books, and I *can* stop thinking about it!"

From the dead fire pit the men dug foil-wrapped potatoes, crusty and cold. At the pond, they chomped into them, but they did not fortify the heart. Chewing, willing their chambers to fill, to empty, to fill again, they tried to outmaneuver their autonomic nervous systems by quick movement, taking up different vantages along the shoreline, finding that some afforded better angles into the water than others. This was enough for the moment, because everybody knew they could always return to the marsh if need be. Even Mr. Ruthbar pointed and cooed, like an honorary widower.

Keillor, wagging the riding crop, was only half kidding when he said, "That looks a little like Jessie's horse, like its head, you see?"

Zingman's ankles stung zestfully, as did the bones highest in his feet, and this gave rise to a fresh possibility, that although the woman certainly couldn't understand how, Steffi's words were nonetheless—in view of the cave and then the marsh—right on target.

Instead of voicing this heresy, however, he used the vibration in his fine bones near the ground to start his mind spinning extrapolations in the case of Sheila Glennon; he thought he should do a book called, *Into the District Gale.*

Of course—the new book could wait a minute—it was easy to make fun of SORW, but then wasn't it even easier to ridicule a man with an extra set of eyelids, semi-transparent? Steffi's superficial, searching eyes had helped Zingman, just now, to recognize that with practice and in the best of circumstances, perhaps a nictating lid can serve as a fish-eye lens, being more inclusive, widening the optic angle.

He glanced down at his left ankle, at the ring of pale hairy skin just above the sock, and wondered if a tiny pair of wings might pop forth. He laughed, but bent over and pushed his sock down, checking lower, scratching.

After a minute, Reese sighed. "To think, they almost left us."

Taking along a baked potato, as though it might rescue him yet with its starch, Zingman split from the others to check again upon Matthew Glennon, who was now sitting on a new hillock, farther out, where the mist was even thicker, beside an up-reaching dead tree worthy of a sleek resident bird of prey or at least a black-and-white photograph. He shook his head when asked if he was planning to come in. "Aren't you cold?" He still wasn't talking, but he did catch the unwrapped potato skillfully on the fly, then raised it in mild thanks.

When Zingman got back to the group, they were gazing down into the water, distinguishing much of value, and Tenzer was reciting more of the old Rilke poem. "'Of course, it is strange to inhabit the earth no longer, to give up customs one barely had time to learn . . . no longer to be what one was . . ."—Zingman checked his other ankle for wings—"'. . . to leave even one's first name behind, forgetting it . . . Strange to see meanings that clung together once, floating away in every direction . . .'"

From the pond's opposite bank, sixty feet away, came sarcastic applause. Mr. Ruthbar let out a yelp and sat down.

"Miss me, partner?" shouted the scrawn, who stood beside an amateur fire, casting more smoke than flame. She started up again, but at least this time she was dressed, and left alone, like a spindle on her own side, so that hardly had to hear her ranting at them across the water. "Oh, this is rich, you're leering at the prizes—a classic little scene, men praying at the altar of the ideal woman. Meanwhile, HERE I AM, LOOK AT ME! I've got 'a face only a world could love,' to quote my funny mother on the subject. But no, feast your eyes on the pieces instead, please, it's what you do, it's what I've come to love. Speaking of love, you claim to miss your wives, and you'll even use their names in that way, ah that way, but loyalty sloughs off like a snake skin at a moment's notice, doesn't it? And the new skin is alive, I'll say it is. Sure, play dumb—one of you knows what I'm talking about; hey, I can never recognize the guy the morning after, and you're interchangeable, anyway. And spoiled, but guess who ends up with the spoils?"

Zingman was proud, how they treated her like a minor climatic phenomenon, each guarding his heart against brainless castigation as if holding a hand around a match flame in the wind.

Mr. Ruthbar, though, got up and took off, hunching and glancing upward again and again. "That's right, Chicken Little," the scrawn yelled. "Run! But don't forget, I didn't make you do anything down there you didn't want to do. The rest of you, your wives may've walked, but look at this, we've all stepped into a sweet situation together. Me, I feel like I've climbed through the eye of a needle."

Zingman followed Mr. Ruthbar to the low rise from yesterday, sat beside him. Alexander was not fishing here today. Under the trees, Mr. Ruthbar relaxed. Zingman pointed out the sunken branches, and while he was hunting for the drowned shapes—not enough light—it was Mr. Ruthbar who pointed out a shadowy creature whose tail drove it onward but whose fingers, gripping a branch, held it back.

Soon, the others arrived, still minus today's separatist. It was colder here beneath the pines, and after ten minutes on the hard ground, they began to go numb.

"You'd probably rather I got sucked down a drain for good, am I right? Down the tube, eye of a needle—heck of an upgrade for me, yeah?" This time, she was high above them, having scrambled up the Valley wall, and looming larger; she'd put on several blankets gained by a sometime raid on the Cobsite, and now she flaunted them like a shroud. "Keep looking into the water, yes, keep on watching my prizes. You'll find no two are quite alike." Zingman pretended not to see her rubbing and patting her belly. "Are you familiar with the term 'parthenogenesis'? Didn't think so, all you know is, 'She's full of herself.' Well, guess what, guys—same diff! Oh, I may be in for a tough labor. 'Tough'? I'll say so! If you want me to be honest—and I sense that you do—when has sex ever not been suicidal for me? But hey, don't answer that. I know what makes your crickets tick. Yes, I stole your matches, I confess, but here's an invitation. Swim over to my fire, often as you like, and I'll punch your tickets. We're on the brink of November, with this heavy cold front, and I'll need to keep producing."

In return for pumping their hearts, the men received the depths, gradually emerging, with contours perhaps familiar, like topiary. Certain dark shapes stirred; others would not, and then there were hollows in between, but even these were encouraging.

The men remained absolutely still on the hard ground, as though to aid the underwater shifting. And they let the cold travel up their backs and out their legs.

"My motto?" she projected. "'Adjust!'"

And this numbness, Zingman thought, makes us feel wise.

Selections from "The Off Beat," by William Stennhouse III

October 29...VALUABLE SHARK, OTHERS, PERISH IN SEAQUARIUM SPILL

October 30...ANTHRAX SCARE FORCES SHUTDOWN OF DISTRICT FIVE RESERVOIR

October 30...NEW BRUNSWICKITE, PROTEGE, IDENTIFY KILLER, CITE MOTIVES

October 31...UNSEASONABLE TEMPS BLAMED ON NATURAL ODDITIES; RANGERS REPORT HIKERS' STARTLING TALES; NO EVIDENCE PRODUCED

November 1...TRAPUKA ARRAIGNED ON MURDER CHARGES, DECLINES COUNCIL

November 1...SUSPECTED CONDOR PREYS ON PORTLY

November 2...ZOOLOGICAL COMMUNITY WITHOLDS JUDGMENT ON LOCAL CATCH; FISHERMAN ALEXANDER SWATHMORE HAILED

November 3...CURIOUS FLOCK TO REMOTE POND

November 3...ZOOLOGISTS WARN OF CONTAGION, TAMPERING; POND QUARANTINED

November 4..."WIDOWERS" TO WORLD--"BUT WE LIVE HERE NOW"

November 5...HORROR AUTHOR SEEN SWIMMING AMONG "MONSTERS"; REMOVED BY OFFICIALS; BOOK SALES SOAR

* * *

November 6...

CAPITALISM ALIVE AND WELL IN SKOONLET VALLEY; ZINGMAN REMAINS TIGHT-LIPPED

Police were out in force again today, shutting down booths and blanket-top concessioners camped near the cordons around "Swathmore Pond."

No one is allowed beyond these ropes. No one, that is, except Zingman and his so-called "widowers' group."

Entrepreneurs from around the region and as far away as Texas have become bolder by the hour for the past four days, as news of the Skoonlet Phenomenon has spread.

"It's getting to be a real side- show atmosphere out here,"said State Police Sergeant Dan Thom-pkins. "I mean, you've got your buttons and t-shirts and baseball caps with pictures of sea mon-sters and mermaids, of course. But now, we're starting to see more unique types of merchandise cropping up.

"We caught one guy from New York City," Thompkins continued, "selling designer fishing nets in all colors of the rainbow, which were doing a brisk business until we impounded the stock.

"A couple from Houston heard that piece on National Public Radio and hopped a bus, to put a stop to what they feel is a clear case of demonic occupation. They're handing out pendants--a circle with a fish inside, an apparent symbol of Christ.We kind of hated to ticket them,because they were already getting such a rough reception from the crowd, you know."

Meanwhile, "The Off Beat"has uncovered other creative ventures operating in the Valley that have so far managed to elude Thompkins and his troops.

Children employed by a shadowy concern in the city have been milling through the crowds hawking miniature wooden boxes patterned after fisherman Alexander Swathmore's much-photographed cardboard box.These miniatures even sport the same Dewars Scotch logo.

Some buyers are even catching diminutive specimens of their own in other ponds and streams, claiming to hold in their hands the next great discovery but refusing, ala Swathmore himself, to remove the lids without payment and recognition.

But the prize for Yankee ingenuity must go to those who are distributing blue and white banners with the words, "WE LIVE HERE NOW" emblazoned on them, a clear reference to the tearful and manipulative statedelivered by one of the grandstanders who have so far resisted relocation from their beachhead,aiding author Ross Zingman in his boldest, most shameful bid yet for notoriety.

Not coincidentally,the banners bear a striking resemblance to those that festoon a certain downtown automobile dealership. Though Zingman cannot be blamed directly for this, his Pond of Horror Hoax has set everything else in motion.

Sergeant Thompkins's face was haggard early today as he told how profiteers have booed him and his men, even throwing pinecones and clods of dirt. "We have a job to perform, don't we?"

Thompkins further related an incident in which they were forced, late last night,to place under arrest members of a local Baptist church, who had brought a vanload of the physically challenged and attempted to storm the cordons. At his news conference,Reverend Lippincott was unabashed. "They are the halt and the lame. They simply wish to bathe in these waters alongside those less fortunate than themselves." At last word, bathing privileges had not yet been granted.

"But not everyone is so aggressive,"Thompkins clarified. "We estimate upwards of five thousand individuals in the field half a mile from the site, who are taking a more relaxed attitude, camping overnight, singing old tunes like, 'Age of Aquarius' and 'Octopus's Garden.'"

Indeed, this reporter has witnessed many such acts of self-expression. Dancers are gyrating to African drummers. Much poetry is being read--and shouted. But by far the healthiest audiences have been drawn by several guitar- strumming songsters, such as the young man with long purple hair who played rousing protest songs(of obscure current application) such as,"We Shall Overcome" and "Alice's Restaurant." He was accompanied for a time by a jubilant woman identifying herself as Henrietta Lacks who,following several beers, told a crowd infected by her enthusiasm if not by her talent, "Hey, just call me Rosy!"

And through it all, Zingman and his dubious crew bide their time, letting the world come to his adoptive doorstep.

Ok, I know what you're thinking: this reporter himself is becoming Zingman's most effecttive publicist, even as regional and national news outlets arrive and scurry aboard the bandwagon. Perhaps. But this state of affairs will crash down on him, at the moment of exposure. As if he comprehends this only too well and is trying to soften the eventual blow, he and his weepy cohorts have now begun an odd campaign-- handing out roasted corn on the cob.

They husk hundreds of ears during the day, making ready for camp -fire roasts by night, pass them over the cordons to grateful if envious bystanders.

It won't work. I've infiltrated by devious means and observed from secret vantages, and Zingman's face reads like a dictionary of disappointment and flowering guilt.

Late in the afternoon, as though on cue, our temperature fell to 27. The not so merry band gazed out upon Swathmore Pond from their perch of privilege, as a thin sheet of ice began to form.

Printed in the United States
2468

9 780738 834191